The French Woman's Ghost

The French Woman's Ghost

A light-hearted murder mystery, romance,
and ghost story set in 19th century England

B.J. Van Horn

Completed by Mike Van Horn, Rebecca Van Horn,
and Eva Shoshany

Copyright 2024 Mike Van Horn
Published by The Business Group Publications

Cover by Shane Colclough
Book produced by William M. Van Horn

Acknowledgements

Thanks to all who read parts of the manuscript and gave us great ideas and invaluable feedback: Josie Papendick, who helped flesh out the 19th century London locations, Taylor Mannes, and our other beta readers.

Thanks to cover designer Shane Colclough, who captured the essence of two of the main characters.

Thanks to my brother William for producing a professional-quality book we are proud of.

Tribute to the Author
BJ Van Horn (1949-2023)

This story began with a hike up Ring Mountain in Marin County, north of San Francisco. Mike and BJ found a large boulder embedded in the hillside with a crack that looked just like a dagger. Here's a photo of BJ sitting next to that rock. A story had to emerge from that cracked boulder, and BJ wanted it to be a ghost story. It took a number of years for the cast of fascinating characters to emerge and tell their stories.

After a decade of developing the manuscript, the story was within a hair's breadth of completion when BJ unexpectedly passed away (in October of 2023). To honor her memory, the rest of us in her writing group (husband Mike, daughter Becky, and fellow writer Eva) decided to finish the project and publish it. And now here it is: BJ's ghost story, finalized by her three ghost writers.

At the end of the story is a table
showing the main characters
and their relationships.

Prologue

From the Journal of J. Edmund Symme, Barrister, London
In my 34th year of life upon this earth—anno domini 1896—I was fit for nothing save the practice of law. My mind was keen as a scalpel and as merciless, slicing through the intricacies of the justice system until nothing was left save what served my purpose. My indifference to everything but how best to use my wit to my clients' benefit, cut through human hopes, dreams, and follies until only shreds remained like ribbons to decorate my courtroom victories.

Yet, I began to find less and less satisfaction in my practice. Where once I enjoyed the acclaim—even the notoriety—it now left me restless. The exhilaration of victory paled. I became difficult with my clerks, aloof to my excellent household staff, and impatient with humanity in general. It was my fate to have personal daemons conquered, competitors defeated, adversaries subdued. In short, I was constantly irritable and most mightily bored.

But no matter—I was in tremendous demand, both as barrister and bachelor. For the women of London, married and unmarried alike, seemed to find me irresistible. They reminded me of my poor mother: titled, beautiful, and completely empty-headed, morbidly subordinate to her mate. She was besotted with my horrible father, a simpering, weak-willed fop who considered himself a man of the world. Thank God they both suffered from wanderlust and then early death; they left me mostly to myself and the tender mercies of public boarding schools, and then to University.

Which is where I acquired the only two individuals whom I have ever called my friends: Christopher Banks, who came to me as a grace from God during my excruciating tenure at Eton, and Regis, who joined my household some years later, after I read at Oxford. Banks took his degree in medicine and is now my physician as well as my confidant. Regis, of course, is a most immense and magnificent Great Dane of unusual intelligence and temperament, who shares my London home and most of my meals.

It was in the spring that I began to dream. No, not that grand flight of the soul toward some lofty attainment—I had long since left those pastimes to the simple-minded. No, dreams that would come to me in sleep. Before then, I don't know the last time I could remember dreaming; perhaps at the onset of puberty, when lustful impulses sent ripe-thighed damsels parading behind my fluttering eyelids on a nightly basis. I do remember a childhood dream of large, toothy insects chasing me around my nursery, but that was very long ago. No, these recent dreams were neither lustful nor threatening, just vivid and, well, provocative in nature.

For example, in one dream there appeared before me a sunny summer garden, flowers abloom and bees buzzing. I heard Regis bark and when I turned to see, I found him next to me on a wooded hillside on a starry night with a full moon. Again, sounds caught my attention. I heard a woman laugh and then cry, an angry man shout curses in the dark. Rain and wind suddenly lashed down and soaked me through inadequate clothing. And then the scene changed again and I was ambling upon the same hillside on a fine day, Regis gamboling ahead as I forded a shallow stream. I looked forward to getting somewhere important.

When I awoke from dreams such as this, my curiosity was aroused more than by events in my waking life. And for some reason, as I would attempt to resume my rest, thoughts would turn to childhood visits at Owlswood, our family house in Yorkshire. I would remember fine times in that old house and the games I would play among the fountains and gardens of my grandfather's domain. The family stopped going there before I reached my 10th birthday—why, I was never told. But I remembered well that sour, stern old knave, my grandfather, and his fondness for smacking my legs with his riding crop at the slightest provocation (often just the sight of me) and his absolute edict that I should be let nowhere near his precious glasshouse (so of course I threw stones at it every chance I got). I disliked him immensely, but at least he was a man—unlike my father, who was not even worth disliking, to my mind. I certainly hope to exhibit the backbone he never had. I hope to escape any lingering curse of his vacuous tendencies, and accomplish something meaningful with the time I'm given.

1
London Barrister

If passers-by on the street had cared to look up, they would have seen London's most famous barrister standing motionless, framed in the library window of his Berkeley Square abode, with the front page of the *London Times* crumpled in his fist and his gaze fixed on the trees of the park across the avenue. Although servants had entered the room several times, he had not noticed them. He had not noticed the fire built, nor the brandy poured, nor the scattered and torn pages of the Times picked up, smoothed and refolded, and placed discreetly on the marble table. The servants were pleased not to be noticed when the master was in such a mood.

The huge dog lying near the hearth shifted his weight and looked at the man dejectedly. He groaned and, when ignored, churned the Persian rug upon which he lay briefly with his paws and then was still. He could tell, there would clearly be no walk together along the river path tonight.

The doorbell rang, and a tall, elegantly dressed gentleman was admitted and shown into the library. Edmund Symme took no notice. The visitor greeted him and, receiving no reply, easily and with good grace made himself comfortable in a chair with a glass of brandy, and simply waited. The dog, Regis, moved his great bulk to settle with his head on the man's knee, and sighed.

"Regis, old boy, you've had no walk with your master today I take it, and not much hope of one, eh?" The visitor scratched the big dog's ears and the beast looked at him with sad eyes and sighed again, apparently confirming this statement. "Ah, well, some weighty business is afoot here, no doubt," he murmured, "so you and I are to be completely ignored."

Edmund continued to stare, lost in thought, out over the green of the treetops. His steel blue eyes were hard and almost colorless with concentration. "Damn," he murmured softly as his clenched his fist tighter around the newspaper. "Bastards—ignorant bastards, all of them."

"I must say that I had no idea my parentage would come under attack when I accepted the offer of a pre-dinner drink." A wisp of fragrant smoke curled upward in a graceful spiral as the seated guest lit his pipe.

"Quiet, I'm trying to think!" Edmund snapped absently, at last acknowledging their presence. "This rubbish—what rot passes for journalism!"

With this, he crammed the offending page into a ball, turned, and threw it with force into the fire.

"Damn!"

The guest looked at Regis, who was startled by the action, and stroked him comfortingly. Then, unperturbed, he queried, "For God's sake, Edmund, are you prepared to tell me what is bothering you or shall we engage in light fisticuffs right now? Bastards, indeed."

Edmund began to pace, gesturing expansively as he spoke.

"The courts are becoming bloody circuses, and the papers seem to regard me as nothing more than ringmaster! Are we to become tools of social propaganda? Is there no respect for the Law, for Justice? These jackal journalists are nothing but. . . oh, I say, good evening, Banks. I didn't see you come in. Are you well this evening?"

"As you see me, but a damned bastard, I believe you said—oh, that's what I am, not how I am." He smiled affably. "I'm well, thank you."

"Did I call you a bastard? That's impossible, Kit, but I admit— I'm distracted." He saw the remaining section of the Times on the table and snatched it up. "These newspapers are appalling, they'll print anything!" He accepted the snifter Banks had poured and took a sip. "Thanks—I may need more of this before the night is over."

"The opinions and comments of London at large—that rubbish in your hand included—have up to now rolled off your tender sensibilities like water from a duck's back. What now has changed, pray tell?"

"I don't know." Edmund shook his head and sat down heavily. "It's strange, Banks. I'm annoyed all the time. I'm so restive, so . . . so disillusioned. So bored." He almost groaned out the word.

"Things are going that well, eh? You have no worthy challenges, is that the problem?" Banks asked jovially.

"Perhaps. It's all too true that I feel little excitement about my work of late." Edmund frowned. "You're a doctor, can you give me a tonic for this kind of malaise?"

"Brandy works as well as anything. But this seems more than superficial unhappiness, does it not? You may be suffering from a malady this lowly physician has not been fortunate enough to contract."

Banks sipped from his snifter.

"And that is?"

"Success. Fame and fortune. Too much luck, too much brilliance." Banks looked at his friend intently. "Your clients come from the oldest, richest, noblest, most privileged families in England. These same jackal journalists you so decry have written you into legend status, allowing you to charge magnificently inflated fees. Any trial you undertake becomes a cause célèbre. You used to find it exhilarating, but now all that has become displeasing to you. Poor fellow."

Banks chewed on his pipe as he spoke.

"You think my discomfiture trivial, then?"

Of all the opinions in London, Banks' was one that mattered to Edmund.

"Not at all. But hardly cause for alarm or depression." He leaned forward and continued, "You work too much, and too hard. You lose yourself in your cases, take them personally. Everyone needs a time of rest." He leaned back and thought for a moment. "Perhaps a change of scenery is worth considering. An extended trip abroad or a hunting safari in some exotic clime? A complete change of pace might be the restorative you seek."

"Cramped, uncomfortable trains, abominable sanitary conditions and dead beasts. Not appealing."

Edmund shook his head.

"An odyssey on the high seas, then, perhaps to the Americas?" Here was a trip that Banks lusted after himself. "As a mark of my high esteem for you, and at great sacrifice to my patients, I could accompany you, if you like."

"Shipboard for weeks? Inactivity always annoys me, Banks, and the Americas are populated by savages." He paused briefly; his mind captured by some thought. "I read somewhere that the suffragists are incredibly active in the Americas," he mused aloud. "Can you imagine giving the vote to women? Most of the women I

5

know are in no way capable of reasonable thought, much less a sane choice in politics. I'd never expect to have a stimulating or companionable evening of political discussion with a woman—Lydia, case in point."

"We cannot judge the entire female population of England—or the Americas—by the standard of Lady Lydia Grenfield, Edmund, and thank God for it." Banks' eyes began to twinkle. "But there's an adventure for you: word has it that you are considering a voyage on the seas of matrimony—is that correct?"

Banks kept a straight face but his eyes were full of mischief.

"Et tu, Brute?" Edmund looked at Banks accusingly and sighed. "I suppose it's time, isn't it, Banks? Family can be safe harbor on the sea of life, I hear. Or a millstone 'round the neck'." Edmund rubbed the back of his own neck absently. "I've been seeing that glint in women's eyes more and more these days, and I get it all the time from Lydia! I feel my neck being fitted for a millstone. Oh God—I'm not looking forward to this soiree tonight."

"You ungrateful cad. The lovely Lady Lydia Grenfield and her parents, throwing a dinner party to show you off like a prized stud stallion soon to be acquired by their stables—how could you be anything but thrilled at the thought?" Banks grinned. "I can just see old Grenfield now, into his cups and hinting and winking about when you shall become his son-in-law. 'How economical it will be to have a barrister as member of the family, I shall do as I like and he'll get me off, ha ha ha!'" Banks imitated the blustering codger well.

Edmund nodded gravely. "God, the man is an idiot."

"I agree. However, it is a party and you don't seem much in a celebratory mood. Can you cast off your pall sufficiently to be a charming guest of honor?"

"Have I a choice?"

Edmund looked glum.

"No, actually," replied Banks cheerfully. "So, let's be off. Get your hat; let us not keep the charming family Grenfield waiting."

Edmund accepted his gloves, hat, refused a coat, and instructed his butler to be sure Regis was given a good walk before dark. As he closed the front door behind them, Edmund's brow furrowed.

"God's teeth," he groaned as he pulled on his gloves, thinking of the evening's festivities. "Christopher—in all candor, have you ever seriously considered marriage?"

"Considered it!" Banks exclaimed. "I dream of it." Edmund's dubious stare moved him to elaborate. "Nightmares, of course, and I awake in a cold sweat screaming for whiskey!" He opened the door. "Come on."

Since the evening was mild, they decided to stroll through the pleasant twilight instead of hailing a cab. They ambled along Farm Street, presenting impressive figures in their well-cut evening clothes, engaged in animated conversations. Even on bustling London thoroughfares, the fair aristocratic-looking Banks and the dark, brooding Symme drew interested stares from other pedestrians as they passed by.

"You know, I remember these black moods of yours from our wrestling days at University," Banks abruptly announced. "You'd become depressed after too many wins and a cold ferocity would descend upon you. Woe to the next opponent, mind you, but you'd often go after some brute of a challenger in a heavier weight class to make it interesting for yourself. You remember that one from . . . where was it, oh you know the one who growled constantly. I thought I'd never set your shoulder straight after that one!"

"Humph. The man was hairy like a bear. I believe he went on to medical studies—most particularly brutish university students do," Edmund replied. "Black moods indeed," he scoffed. "How ridiculous."

They passed an old, stately church, lit for evening service. Edmund became thoughtful. "Banks, what do you think of Lydia? As a woman and possible wife, I mean."

"Really, Edmund, is this a serious question?" Banks asked, looking askance. "Why ask me? Why ask anyone? You must make your own decisions in these delicate matters, although I daresay you have a vast number of willing candidates available to you." He shook his head. "I could never comprehend why you appeal to so many women, but appeal you certainly do!" Then he added more seriously, "So why focus on one who'll keep you giving parties and paying large bills to your grave, for god's sake?"

It was true, much to Edmund's dismay and total puzzlement, that he was irresistible to most women. After several brief and discreet, but hardly satisfying, affairs, he had taken up with Lady Lydia Grenfield. They had met through her father, after Edmund had counseled him to avoid a business entanglement that had proved

7

disastrous to those who had not the benefit of such sage advice. Lord Grenfield had been a distinguished military man with a long career in Her Majesty's Navy. Now reduced to a rather doddering old age, he still fancied himself a force to be reckoned with in business and politics. And so it had come to pass that Lydia, her mother and father, and in truth her entire extended family had decided that Edmund would be the ideal son-in-law, from both a romantic and legal point of view. Edmund remained unconvinced.

"She is quite beautiful and of very good family, you know," Edmund countered, addressing his own misgivings more than Banks' words. "She is exceedingly well-bred, has many social graces and skills, and a well-run home has some appeal, has it not? Giving parties and spending cash—that's what women do, isn't it?"

"You have a highly competent housekeeper," Banks replied wryly. "You have a fine dog with excellent breeding. Those are niches already filled in your life, Edmund; you don't need a wife for those reasons. Remember the adage, 'marry in haste, repent at leisure'?" Banks looked at him incredulously. "You really are in a state, my lad, you must get a drink immediately before your brain turns to porridge."

When they arrived at the Grenfield home near Grosvenor Square a few minutes later, Edmund found his humor slightly improved. Once inside, Banks quickly surrounded himself with pretty women and left Edmund to the ministrations of Lady Grenfield the elder. Edmund, in turn, submitted gracefully to the fawning of his hostess, who made tedious introductions to all her distinguished gentlemen guests and their bejeweled ladies.

"May I present J. Edmund Symme, famed barrister and charming admirer of my daughter Lydia," she gushed too many times, her hand firmly planted in the crook of his arm so no escape was possible. "He attained another stunning victory this week!"

He was rescued only by the appearance of the younger Lady Grenfield at the top of the center staircase. After bidding good evening to the crowd at large and making sure she was noticed, she glided down the staircase and held out her hands, crying "Edmund, darling, how wonderful to see you!"

Lydia always made spectacular entrances, and tonight was no exception. Every eye was upon her. She was dressed in a gown of light green satin gathered tight onto her fashionably tiny waist; the skirt flowed full and voluptuously to the floor. Her neckline was cut in a deliciously low décolleté, with several fresh white gardenias pinned along the bodice. A single emerald hung from a gold chain around her neck and her earrings were emeralds surrounded by diamonds. In her beautifully coiffed golden hair, another gardenia nestled over her right ear, and her satin gloves had been dyed to match the color of her gown. Her patrician face, impeccably rouged and powdered, was radiant, as always. Her violet-blue eyes seemed especially bright as she surveyed the attentive crowd below, and her perfect smile lit up the entire foyer. She seemed to float down the stairs to where Edmund awaited.

As he took her hands and bent to kiss her cheek, Edmund remarked to himself on what a disagreeable shade of green she had chosen. However, he also noted the rise and fall of her creamy bosom as she whispered to him, "Darling, I can't wait until we're alone!"

Actually, he wished he were alone, but acknowledged her remark with a kiss on her other cheek and another glance at her cleavage, whose gentle curves piqued his interest and somewhat soothed his discontent. After procuring a glass of champagne for Lydia, and a second for himself, he mingled with the assembled admirers and breathed a sigh of relief as dinner was finally announced.

By the time the main course was served, he felt that his growing impatience with this glittering company must be plainly visible. But no one seemed to notice the distance in his eyes or the increasing coldness of his manner. Least of all Lydia, who was holding forth on the value of bloodlines in people as well as horses. Every few minutes she would coyly place her hand in his lap and allow her fingers to wander indecently. His boredom rose, and even though she punctuated her caresses with discreet breaths in his ear several times, his ardor did not. He was growing more and more irritated by the voices around him and suddenly wondered if he had drunk too much.

"I feel certain that Edmund is a perfect example of impeccable breeding, even down to his very stubborn streak, which is common to most 'thoroughbreds.' He refuses to let me trace his genealogy, even though I recently researched a family tree for Lord Rochemont back almost to the Battle of Hastings!" Lydia pouted delectably.

Her one claim to scholarship was composing family trees, with the help of a smitten junior assistant Royal British Genealogy Librarian.

He brought her fingers to his lips and suppressed the urge to bite them, kissing them lightly instead. "Lydia, my sweet—really, don't submit your guests to a history of my recalcitrance."

He decided that, no, he had not had nearly enough to drink after all.

"Nonsense, Edmund, they're fascinated by everything about you, as am I. All London is fascinated with you, you've captured our imaginations. And you cannot disagree that every titled family should make use of the marvelous records of civilization now at our disposal . . . "

It seemed to Edmund that Lydia's mouth took on a life of its own, not caring what it said, but just wanting to continue moving.

". . . and you, never having really known your forebears, need a record of your ancestry and the passionate (dare I say regal?) bloodlines and extraordinary intellects that combined to form the house of Symme!"

Lydia beamed at him, and he felt he must bolt from the table if she said another word. To prevent such a course of action, he leaned over and placed a long, vigorous kiss upon her finally still lips. The assemblage tittered and clapped appreciatively, and Lydia, regaining her composure, looked at him with becomingly demure adoration.

"Edmund, darling, you're so impetuous!" she exclaimed breathlessly.

Then she quickly appraised the effect his action had produced in her guests, and her smile became even more brilliant, as every eye was focused on her. Never one to permit being the center of attention elude her grasp, she continued.

"You see my own darling Teddy-Wink—you don't mind if I share my private name for you, my love—had the misfortune to have parents and grandparents who died at a very early age, except for his marvelous paternal Grandmama, who traveled all over the world after the passing of her spouse and had no time at all to spend with dear Teddy. Poor little boy!"

Of all the pet names Lydia had ever called him during intimate moments, "Teddy-Wink" was the most unacceptable to Edmund, and he made his disapproval clear upon many occasions. At this moment, an epiphany occurred within him: he saw all too well that here was a woman who cared naught for the feelings of her suitors, but merely wore them, much as she wore jewelry, as ornaments to enhance an already stunning appearance. Edmund Symme was simply the most prized ornament, to be used to greatest advantage and kept exactly where she could always be sure of finding him.

As she glanced coyly at him once more, proud of her witty and charming conversation, she became suddenly alarmed at the complete and utter coldness she found in his eyes. She shivered unconsciously at the strength of the dislike in his face, then, a bit perplexed, she composed herself, glanced imploringly at her mother who caught the signal and announced to her guests, "Ladies and gentlemen, shall we retire to the drawing room for coffee and brandy?"

As the others rose, Edmund sat completely still and held Lydia fast in his gaze. When the last of them had filed out of the room she spoke.

"Edmund, you're not angry with me, are you?" she pleaded prettily. "You seem suddenly cross, darling. Oh, don't be cross with me."

His eyes remained hard for a moment, and then a slight smile slowly spread across his lips and his shoulders relaxed. Lydia, too, relaxed and offered her mouth to him, eyes closing to fully savor his kiss. He hesitated only the briefest moment, then bending toward her slightly, took the glass of wine from beside his plate and poured it into the crook of her breasts. He saw that several drops had splashed onto the gardenias on her dress, looking like drops of blood against the white flower flesh. He rose and kissed her hand.

"No, Lydia, I'm not angry with you. I'm done with you. Good night, Lady Grenfield, and goodbye."

He bowed slightly and left the room.

Lydia's eyes popped wide open as the cold liquid trickled down her skin and began to soak into the satin of her bodice. She made a few strangled noises in her throat, then rose and rushed after him. But Edmund was across the foyer and out through the front door before anyone could ascertain what had happened, and the startled servant was left scurrying to find his hat and gloves—and then to wonder what in heaven to do with them.

2
Finding a Pub

Edmund strode vigorously along the street, without thinking where he was going, now and then breaking into an exhilarating jog. He barely glanced at the well-kept residential streets lined with staid, imposing mansions, or the well-groomed parks, toward the teeming hub of the city. As he passed the Marble Arch, he slowed to a stroll, hands in pockets and eyes searching for a landmark. This was an unfamiliar part of town, and he wondered what sort of neighborhood he had wandered into. He pulled out his pocket watch; the face read 10:54 pm. Not so very late, but . . . perhaps not a good time to be lost.

As he walked past Hyde Park, he heard quick footsteps in the stillness. He looked back in the direction from which he had come as they grew louder and more distinct. A man's footfall, no doubt about it. He could see a figure silhouetted in the light of the street lamps heading toward him, still several blocks away. The man was tall, well-muscled. A feeling of alarm momentarily claimed him, but he calmed himself and stepped into a shadowed doorway, and waited. The footsteps stopped, then started again as the figure moved closer. Edmund stood poised for action and held his breath as he watched the figure come into the lamplight . . .

"Banks! For God's sake, man!"

"By Jove, Edmund, what an exit! The entire city will be talking about it tomorrow, and you will again be the darling of the society page." Banks' mellow, though now slightly breathless, voice cut through the chill. "Say, old man, I had a devil of a time catching up with you—I had no idea you were in such good condition."

"You almost scared the life out of me just now!" Edmund exclaimed. "Could you not have called out to let me know it was you?"

"I didn't see you; you were hiding in the doorway like a bloody thief! Good God, man, whatever is possessing you?"

"You saw what happened at Grenfields?" Edmund inquired.

"I saw the aftermath, and surmised the rest," said Banks, regaining his breath. "All Grenfield's visions of bouncing tiny barrister grandsons on his knee—up in smoke! Again, I ask, whatever possessed you?"

Edmund hesitated a moment.

"I cannot even venture a guess. But I think I've decided against that marriage!"

They began to laugh heartily. Banks announced that now a stiff drink was truly in order, so they continued down the street in search of a suitable pub.

"This is not a likely area for a friendly tavern, Banks, and we are definitely lost. We may have wandered into Marylebone. I think it best to set our minds to finding a cab and returning to my house, wherever in the world that might be from here, and the brandy within it." Edmund was not keen on disreputable drinking establishments in the middle of the night. "Damned imprudent to wander the streets hereabouts."

"Come, old man, first you complain of boredom, now where's your spirit of adventure?" Banks asked genially. Edmund simply raised an eyebrow. "We'll be perfectly safe and very happy in the next pub we discover," Banks continued. "Trust me. And to prove my point, I can hear what promises to be a very congenial crowd nearby."

Following the sound of voices, they shortly found the Bull and Bear, and although its dank and smoky interior looked somewhat grimy, Banks decided it would do nicely. Once settled at the bar with brandies in hand, they grinned at each other and clinked glasses.

"To us, my friend," Banks began, "and to the many lovely women and professional victories in our futures." Edmund winced, but drank the toast nonetheless as Banks continued. "I must say, this evening has been an unexpectedly entertaining one, especially the latter portion. However," he added, "I fear I shall soon be summoned to treat the elder Lady Grenfield's nervous prostration, or vapors, or some such, resulting from your inexplicable behavior—which may prove the most entertaining part of all."

Edmund looked squarely at his friend. "So, Dr. Banks, have I lost my senses at last? As my physician, what would you prescribe for my fragile health and sanity?"

"You're as fragile as an ox, my friend, and you've a reputation for driving others mad, not yourself. Lydia is most probably in hysterics, even as we speak."

"Don't you believe it," Edmund grunted. "She'll soon design some profit from the whole thing. Lydia. My God, I'm glad that's finished. I don't know, Christopher, she used to fascinate me, arouse my lust at least. But now . . ." He shuddered and ordered another round. After a quiet moment he said, "I can't believe I was considering such a marriage. But quite seriously, I do seek your counsel. I've been having strange dreams of late—dreams of, well, many things, but among them, idyllic settings in lush countryside. Perhaps I'm longing for some time in the country—fresh air, rabbits for Regis to chase, long rides in the meadows—that sort of thing. Time away might do me good. No newspapers or vacuous, scheming women about!"

"A fascinating notion to be sure. Where exactly do you . . . uh oh, what have we here?" Banks looked over Edmund's shoulder into the barroom, and Edmund turned to look as well.

A youngish man had just risen from his seat in a dark corner and started toward them. From his worn, stained clothing, hard body, and gang of similar men at his table, Edmund surmised that he was a laborer. From his angry, sulking face, Edmund guessed that he felt ill-treated by life in general, and people with money in particular. It was obvious that he resented their presence in his favorite drinking establishment as he approached them, tankard in hand, and spoke loudly to his comrades behind him.

"Now will ye look at these two nancies! Slummin' now, are we gents?"

He looked them up and down and made an exaggerated bow.

Edmund noted a number of lost and blackened teeth as the man grinned maliciously, as well as his fist clenching nervously.

He's ready for a fight, Edmund thought to himself, *and he thinks we are sodomites.*

"Not at all, my good man," said Banks, the peacemaker. "Have a drink with us, won't you?" He smiled his friendliest smile. "Barkeep, another for this gentleman."

The man's eyes narrowed and he replied, "Drink! With you! Me and my mates don't drink with nancy-boys."

Edmund could see several figures rise from the corner table—menacing shapes moving closer like wolves to prey. *Wonderful,* he thought as he scanned the room, *I wonder if Banks knows what's hap-*

pening here.

"Oh, nonsense, a drink's a drink. Barkeep!" Banks summoned.

But before the owner could respond, the laborer flung the remaining ale from his mug into the young doctor's face, then grabbed him by the lapels and slammed him hard against the bar. It was then that Edmund's right fist broke the man's jaw and sent him sprawling.

Instantly, the dark shapes were upon them. No university wrestling match this; these three were street brawlers, mean and dirty fighters coming to the aid of a comrade oppressed by the upper class. One burly specimen bellowed like a bull as he charged Edmund, only to be sent over the bar and into the bottle rack. Edmund leapt over on top of him with a resounding thud, the two scuffling violently as they disappeared from sight behind the bar.

By this time, Banks had cleared his vision and defended himself with his fists. A second man grabbed him from behind and pinned his arms while the one he had been fighting delivered several strikes to his face and mid-section. Banks managed to kick his attacker senseless with a well-aimed blow to the head, but could not break free of the man holding his arms until Edmund, having left his own opponent groaning on the floor, broke a bottle of whiskey over the villain's head, rendering him unconscious.

The sound of police whistles came from outside caused panic in the bar. Out of the corner of his eye, Edmund saw the barkeep exit through a backroom doorway hidden by a curtain. He grabbed Banks by the arm and ducked out the curtained door into a dark, refuse-filled alley. They ran down the shadowed streets, careful to scout for bobbies at each corner, and soon heard police whistles only in the distance. They slowed to catch their breath.

"Will you ever bloody learn that it's no bloody good to speak to bloody strangers in bloody pubs?" asked Edmund, holding his bruised ribs and wincing. "I can hardly draw a breath." He looked at his comrade and commented, "By God, *you* are an attractive sight!"

Banks' face was taking on the appearance of raw meat.

"Well, I think I held my own quite credibly," he retorted. "On the other hand, Teddy Wink, you certainly look the worse for wear. Quick, hail that cab or we'll never find another!"

The cabbie looked dubious as he viewed these potential customers, but then decided that their evening clothes bespoke a higher station in life than their disheveled condition. He stopped his horse and allowed them to get in. After receiving the address of their destination, he inquired, "Do you wish to go 'round to hospital first, gentlemen?" But they assured him that their own beds would do.

The steady rhythm of the horse's hooves on the cobbles was soothing, and the two passengers leaned back against the rough fabric seats and did not speak.

After a few minutes, Edmund said, "I can't take many more of these evenings on the town with you, Banks, that's a certainty. I think it may be time to leave London."

"Are you afraid the papers will skewer you, should they get wind of this? I don't think you were recognized back there," Banks chuckled softly. "Are you leaving forever, or just until Lydia marries some poor fool?"

Edmund's voice was soft. "Remember the dreams of rural life I mentioned? I've just this moment decided to go to Yorkshire for an indefinite time. A sabbatical, if you will."

"Yorkshire? You have a family home there, do you not? Rabbits, fresh air, lush countryside?" inquired Banks. "Well, Regis will certainly approve! You've not been there since I've known you, though you've spoken of it before. The place must be in a dreadful state after being closed up for such a long time."

"No, not really. My grandfather's will stipulates that the house should be kept open at all times; he even named a village family as keepers. And the place has all the modern conveniences, again gratis of grandfather's will. He had a true soft spot in his heart for that house—plenty of room in the old bastard's heart since no people had places there. But you're right—it's been decades since I've seen it."

"So why go now, Edmund? For the sake of a few disquieting dreams and a broken affair?" Banks grimaced slightly and dabbed at this split lip. "I have difficulty picturing you as country squire, I must admit."

"I don't know why, Banks. I just know . . . that solitude beckons. The house beckons. *Something* beckons. I think I've been dreaming about that house, although it's hard to remember those dreams."

"Do you intend a hermit's life, or shall I visit you there?"

"Of course, old man, after I've got settled in you'll be the first to come. I'll take a day or two now to look after affairs here, and then I'm off. I'll send word in the morning to expect me for an extended stay." His voice drifted off. "It's exactly what I need."

After the cabbie left him at the curb, Edmund waved good-night to Banks, entered the dark hallway of his house and found Regis awaiting him just inside the door. It was so still, he could hear the big dog's tail swish as it wagged a welcome.

Climbing the quiet staircase, Edmund began to feel weary; emotional and physical fatigue grabbed hold of him with incredible force. His bedroom was dark except for the warm light thrown by the carefully banked fire. In front of it, he saw a glass of brandy on a small silver tray next to his favorite armchair, and a freshly pressed nightshirt lay across his turned-down bed. Thank God for competent servants, he thought, and chuckled to himself as he remembered Bank's comments about not needing a wife.

He relaxed into the welcome the room seemed to bid him, then left his evening clothes—rather the worse for wear—in a heap on the floor and settled himself naked into the huge four-posted bed. Even before the eiderdown stopped rustling, the deep black velvet of sleep enveloped him and soon he found himself in a beautiful dream garden at a warm dusk.

Again, this familiar garden, exactly where, he did not know. Past the manicured hedgerows his gaze traveled, to the ornate gazebo beyond, where the slim figure of a woman leaned dreamily against the trellis. She was vague and indistinct among the greenery, but he could tell that her hair was loose and glowing red, and she was gowned in creamy lace. Her arms were full of flowers. She must have been gathering them, taking a moment to rest and daydream. He moved closer to get a clearer look at her, straining his eyes through the twilight. Suddenly, she caught sight of him and was, for an instant, startled. She stood returning his stare and he thought he could see a slight smile play around the corners of her mouth. Then she moved rapidly across the garden path toward the carriage drive.

Edmund ran after her, wanting her to wait for him. But she continued quickly on, and giving a look over her shoulder, continued out of sight. He kept up his run, hoping to catch her. All at once, he heard a scream—long, high-pitched, terrified. He reached the drive just in time to see a carriage hurry away, making grooves in the gravel behind it. Along the drive, in the vehicle's wake, lay a spray of gardenia, their white petals bruised and mauled by the wheels. There was no sign of the red-haired woman.

As he bent to gather a crushed blossom, his head began to swim and, before his eyes, the scene changed to a dark London street, glistening as if after a heavy rain. The streetlamp threw light on carriage wheels as they crushed the gardenia on the cobbles. The strong flower fragrance assailed his senses as he watched in horror as drops of blood appeared on the creamy flesh. He could feel the anguish of the bloom as it was broken against the rough stones, hear the scream — that scream, shrieking in his head . . .

He sat bolt upright in his bed, heart pounding, ready to spring out into the hallway to find the source of that scream. Then he remembered he had been dreaming, and shook his head to clear it. "My God," he murmured softly and slipped out from under the bedclothes to the floor and over to the brandy, still waiting in its crystal snifter. He downed it quickly and then padded back to bed, deciding to have no more dreams that night.

3
Remy

"Damnation."

She had begun weeping again, her hanky nowhere in sight, tears streaming and nose running. She dropped the letter she had been reading onto the table, lifted herself off the chair and grabbed a sacking dishtowel from the sink. As she dried her hands and blew her nose, she wandered into the parlor, catching sight of herself in the large framed mirror above the sideboard.

"Ugh," she thought and tried to capture the strands of reddish hair that had escaped their pins. The cottage was too quiet; the rooms too empty. She stared at her reflection dully.

She noted how the face staring back from the mirror was not typically British; the brow was clear and high, and the skin lightly tanned rather than milk-white. A few freckles peeked out here and there, and the unusual hazel eyes were now green with weeping. While the red in her auburn hair was not overly noticeable, her mouth was "overly generous" by British standards—though the French might say, "*delicieuse.*" She smiled slightly to think of her French father, how he delighted in his wife and daughter, his two "*jeunnes filles charmantes et delicieuses.*"

Two cats jumped up onto the sideboard. The larger portly beast, orange except for four white paws, nudged his head into her gently and purred. The smaller tortoiseshell chirruped a greeting, then settled quietly and began to clean her whiskers. The woman smiled slightly in spite of her troubles. "Boots, do you think I have some food with me?" she asked as she smoothed the orange head, and then, "Pyewacket, a lady must keep well-groomed, no matter what the circumstances, and you are doing better than I."

They both looked at her sagely.

Returning to the kitchen and her seat at the table, she took up the letter and continued to read.

I can only imagine how trying this time is for you, my dear, and I will do all I can to see that you may return to studies at the earliest possible moment. The London School of Medicine cannot afford to be without one of its best students. Do not let your difficulties dissuade you! We have sometimes talked about my student days at Edinburgh, when our male 'colleagues' and professors sought to make life hell for us females—the nasty pranks, attempts at disparagement, and the supercilious attitude of the arrogant male focused on we seven. But we did prevail, as I know you will prevail now. Remember, all women require is a fair field, and no favor, to prove their worth among men.

The woman paused, looked up and snorted. " 'A fair field and no favor' indeed—and fairies dancing in the garden, as likely." She shook her head and continued reading.

Please accept my deepest condolences on the death of your mother; I believe no one could have had a better nurse, or a more devoted daughter, than she had in you during her final illness—which, I know, came upon her so suddenly as to leave you both unprepared for the unhappy outcome. As we have come to know, such a circumstance is often a blessing. You have our prayers and are ever in our thoughts, and you have only to ask for what you need. When my own dear father died many years ago, I thought I, too, would be required to abandon my dream; I was called to return home, rather than stay in America to study at Blackwell's School. Family obligations influence our decisions most strongly and we cannot abandon them. But the path finally opened before my feet, as it will open soon for you.

Keep your spirits up, dear girl, and be gentle with yourself. Know that I am working strenuously for your return to us; I continue to press for scholarship monies among our supporters and friends. Know, too, that your classmates and I wish you peace and strength at this time. Please write soon and tell us how you fare. We look forward to the day we are together again.

Your true friend always,

Sophia Jex-Blake

When she looked up from the letter, the two felines were spread lavishly across the tabletop, staring intently at her. "You know mother would never have allowed you such liberties—do I seem less stern?"

Both furry heads turned sharply to the window behind her, ears twitching and eyes alert. She rose and turned to peer out the kitchen door, which was open to the mild mid-afternoon warmth, and saw visitors approaching. She rose and quickly splashed some water on her face at the sink, dried it, and smoothed her dress as she stepped onto the threshold. Her expression softened and she smiled.

"Well, what do I see? Is that Molly coming to my house?" she called, stepping out onto the entry stones and waving at the small approaching procession. Taking the lead, moving with a lopsided gait, a girl of about six years of age made her way up the path, hobbling on a crippled leg. Close behind her proudly marched a huge goose, a flower garland loosely circling his snowy breast. The cats immediately disappeared; the goose was not a favorite of theirs. Behind him came two women, the younger slim and tall and holding the arm of the elder, who was small and wizened and carrying a basket. They entered the front yard and came up the walk.

The little girl threw herself into the woman's embrace.

"Yes, it's Me, and I've come to visit you!" she exclaimed with a big hug. "Nana and me mum are here, too, and General Gander!" She pulled back and looked up, smile fading. "You've been crying. Again." Her little face clouded with concern. "Auntie Jeanne, are you sad today? Because I brought you something to make you glad—see?" She offered a fistful of pinkish flowers. "They're c-o-l-u-m-b-i-n-e, Columbine! For you!"

"Thanks to you for the lovely presents, all three: the flowers, your good spelling and . . . your presence!" She raised her eyebrows in a question, and got her answer.

"P-r-e-s-e-n-c-e!" cried Molly, giggling with glee.

Jeanne accepted the bouquet and a kiss on the cheek, and continued, "Yes, I was feeling sad today, and now I feel much better—for seeing you, and for your thoughtfulness."

"Oh, I just got them in the field when the General was eating snails there," Molly replied offhandedly. "The color made me happy, and so I knew you would like them, too." She looked toward the kitchen. "Do you have any muffins, Auntie Jeanne?"

"I'm afraid not, but come along inside and take a look in the pantry." The two women, who had lagged behind, reached the doorstep and embraced Jeanne in turn.

"How do you, Jeannie girl?" asked Nana, the elder, as she entered the kitchen. "We've not seen you much this past week."

"She does well enough, and will be even better once the kettle is on," Annie smiled. "We've come to have some tea—does that suit you?"

She pulled out a chair for her mother-in-law at the table.

"Ah, well, it so happens I'm free this afternoon, the Squire

21

and the Bishop having sent their regrets, so I'll put the kettle on," laughed Jeanne. "But, I'm afraid you'll find my hospitality wanting. I have tea and milk—and some bread and honey —but there's not much else in my cottage."

"Don't bother about it, we came prepared," her friend replied. The older woman placed the bentwood basket on the table, opened the crisp white towel, and revealed several plump crumpets and scones.

"We made too many," she said, "and I thought you could make use of them. A few eggs underneath, too, just from this morning. And I brought this along just in case."

The grandmother winked and reached into the pocket of her skirt, drawing out a pot of strawberry jam. They all laughed like young girls and settled themselves at the table, Jeanne having brought cups and plates from the shelf.

"What a feast we shall have!"

Just then Molly thumped back into the room.

"I don't know, Auntie Jeanne, that pantry is EMPTY! Nothing there even for mice!" She looked disappointed. "And I'm hungry."

"Then you shall have some crumpet and jam, and some lovely tea, before the mice can get them."

The little girl's eyes opened wide as her mother sliced a huge crumpet and began to toast it at the stove. Having clambered up on to a chair, she waited politely while Jeanne handed her a napkin and brought a small glass of milk and the warm buttered crumpet. Molly began to eat solemnly and efficiently, watching the progress of the table being set.

"Do you miss Auntie Aimee, Auntie Jeanne?" she asked between bites.

"I do, yes, I miss my mother very much," Jeanne answered. "It's very strange to be in this house without her. Sometimes . . . sometimes it feels like she is still with me, and, it's true she is with me, here in my heart and my memories. But I still miss her very much."

"Are you an orphan now?" Molly continued, taking a sip of her milk.

"Yes, I am an orphan. Perhaps that's why I am feeling a bit sad, as well."

Molly reached over and patted Jeanne's hand with her buttery fingers. "Don't be sad—we'll take care of you. You can be in our family. You don't have to worry." She looked out the window. "Even General Gander likes you, and he hardly likes anybody!"

The goose raised his head and poked it inside the door upon hearing his name, honking inquisitively, then returned to scouring the plant on the flagstone for tasty pill bugs.

While the tea sat brewing, conversation turned to lighter matters and the women talked briefly of the latest village gossip— mostly the foibles of men and the hardships of women, the difficulties of raising families, the snits between neighbors. When the tea was ready, they, too began to eat and drink with pleasure—and Jeanne found her appetite heartier than expected, perhaps encouraged not as much by the delicious baked goods as by the friendship that filled the room.

"Mum, I am finished." Molly announced to Anne. "Thank you, Auntie Jeanne, it was very good." Pleasantries handled, she turned to her mother. "May I go see the new kid in the barn, please?" Molly pleaded.

"Yes, but mind to close the gate," Anne said.

Molly left the table and three sets of eyes watched the tow-headed girl as she made her way slowly out of sight, goose at her side.

"Now General Gander, you must behave—you mustn't frighten nanny's baby goat with your bad temper," Molly chastised. "No hissing, no nipping, nothing but your best manners."

The goose followed her obediently, honking softly, apparently heeding every word.

"Jack still dotes on her, does he?" Jeanne asked softly. "She is such a treasure."

"As if she were his own, and she has become his own," Anne replied. "We will always remember Sarah, but we have forgotten that Molly isn't born of our own blood. We love her so much." Anne's smile was brilliant. "And it seems clear that we've now adopted you, my girl! No orphans at this table!"

"Well, it would be good to belong *somewhere* in this world!" Jeanne sipped her tea pensively. "In London, I was the stranger from the country, hay in my hair and mud on my shoes, trying to challenge my betters and become a physician! What cheek! And thinking myself as good as any man, in the bargain." She shook her head and smiled ruefully. "And now the people of my own village, my home—they feel I left to put on airs and look down on them, and that my life among them wasn't good enough—being the local herbalist wasn't good enough for me. Now they see me taken down a notch, they think I've failed. Perhaps I have." When she looked up, tears were building in her eyes. "And now I've lost my mother. I tried, but I couldn't save her . . . just like I tried to save Sarah. I lost them both. Again, I was lacking, I didn't have the skill, I didn't have . . ." She caught her breath before she could sob. "Maybe I am a fool to think . . ."

Anne took Jeanne's hands in her own and squeezed them gently. "None of that. You belong with people who care for you. Such as we. Don't forget that, even when you're a doctor." The two friends looked at each other in camaraderie. "Or . . . when you have a good man in your bed and babes in the cradle!"

Anne loved to tease her.

"Oh, little chance of that, my girl," retorted Jeanne, "no jumping from the pan into the fire for me! You'll never find this woman living by some husband's leave, subject to his will and whim. Even a warm bed and a good man like Jack—I aim to make my own way in this life."

She smiled as she spoke, though, as Anne shook her head and the old woman clucked in amusement.

Changing the subject to a more neutral ground, Anne continued, "So have you been up to the Symme house recently?" she queried, sipping her tea and smiling slyly. "Have I done myself proud or not?"

"I was there yesterday. Thank you, everything is in perfect order. You did magnificent work. And I'll be moving in there tomorrow, and spending some time with Samuel on the garden, as we need to make some improvements there. And I'm glad to give you this." She rose and fetched a small packet from her writing box. "I was planning to walk over to you this evening, but you've saved me the trip." She handed the packet of coins to Anne. "I can't say how much I appreciate your taking this on for me."

When Anne hesitated, she continued, "We had an agreement; there is no shame in being paid for your work. There would be shame for me, in not paying you for what I should have done myself but could not." She waited a moment. "Please, Anne, don't be stubborn."

"You know I would have helped Aimee anyway. Why should you pay me?" Anne asked.

"Don't be daft. Mother was too ill to work for some while, and by the time I came home she needed all my attention and the Manor House was the least thing on my mind! The Symme endowment pays us, and I'll not take money for what I haven't done. If you hadn't been willing, I could never have handled everything myself. And then the prodigal son would have had to sleep on musty sheets and walk on unpolished floors; heaven preserve him from such misery." She chuckled, then turned serious. "We'll talk no more of this, Anne, take it. And . . . since I need to engage a cook, will you be interested?"

"Oh, I don't know about that, I'd be glad of the money of course, "Annie replied, taking the packet from Jeanne's hand, "but I couldn't stay on when the harvest begins, and I won't spend my nights away from home." She thought for a moment. "What about Cassie Miller? She's one of the best cooks I know, and a widow is always glad of extra coin. And now that she's taken in her sister's girl . . . Can she be at home at night?"

"It could work out—especially if she brings Rose with her to help during the day and then with clearing up in the evening," Jeanne replied, thinking out loud. "She'll be paid, too, of course, for her time and work. Then they could leave right after the meal was served. And with only one person to feed—well, it won't be lengthy to present. They would have to be back early in the morning, but . . . What do you think?"

"Speak to them—they're both dying to get a look at the fine city gentleman anyway, as I am myself!" Annie laughed. "Master Edmund—all grown up and a famous person. Never would have credited it, myself."

"I remember that boy," the elder woman began, "so now he's master, is he? What business brings him back after all this time?"

"No idea. I did not like him when he was the son of the house, and I doubt I'll like him now. I am surely not privy to his plans," began Jeanne wryly, "only to the information that he plans to arrive soon, and stay for an indefinite period. Beyond that, we shall all find out in good time." She became thoughtful. "I shall need serious conversation with him about the future of the housekeeping arrangement."

"Planning to beard the lion in his own den, eh?" chortled the old lady. "But tell me—have you started dreaming again, Jeannie, since you're home?" She looked concerned. "Any troubles with that?"

"Nana Cooper, dreams are the last thing that trouble me. I have enough trouble with waking life and the events that occur in it!" Jeanne replied lightly, but felt somehow off-balance at the mention of her dreams. How would Nana Cooper know if her dreams had returned, she wondered?

"Well, this visit today is not just because we hold you dear in our hearts, and we do—it's that I feel beholden to you for the lessons you give my granddaughter," the old woman began. "Now, don't protest, take heed from your own words—you need to be paid for your work. And I cannot pay you in coin, but I'm here to do a reading for you. Some say that is worth more than gold. Clear the table and we'll be about it."

Nana Cooper was famed both as a midwife and as a Tarot reader, and people from far and wide sought her skills. Her mother and grandmother before her were renowned for their talent with the Cards. Jeanne knew she could not refuse the woman's kind offer without risk of offending her; and while she had long ago left behind any beliefs in the superstitions and occult practices common to village life, she admitted to herself that she was curious, though slightly uneasy, about the reading.

The table cleared, and the women settled again, she was told to shuffle the deck and select five cards. She did so, and the cards rested face-down on the table for a moment. Then Nana turned over the first card, and began.

"The Hierophant speaks of a man who cometh— a dark, brooding one. A man you do not yet know well. He brings wealth. He brings trouble."

Hardly a revelation, Jeanne mused, thinking of the imminent arrival of the gentleman Symme. She smiled slightly and glanced at Anne. *Why, she's mesmerized*, she thought to herself, *she hangs on every word.*

"The High Priestess next, a card that speaks influence from an unseen world, and unseen power that comes from a woman. There's danger here. A place, a house—some danger, it is not clear. Are you sure you haven't started 'dreaming' again, Jeannie?"

The old one looked at Jeanne's startled expression, nodded, and returned to the cards. The gnarled fingers turned over two more cards—Five of Cups, the Tower—and spoke gravely of what was written there. She seemed troubled by what she saw.

Finally, the fifth card lay exposed and the old one was silent, seemingly lost in her own thoughts, until finally Anne touched her shoulder. A skeleton dressed in armor, mounted on a steed, leered merrily up from the table. She looked intently at each previous card, then moved her finger to tap the last card. She trembled slightly and opened her mouth as if to speak, but remained silent. The air hung heavy around them, and finally the old woman shook her head gravely and said but four words.

"These cards speak Death."

*   *   *

In the Symme London townhouse, things had quieted somewhat and preparations for Edmund's departure the following morning were complete. He sat in the drawing room, brandy in hand, reviewing matters with his butler.

"Mr. Carlisle is in charge of all pending cases and legal matters, and of course, he is most capable and has my complete confidence. There is nothing requiring my personal attention for the moment, and for at least several weeks. Should anything arise regarding household matters, either he or Dr. Banks should be contacted immediately. They know how to reach me, if necessary, as do you."

"Yes, sir, I know how to reach you, should the need arise." Wilson stood beside the armchair in which Edmund was seated. He cleared his throat. "Mr. Symme . . ." he hesitated.

"What is it, Wilson? Please continue."

"Sir, it pains me to think of you in such a . . . primitive environment without benefit of my services, or at least a valet to assist you. Who will see to your wardrobe needs, your menus . . . truly, sir, I am concerned."

Edmund smiled and rose.

"Wilson, be calm. I travel only to Owlswood, not a far-off jungle. This is a family home, not a frontier."

"Yes, but, sir—it's in Yorkshire. The place is wild yet, sir."

"No, there is a town nearby, with a Post Office and a telephone—two, I think, one there and one at the Vicarage. We have boilers and hot water, the privy is no longer in the yard, and the bathtubs have faucets and are quite amenable to soaking. There is a butcher, and groceryman, and most probably a very capable constable. I shall do quite well."

"But your meals, your clothing . . ." Wilson grew slightly more fretful.

"I will not be dressing for dinner, and I will certainly not be entertaining anyone—until Dr. Banks makes his arrival and I don't worry about him—and I believe we can get the laundry attended to adequately. I do have a housekeeper there, Wilson."

"I feel you are making light of my concern, sir." Wilson seemed slightly abashed.

"No—no, I hold your opinion in high regard. I appreciate your concern and your attention to your responsibilities. However, I will not be gone for such a long time, and it seems unwise and especially unkind to disrupt the life of this household just because I go away—and not very far away—for a rather short time. Weeks, Wilson—maybe a couple of months. That's all. Be at ease about it."

"As you wish, sir, however, please know you need only send word if you arrive and change your opinion. I do not mind train journeys and I have a quite good long coat."

Edmund thanked him and bid him good night, and kept his amusement to himself until the door shut quietly. Then he waited a few seconds, and began to chuckle. "Wilson, you old mother hen! Whatever can befall me at Owlswood? Whatever happens in the country, for pity's sake?!"

*   *   *

Visitors gone and the washing-up done, Jeanne again sat at the kitchen table, writing box before her. She was tired, but felt the need to respond to the letter from her London mentor. She smiled slightly, took up pen and paper, and began her response.

My Dear Professor Jex-Blake,

Your letter did much to buoy my spirits, for I confess I feel somewhat overwhelmed. I never expected, when I returned home several weeks ago, that I would see my mother out of this world and into the next. It has been a great shock, more than I had imagined it would be, and now there are many things I must see to.

Not the least of which being my family's ties to the Owlswood house through the will of John Symme. There is an obligation upon us—now upon me—to care for the house in return for a very generous stipend. My mother was only too happy to fulfill this duty, as she had little interest in life outside our village and, as I have mentioned, color had drained from her life upon the untimely death of my dear father.

28

The stipend kept her comfortable and even allowed me some money for my studies. However, now I am left with this burden and I must find a way to disengage; I am neither a housekeeper nor the village idiot, which I would needs be to remain here in service.

To make things worse, after many years, the current heir has decided to live in Owlswood for some indefinite time—beginning within a day or so—and I must prepare the house and serve him for the time being. With these preparations at hand, I have had no time since the funeral to consult with a lawyer about discountenancing the will. Sometimes I feel that I will never be able to return and achieve my goal of becoming a physician. Sometimes I feel—unknown forces bar my way.

When my mind is most troubled by these matters, I remember the stories of how you and the others fought for your rights—even at the risk of your lives, as during the Surgeon's Hall riot, and how you kept going when all obstacles seemed overwhelming. It gives me solace, and a glimmer of hope, and it stokes the embers of my courage, though they burn low.

I have no idea of when I might return. Rest assured I will do so at the earliest possible opportunity. I do not rely on your largesse, nor your efforts to obtain scholarship monies; I feel strongly I must pay my own way, in my own way. This is no reflection on your kindness or your work on my behalf, and the behalf of worthy others. Many things must be arranged, so I can only say I will keep you apprised and hope I do not fall too far behind. Your faith in me sustains me, even from afar.

Tell Margaret I dream of her spice cake (warm from the oven and slathered with clotted cream, of course) and the day when we are in the common room again, eating huge slabs of it with our tea and trading ideas for a better world.

I remain your friend and most grateful student,

F.J. Remy

The letter addressed, sealed, and readied for its trip to the post office in the morning, Jeanne doused the lights and made her way to her bedroom. She was tired, unsettled, but ready for sleep. Under the eiderdown, her last thought before falling into slumber was a vague prayer, to whatever god that may be, that she should have no dream—especially that particular dream—this night.

*   *   *

In the black sky overhead, the moon was surrounded by a hazy ring—a Blood Ring, the old ones called it. The ancient crone could hear shallow breathing, quick and panting like an injured animal. Her rheumy eyes narrowed and shifted warily to steal a glance at the figure in the shadows.

Across the table between them lay the cards, pictures gleaming in the candle light. The old one wiped leaking spittle from the corner of her mouth, then pointed a wizened forefinger at the cards and whispered, "I see . . ." She paused and strained to see into the darkness, as if considering whether to go on.

The shadowy figure shifted slightly, then softly said, "Dites-moi tout, Bon Maman."

When the crone failed to obey, the figure leaned into the candlelight and hissed, "Tell me all—everything!"

The young gentlewoman's eyes were unnaturally bright and her cheeks high with feverish color even in the light of two meager candles, whether in illness or deep distress the old one could not tell.

"Alright, good lady! Calm thyself now. I see . . . a tall man, a handsome man. His hands—there is much blood and . . . the knife! The knife lies there!" Her ancient face looked pained as she continued. "These cards speak Death. I see death . . . very soon."

"Ahhh."

The sound was more a release of breath than a word. The young woman leaned close in to the cards, fixing them in her gaze as if confirming what she had just heard. Her loosened hair shone deep red against her milky skin in the light from the candles, framing great beauty even in her despair. She tilted her head slightly and whispered, "Mon Dieu—what shall I do?" She began to moan and to rock slowly back and forth. As the shawl slipped on her shoulders, moonlight shone through the cottage window and illuminated the tiny face of the baby at her breast.

The old one felt ill at ease. She had made many readings of Tarot for many people, but this time—this was strange. A madwoman sat before her. She looked quickly over her shoulder at some imagined movement outside the cottage window, then shivered as she quickly said, "Let me read again, good lady. We need . . . "

The slender hand commanded silence. "Non, bon femme, c'est ca. The cards speak only what is so." She stopped rocking and rose slowly. "I know what I must do. Now here is what you must do." A cloud passed across the moon as she came to stand over the old woman; but her eyes glittered even in the darkness as she thrust the child into the Tarot Woman's arms

30

and spoke. "Take her. If I do not return, find her a mother—one uncursed! Not one such as I."

As she took the lace shawl from her shoulders and wrapped it around the infant, a tear fell from her eye onto the child's cheek. She kissed the tiny face with a sad but calm smile. "Adieu, ma petite. Be well. Be happy, until I return for you," she whispered and smoothed the little head with her hand.

Her faced again became crazed as she commanded the old woman, "Do it! See that it is done! Or I shall know and surely have my revenge on you and this hellish village!"

With that, she flung open the cottage door and ran. The blackness swiftly swallowed the slight figure as the old woman crossed herself and hugged the now screaming, red-haired child in her arms.

The young woman ran and ran, every breath bursting against her rib cage. She ran to become part of the night, part of the deep, cool, comforting darkness. She ran to lose herself—to lose the sound of wailing that rang in her ears. She ran to become one with the night and then . . .

Through the darkness she saw a pale shimmery light. A shape—what was it? The Stone! Le poignard en pierre stood ahead. She slowed and peered through the velvet night to see . . . "No!" she screamed. "Mon Dieu, donne-moi le courage! Donne-moi le vengeance! Ayez pitie de moi! Ayez pitie!"

The wailing grew loud again. She clutched her head and looked up at the moon above her. The wails . . .the wails!

Jeanne woke in the darkness, alert, sweaty and frightened, and realized that the screams that woke her were from her own mouth. Settling herself, she calmed her breathing and swung out of bed to find some water.

I can't believe it has started again, she thought, *I thought when I returned, the dream would leave me. Why does it come, night after night?*

After a brief time, calmer, she returned to bed and decided to dream no more that night.

4
Owlswood

It was only five days after the ill-fated Grenfield dinner party when Edmund and Regis climbed aboard the train in the dark pre-dawn hours and settled into their private compartment. Edmund had brought a suitable amount of reading material, but soon found the steady rhythm of the engine and the emerging rural countryside outside the window too engaging to ignore. He had always enjoyed travel by train, and now he found himself dozing and waking in turn, opening his eyes to an ever-changing and ever-more lush and calming view. "I think this was a good decision, don't you, boy?" he asked Regis as he leaned across the narrow aisle to where the dog reclined luxuriously, paws crossed, on the bench seat facing him. Edmund scratched behind the soft ears in just the right spot to elicit a canine groan of pleasure.

Despite having to transfer in York, the local train was early into Thornton Dale. Even so, the cab engaged to carry Edmund and Regis to their destination was waiting when they arrived. Predictably, Regis was far better behaved than his master at the station, where Edmund—ever impatient with incompetence—proceeded to softly but thoroughly berate the unfortunate driver and his assistant, neither of whom could find the right trunk among the other luggage. The big dog sat quietly, and with polite reserve accepted the affection heaped upon him by a small fellow traveler of about four years of age, who was also waiting for luggage to be found and loaded into a cart. The boy hugged the dog and was kissing Regis' nose when collected by his frazzled mother and taken off home.

At last, luggage loaded and grace restored, Regis and his master climbed into the carriage and set off for Owlswood, some miles northeast. The countryside was green and pleasantly rolling; every bush and tree seemed bursting with life. The fresh country air was filled with pockets of blue mist that rose from the hollows to dissipate in the afternoon sun. The sound of the horse's hooves on the macadam was soothing after the noise of the train, and birdsong drifted on the air. "Quite idyllic, eh boy?" Edmund said as he stroked Regis' head and relaxed into the ride.

About two miles from his destination, Edmund stopped the

driver and instructed him to continue on and deliver the luggage to the house, where someone would be waiting to receive it and direct them in its unloading and placement. He and Regis would walk the final distance to take full advantage of the remainder of the day—and to get a better sense of the lay of the land. He felt foolish admitting it, but waves of childhood memories came flooding back, filling him with heady euphoria.

They soon left the main road to do some real exploring; Edmund circled around off into the trees, relying on memory and instinct to guide him. When he felt he was close enough to the house, he took zigzags and overgrown paths to revisit his old haunts—the huge patch of blackberry bushes where he'd escape from his nanny and sit, undisturbed, under pricks of the doming vines with his toy soldier armies; the stately copse of oak trees where he would climb and hang from branches with his playmates on sunny afternoons; the little rise that seemed like such a fine hilltop for a game of "king of the mountain." He threw sticks for Regis and became so caught up in his explorations that he was surprised to note that a good two hours had passed since leaving the carriage, and that his shoes were caked with mud, his waistcoat streaked with dirt, and his trousers torn in one or two places. He dusted himself off as best he could, and he noted he was only about a quarter-mile from his destination. He realized, with some surprise, that he was looking forward to seeing the old house.

When he came into the clearing of the ancient summerhouse gazebo, and saw the fountain on the stone terrace some distance beyond, he grinned and began to trot toward it. "Come on, boy, let's go! Oh, Regis, you should have been with me then—what fine times we would have had! And that fountain—I used to sail my toy boats in there and wade about with them, driving my nanny absolutely mad!"

Man and dog trotted easily over the grass, slowing to a walk a little ways from the house. As they came closer, Edmund began to catch snippets of conversation between a man and woman. They stood just beyond a small stand of trees. He couldn't see them directly, but their words became clearer as he approached. He walked slowly and quietly so as not to disturb them.

"Samuel, this patch is just not doing well. Have you any recommendations?" The woman spoke in a pleasant, melodious voice.

"Ah, Jeannie my girl, I know exactly what's needed here —a

33

good bit 'o ticklecock, dug in deep and watered well. That'll do the trick!" The man's country accent was pleasing to hear. "I'm sorry, luv, I dinna notice before—I should have been watchin' closer, eh? But it won't take much time 'fore things are wild with growing. That should please the new master, alright. "

"Can you take care of it for me? Will it be costly—the ticklecock?" There was a touch of a laugh in the woman's voice.

"Oh nauw't much, I reckon—manure is pretty cheap at the old Foster place and we need just a cartload or two. The sun's a bit low in the sky now, I'll see to it first thing on the morrow."

"My thanks—and another thing about tomorrow—can we be sure of . . ."

A loud crash, followed by a furious feline shriek and a heart-rending howl, interrupted the conversation. All at once, Edmund found himself face to face with the owners of voices he had eaves-dropped upon: one, an elderly, though quite spry, man in garden-er's clothes, and one, a tall, slender, crisply-dressed young woman who looked at him first with escalating degrees of surprise, ap-praisal, and finally, concern.

"What the devil . . . !" Samuel exclaimed, " . . . get yourself out of the way, man!" Then he strode on with his companion hastening beside him. Edmund took pains to catch up with them.

All three hurried to the far corner of the garden where stood the ruins of a most impressive *orangerie* glasshouse, attached to the southern wall of the manor. It had been sadly neglected, many panes shattered and not replaced, the shelving beginning to show signs of rot, the lower beds covered in debris. Only a small portion was left intact and obviously in use; the door was open, and upon entering, they found a dirt-covered Great Dane, sprawled among shards of shattered clay flower pots. Regis lay woofing playfully at a large, fat, white-pawed orange cat who spit at him from a high potting shelf. The fur of the cat's back stood straight up as he hissed and swatted at the big dog with one of his white-stockinged paws, ears laid flat against his head. The dog seemed excited but playful; he had received a right good swap of the claw across his muzzle and was alternately whining piteously and woofing with delight at the play.

"Regis—Come!" commanded Edmund. Regis immediately came to his master's side and sat, panting, managing to look happy and sheepish at the same time.

"This dog is yours, then?" The young woman turned on her heel to face Edmund. "One would think the owner of such a large animal would teach it better manners." She had picked up a stout-handled hoe as she had entered, not sure of Regis or the possible need for defense.

"The dog is mine, yes." He felt annoyed at the criticism. "And how would you expect a dog to behave when attacked by a spitfire cat?"

"Attacked? The cat did not attack, nor is he accustomed to being accosted by a strange animal ten times his size. This is his home, sir, and I take it your unruly beast chased him into this glasshouse and up onto the shelf, where he was forced to defend himself and his territory." Her eyes flashed but she maintained complete control and looked at him with cool appraisal. "And may I ask what exactly you and your dog are doing on this property?"

"I take it I am addressing the owner of this house, then?" Edmund was seized with mischief and, admittedly, the desire to take this self-possessed young woman down a notch. He decided to test the mettle of his staff—he assumed she was part of his staff.

"I am charged with the care of this house. And you have not yet answered my question." Her eyes kept calmly focused on his.

"Where is the owner, then? I'm not used to dealing with servants, I'd like to speak directly to him immediately." Self-possessed woman, he thought to himself, and straightforward enough.

"You will deal with me, sir, and provide me with reason as to why I should not have you detained by the local constabulary for trespass." She looked at his disheveled and dirty clothing as she continued, and Edmund noted that she tightened her grasp on the hoe. "Best hurry with your answer as I am not used to being put off by ill-mannered strangers."

Her voice did not raise and her manner did not change, but the intensity of her gaze made Edmund extremely uncomfortable and increasingly annoyed, until he realized that her tenacity in looking after his own interests should inspire his admiration. He thought he'd better set things straight.

"My apologies. I seem to have created a false impression here, not to mention a devil of a mess!" He smiled what he thought was his most winning smile.

"You have my full attention." The woman remained unsmiling.

"Watch yerself, young fellow," the old man cautioned. "I can be off t' fetch Constable Pryce in a trice. Shall I go now?" he asked the woman. He, too, was armed with a stout rake snagged from the tool rack.

"Just a moment," Edmund spoke quickly. "When you hear me out, you'll certainly need no constable. The owner of this estate has to the moment been 'in absentia' in London, is that not correct? He is, however, due to take up residence in the house at any moment and you have been making things ready for his arrival. In fact, his luggage has not long ago arrived without him. "

"Any poacher or trespasser on these grounds could have seen luggage delivered. I hope you have more to say than that." She tilted her head slightly and arched one eyebrow.

"I do. Yes. Well. The luggage has the monogram of JES on each piece which stands for J. Edmund Symme, the owner of the house. And you, miss, are no doubt a member of the caretaking family who was named in John Symme's will—John Symme being the grandfather of the present owner. "

"And you are?" Her tone softened slightly.

"Allow me to introduce your employer and his rowdy dog; J. Edmund Symme, at your service, and Regis, whom I assure you has impeccable manners when unprovoked."

Edmund bowed slightly and offered another brilliant smile.

"Neither man nor beast needs impeccable manners until provoked." She looked at him for a moment, evaluating what he had told them, then continued drily. "Mr. Symme, I'm afraid we are not used to such spectacular entrances."

Edmund replied almost in a murmur, "My specialty up to now has been spectacular exits, but," then speaking out more directly, "I assure you I take no offense at your concern for the welfare of my property, Miss . . . your name?"

"Remy. And this is groundskeeper Samuel Cox."

Edmund extended his hand to the man. "I remember you! You were here in my grandfather's time, were you not? Had quite a large staff of gardeners as I recall. I'm very pleased to see you're still here."

"Aye, it may be my father you remember, Head Gardener, and I his foreman. And I remember you, Master Edmund—quite a nuisance of a lad you were then, much smaller of course." Samuel shook the offered hand firmly. "Yes, we had many more bodies that time, lookin' after the place. It's just me now. So, if things are not up to your likings, I'm letting you know why in advance."

Edmund nodded. "Well, I would be most pleased to get into the house and settled. Shall we?"

He gestured toward the manor and began to walk, Regis steady at his side. As soon as they had left the lawn, Puss-in-Boots was coaxed into his mistress' arms and soothed with gentle stroking. He then leapt to the ground and was off to the house, running through the hedges and keeping one eye out for the intruding canine.

Remy and Samuel followed their employer across the grass and up onto the brickwork terrace just in time to see Regis stand on his back legs and take a long drink from the lowest fountain tier, almost submerging his entire upper body in the cool, gurgling water. Then he got down, gave himself a quick shake, and took off after Edmund into the house, sopping forepaws and all.

"Oh, my" exclaimed Jeanne under her breath, "The floors were just yesterday polished!" She sighed deeply. Then she turned to Samuel. "Well, what think you of our manor lord?"

"Nothin' much to think yet, my girl, exceptin' that he likes dogs. Best to give the man a chance—he was a spirited wee boy, alright, and maybe he's a decent man. Time will tell." He stopped and seemed to think of something. "Didn't you know him when you were both small? He didn't say he remembered you, but I seem to recall you two in mischief together."

"We weren't supposed to play together, but sometimes did. I was glad to have reason to avoid him, though—he was very bossy." She shook her head. "Maybe he won't remember the time I . . . oh well."

"Don't fret on what hasn't happened yet; people change over years. Well, I'm off now, luv. Ticklecock be here tomorrow, right, first thing!" Samuel tipped his cap and made his way off.

Remy thought it best to find her employer and see if she could be of assistance. She made her way into the house and noted with satisfaction the way things looked: everything polished, gleaming, flowers in the great room, all in proper readiness for a homecoming. She was sure J. Edmund Symme would be pleased, even though their first meeting had taken a turn neither had expected nor appreciated. She found him on the landing of the stairway, looking at the portrait of John Symme that dominated the foyer. It was a dark and somber painting; its subject looked out, brooding and unsmiling, with apparent displeasure on any who would climb this stair. A sad-looking, angry man, Jeanne had always thought, I wonder what hurt him so?

Edmund seemed to be having similar thoughts as he studied the face. Then he noticed her and turned. "My grandfather's portrait, much as I remember him from my childhood. Well, Remy—Remy is it? I should like to take some time to freshen up and then I expect you will make yourself available to go over the daily routine I intend, as well as some other matters. And now I would like to see my room."

Edmund was pleased when the door to his bedroom suite was opened and the key handed to him. The huge four-poster bed of cherrywood shone, the bed itself laid with a goose eiderdown. Its burgundy spread and canopy matched the draperies on the windows and the fat cushions in the window seat. There was a huge fireplace with a black marble mantelpiece on which stood an exquisite silver-cased clock and several highly-polished silver candlesticks. Before the fireplace, two large and comfortable arm chairs stood, also upholstered in rich burgundy fabric. There was an offset alcove to the side, and in it, a writing desk and matching chair. A small sideboard on the far wall held a silver tray with crystal decanters of various liquors, a crystal water pitcher, and two goblets. On the other side of the room stood a great armoire with a large oval mirror in its door, and a wash stand topped with the same black marble as the mantle. There were small crystal vases of fresh flowers throughout the room. A door led to a small private bath.

Edmund's trunk and valise had been deposited next to the armoire. Remy entered the room and flung open the windows nearest the bed, which looked out over the fountain and lawn area beyond.

"I was not sure you wanted your belongings unpacked, Mr. Symme, as we had no word about your bringing a personal valet. I thought it best to inquire first." Remy came to stand before him.

"Ah. No, quite right. My personal staff is remaining in London, I couldn't inflict the country on them." He spoke absently, seemingly unaware of the implied insult. "I shall tend to unpacking myself. Have you engaged additional help—a cook and a housemaid?"

"I have made tentative arrangements, as I was unclear about your desires in that matter. Would you care to interview or do you leave the choice to me?"

"Good God, no bloody interviews!" Edmund looked a bit embarrassed at his exclamation, but continued. "Pardon my vehemence. I am here to get away from all such activities, Remy, to simplify my life for a while. You engage all help needed, and you are responsible for them. Understood?"

She inclined her head slightly in assent, and he continued. "While we are on the subject, I have breakfast each morning at 7:00am sharp. I do not myself take luncheon, but will have tea at 3:30, dinner served at 8:00pm. All my meals are substantial in nature and I expect as full a table service as you can manage during my stay here. I trust you can take care of menus?" When she nodded again, he continued. "Be sure tea and coffee are available at each meal. I am not particularly fond of organ meats, except for sweetbreads occasionally; see that cook is so informed. I think that's all—oh, and no more flowers in my room, please, although the ones in the rest of the house are fine. Thank you, Remy, that is all."

She looked at him for a moment, then said, "Yes, sir," as she turned to leave. "Oh, and Mr. Symme," she paused on her way out, tossing over her shoulder, "welcome to Owlswood." Shaking her head in disbelief as she went downstairs, she thought, "*Arrogant, unpleasant man!*"

*　　*　　*

Edmund unpacked quickly and, after his much-needed bath and change of clothes, began to explore the house, refreshing his memory, Regis at heel. Only some of the rooms had been kept open for use—the house was of normal size for a country place, designed to accommodate a large extended family but not suited for formal entertaining. The upper two floors remained closed off, their rooms locked tight. Grandfather Symme had always taken the top floor of the house as his own, demanding solitude, and Edmund doubted anyone had set foot up there in the past two decades. The main floor, with all of its living space in the great room, dining room, library, music room, kitchen, and cook's quarters, had been kept up beautifully.

The floor with his room was just above, and there were three other bedrooms open and ready. Edmund recalled that he was settled in one of the larger rooms. He peeked into the two rooms down the hallway from his door and found them to be similar in furnishings, except that one was very femininely done with flowered patterned chintz. The other was more like his room, but done in deep blue and not as large. He looked into the third room, quite a bit smaller than the others and located at the far end of the hallway next to the service stair, and was surprised to see Puss-In-Boots lying luxuriously across the bed, enjoying the rays of the waning afternoon sun.

"Definitely lived-in, wouldn't you say? And by our feisty housekeeper, apparently. Installed herself in a family room, has she? Most unseemly," Edmund muttered to himself.

He continued down the stairway and paused again before the portrait on the landing. "Well, grandfather, you great ogre, I'm come back to the family home." Edmund spoke aloud. "You were an arrogant old knave in life and I never liked you much, but you have my unending gratitude for your will and the upkeep of this house." He bowed slightly and continued downstairs.

After poking around on the ground floor and finding the rooms familiar (but somewhat smaller than he had remembered), full of flowers in huge vases, furniture polished with beeswax scented with lemon, Edmund entered the library. Ever since childhood, he had loved this one room with a passion. He used to scramble up onto the seat in the big bay window and nestle there with a book. He would be so quiet that adults using the room would often not be aware of his presence, and he would overhear many supposedly private conversations. Most of the time he would just shut the voices out, but sometimes he would be privy to quarrels and confidences between his parents and grandparents, many of which he did not understand. And the books! Every inch of wall space was lined with shelves filled with books of every kind! The earliest friends he had were books from these shelves—adventure yarns, stories from holy scripture, even Grimm's Tales. He had left Owlswood long before his tastes had matured into Yeats, Milton, Socrates, and social commentaries, but his quest for knowledge and joy in the written word was born and nurtured in this room.

His eyes scanned the bookshelves and were delighted to see his "old friends" still occupying their niches. The volumes were dusted and well-cared-for, much as he had found the rest of the house. Still prominent were the Moroccan leather-bound classics that his grandfather would not let him touch—which he now took down and perused with pleasure. On a far, high corner shelf, Edmund could make out books with French titles on their spines, and he wondered for what reason his forebears had interest in French literature—much less literature *written* in French. He remembered them as astute managers of financial affairs but rather philistine in their tastes and certainly never linguistically sophisticated enough to read Diderot and Madame de Genlis *en Francais*.

Edmund reflected on the disregard in which he held his recent ancestors: his father Nigel, a rather remote and ineffectual man who did nothing much during his lifetime but sire Edmund and die young; his grandfather John, who was withdrawn, cold, and brutally impatient. Old Symme was feared by everyone, but especially his only grandson who was filled with enough questions and high spirits for three boys his size. That left the most questionable and obscure of the lot, his great-grandfather Alistair, who managed to amass a magnificent fortune and, in so doing, earned his reputation for ruthlessly destroying anyone or anything foolish enough to get in his way.

He remembered that he had not seen the house from the front yet, so out the heavy mahogany door and down the stonework steps to the front drive he and Regis went. "No more major excursions until tomorrow, dog, but a quick turn around the grounds will do us good!" The drive was a graceful semi-circle framed by flowering fruit trees and Edmund could see the massive black iron grillwork entry gate and fence along the road some hundred meters away. His feet crunched gravel as he began to walk.

He was suddenly seized with a disorienting sense of déjà vu and a knot in the pit of his stomach; he stopped and looked around him. He could see nothing amiss, but he felt off balance, nauseous. Regis sat and looked at him inquiringly, hoping this was not the end of the walk.

Edmund shook his head and continued along to the place where the drive branched off, one side curving toward the entry gate, the other around to the back side of the house. "I've been here—this exact place—very, very recently." He again turned and looked all around him. "But that's impossible." He paused, then started to walk again. "Come, Regis," he called.

They continued their quick loop around the main house, Edmund recovering enough to note with pleasure the compact but verdant vegetable and herb garden, bordered by rose bushes, standing close outside the kitchen door. Someone knows this soil, he thought to himself, must be Samuel's doing. They came again to the fountain, took a quick turn through the small maze of privet and rosemary bushes, and came into the house by the door they had first used to enter that afternoon. The floor showed no evidence of their recent soggy entrance. The afternoon was fading into dusk, and a slight but chill wind began to ruffle the trees.

Feeling somewhat more himself, Edmund headed down the hall toward the library, where he encountered Remy, emerging and closing the door behind her, a book in hand. Regis continued to her side and nudged her free hand, demanding to be petted. She smiled and obliged, and somehow this familiarity on the part of his usually most discriminating companion annoyed him.

"I shall take dinner in this room today, Remy. You will be kind enough to bring a tray. I assume something will be ready at the designated hour, even without a cook? Something cold is acceptable under the circumstances." He spoke commandingly, perhaps because he felt a bit uneasy. Before she could reply, he continued. "And while you are here, I should like to know why you have that book. Are household staff normally allowed access to private libraries in Yorkshire?"

She looked at him calmly, still scratching Regis behind the ears. Nearly as tall as he, her eyes met his straight on. "In other houses, I know not. However, if you will recall the provisions of your grandfather's will, Mr. Symme, you may remember that my family has been afforded the use of this library, and all books herein, 'as long as Owlswood shall stand'—if I may quote the exact words. Therefore, I have this book because I read quite ravenously and I plan to read it. As I understand it, I do not overstep, unless, of course, you intend to countermand this specific codicil provision?"

Edmund, caught being somewhat stuffy even in his own eyes, paused. "I seem to recall that line, yes. Thank you for refreshing my memory. It has been some time since I concerned myself with the affairs of this house, but of course, the will stands as stated. However, another matter if you please," he went on as she made move to leave. "I have found that you are installed in a room on the second floor, rather than in the servants' quarters off the kitchen. May I inquire why?"

"Of course, sir, you may. Even in the country, it is unwise for a woman alone to be the only inhabitant of a house and grounds such as Owlswood. While the house remained uninhabited by your family, Samuel Cox, a widower for some years, made use of cook's quarters. He did so, not only to keep good track of security, but because he would often work from before daybreak to just after dark. This is a large labor for one man, even a young man, and it often takes Samuel many hours to accomplish his work."

"Very sensible, yes—but didn't Samuel's family have a cottage on the grounds? I seem to remember a groundskeeper's lodging not too far from the house."

"Yes, you recall correctly. However, that cottage fell into disuse and has not been livable for some years. Therefore, Samuel lodges next to the kitchen, and the housekeeper was 'installed', as you say, in the former lady's maid's room in which I now stay. Since the house was not designed for a full complement of servants, we have no other below-stair lodging." She paused for a moment, meeting Edmund's discomfited gaze. "Would you have Samuel leave, Mr. Symme? He shall be gone as soon as you give the word, and I would also relocate immediately, upon request."

"I had not considered that. No, of course he shall stay. But now that cook will be coming . . ." Edmund was unsteadied by her cool composure and the absolute logic and good sense of her actions.

"There will be no problem. Since we spoke earlier this afternoon, I have engaged a cook to start tomorrow, who lives nearby and who prefers to leave each night to be with her family. The maid also will come from the village each day. Am I to understand, then, that the arrangements as they stand are acceptable?" Her eyebrow arched slightly with the question.

"Everything seems to be . . . acceptable. Yes. However . . . I am puzzled about something. I was expecting rather a more mature individual in the post of housekeeper. Someone with more tenure and experience." He looked at her closely. "Can you enlighten me here? *Are* you the official housekeeper?"

Remy returned his look. "Yes, I am. Until very recently, however, my mother was the 'official' housekeeper here and I assisted her at various times. She has now passed on." She tried to keep the catch from her voice. "So, again, as per the stipulation of the will, I am the family member entrusted with the care of Owlswood, officially." She stressed the last word drily.

"Ah, very unfortunate news. Condolences on the death of your mother," Edmund paused. "So, you are very inexperienced in this role?"

Anger rising, she kept her voice steady. "I am more than capable of running this household, Mr. Symme. I have assisted my mother for a number of years, and my grandmother before her, and I grew up here. While no owner has used the house for many years, I am fully capable of directing the staff in your requirements. You will be most satisfied with everything during your stay."

"Ah, well, good. I rest assured of your competence. Under the circumstances, however, I feel it incumbent upon me to review the house ledgers and account books, which I have only attended to most cursorily in the past. May I rely on seeing them sometime tomorrow?"

"Of course, sir—and after an entry for the delivery of ticklecock tomorrow, the accounts will be completely up to date." She felt her cheeks color with annoyance, but also smiled inwardly at Samuel's colloquial word for manure.

"Very good, I shall meet with you immediately post breakfast. And again, my sympathy for your loss."

She nodded in acknowledgement.

"Thank you. If that is all, dinner will be brought to you here at 8:00."

Remy turned and left. *What a disagreeable man,* she thought again as she quickly walked away. *What an absolute, arrogant ass!*

"What a disagreeable female," Edmund muttered, looking after Remy as she left. "You seem to like her quite well, you traitor," Regis laid his ears back and looked guilty, "but you never were a good judge of character. She is headstrong, rather outspoken. Certainly doesn't seem like a servant at all. Much younger than I had expected. Country people are a different breed, one must suppose, but a servant who doesn't know her place may know little else. And one who is interested in French literature—I believe that was a volume of Rimbaud. Very odd, indeed."

He entered the library and felt soothed almost immediately. Thinking to get a good hour's read before dinner, he scanned the shelves until his eyes were drawn to several tall, slim volumes bound in sky blue leather with gold lettering. He picked one up and read, "Symme Family Chronicles Volume I" on its cover.

"What's this? Family chronicles?" His interest piqued, Edmund crossed to sit in the armchair nearest the fireplace and began to read the entries, all in neat script, of what seemed to be a personal chronology of family events written in a beautiful, and obviously feminine, hand. Although some mention of business was made, most of the entries were about family members, gatherings, and anecdotal stories—the kind of information interesting to mothers, grandmothers, and new wives. Edmund found himself fascinated, though, because he had stumbled upon more insight into the personal lives of his forbears than was ever before provided. The book was filled, too, with names of the families and friends invited to stay at Owlswood and whose lives and fortunes were interwoven with those of the Symmes. Edmund was utterly absorbed through the entire first volume, then was about to rise and get Volume II when he heard a discreet tapping at the door and Remy entered, dinner tray in hand.

"Good evening, Mr. Symme." Edmund glanced at the mantel clock as she placed the tray on the small reading table next to his chair, "8:00."

"Good evening, Remy." He inspected the tray and noted a small cheese plate with fruit, several slices of warm bread with a tub of butter, and a bottle of claret in addition to a covered soup plate, from which came a deliciously savory aroma. "I thought the cook was coming tomorrow?"

"That is correct, sir. I prepared the meal. This is cassoulet, one of my mother's recipes, which I thought acceptable for tonight. I hope all is to your liking. *Bon appétit*, Mr. Symme. I will leave you now, and collect the tray before I retire."

"No need to return, you are dismissed for the evening, Remy. Goodnight."

"As you wish, then. Goodnight." As she turned to leave the room, Edmund called after her.

"Ah—before you go." She stopped and turned to face him. "Do you see, there, across the room on the fourth shelf near the corner, a leather volume in blue? Please fetch it here."

Remy bridled slightly at his tone, walked to the shelf, selected the requested volume, and turned to bring it to Edmund. As soon as her palms touched the leather, she began to pale and her eyes took on a far away, glassy cast. She felt out of time, past the walls of the room, in some long dark hallway. She took a few steps and then stopped, and tottered, catching herself on the back of the desk.

"What's wrong?" Edmund rose from his chair and hurried over to her. He took the book from her free hand, set it down on the desk and took her arm to guide her to a chair. "Are you all right?"

45

She drew breath, blinked her eyes several times, and seemed to regain her color and composure after a moment.

"Yes. I am all right, Mr. Symme. Thank you."

"Are you certain—some water, perhaps?"

Edmund was neither convinced of her recovery nor pleased at the prospect of a fainted servant woman sunk onto the library floor.

"Forgive me, I . . . I am very much recovered and apologize if I have distressed you. Please give it no more thought. Goodnight."

She straightened, let go of the table and quickly left. Edmund watched her go before erupting.

"Bloody hell, Regis, what next! A newly-coined, headstrong housekeeper prone to swoon—Wilson was right, I should have brought him. Damn it all, my luck with women never changes! Hrmmp."

He stomped around the room briefly, but soon the aroma of his dinner tray enticed him to be seated. He began to enjoy his dinner, feeling better and better with each mouthful, and he relaxed.

"She can apparently cook quite well; I'll say that for her at least. I hope the 'official' cook can do as well," he said wryly, remembering the earlier conversation. After finishing his cheese and fruit, he rose and retrieved the slim blue volume that had caused Remy's swoon from the desk, poured himself a large snifter of cognac, and settled back into the voluminous leather armchair to continue his reading.

As Remy closed up the kitchen and prepared to retire, she was fuming. "*Not now, not again,*" she thought angrily, "*I must not lapse into...This house, this place always brings them on.*" She mused aloud. "*I cannot afford to start 'seeing' again, it mustn't happen. Why do they come? They must leave me alone!*"

Her emotions in a jumble, she climbed the stair to her room and locked the door. *And to have it happen in front of that man!* she thought has she brushed her hair. *What an arrogant, disagreeable person he is, employer or not! It takes no visions to see that nothing good will come of this.*

*   *   *

After consuming all but the last swallow of cognac, Edmund felt very contented indeed. An unexpectedly excellent dinner, he had to admit, and he was absorbed and most entertained, in spite of himself, by reading the anecdotal richness of the little history of his forbears, handwritten in the slim little book. Nevertheless, his eyes began to tire, and he could see the moon rise through the library window. He was growing sleepy and several times vowed to leave for his bed as soon as the page was finished, but he continued on, intrigued by the stories that unfolded. He found himself particularly taken with an amusing section on—of all people—his despised grandfather! He was actually chuckling to himself when suddenly he felt a cool, delicious breeze on his skin. He looked up to see the lamp flicker briefly, though no window was open, and then he noticed a sweet gardenia scent.

His eyes, so tired and hot just a moment before, felt relaxed and easy. His shoulders and chest, cramped from sitting so long, suddenly felt cool and liquid, as if gentle hands had kneaded the muscles into a soothed and comfortable rest. A great sense of well-being came over him, along with a feeling of . . . intense expectation. He could almost hear a crackle of electricity in the air, or was it the rustle of heavy silk?

He sat up, alert now, and saw in the dark air just above mantelpiece and glow of the dying fireplace embers a shimmering of light. It grew brighter as he watched, and a form began to emerge. As the rustling became louder and the scent of gardenia stronger, he saw in the light, the shape of a woman growing ever more distinct. She was clothed in a dress of peach silk and creamy lace, in a style of long ago, and her cascading flame-red hair was dressed with gleaming combs of pearl and sprays of gardenia. Her bodice, cut low on her shoulders to expose a gleaming décolleté, displayed more creamy-fleshed gardenia nestled in the cleft of her bosom. She perched prettily on the mantlepiece, and looked at Edmund with an amused expression, leaning forward toward him so even more of her breasts were visible. Edmund's eyes grew wide and he stood up in amazement. The lady made no sound, but leaned ever closer as if to touch him. His mouth gaped like a hooked fish, but he could make no sound. Then he smiled slightly and bowed, which seemed to delight the vision before him. She pouted her lips sensuously, and with a mischievous gleam in her sea-green eyes, raised one elegant, graceful hand to blow him a kiss, and disappeared!

Edmund felt knocked senseless. He almost swooned and recovered his balance with difficulty, shook his head, and wondered if he was . . . overtired. He looked at the brandy snifter and then examined it closely, wondering if something had been . . . but no, he had poured it himself. What the devil just happened? He flopped back into the armchair and tried to put his thoughts in order. He was not asleep, he was not drunk, he was not drugged, and he was not crazy. And yet, there was no doubt he had just seen the most beautiful woman he had ever laid eyes on, there before him, coalesced out of thin air, like a dream or a . . . spirit. And not only had he seen her, but felt her, been enveloped by her! What an experience! And although she had said no word, he could hear words in his head saying, *"Bienvenue, Chérie, je suis enchantée a vous voir, enfin*! Finally, my dear, we meet!"

My God, Edmund thought, suddenly unsettled and shivering; it's time for bed.

5
Fleur

The next morning, having slept well, Edmund almost convinced himself that the vision of the previous night had been no more than the trick of an over-stimulated mind. He decided he was hardly the kind of man to hallucinate, and since the experience had lasted but a brief moment, he talked himself into discounting the entire thing. After an unnecessary hour post-breakfast, looking over the household account books—impeccably accurate and clear—Edmund was satisfied that Owlswood was indeed in good hands, and Regis got his promised outing into the countryside. Instructions were given that they would not be back for tea, but Edmund would have dinner at the appointed hour that evening, and the pair set out in great high spirits.

The weather was gloriously fair and warm. Regis pranced and ran and leapt over the hedgerows, scattering quail, always turning back to see if his master was coming. As they continued together over the meadow toward the wood, delicious scents came to them. To the man, the perfume of honeysuckle, mint, and heather. To the dog, spoor of rabbit and weasel and deer. They were absorbed in the lush surroundings and spent a good hour exploring before coming upon the stream, there pausing to drink and rest.

Edmund was delighted to revisit the pollywogs thick in the shallows at water's edge; he lay down on the cushiony mossy bank, propped on his elbows, to watch them. Ever since he was a boy, he loved the roly-poly little beings, some with just a hint of leg at the junction of round body and serpent-like tale. He loved to see them swim in unison this way and that, their dark, velvety bodies plump and swift through the water. He was fascinated at how they would come to rest on a flat stone and lie motionless as the clear water moved over them. Did their tiny brains have any idea what was about to become of them; did they know that they swam on the brink of a major life change? Do frogs remember pollywog days?

He yawned and stretched, then gathered a pebble and tossed it—plink!—watching the ripples sweep away, rocking pollywogs and startling hovering dragonflies. He laid back and watched the clouds for a while, finding shapes in them as he did when he was a boy. Not one law book up there, he thought, not one judge, not one gavel, not one brief, not one newspaper, not one ancestor.

He tried not to think of his hallucination of the night before, but with little success. So he put the case to himself. Point: Simple overstimulation, of course, coupled with childhood memories, a disconcerting servant, and general fatigue from travel, manifested in a realistic daydream. *Point: I am a man of intellect and stature, keen of mind and instinct, not a madman—nor is there hereditary madness in my family. Point: One does not go mad in the library over brandy and ancestral stories. Absurd . . . But she was so beautiful . . .*

"And that most unexpected book!" he said aloud. "And the library, just as mesmerizing as when I was a child! It's almost as if a spell comes over me in that room. Well. Summary: I needn't worry about myself—it was merely a passing episode, like indigestion from a too-rich meal. Case closed."

All was peace and tranquility for some time. Edmund dozed contentedly until he was disturbed by the sound of men's voices further down the riverbank. They grew louder and more raucous—at least three, from the sound. It annoyed him at first; after all, this was his spot, on his land, and no one should intrude. When the sounds came no closer, he relaxed again. Perhaps these are neighbors, he thought; trespassing, probably, but to be expected since the house has been unoccupied. He stood up and brushed the grass from his trousers and, feeling curious, set off at a casual stroll toward the sound.

Perhaps I should introduce myself, he thought. As he drew closer, the voice of a woman joined the men's. She seemed to be arguing with them, calmly but intensely. His interest was piqued and he moved a little faster. Then he heard the high-pitched scream of a child. Regis growled low in his throat and bounded off in a spray of water, Edmund at a run behind.

When they reached the clearing, Edmund found an ugly scene. The stream pooled around a horseshoe bend full of willows, and there he saw the young men, perhaps the eldest a man of four and twenty, manhandling a very small girl and a furious woman. A broken slate and smashed basket lay tossed aside on the bank. A huge goose attacked the men from every angle, honking and hissing and furiously flapping its wings as it tried to bite the one who had the child dangling by one arm. One of his companions took a stick from the ground and began to chase the goose, and when a blow landed, laughed loudly in triumph. Edmund noted several small animal snares dangling from the man's belt. Poachers, of course.

The woman commanded, "Let the child be! Kane, stop this! Get off, get away from her!" When she was ignored, she leapt upon the back of the one holding the child, pummeled his head, and finally raked her fingernails across his face, leaving bloody gouges in his cheek. The third man sauntered over to the aid of his companion, grabbed the woman's arms and wrenched her off. They were all shouting and the child continued to scream in pain and fear.

"Bloody goose! Nip me, will you! I'll break your legs!"

"We don't need devil spawn among us! Throw the girl in, Kane—let's see if she floats or sinks, like a witch!"

The man whose face the woman had scratched looked at her with disdain. He had a proud, cruelly arrogant face and dressed in somewhat better clothing than the other two.

"Time enough for that later," he said.

He dropped the child into the dirt, wiped his face with his forearm and spat at the woman's feet.

"We want no witches, and no fine city ladies who think they're better than us—with poisons and potions, lying and riling up our good women with false ideas. We know how to deal with such women, always have!" His eyes glinted maliciously. "And it's said, anyone who draws my blood and leaves me living must pay. A man would pay with his own blood, but . . . you will pay differently, and hope I find it good enough."

He drew a blade and began to slice the buttons off the front of her bodice, exposing her camisole as the fabric parted.

It was then that Regis barked his stentorian warning and was upon them. He leapt at the closest, the man with the stick, and hit him full on the chest with his paws, knocking him to the ground, and began tearing at the hand holding the weapon. Edmund was close behind, and having picked up a stout fallen branch, he swung it so hard that when it contacted the head of the man with the knife, it broke in two and framed the fellow's unconscious body as it fell. Edmund then turned attention to the large, brutish boy who was twisting the woman's arms. As the woman ducked, he spun around and hit him full in the face with his fist and heard a crack—whether the brute's jaw or his own knuckles, he couldn't tell. A trickle of blood, and a tooth, came from the boy's mouth as he hit the ground.

Edmund called Regis to his side and surveyed the three bullies, one groggily coming to and the others conscious and nursing various wounds.

"Good God, what kind of men are these!" he exclaimed out loud. "Besides being poachers and thieves!"

It was only then that he took time to look at the woman and was startled to recognize her: Remy! She was cradling the child in her arms, soothing her with soft sounds, and returning his look of amazement.

His surprise replaced by indignation, he addressed the wounded attackers.

"See here, just what do you bloody imbeciles think you're doing? How dare you attack a member of my household?!" he demanded.

"Who the hell are you? What's it your business?" The big one whose tooth Edmund knocked out spoke.

"I—you village idiot—am the owner of this land, and this dog, and the employer of this woman. And you, sir, need to learn manners!"

Edmund grabbed the youth by his shirt, and yanking him to his feet, punched him hard in the midsection, and pushed him into the water. One of the others made a move to come to his aid, but Regis bared his teeth and snarled a warning, hackles raised, and the man backed off nervously.

"Either one of you other cowards care to take on a grown man instead of a woman and a small child?" Edmund challenged as the waterlogged bully sloshed out of the shallows. "And I see you've been setting snares—poaching? I'll have you all before the magistrate on the morrow. Wait—stop, you bloody ruffians!"

They had gathered their wits and were half stumbling, half running into the cover of the trees. Regis pricked up his ears and looked at Edmund questioningly.

"Stay. Let them nurse their wounds. We'll find them later."

He watched as they disappeared over the rise, then turned to Remy and the child.

"Well, ladies, what happened here?" he demanded.

"We were . . . accosted."

She hesitated and then decided more explanation was required.

"Cook needed a few things from the village, and I offered to go, since I wanted to see Molly and her family. While we took time for a short walk and a reading lesson, there were uninvited visitors."

"Just like that? Why?"

When Remy shook her head wearily, Edmund continued, "Never mind now. I think we'd best leave here, just in case they regain their courage. Can you walk, Miss Remy?"

"Yes, of course." She rose awkwardly and handed the child into Edmund's arms. "Here, please take Molly, will you," she stated more than asked, and quickly adjusted her blouse and smoothed her skirts.

Edmund, startled to find a small weeping girl clinging to his chest, gingerly folded his arms around her and turned his attention back to Remy. Apart from looking tousled and dazed, she had suffered only minor bruises, in addition to the assault on her clothing.

"Mr. Symme, how did you come to find us?" Before Edmund could reply, she cried "Oh, no!" as she saw the injured goose, feebly twitching on the ground. She rushed to gather up the poor beast in the folds of her shawl. "Bloody bastards—damn them to hell!" She spat the words from between clenched teeth.

Edmund's eyebrows raised at hearing such unseemly language from a female, but had to admit that she was entitled to it.

"Yes. I heartily agree. But let's be off now before any further unpleasantness occurs."

* * *

And so, they set off toward the village. Remy gently adjusted the goose in her shawl, cradling it in the crook of her arm, quieting it with her voice. The child soon stopped whimpering and snuggled into Edmund's shoulder, as the rhythm of his stride lulled her into a sleepy state. Her flax-colored hair was very soft and smelled of hay and lavender.

"So, off for a pleasant afternoon were you, when your unexpected visitors arrived?" he spoke softly to Remy. "You called one of them by name; do you know the others?"

"Yes, I know them." she replied grimly. "Kane is the son of a landowner nearby; the others are boys from the village. "

"Boys! You have nasty large boys in this shire!" he snorted. Catching her wry look, he continued. "Why should they bother you?"

She sighed wearily. "Well, for one thing, I am persona non grata since I left the village over a year ago. I went to the city, I went to be educated, I have strange ideas, I think village life and village men aren't good enough for me. Worse, I share my ideas with other women."

She nodded at the child. "For another, this little one carries the mark of the devil, and so is fair game." When Edmund looked puzzled she added, "The clubfoot."

He looked down at the legs wrapped around his middle and felt with his free hand the deformed limb.

"Ah." *They are idiots*, he thought, *heads full of ghosts and superstitions.*

"She's marked by the evil one, her mother probably a witch but certainly of loose morals, and General Gander is her familiar, of course." She looked fondly at the goose in her arms. "Brave champion-heart notwithstanding," she said ruefully. "Ignorance and cruelty are a way of life for some. Many fear and hate what they cannot explain. And use power over others for sport."

"You seem to have escaped succumbing to superstition and ignorance," Edmund replied, "though coming from the same village."

"I've never been a tractable student in the demeaning of women or children, or of the weak by the strong." She looked straight at him as she spoke, the color still high in her face. "I don't fancy the occult explaining reality."

"Indeed." Edmund replied and a hint of a smile flickered on his lips. "Is the child a relative of yours?"

"The dearest friend of my girlhood gave birth to Molly. It seems she conceived the child with no husband, no betrothed, and moreover, she refused to name the father. Gossip has it that a man came to her in the moonlight, at midnight on the Sabbath, only once." She smiled sadly. "It was a difficult birth. She died because midwife Cooper was too ill to come, and no other would attend the birth of a child conceived of the moonlight man." She turned her face away, scanning the sky. "I was the only one there with her, and I couldn't save her; I didn't have the skill. Then Annie came and helped me, and took the baby as her own. Since the clubfoot is obvious proof of the curse and reminder of the sin of her mother, Molly has had a difficult time."

"Why was she so afraid to name the father, your friend?"

"I never understood why. The son of a rich man, perhaps, or the town bully, or someone married. Or she was forced and afraid of more abuse if she spoke out. Anyway, these things are always the woman's folly and burden, aren't they?"

She expected no answer.

"You don't believe in superstitions and the occult, then, though your neighbors do? That's a fairly enlightened opinion."

He found himself interested in what she thought, for some reason.

"I admit there are many things I do not understand," she replied. "But I do know that the man who fathered Molly was flesh and blood."

"The man should have come forth." He felt somehow embarrassed for his sex. "If he had a shred of honor in him."

"Yes," she agreed. "He didn't. And Sarah had to pay. Women always pay,"

"A cynical viewpoint, Miss Remy." Edmund commented.

Remy looked at him sharply.

"I am quite cynical, Mr. Symme, toward a society that places limits and unfair burdens on its distaff members. Any woman with half a brain, who is aware of what goes on around her, cannot help but feel the same."

Edmund's interest was piqued.

"I know a fair number of women who do not share that view— women who are most pleased to live and even thrive in the society you criticize so vehemently."

He could not help but think of the women he knew in London, Lydia and those like her, who seemed very contented with their lot and even seemed to make the most of it.

Remy smiled ruefully.

"And I wager they are women who live by the leave of benign protectors—fathers, husbands, brothers—who treat them like beloved pets. And like pets, they are expected to look impeccable and behave prettily, not speak too loudly or too long, and certainly not express any dangerously unusual thoughts. Yes, for some fortunate birds, the cages are gilded and comfortable, indeed, but they are still caged and still controlled by keepers."

Edmund stopped in his tracks and turned to face her. He felt his rhetoric warming up.

"I beg your pardon, but this is intolerable conversation! You, a housekeeper in an obscure village, castigate fine men for protecting and caring for their women, and compare the women to pets! These women are the mothers of the future leaders of this great nation, responsible for the current apex of civilization we enjoy! What better place of honor could be theirs?"

"A place of their own choosing, not one assigned them," Remy retorted, heat rising in her voice. "You speak of motherhood as a holy calling, but what rights do mothers have? And are all these husbands fine, decent, upstanding paragons of virtue who live only for their wives and children? I think not, sir. And I think you well know it. Don't tell me you haven't seen it yourself."

Edmund was uncharacteristically speechless. And when he remained silent for a moment, Remy continued scornfully, "Mothers of the leaders of the nation, are they? And they cannot vote on how the nation is led—or any other matter that affects them."

"Hah!" Edmund cried, "I knew it—a suffragist. God bless us, you women are everywhere, even in my own household! Look here, you seem to forget that our glorious Queen is a woman—a woman who occupies the highest honor in the kingdom."

"An accident of fate, elevating one woman to a throne, compensates for widespread and century-old injustice?" Remy looked at him squarely. "Do I look like a fool, Mr. Symme, that you say such things to me as serious argument?"

Edmund had no answer. They continued walking in silence for a few minutes, each lost in their own thoughts.

"Those 'boys' were turning their attention on you—you know that." Edmund began.

"Yes. Thank you for helping me." She flushed. "It would have been much worse for me if you hadn't."

"Worse indeed, by my oath! You'd have been rap . . . in a very serious situation. What made you stand against them, all by yourself? You should have run off and found help for the child."

"Don't be absurd—how could I run?" She looked at him, astonished. "You were only one against three, and you didn't run."

"Yes, but I am a man!" Seeing this comment made little impression he continued, "And I had a stout stick and a very large dog with me! It's a very different thing!"

Her eyes blazed and she turned to him again.

"I would have given as good as I got, and Kane would be missing a . . . even if in the end I was . . . well . . . And then Molly would have gotten away in the distraction."

"Distraction! You are a foolhardy woman, Remy. Your headstrong actions could have cost you dearly. You could have been violated and dishonored."

Edmund had adopted a stern tone, like a schoolteacher whose task was lecturing wayward boys.

"I would not have been the one dishonored by the act. The man who did it would bear the dishonor," she replied in a measured voice. "With all due respect to you as my employer, let me be clear. Since the death of my father, I have been accountable for my personal actions to no man, Mr. Symme, and I owe no account of myself to you in matters other than my employment." She stopped walking and faced him. "But I am indebted to you, and most, most grateful, not only for myself, but for Molly as well."

Her face had softened and Edmund could see tears welling up in her eyes.

Edmund was not used to such female straightforwardness and he felt somewhat flustered.

"Well, I'm most glad we came along, although the credit belongs in large part to Regis."

"Yes. A fine, brave beast. Thank you, Regis."

Remy smiled and caressed the dog, who fairly shook his tail off with pleasure, and then they continued on.

"I'll give testimony, of course, when you bring charges up before the magistrate, although I will attempt to avoid asking testimony of you when I indict them for trespass and assault against my estate. I believe there to be enough circumstantial evidence to indicate poaching."

He wanted her to know he was no snob in matters of justice.

She almost laughed as she replied, "I had forgotten that you were a barrister. Do you truly suppose the magistrate would be inclined to make room on his docket for this matter? After all, nothing happened."

"Pardon? You cannot be serious!"

"No animals were taken. No . . . violation occurred. And I doubt the child's family will want to pursue it—but I will speak with them. You, of course, must do as you see fit."

"This is a clear case of criminal action! Assault, and on my land! The magistrate must prosecute!" Edmund declared. "And what do you mean, the family will not pursue it? Will *you* not pursue it?"

"There are menfolk in the family who will deal with the matter, without benefit of the magistrate's wisdom." She looked at him with candor. "Truly, it would be best to leave it."

"And you—do you also have uncles and cousins to champion your cause? I would have thought you'd be the first to fight your own battle, instead of . . . "

Remy cut him off.

"And you think I should let 'the law' fight it for me? What exactly do you mean to say—that the law will protect Molly, or me, from such assaults in the future? Will it not make me out to be the foolish and irresponsible one, the temptation at the pond, and reflect poorly on the memory of my widowed mother? Did I not invite such trouble by being in such a remote place, with no man to protect me? Kane comes from a wealthy land-owning family; I am a poor upstart woman. All the law I've seen counts sovereigns in the purse and male as a gender before anything else, and hardly stands guard over small girls and their pets on dark nights!"

"Now I must protest! You speak nonsense! The law was conceived to protect any citizen of the land from actions such as these, especially to help the weak stand against the strong. But the law is only as strong and alive as the Englishmen who uphold it! You must see that . . . "

"I see that solicitors and barristers line their pockets with gold, and judges dispense all the law money can buy, but the good Englishmen you speak of still languish in debtors' prisons and lose their farms when they're ill—all according to law—and that Englishwomen have no say at all in what goes on in the government!"

She gave him a fierce look, and he pressed it no further as they again walked apiece in silence.

Taken aback by her vehemence, he fell back on his expertise in calming agitated witnesses and asked, "Can you heal the goose, Remy?"

"Yes, I think so—he's a hearty bird with a strong spirit. His injuries look worse than they are, and proper herbs can work wonders." She stopped walking. "This is where we part. Thank you again for your assistance and for your kindness to the child."

"No, I'll accompany you all the way." He looked at the little girl. "I think she's fast asleep."

"She's awake, and can walk," Remy replied before speaking softly to the girl. "Come, we must get the General back home so I can fix his wounds."

With that, the child came alert and wriggled out of Edmund's arms. But first, she gave him a soft kiss on the cheek, and smiled slightly as she said, "I like you, sir."

Surprised and unexpectedly pleased, Edmund replied, "Well, Mistress Molly, I am glad of that."

Edmund began to protest again but Remy interrupted him. "Really, it's best we go on alone. Being brought home by the master of the big house will not help Molly in the slightest."

Seeing the wisdom of her words, he acquiesced.

"As you wish, then. Don't try to get back to Owlswood tonight, just come tomorrow if you're fit enough." He paused. "You could do with some rest, Remy." Then, feeling too soft-hearted, he stiffened. "I have no wish to lose your services due to indisposition. Take rest this night and return tomorrow."

"Tomorrow, then. I'll be there in the morning. Good day, and many thanks, Mr. Symme."

She looked at him somewhat gravely for a long moment, then as a smile spread into her eyes, she nodded, and was off.

Edmund watched them disappear through the wood. *For a humble servant of the law and officer of the court, he thought, I've had my share of fisticuffs recently. And why did I come here—for quiet and rest? For solitude and comfort? Certainly not to be plagued with village ruffians and opinionated servants.* Then aloud he whispered, "These damned women breed nothing but chaos!"

Man and dog made their way back to the house as afternoon shadows cast strange images across the lawns. Entering the main hallway, Edmund found a letter on a salver on the entry table—from Banks, announcing his arrival at the end of the month. Very pleased, Edmund had just enough time to wash, tend his discoloring knuckles, and catch a short nap before dinner.

In Remy's absence, Cook served him in the dining room with some nervousness but great good cheer. She was a sweet, round, rosy-cheeked and motherly woman; she fluttered around Edmund to make sure he had enough of everything he needed. When he complimented her meal, she smiled widely and decided he was a wise and charming young gentleman, indeed. After she took her leave of him to return home for the night, Edmund poured himself a large snifter of cognac and settled into his favorite library armchair for another quiet evening of reading.

He felt a brief moment of trepidation—wondering if he might be prone to another "visitation" due to his rather tumultuous afternoon—but shook it off quickly.

He returned to feeling calm and relaxed, with good news of Banks' visit and a fine dinner adding to his comfort. He decided to start his evening read with an old friend, Marcus Aurelius, and turned to his favorite section in *Meditations*. But soon he felt bored with ancient wisdom, set aside Aurelius, and his hand found its way to the smooth, cool cover of the Chronicles, Volume II. He read for almost an hour, greatly entertained; then gradually he noticed the fresh, yet heady scent of gardenia growing stronger with each breath he took.

He paused in his reading and breathed in the air, savoring the sweet perfume. He looked around—all around, quite thoroughly—and seeing nothing unusual, he relaxed back into his chair and his reading. He felt so wonderfully calm and at ease. He began to smile, and then to laugh out loud, as the words before him told yet another story of his grandfather. He set the book on his lap and laid his head back against the chair, picturing the scene portrayed in text and laughing again. Just then he became aware of a small, elegant hand resting on his left shoulder and heard inside his head the words, *"Tres amusant, oui?"* He turned slightly and saw the silk-clothed lady of the night before, seated on the arm of his chair and leaning as if to read over his shoulder, smiling brilliantly at him. Her green eyes sparkled with delight. He stared into those eyes, mesmerized, for several seconds and then leapt to his feet.

"Lady!" he exclaimed.

Flustered, confused, and again, not believing his senses, Edmund was at a loss. *How does one act when addressing one's hallucination?* he wondered. He took the plunge.

"Madame, I am honored," he said and bowed slightly.

"Enchantee," the lady replied, smiling even more brilliantly, and extended her hand to him. Noting his hesitation, she laughed and

wagged a finger at him. *"Vous avez trop peur* . . . ah, you are too timid! I will not pinch you!"

Again, the beautiful, elegant hand was extended, and Edmund took it and kissed it lightly. His lips felt the cool, incredibly soft gardenia petal skin beneath them. *Can this be?* he asked himself. *Am I dreaming?*

"No dream, *Chérie,* it is I. Do you like *mes contes?* My stories about your family?"

"Your stories? You wrote these stories? You knew my family? My grandfather?" Edmund blurted. His voice sounded strangely loud in the quiet of the room.

"Ah, yes, I knew him very well, *Chérie.* He was, once, one of my favorite men in all this world." She tilted her head, then looked at him coyly. "You doubt this? If so, I can tell you more about him, much, much more, *oui?"*

"No!" Edmund barked.

The lady looked startled, then perplexed.

"No, I mean, I would never doubt any word of yours, lady. I would never doubt . . . "

Her silvery laugh floated on the air. "You prefer to speak, no? Instead of hearing me in your mind? *Oui,* I can speak, *Chérie!"* Her voice was musical and sweet. "And I know what you doubt, *ex-actement*—you doubt I am here, *n'est ce pas?"* She rose and walked around the room. "You can see me, yes? You hear my voice, you smell my perfume, do you not?" She came closer, until she stood within inches of Edmund's face. She tilted her face up to his and whispered with a pout, "Would the touch of my lips on your yours banish your doubt?" Her lips parted slightly and Edmund thought he could feel her breath on his mouth. His heart began to beat faster as he bent ever so slightly toward those lips . . . . . .

"Ah, no, no, no, but I embarrass you!" She pulled away and returned to her seat on the arm of the chair. "Shame on me, I am always the impetuous one, *oui?"* She was quite businesslike now. "Come, tell me how may I convince you I am here."

Here, Edmund thought, *is a challenge to best the finest minds on the earth: how to assist a hallucination to prove to its host that it is real, and in so doing, prove the host's own insanity. Or, how to convince the hallucination that it was not real, and therefore prove the host perfectly sane but grossly over-stimulated. But if she is convinced she is not real, she may leave and then I would lose the opportunity to . . .*

"Come, come, what is all this intellectual chatter? This is a simple request, *non*?" She looked somewhat exasperated and waved her hands in the air. "Shall I move something around the room, or find something you have lost, or build up the fire, so?" She blew gently toward the embers in the hearth, and they burst into flame. Delighted, she laughed. "So, what shall it be? Or do you prefer to think yourself mad?"

"Lady, I am at a loss—as you can see." Edmund shook his head and laughed at his own discomfiture. "Whatever I ask, I'm sure you will do but, since it's all in my own mind, what would be proved?"

"Ahhh," she nodded her head sagely, "now I see your problem. Hmmm." She thought for a moment. "So, you believe you alone have me inside your little brain, eh? No other can see me, or hear me?"

Edmund nodded. "Yes, exactly."

She looked around the room, and then a smile began to play at the edges of her lips. She pursed her mouth and whistled shrilly, and Regis, who had been sleeping by the fire, leapt to his feet and looked around expectantly. When his eyes reached the spot where the "hallucination" was sitting, his tail began to wag and he walked briskly over to stand before her.

"Sit!" She spoke. Regis sat. "Lie down, dog!" Regis lay down. "Give me your paw, now," she bent down to take the huge paw in her small hand and smiled as Regis licked where her face seemed to be. "Do you think this dog is mad, too? He sees and hears me quite clearly, *n'est ce pas*?"

Edmund had to admit, Regis seemed quite convinced the Lady was real.

But the conflict between his own senses and his logical, law-trained mind was about to drive him mad—if he wasn't already mad. Talking to a . . . an apparition! He sat down and tried to think.

"Never mind, you'll get used to me, *Chérie*," the Lady spoke again. "But such a young and handsome man, to be so shackled by intellect and so unmoved by your own experience . . . Well, I do not need to come again, if you wish."

She looked at him with pity. "I do not want to trouble you so very much, but I thought you were—*comment se dire*—a sympathetic heart. A soul such as my own . . . but perhaps . . . Is your imagination so lacking that you cannot see past what you think?"

"No, please! I . . . " he stammered, "I just need some time to grow accustomed to the . . . situation. This is a new . . . thing for me." He smiled apologetically. "I'm sorry if I offend."

She smiled to comfort him. "No, no, calm yourself. Perhaps if we just engage in conversation . . ."

And they did, for almost an hour, just talk about the Chronicles, the house and its history, and Edmund found himself opening to this vision as he had opened to no one save Banks. They laughed much and shared thoughts on many things, and then, abruptly, the lady rose to leave.

"Now it is time, *Chérie*. The moon is almost set, and I must leave you."

"Ah . . . so soon? I have enjoyed this night so much." Edmund felt shy. "Will . . . will you visit again?"

The lady looked at him slyly. "If I am just a vision, you can summon me at your will—you need not ask me."

"I know not what you are, or who, but I know you are . . . enchanting. And I know you do as you choose, not my bidding. I wish you to come again."

"Then I shall consider it." She smiled and tilted her head. "*Au revoir!*"

"Wait—who are you? May I know your name?" Edmund wanted to delay her departure in any way he could.

"Oh, you needn't know my name for now. Perhaps in time . . .what would you like to call me?"

"Belle Dame! You are La Belle Dame, just as in the poem!" Edmund exclaimed.

"Ah—you are a student of Keats. La Belle Dame . . . are you also familiar with Edward Malory, from whose pen come the Arthur legends and the story of La Belle Dame?" She turned as if to leave. "Did you know that Malory was condemned to prison for rape and murder?"

"He was?" Edmund was startled by her words, and shivered as he viewed the cold hardness that passed across her face as she spoke. "I meant no harm, Lady . . . "

"No, *bien sur* . . . I like your name for me, and the poem from which it comes." Her eyes again sparkled but her smile seemed sad. "*A bientot!*" And she was gone.

6
Fleur Blooms

The fortnight before Banks' arrival passed quickly and Edmund became more and more comfortable at Owlswood, taking time to walk the property each day—sometimes with Samuel as guide, always with Regis—and became interested in the land and its richness as never before. The woods teemed with small game, the streams ran clear, some with promising populations of fish. Samuel had taken his duties seriously through the years, employing young men from the village to handle the more strenuous work of tree thinning, brush clearing, and keeping the gardens clear and ready for his expert attentions. *Another gift of grandfather's endowment*, Edmund thought wryly, *Too bad he was so objectionable while alive; I quite like him now he's dead.*

There was no further trouble with the locals. He somehow got the impression Samuel had a word with the local constabulary, unofficially of course—and his housekeeper maintained a calm and almost deferential, for her, demeanor while the household ran seamlessly and comfortably. Finally, some calm began to emerge.

Yet, he rarely felt calm. While the exercise of tramping the grounds gave a physical satisfaction, and learning about his estate stimulated his mind, he was irritated, restless, often snappish, waiting for the sun to fall low in the sky. At nightfall, he found his spirits rise and his heartbeat quicken. Although he continued to look forward to his explorations of Owlswood grounds by day with great pleasure, they were eclipsed by his relish of the nightly visits of La Belle Dame. So much so that he had adjusted the dinner hour to an earlier time to "retire to the library for study and thought." Cook was ecstatic, as she arrived home to her family and cozy fire earlier at night, and the serving maid was happy to leave early as well.

Remy was at first surprised, then increasingly concerned at the changes emerging in Mr. Symme. He became more remote and irritable, as if that were possible. He seemed obsessed with spending time the library; he could be heard speaking out loud in the quiet hours of the night—for what reason? She worried, but kept her own counsel.

Edmund began to regard his nightly "visitation" with the pleasure heretofore reserved for spending time with a colleague or old friend. He found, to his surprise, that La Belle Dame was quite well-read and shared his affinity for Marcus Aurelius. The time spent in discussing the Meditations sometime soothed, often stimulated his mind. La Belle was also possessed of a wry wit and raucous sense of humor, which manifested in some interesting and somewhat ribald stories of her life before, and at, Owlswood. She would entertain him with anecdotes that he could not believe were entirely true, however . . .

"Were you there, *Chérie*? *Non*, well, I was there!" she would admonish him. "Do not doubt an eye-witness!" And then she would laugh delightfully, even when Edmund would retort, "I never trust eye-witnesses, Lady, they are notoriously unreliable—take my word for it!"

Sometimes she would speak of her life before she came to Owlswood.

"When we lived on the island, I thought I was in heaven! The sky, the water, the flowers all crowded my senses with beauty. The natives called it Martinina, island of flowers. And the music! Music everywhere on our plantation, and dances and parties! My father brought me up as a free spirit—I think you say?—and I was finely educated but also permitted my liberty to wander, explore, be alive. You know I read Latin, and Greek as well, and I also had the most beautiful horse! So swift, so fearless! We would race the wind itself, on the cliffs overlooking the bay."

Her eyes sparkled and her cheeks flushed with color.

"My mother Marguerite was Creole, you know this term, yes? My father Olivier loved her greatly. But she never recovered from my birth. He took a mistress—he was still a young man—and so my brother was octoroon. On yes, I had a brother, his name was Armand. He used to travel with Papa as his 'valet' and we would laugh so hard at the raised brows!

"But Paris—I loved Paris. When Maman finally died, Papa was inconsolate—so he took Armand and me to Paris to sooth his aching heart, and ours. I don't like sea voyages, but Paris was worth it. The museums, the Champs, the theater, the soirées—I fell in love with the City of Light. It lit up my heart and my very soul."

Then, with a sea change in her eyes, she would state, "Enough

66

memories! What do you make of these words of Aurelius: 'He often acts unjustly who does not do a certain thing; not only he who does a certain thing.'"

And they would discuss the classics until the moon set.

During daytime hours, the neglected glass house particularly fascinated Edmund. He began to remember running through the rows of plantings and potting benches during games of hide-and-seek, and how Nanny tried to find him and grew cross, and how he always wondered why there were no really good edibles growing there—just things like strange citrus plants and a few straggly-looking bushes with an occasional small, stunted white flower. A fragrant bloom, though—what was it?

"Samuel, you knew the glasshouse when it was in full use, didn't you?" he asked during one of their daily walks along the property line. "You were at Owlswood when my grandfather was master here, and also my father?"

"Aye sir, and for a time with your great grandfather. I was just a lad runnin' after my father then, helpin' and such. Da' was Head Gardener." Samuel leaned on his walking staff and looked out at the fields stretching before them. He smiled at his recollections. "'Twas a long time ago now. Aye, sir, that was in the glory days of the old glasshouse—the *orangerie*, 'twas called—and the gardenias. Ah, the flowers they grew in that glasshouse would make your eyes fill with tears of wonder, they would!"

"Tell me," Edmund prompted, leaning on his own walking stick.

"Oh sir, a spectacle it was—yards of white fluffy flowers, beaded with dew just as if they were out in the meadow natural as you like. And the smell—it like to knock you down sometimes when you opened the door and went in!" He shook his head slightly and smiled again at his thoughts. "They brought every high-toned specialist from the best botanic societies in Europe to get it going, just to get it right so they could have them gardenia all year, every blessed season, even dead of winter. We had special chimneys and hearth built, just in case. And a boiler and water pipes to warm the air! That was a time, it was."

"Why all the trouble for a flower?" Edmund puzzled.

The old gardener's voice became soft, and his eyes glassed over as he stared at the sky. "For her, of course. It was for her."

"Who? Not Grandmama—I can't picture her caring a whit for gardenias! You must be joking!" Edmund laughed out loud.

Samuel turned to face him.

"No, lad. For *her*, the French woman. D'ye not know about the woman? Girl, really, she was only just more than girl when she came here. Beautiful, sweet thing she was. And she loved gardenia more than any other flower."

Edmund felt his heart begin to race.

"The French woman? What French woman? Who was she?" he asked through the catch in his throat.

"Ah, she was the most charmin' creature you could imagine—your great-grandfather's ward. One of his old cronies—pardon, sir—was a very rich French gentleman with a sugar estate on some godforsaken island. Someplace. Martinique? Since he was a widower, he was very concerned with the future of his only daughter and asked old-man Symme—beggin' your pardon, sir, Mr. Alistair Symme—to take care of her if anything should happen to him. Apparently, a good decision because he died in some kind of heathen uprising in that far-off place and the young lady came to live at Owlswood."

He continued, "Before he was killed, the father brought her to France for schoolin', and then felt a time in England would polish her up, so to speak. What better place than his old friend's household—first in London and then Owlswood? So, he left her in the Symme keeping, supposed t' be for a year, and returned to his foreign place. And the young lady—a lovelier soul you could never imagine—and beautiful! She graced this place like a jewel. Your grandfather, John, was quite smitten with her—every young man for miles around was, 'course—and I always thought they would marry but . . . it is too sad to remember . . . and then the life went out of him and he married some arranged match."

The old man's voice trailed away. He shook his head.

Edmund felt the blood drain from his face and his breath quicken; dizziness threatened to overtake him. He leaned heavily against a stone post and demanded, "What happened? Tell me."

Samuel looked at Edmund sadly, then with alarm. "Sir—are you quite well? You look as if you've seen a ghost—sit!." The old man took Edmund's arm and guided him to sit on the stone marker fence nearby. "There, that's right—here, drink this." He handed Edmund his flask of cider and watched as he took a swallow. "There now, better sir?"

Edmund nodded. "Tell me, what happened to the French woman?"

Samuel shook his head. "With all due respect, I will not. Not now—we need to get on back to the house. Do not press me, 'twill do naught, I'm determined, sir. Here, lean on me and get yourself steady on your feet."

Edmund accepted the help and stood.

"What happened to the woman?" he again asked.

Samuel set his lips firmly. "Not now. We need to be off. Come."

He took Edmund's arm and they set their course for the house. Edmund heard a soft mutter as they walked.

"Best to speak no more of it anyway."

By the time they were halfway back to the house, Edmund had recovered himself and was striding normally along the path. His continued demands to know what had become of the French woman fell on deaf ears, and he finally conceded that his oratorical skill and assertive courtroom manner had absolutely no purchase with Samuel. He ceased his questions and they walked in silence.

When they passed the glasshouse, Edmund halted. Samuel stopped, too, and looked at him stoically, expecting another onslaught of questions. Only one came.

"What would it take to bring the glasshouse back to its prime, and fill it with gardenia?"

Startled, Samuel replied, "A fair piece o' work, and a great dollop o' cash . . . sir."

"Put together an estimate of what you need, and how many workers you want. Give it to me in two days. Have Remy help you with it—have her write it down and present it to me for review." Edmund looked at him. "Do you understand?"

"I do, sir. I will." If Samuel's weathered face could express surprise, it would have. Even though he had lived through many unusual and amazing happenings at Owlswood, this was one of the most surprising.

As evening darkened into night on the day of Edmund's questions about the glasshouse, he grew nervous. He longed to ask La Belle Dame about the glasshouse and a million other things swirling in his mind, but he feared her reaction. Would she be reluctant?

Angry? Embarrassed? Would she decide not to visit him further?

To calm his anxiety, Edmund drank more wine at dinner—and after—than he had intended. He felt sleepy and dull as he took to his armchair in the library, tipsy but still anxious and somewhat annoyed with himself. He tried to read, but could not concentrate. He sat in the deepening darkness of the library and simply stared into space. Suddenly, the air became cooler and the scent of gardenia roused him slightly.

"Eh, la—what is wrong with you, *Chérie*? So quiet, so subdued. And what is that disgusting liquid in your glass?"

La Belle Dame appeared, perched on a table edge, her musical voice cutting through his torpor.

"This? Well, it's some sort of claret, or something—just what I had sent up from town. Why do you ask?" He looked at his half-empty wine glass on the table. "What's so disgusting?"

"*Chérie*—the color, the nose, the . . . gross attributes of a very poor vintage! What do you mean, you had it sent from town? What kind of wine is it? Have you not been to the cellar?" She looked scandalized. "Are you insane, *Chérie*?"

"The cellar?" Edmund repeated dully. "Owlswood has a wine cellar?"

"*Mais oui, bien sur*—a very good wine cellar which I helped to create! Oh—oh no, *Chérie*, tell me you are not one of those Englishmen who cannot drink wine properly! Oh *mon dieu!*" She rose and brought her hand to her head in a gesture of distress, then twirled around and cried, "I should have known." She looked at him severely. "Go!" she ordered. "Go *immediatemente* to the cellar and look carefully in the third rack from the back wall left. Bring here a bottle of the St Croix du Mont—no, no the Chateau Lafite-Rothschild of Pauillac—1827. Open it carefully, pour and let it rest in your glass —*do not taste it!*—until I return. I will come back in exactly two hours. *Allez!* Go!"

She disappeared from the room.

Edmund remained seated, mouth open, for a moment, and then looked at his glass again.

"By all the saints, what is going on here?" he asked the empty room.

He was torn between his reluctance to be ordered around by a figment of his imagination, and the feeling of incredible curiosity and interest her commands seemed to produce. His spirits lifted. The next moment, his decision was made, and he strode from the library into the hall, calling for Remy. She emerged from the kitchen.

"Where is the door to the wine cellar? And did you know we have a wine cellar?" Edmund demanded.

"Yes, sir, I do know that Owlswood has a wine cellar. The door is at the end of this hallway, and here is the key." She handed him a large key from her key ring. "However, the wine you had sent from London is actually in the buttery; it didn't seem as if it needed special storage. Shall I retrieve a bottle for you?"

Edmund looked at her crossly.

"You, too?" he asked.

Seeing the startled look on Remy's face, he continued, "I want a specific bottle from the wine cellar—I'll get it myself. Be so kind as to provide a fresh glass and corkscrew in the library, then I'll not need you further this evening."

He stomped off to enter the bowels of his house, on a quest set him by a phantasm, to obtain a bottle for a tutoring session on the finer points of wine.

While in the chilly and church-like confines of the cellar, Edmund discovered two full walls covered with wine racks, each with 100 cradles or more filled with French and Spanish wines that even to him, appeared to be of some distinction. Braving the cobwebs and several very large, rather angry-looking black spiders, he carefully searched for the Chateau Lafite as La Belle Dame had directed. Carefully removing the bottle, he dusted the label (coughing several times) to be certain he had the correct vintage, and made his way from the subterranean trove of riches to the library. There, he found a gleaming clean glass, a hand towel, and corkscrew. Taking care to open the wine without damaging the cork, he poured it into the glistening glass, and sat down to wait.

True to her word, La Belle Dame returned exactly two hours after the wine had been poured; she looked delighted.

"Ah, *Chérie*, now we will begin!"

Her eyes sparkled as she settled herself on a nearby pedestal (shared with a bust of Henry Brougham, who also looked delighted at her company), adjusted her voluminous skirts appropriately, and clasped her hands in teacher-like fashion. She looked at Edmund.

"*Alors, Chérie*, lift the glass by its stem and bring it to your face.

Bien, bien, do it!" She gave the direction. "Now, swirl the liquid vigorously but carefully in the bowl. *Bien.*" Edmund did as she had bid him. "Now, hold the glass to the light—what do you see?"

Edmund took a good look at the glass and its contents. He saw a deep, opaque burgundy color that seemed to coat the inner sides of the glass with rivulets.

"Beautiful, no? What does that color remind you of?"

Edmund felt foolish, but he also felt he had no choice but to cooperate. He looked at the wine.

"It reminds me of . . . of the velvet curtains in our small sitting room when I was a boy. I used to hide behind them and wrap myself in the softness while at play with nurse . . . and the sun sometimes shone on the fabric and made it warm to my touch." He was amazed at the memories that flooded to him. "The sunlight made them look like . . . like red gold."

"*Bien, tres bien, Chérie.*" She clapped her tiny hands. "Now, swirl it again and take a deep breath of the fragrance."

Entranced, Edmund did as he was told and allowed the scent to enter his nostrils.

"Well? What do you smell?" the lady asked.

Feeling something between bewildered and stupid, Edmund replied cautiously, "I smell . . . wine?"

"*Ah, mon dieu, quelle betesse!* *Chérie,* close your eyes, swirl the wine again, and now tell me . . .*"

Edmund followed the directions.

"Now tell me—do you smell faint chocolate? Do you smell some fruit? Tell me—what do you smell? Keep your eyes closed!" she commanded.

Edmund swirled the wine in his glass again, almost despairing of the task. *I smell wine,* he thought, *what else is there to smell?*

Then, suddenly, his mind seemed to release and surrender to his senses, and he was enveloped by the scent of freshly bruised cherries wafting on a summer breeze, then a slight fragrance of strong coffee. He shared this with La Belle Dame.

"Ah, very good, *Chérie.* What else?"

She had him swirl and sniff three times more, and each time he found another interesting fragrance in the liquid in his glass. He was amazed.

"Now, *attencion*! Now you must take a small sip: swirl it in your mouth, just as you swirled it in the glass. Let it rest against the back of your tongue. Now!" The lady leaned forward in what seemed to be excitement. "Keep your eyes closed!"

Edmund took a sip; he swirled and let the wine rest in his mouth for a few seconds.

"Tell me what you taste," his tutor urged.

Edmund swallowed, and kept his eyes closed. "I taste grapes, of course, but also . . . also lavender and some heavy sweetness. Honey? And something musty, dark—mushroom?"

"And what do *you* see, now," the lady pressed.

"See!" Edmund hesitated. "I see . . . a sunny hillside, trees, some larger hills, grass and . . . and there is water nearby."

"Ah" the word was almost a sigh as she said it. "Now, *Chérie*, now you have had your first true taste of wine. It is one of the things I miss the most."

Edmund opened his eyes slowly, to find her looking wistful and sad.

She continued, "To really taste the wine is to take a sip of another moment in time—a happier time, perhaps—captured in a bottle. How many people put their souls into growing the grape; how many smiles came during the harvest, how much laughter surrounded the first taste of the *nouveau* cask, how many love affairs were sparked in the eyes of the men and women who toiled together?" She paused. "We French have a saying: In water one sees one's own face, but in wine one sees the heart of another."

She seemed lost in her thoughts for a moment, and then continued softly, "Although wine, like life itself, can turn to vinegar."

Edmund felt a wave of sadness for her. "I wish I were a better student, Belle Dame. I am a disappointment to you, I fear."

She only smiled slightly and shook her head. "*Ca n'est fait rien, Chérie*, you are no disappointment. Not like your father."

"You knew my father?" Edmund was taken by surprise. "You knew him, too?"

Her eyes, still slightly glassy with tears, did little to soften the wry expression on her face. "*Oui*. I knew him. He was . . . unacceptable."

"Unacceptable? Explain, please."

Edmund came to attention.

"He fainted easily." Her hand moved in a graceful gesture of dismissal. But when she saw Edmund's face, she sensed he wanted more. "Your father, he aspired to nothing, he settled for less. He was afraid of . . . everything. He lacked courage, he lacked imagination. I found him unworthy."

I can see she knew him well enough, Edmund thought, *she describes him perfectly.*

"I feel I should mount some defense of the man, Lady, if only to admit the possibility that the bloodline I carry may possess some more admirable qualities." He paused. "However, I too found my father unacceptable."

He inclined his head in apology.

"There is no taint on you, *Chérie*. Many excellent, as well as unworthy, qualities of character skip generations, as we know," she smiled slightly. "And your bloodline is one I cherish."

She seemed again taken by a great wave of melancholy. She closed her eyes and was silent for several heartbeats.

"If only," she said quietly, almost to herself. "If only things had come to pass as my heart desired, your father should have been saved from his abject mediocrity and you . . ."

"And me?" Edmund asked sharply. "What about me?"

The Lady looked at him intently, a struggle faintly visible on her face. She seemed to be on the verge of some pronouncement, but then caught herself and said only, with a bit of sparkle returning to her eye, "Why, then you and I would have met far sooner than we have, *Chérie*. Far sooner. And that would have pleased me so very much."

They remained in companionable silence for some time. Then, wanting to know more, Edmund ventured to ask a question that had come to him that morning.

"Lady, do they speak of you here as the French woman?"

In a moment of sudden and unexpected anger, the Lady's eyes flashed and she demanded icily, "Who told you that? Who is speaking of me? What lies do they tell you?" She came down from her perch atop the fireplace mantle and began to move through the room. "Who? Tell me!"

Edmund was shocked by the change in her. He felt he was a schoolboy again, stammering out an answer to an angry don.

"No, no one has told me anything! I . . . I was only . . . I decided to bring the glass house back into use, repair it and grow things again, and Samuel told me it used to be filled with the French woman's gardenia!"

The Lady stopped, seemed to quiet herself, and replied, "Samuel was a fine boy, and now is a good man and skilled gardener. What else did he say?"

"He refused to say anything more. That's why I'm asking you." Edmund said in explanation. "Are you the French woman?"

She looked at him with amusement. "*Alors,* I am obviously French, *oui,* and we can agree I am a woman, *n'est ce pas*? And the gardenia in *l'orangerie*—the glass house—were for me. So, I suppose I am this French woman." She continued, "And why do you decide thus, to rebuild? It has been neglected to ruin these past years, another thing for which I credit your father."

Edmund felt uncharacteristically shy, and resisted admitting the true reason; he wanted to please her.

"It seems a shame to have it in such disrepair," he expounded. "I understand it was a magnificent part of the house in its day. I believe it was the first glasshouse—er, *orangerie*—in the shire to have a set of warm water heating pipes, and that the angle of exposure provided by the construction was at the cutting edge of technology at the time it was built."

He hoped he sounded sufficiently scientific and detached.

"When I first came to Owlswood, *Chérie, l'orangerie* was filled with citrus—orange, lemon, citron—and they provisioned the kitchen with fragrant fruits almost all year long. The trees were pruned to remain small, and so beautiful when they were in bloom—the scent of orange blossom was so lovely!" Her face continued to soften with memory. "But when I told Jean that I longed so for gardenia—they used to grow everywhere when I was a child—he made it a quest to fill the place with them. I remember when he brought me to the door—it was my *anniversaire,* my birthday—and he took my hand and said, 'Close your eyes, I have a surprise for you!' I could tell before I opened my eyes what had been done, because the fragrance was so sweet. And then I saw—and he told me, 'You shall have gardenia every day for your room, your hair, and you will see them and know how I love you.'"

"When you speak of Jean, you mean my grandfather, John Symme, don't you?" Edmund asked.

"*Bien sur*, but of course—my own, my heartbeat, my only one . . ." She stopped abruptly. "Betrayal comes in many ways, *Chérie*. He has had use of my heart long enough. I move on."

She looked sad for another moment, then seemed to recover herself.

"Your little brain can acknowledge that I was once alive, but now am not, no?" she asked. "That means I am, how do you say, a phantasm, a ghost *en anglais*, non?"

When Edmund could only nod, she continued, "But I remember—I remember many things. Ah *Chérie*, what I remember!"

"What do you remember, Belle Dame? Tell me," he requested, enthralled.

She closed her eyes.

"I remember the caress of the wind on my face. I remember the warmth of sunglow on my back, the feel of warm flesh against my own." Her face was luminous. "Can you remember the pulse of your mother's heart, beating against your cheek? Can you recall the taste of your lover's lips, the moistness of her breath as she bends to you?"

Tears formed at the corners of her eyes. She opened them and looked at him with longing. "I can almost feel again, through you. You bring me . . . memories. Memories that touch my heart. Things of the spirit—they pale without the body, like only one side of a coin. An exhalation with no breath in." She suppressed a sob. "Savor these things, *Chérie*, pause and savor. Because they disappear with your own last breath."

She turned her face upward and opened her eyes. "I remember also . . . I remember the *poignard en pierre*! *Ah, mon Dieu*," she began to wail, "*mon Dieu, mon Dieu, ayez pitie* . . . "

And she faded from view.

7
Banks Comes to Visit

"This place is utterly beguiling, Edmund," Banks commented, smiling broadly as he surveyed the woodland spread out below. "I can't see why you haven't come back here sooner."

He had arrived, as expected, only several days before and was pleased to be in such picturesque country. They were on a walk through the estate, paused on a scrubby knob above the valley through which the river meandered.

"Well, my memories are not the best, old man," Edmund replied, "As a youngster, I really wasn't all that happy here most of the time." When Banks looked surprised, Edmund continued, "We lived in the London house, of course, but came here regularly for long stretches. It was my grandfather's *demesne*, and he was a very unpleasant and, frankly, frightening man."

"What was so frightening about him? I can't imagine you as a child who frightened easily!" Banks chuckled.

"Oh, I don't know, Banks. He was a mean old bas . . . bloke. Always melancholy or angry—he seemed like he'd love to get at me with a horsewhip every time I crossed his path, so I kept to myself and outside, away from everyone." He shared a smile with his friend. "No one seemed to miss me, least of all old Grandpapa Symme—he seemed distracted and most preoccupied all the time. He stayed mostly in the library but sometimes he ventured into the glasshouse—what he was doing there, I can't possibly imagine, certainly not getting his hands dirty. He was cold and dismissive with my father—which I understood perfectly, even then, my father being who he was. And, of course, I was nearly always here with my parents, insufferable beings that they were. Unbearable."

"Poor little mite, you could have given a bedraggled soul like David Copperfield advice, eh?" Banks chuckled as he stroked Regis' great head. "Why have you embarked on reconstructing the glasshouse, then? It seems like a complicated and lengthy business, and certainly not an endeavor based on fond memories."

"Do you think it's so strange? Why?" Edmund asked sharply. "What business is it of yours, anyway, what I choose to do with my house?"

"Easy, old man, I'm just curious," Banks was surprised at the vehemence of the response, "I don't take *you* for a gardener, either."

Edmund went on more calmly, "Well, it seems that in its prime, the *l'orangerie* was one of the best of its kind in the area. A very sophisticated boiler and water heat system kept the place warm enough for even tropical plants all year round. I'd like to get it back into condition." He continued musingly, "Of course, when I was a boy there were very few interesting things growing in it—I think the housekeeper or cook used part of it for herbs and a pottage garden, but not much more. It is a disgrace that the family let it deteriorate. I'd like to put it right."

"What shall you grow there?" Banks asked absently, looking out at the horizon.

"Gardenia . . . oh, and, well, citrus of course and . . ."

"Gardenia! What infernal use does a famous hard-hearted London barrister have with gardenia?" Banks exclaimed and began to laugh. "Surely you are jesting with me."

"Let's be off," Edmund snapped.

He stamped his walking stick and headed down the hillside, barreling through bracken like an angry bull.

Banks looked after him for a long moment, then followed and caught up with him at the river.

"Something bothering you, Edmund?"

"No, of course not. What a question." He looked up-river. "Shall we follow the water for a stretch—it's quite shady along the bank and we can see if it looks promising for a bit of fishing, if you like."

Edmund kept his voice and bearing even, and managed a smile.

"Yes, let's do—lead on, *mon vieux!*"

It was a pleasant trek along the riverbank, and Edmund pointed out his polliwogs in the shallow pools created by the meanders. Soon, they came to the place where Edmund had encountered Remy and her attackers earlier in the week. He told Banks the story, praising Regis for his part in the matter, and then commenting, "Can you imagine the gall of the blackguards, on my property and about to take advantage of my housekeeper! I will say, Regis was not the only one whose hackles were up! Who ever heard of such cheek! And probably intending to poach after their monstrous behavior was done!"

"I had no idea I was enjoying the hospitality of a defender of the realm's holy womanhood," Banks commented drily. "I am indeed humbled."

"Well, you appear to be the only one. That woman seemed to think I was looking after myself and my own interests—and do you know, she actually told me that the law had no interest in the well-being of women and children."

"Perspicacious of her, wasn't it?" replied Banks. "This is Remy, your housekeeper, of whom you speak?"

"The very one—and what do you mean, 'perspicacious of her'—you can't tell me you agree with her!" Edmund looked amazed.

"But I do—well, at least I see her point. You know, Edmund, you have never taken on a case involving a woman or a child, or a poor man, although there's plenty injustice in those quarters. The high profile, high complexity, high compensation briefs pique your interest. And you are brilliant in resolving them." Banks was smiling, but he spoke seriously. "However, you have no knowledge of what happens in the common courts. I have seen people without money, or influence, or social standing, or public goodwill brutalized by our legal system—why, take my sister! Had the Lord Magistrate not been afraid of scandal, she would have been committed by that bastard of a husband—may his soul rest at the bottom of the Styx—and never would have recovered her dower and become able to re-marry."

"Oh, this is too much—really Banks, what has happened to your brain? A few weeks without me in London and it begins to rot!" Edmund was now mightily irritated. He stopped walking and turned to face Banks. "You know I would have overturned heaven and earth to make sure Dolly received justice! It just so happened that . . ."

"That you had an investigator who unearthed the less-than-wholesome facts about our Magistrate's family involvement, and put his feet to the flames!" Banks came closer as he continued. "I mean no criticism of you, nor do I question your integrity, you must know that. Don't you see, Edmund, perhaps the reason you became so discontented with life in town—enough to come back to Owlswood—has to do with coming back to why you chose the Law as your life. Justice for only the wealthy and prominent was never your aim, as I recall. Justice for its own sake, justice for all, for the overlooked, the common man, the ones left to get by as best they

can, the ones our great society neglects. Perhaps you could personally care about something, some principle, someone, again."

"Oh, please Banks, no oratorio. Don't use my decision to take a
sabbatical as evidence of some great life turning point, some major
disillusionment with my profession, some quest for . . ."

"For justice, Edmund? For truth? For making those rights acces-
sible to everyone?" Banks placed his hands on his hips and continued. "Do you hear yourself? They threatened *my* household, tres-
passed on *my* land, harried *my* employee, poached *my* game—you
were incensed at the injustice to yourself!"

"Banks, where is your logic? If I shoot the enemy in war because
he comes at me with a knife, do I not benefit the whole regiment?
Does the country not prosper because I look after my own affairs? If
I protect my property—animals, household, servants—does it not
do good for the community?"

He began to feel attacked and, incensed, geared up for verbal
battle.

When Banks made to reply, Edmund cut him off.

"This conversation is becoming objectionable and idiotic. I refuse to continue. I will refrain from any further good deeds—the
approbation they incur offends my delicate sensibilities." Edmund
was seething. His knuckles turned white around his walking stick.
"You know, if you were not my guest . . ."

"What about your friend, Edmund. If I were not your friend,
could I speak my mind to you? I can easily leave off being your
guest, but I cannot stop being your friend." Banks looked at him
seriously. "That, I can never stop."

The silence between them ended with two sheepish, broad
smiles, a firm handshake and a rough pounding on each other's
backs. They turned and headed for the house.

*   *   *

They arrived and Edmund led Banks directly through the back entrance to the kitchen, sending Cook into spasms of loud and anxious protestations.

"No, gentlemen, you shan't sit here at the table. I've work to do
and it's not seemly. Nobody told me you would be expecting a feed
at this hour, sirs, the place isn't ready."

She seemed on the verge of an apoplexy when Remy appeared

in the doorway and took charge.

"Cassie, the pottage garden sorely needs your attention—I can do nothing with it, I'm afraid, without your advice. Let me take care of the gentlemen and you take a look."

Cook gladly took the escape provided, still sputtering about gentlemen in the kitchen as her aproned skirt swished out the door.

"Good morning, Remy, I'm afraid we've scandalized Cook," Banks greeted her. "Any chance of some coffee and toast?"

She smiled. "Of course—please go to the dining room and I'll bring it to you."

"No, I'd like to stay here," Edmund declared. "I used to breakfast at this table as a child when I snuck away from my governess—Cook would give me porridge and cream, and toast from the fireplace. We conspired together to evade the authorities of the household."

Noting Remy's raised eyebrow, Banks laughed.

"And now you evade the authorities on behalf of your clients. As the child bends, so goes the man." He looked at Remy and asked, "May we sit?"

They settled themselves and Edmund launched into a reminiscence of childhood times at Owlswood, while Remy busied herself at the stove. Soon, thick slabs of toasted winter wheat bread were buttered and consumed with honey, fresh cheese, and great mugs of steaming coffee. The air of contentment was palpable, and the wholesome food disappeared quickly. Both men ate to almost bursting,

*   *   *

After the early exercise and scandalous mid-morning snack at the kitchen work table, Edmund excused himself and retired to the library for some "solitude and thought." Remy and Cook had disappeared, off to household management tasks. Left to his own devices, Banks decided to explore. He had travelled the hallways of the big house, poking into the nooks and crannies of all the open rooms, scrutinizing various unflattering portraits of Edmund's ancestors (muttering "Good Christ, what a face!" more than once), and decided he would be better off outside. While passing through the main entry foyer he noticed a letter addressed to him resting on the credenza. After opening and reading it, he chuckled softly to himself, refolded it and stashed it in his breast pocket. He continued outside and around toward the back of the house. He was headed out to the gazebo and the maze beyond when he caught sight of Remy working in the herb garden near the kitchen door. He smiled and headed toward her.

"Miss Remy. Beautiful day for gardening, isn't it?"

She was on her knees, dividing a clump of lamb's ears for replanting. She sat back on her heels and turned to greet him.

"Ah, Doctor Banks. Yes, a very beautiful day. Do you like to garden?"

"I'm afraid a green thumb is not one of my virtues. But I take a great interest in herbs and their medicinal properties, and you have a magnificent collection here, I may say."

He looked around admiringly.

"Thank you, they are a passion of mine. I have worked with herbs all my life, and when I was away at my studies, I even had a window box so I could grow them. I experiment with herbal medicaments. My mother was a green woman, and I learned from her." She spoke easily and smiled.

"A green woman? You mean an herbalist?"

"Oh, more than that, Doctor." She wiped her brow with a tanned forearm, and smiled as she explained. "She was a healer, who used herbs to aid health and cure disease. She had a particular frame of mind, and a view of nature that seeks to restore health. She was like a doctor!"

Remy smiled again.

"Ah. May I then consult with you, Miss Remy, on some herbal remedies I have in mind for a certain friend and host, whose disposition is fast approaching that of St. George's dragon?" Banks squatted down to speak to her. "After less than one short week here, I'm feeling a little singed," he said as she suppressed a smile. "I think Edmund needs a tonic for his nerves, at least, if not his health—and ours—in general. Do you not find him . . . distracted? Moody? Often irritable?"

"Most irritable, most of the time," she replied, then considered a moment before she continued. "He appears to be involved in some project of scholarship. He spends long hours in the library, far into the night usually, and seems constantly preoccupied—far away, in a dream almost."

"Ah." The doctor thought for a moment. "That's really not unusual for Edmund. He researches all the time in his work. But here . . . he came here to get away from all that! Well, I assure you he's not such an old bear when he's himself."

"You two have been friends a long time, doctor. I'm sure he shares with you a side of himself not often shown to others."

She smiled slightly.

"Graciously said, Miss Remy, and astutely observed." Banks smiled back with open admiration. "And you're correct: he is a man of many facets."

At this, she laughed out loud. "Do you have a particular cure in mind, Doctor? As you can see, we have many choices." She gestured with her trowel.

"Well, I was going to ask what you recommend. He tells me his appetite is not normal, his stomach is testy, his mood is definitely on edge, and he looks pale to me."

They began a lively discussion of evening primrose, elderberry, yarrow, pennyroyal, lavender, angelica, and several others Banks had no knowledge of. By the end of their conversation, he had a dense green bouquet and specific instructions for the preparation of Edmund's tonic.

"If you like, I can prepare the mixture for you after dinner tonight," Remy suggested.

"Most kind of you, but only if I may assist you and learn how you do it. Agreed?" Banks responded.

"But—will Mr. Symme make use of such a tonic?" Remy asked with some skepticism.

Banks chuckled and said, "You seem to read our mutual acquaintance quite accurately. It will take some persuasion on my part."

"May I suggest, then, that I give half the greens, and my recipe for a very tasty soup, to Cook for the first course at dinner tonight? That way, we can be certain an initial dose reaches the intended recipient, and then you may encourage him to use the tonic thereafter? Do you agree?"

"Brilliant! I am in your debt." Greatly enjoying her company, he asked, "Would you have time to give me a tour of the gardens?" and when she agreed, he offered a hand to help her rise.

As they strolled leisurely across the sunny lawn, he continued the conversation.

"Miss Remy, I find your expertise most impressive. You mentioned studies—where were you educated? Are you a Girton Girl among us here at pristine, stodgy Owlswood?" He put on a look of mock horror. "Lord knows Cambridge University would be proud to have you!"

She smiled wryly.

"Oh, I cannot claim to bring the devilish Woman Question to this idyllic place, at least in its Cambridge form. Girton college holds no interest for me. I studied at the London School of Medicine for Women," she replied, feeling slightly self-conscious as she spoke. "Pharmacologic medicine. "

Banks replied, "Really! Medical studies! With Sophia Jex-Blake? I hear she's got the temper and demeanor of an old war hound—bit of a beast, isn't she?"

"And you heard this from one of your male colleagues, did you, who also holds that women have no place in medicine?" Remy tilted her chin a little higher. He smiled a bit sheepishly.

"*Touché*. Both opinions may be quite unfair, and I do not share the one you mention. Still, apart from possible disagreeable personalities, such study must have had its difficulties."

"Yes, difficulties best not discussed." Her face clouded with some emotion he could not read. "It was not easy."

"But you persevered," he stated gently.

She recovered and went on, "I want to heal, and medicines—how they were concocted in earlier times, and how we may make them better today—are crucial. Study provides the means to uncover puzzle pieces from life long ago, and use them to move ahead today."

"So, you are an historian, as well as a botanist and chemist. Your credentials grow as we speak. I'm impressed!"

"Ahh—you are mocking me, doctor, are you not?" She looked at him intently. "You find this hard to believe, coming from a woman."

He stopped and turned to face her. "On the contrary, Miss Remy, I am prepared to believe whatever you may tell me—with no reservation whatsoever." He did not laugh or seem in the least sarcastic, and looked at her with an even gaze. She felt her entire being melt into a smile.

"Thank you."

They continued toward the gardens, admiring the flame-colored leaves of the woods beyond.

"Miss Remy, I must ask—why did you leave your studies, and whatever are you doing here, as housekeeper?"

She smiled. "Fine and relevant questions, Doctor. Simultaneously, my mother became ill—more gravely than I even knew—and I ran low on funds and could borrow none. Caring for my mother's health, I could not think of anything else. Sadly, she passed all too soon. And when she did, I assumed her charge of caring for Owlswood. I grew up here, you know."

"I didn't know that, Miss Remy!" Banks smiled, surprised.

"Oh, yes, my mother was official caretaker here for many years—as was her mother before her. Our family was named in old John Symme's will as 'the bloodline who shall be employed and entrusted with the care of the house at Owlswood as long as it stands.' A highly unusual codicil, but one my family has taken seriously. And a godsend for us, as a living." She paused. "And since my Mother's recent death, I have fulfilled our family responsibility."

"My sympathy on the passing of your mother. Another difficulty for you." When she nodded and he saw her eyes glisten, Banks continued, "I recall Edmund mentioning that stipulation of the will, and I was surprised at it. But it seems more understandable since I learn your family has long been at Owlswood." He paused briefly. "You speak so fondly of the past. I should think such a lovely and gifted lady would be more concerned with the future."

"Ah—I'm afraid I'm not so in touch with the future, Doctor. It's hidden in the mists."

She seemed wistful.

"Do those mists hold a return to London and more forbidden studies?"

He smiled and his eyes lit with the jest.

She laughed and mimicked peering into a crystal ball. "The future is uncertain, of course, but my greatest wish is to return and continue." She hesitated but a moment. "And to that end, Doctor, may I now ask you to advise me on a delicate matter?"

"Of course. Please do."

"We spoke about the Symme will, from which my grandmother and mother both maintained their post as Housekeeper, and were very pleased to do so." He nodded and she continued, "As I mentioned, the codicil specifies that only immediate family members be so employed. For various reasons, I am not eager to continue in the position. I am most grateful for the consideration, as were they, however you can see that my interests lie elsewhere. I would like to return to London and my studies."

"As well you should."

"I would like to propose to Mr. Symme that one of my cousins take over the post—but you see, she is not immediate family and not of my grandmother's direct lineage. He may not approve. Although we—I—own the house we have lived in, the stipend will be forfeit, a difficult loss."

"Ah—and you wonder what Edmund's response will be," Banks replied.

"I do." She looked at him candidly. "He does not seem a man disposed to unusual consideration, especially toward household help."

"Oh, he can be an old bear, I admit," Banks laughed, "but you do him discredit. I think you can raise the matter with little fear of rebuke, and with every hope of agreeable compromise. Who is this cousin of yours?"

"Anne lives in the village with her family. She cared for the house when my Mother fell ill, before I could return. She is most capable, and most trustworthy."

"With that recommendation, how can he refuse? Really, I think you worry unnecessarily. Speak with Edmund. It will go well, I'm certain. But..." his eyes twinkled, " . . . do not be surprised if he is loath to lose such a capable and graceful presence in his home. He is a practical man who appreciates competence—and grace."

They came to the rose garden where the well-established bushes were riotous with blooms. "Doctor, I would like to stop a moment to gather flowers for the bedrooms—save the master bedroom, of course." They shared a look of conspiratorial understanding. She anchored the pointed end of her flower basket in the soil, and began to select and cut blooms. After a moment's hesitation, she continued.

"Has Mr. Symme ever expressed an interest in the occult, or in spiritualism?" she asked casually.

"Never. I have never known him to waste an ounce of time or

energy on it." He paused.

"Well . . . thank you for a lovely conversation and your sympathetic ear." Remy glanced at the bouquet of herbs he carried. "After dinner, then?"

*   *   *

Banks returned to the house, finding his host looking for him rather impatiently in the back hallway just inside the kitchen entrance.

"By all that's holy, you demand that I drop my scholarly pursuits and meet you no later than 4pm sharp, and then you are nowhere to be found!" Edmund grumbled. "And I see you're getting rather chummy with my housekeeper—what's all that about, Banks?"

He went on with hands clasped behind him, looking and sounding like a stern school master.

"Sharp little eyes, have we?" Banks replied genially, looking out toward the garden. "Yes, I've just had a most enjoyable conversation with her. In fact, I enjoy all my conversations with her. Most interesting young woman."

"Interesting woman? Good God, man, she's the housekeeper! How could you find her interesting? A bit annoying at times, I'll grant you." Edmund twisted around to get a better view of Remy in the garden, as if to make sure they were talking about the same person. "Interesting woman? I seriously doubt that."

Banks sighed and continued. "Where have you been, my friend? She is most definitely a woman (and far shapelier than my wonderful Mrs. Maillot, I can tell you)—and as for interesting, she's been to university and is, in fact, quite knowledgeable about medicinal herbs." Then he whispered conspiratorially. "We were talking about you, you know, and how difficult your disposition has been of late. Did you know she speaks fluent French, and has the most lovely green eyes? Don't tell me you haven't noticed!"

"I have better things to do than notice my housekeeper's eyes," Edmund snapped, "And I would have thought you did, too. What is that ridiculous bunch of greenery you're holding?"

"Ah—a gift, Edmund. Not for your drawing room, but for your stomach. Miss Remy has enlightened me as to a tonic for your sour nerves and hopefully for your sour disposition as well."

"Balderdash," Edmund commented, then asked, "She speaks

French, you say? She speaks well?"

"Quite fluent, old man, it is a cradle language to her; her father was French. Why are you suddenly interested?"

"Well, Banks, I have need of translation." Edmund began guardedly. "There has been a phrase that bedevils me and it seems to be a trenchant comment on her . . . er . . . a very elusive conundrum in law I'm presently researching. Let's fetch this interesting housekeeper of mine, shall we, and see if she can rescue me from my ignorance."

Just then Remy entered the house with her basket of roses, heading for the kitchen.

"Remy, please stop a moment and join us," Edmund called.

Remy left the flowers on the kitchen work table and came back to the hallway.

"Yes, Mr. Symme?"

"Ah, the good doctor tells me you speak French. Is that true?"

"It is."

"Please, then, be so good as to translate the phrase, *Chantez à l'âne, et il vous fera des pets*. Can you tell me what it means?" Edmund asked, leaning back against the wall, arms crossed on his chest.

She looked at him in surprise for a moment, fighting back a smile.

"Well, sir, you have quoted a proverb, very old, somewhat out of use today. If you will pardon the colloquialism, in English it would be, 'Sing to a donkey and it will fart for you.' Similar in meaning to our biblical prohibition about casting pearls before swine, I believe."

"And this is key to some conundrum of legal research, you say?" Banks began to laugh heartily. "What in the name of heaven are you working on?"

He caught Remy's eye and she struggled to keep from laughing herself.

Giving Edmund time to recover from being somewhat nonplussed by her answer, she went on, "Apparently you have happened upon the French disdain for the poor animal in some written work—even Montaigne had little positive to say, if I may quote him: 'Is there anything more certain, decided, disdainful, contemplative, grave and serious, than a donkey?' Of course, he was comparing them to educators, but in general, I find many French men are very much as he describes."

Edmund was silent for a brief moment, then asked coolly, "Do you have any more enlightening information to impart, Remy?"

"No, sir."

"Then you may go. Thank you."

She was dismissed.

After she had gone, Banks said, "Would you not agree that conversation was most interesting? I wager you might concede that Miss Remy is an unusual woman."

"Hmmm . . . most unusual. This is most unusual." Edmund seemed to have forgotten Banks was there. Suddenly he remembered. "Ah, well, Christopher could you excuse me for a time? I find I must attend to something now."

*　　*　　*

When Edmund made no appearance at dinner, Banks finished his own meal and then went looking for him. "He is in the library, no doubt," he told Remy, "so if you'll prepare a tray, I'll bring it in. Oh, and put some of that herbal infusion in a teapot as well."

When the tray was ready, Banks quietly tapped on the library door, then entered.

"Good evening, Edmund, I missed you at dinner." The figure in the large leather chair before the fire was engrossed in his reading, and just waved. "I've brought some food for you." Banks set the tray down on the big table and continued, "Edmund, I have had some rather . . . interesting news arrive by post today. I didn't have a chance to share it with you earlier."

He came across the room and perched on the edge of the window seat.

"Really?" Edmund answered absently, continuing to read. Then when Banks did not proceed, he looked up over his spectacles and added, "Well, am I to assume you intend to share this news of interest? Do go on."

"I wanted to be sure of your attention, Edmund, as this may be of some import to you personally. After you left me today, I attended to some business matters, including correspondence. In the post this morning arrived a packet from my man, Rivers. He writes that a note was delivered soon after I'd left for Owlswood, and includes

89

the note." He drew a small, expensive looking pink envelope from his pocket and waved it at his host. "This note. This note, Edmund, is from Lydia."

"Lydia? Writing to you?" Edmund paused a moment and then began to laugh softly. "Hells bells, has she set her cap for you now? I'd be pleased to give my blessing and see you two wed, no hard feelings, old man." Edmund continued to chortle but Banks did not join in. "Oh, sorry, Banks. Come on, what does she say?"

He set down his reading and turned to give his friend full attention.

"I'm pleased to see you're in so jocular a frame of mind, Edmund. It's a rare treat these days. Let me place a wager with you. When I tell you the contents of the note, you will not laugh. Is it a bet?"

"What does she say, Banks?" Edmund spoke slowly and soberly, anxious at the answer.

"Oh, she says she hopes I'm well, etcetera, and that she missed seeing me at the Rothschilds' soiree. She mentions that her mother had inquired after me and," his eyes shone with merriment, ". . . she informs me that she feels a great need for time away from the city, time in the country. After several weeks of estrangement, she feels strongly the need to 'mend bridges'—I believe she put it—and asks if I would care to escort her on a surprise visit to poor Edmund?" He opened his hands in a gesture that matched his word: "Voila."

Edmund remained silent as the words sank in. His brow furrowed.

"Yes, indeed, old man, this note was delivered to my home not a week after I had embarked on my journey here, and the post delivery here must have delayed it—oh—at least two more days. It says she wanted to leave within the fortnight." He was clearly enjoying Edmund's reaction to the news. He tapped the elegant square with his finger. "Would you care to read for yourself?" When Edmund did not respond, he continued. "Overcome by joy, are we? It's so rare that one finds you speechless, Edmund, it rather takes my breath away." He smiled his most brilliant smile. "Ah, care for some herb tonic? It's good for the nerves. "

"Lydia! Here! My God, Banks, this is intolerable!" Edmund sank further into his leather chair and closed his eyes, waving his hands in the air. "Can't the woman find other ways to inflict herself on society? Why visit me? And after the way she's been treated?

No—you must have misunderstood. She would never come here."

He looked at Banks hopefully.

"I assure you old man, the message is very plain. Here, read for yourself if you doubt it."

He offered the characteristic vellum to Edmund who, after one look and a brief whiff, waved it away and covered his eyes with his hand.

"I don't want her here. She cannot come. I offer no hospitality. How shall I prevent this—what steps shall I take, Banks?"

"She is no doubt on her way, Edmund, so I see no useful strategy. However, since you'll need all your strength, I suggest you eat this wonderful food I've brought you and skip no more meals. And, since the debacle is imminent, I should prescribe a glass of brandy immediately, to be repeated with some regularity until the malady has departed, so to speak." He walked over to the decanter and poured two fingers of cognac for each of them, then handing Edmund his glass, continued, "Come, come, *Mon Vieux*, courage! How bad will it be?"

"It will be bad, Banks."

"Not at all! She'll arrive on her mission of mercy, find you uninterested, and then she'll become bored with the whole affair and go back home. I doubt she has much tolerance for the quiet country life."

"I don't know. Do you really think so?"

"It's difficult to say with Lydia, but that's my prediction."

"God, I do hope you're right, Banks." Edmund brooded for a moment and then, noticing the time, said, "Would you mind leaving me? I'd just like to spend a brief time alone before retiring."

"As you wish. But please, remember to eat something. Just let me take some fascinating volume with me," he reached up and selected a leather-bound book from one of the shelves, "and I'm off to read awhile." He paused. "Are you quite alright?"

"Quite. Good night."

"Good night—and remember my prescription. And don't dwell too much on the arrival of the lovely Lydia. All will be well, my friend."

Banks closed the door behind him.

Edmund leaned back, closed his eyes, and sighed wearily. Soon he became aware of the scent of gardenia enveloping his chair.

"*Que est-ce c'est que vous dire,* 'Lydia is coming?' *Que-est que c'est, cette Lydia?*"

Edmund leapt to his feet.

"Ah. Good evening, Belle Dame. So, you have overheard the conversation? Good, I was planning to mention it to you tonight. How lovely you look."

Edmund eyes couldn't move from the beautiful face, smiling in acknowledgement of his compliment.

She waited for a moment and again asked, "Lydia? "

"Yes, there will be a guest at Owlswood for a short time, and her name is Lady Lydia Grenfield. She will be arriving, well, I'm not sure exactly when, but soon."

"So. It is this way. I am not sufficiently entertaining company, *n'est pas*, to keep you happy? You need another woman to come here?" She seemed genuinely concerned and rather indignant. "A housekeeper, a maid, a cook I can understand, but this one?"

"No, no, Belle Dame, you misunderstand. This lady arrives unbidden by me!"

And that's the absolute truth, by God, Edmund thought.

"Ah, yes? Explain, please."

"You see, before I left London—in a rather abrupt fashion, in fact, to come here—she and I were, well, we . . . ah . . . we spent rather a great deal of time together in various ways. And then I left her behind, abruptly as I mentioned, leaving many things unsaid, if you will, and I rather thought they would remain unsaid but now . . ." Edmund stammered pathetically.

"Ah, you fled from her and now she pursues. Tsk, tsk, tsk, what must she think of herself to do such a thing?" Fleur pursed her luscious lips and thought for a moment. "Can she find no other lover, *Chérie*? Is she plain? Do her teeth protrude—so?" she demonstrated with her tongue against her upper lip. "Is her papa in decline, perhaps? *Trop peu d'argent*, money troubles, eh?"

She winked and shook her head in sympathy.

"No, of course not." The absurdity of justifying a prospective houseguest to a ghostly apparition was not completely lost on Edmund. He began to feel annoyed. "She's a very beautiful woman with straight teeth and a very wealthy papa, er, father. She comes because she chooses to come, and although it's a damnable nuisance, there's no motive except to see me. I assure you, her brain is not capable of ulterior motive."

"Well. Tell her not to come. *Finis*." She waved her hand in a graceful gesture of dismissal. "A simple statement will suffice for the simple brain of this Lydia, yes?"

"Oh, I doubt that. This is far from simple, lady."

Edmund began to weary of the discussion.

"*Chérie*! What could be easier? She speaks English, yes? If not, I will teach you how to say it *en Français*."

"She will not be dissuaded from her journey, I assure you, and she may be en route even as we speak! Anything I say to her will only indicate my interest in her, and the promise of future interest as well."

Edmund began to sound testy, even to his own ears. He paced over to the brandy decanter and poured an indelicate splash.

Fleur watched him intently, then began quietly, "Perhaps you await this 'damnable nuisance' with some pleasure, no? Perhaps you would prefer more stimulating companionship than I can provide. Perhaps the things of the spirit we have shared no longer comfort you—after all, you are mortal, yes? Of the flesh, yes? You require flesh to soothe you?" Her eyes began to flash. "Very well, I understand. I will leave you with your own kind. Perhaps I, too, was foolish to think we could . . . Never mind! You will not be troubled by visits from me anymore! I feel . . . *comment dire* . . . an unkind vibration regarding this Lydia." Before Edmund could open his mouth to placate her, she continued, "Perhaps when the Lydia has departed you will long for your old friends, your true friends. And, who knows, *Chérie*? Perhaps I will have time for you! But a word of caution: mind she keeps to herself in this house. And away from my books!"

In a swirl of umbrage and peach *crêpe de chine*, she was gone.

Oh my God, Edmund thought, *suppose she never returns!*

He was stunned at her anger.

"Fleur! Belle Dame! A moment, please!"

But the library was completely still.

He suddenly felt disheartened. He settled into the leather chair and closed his eyes. *Well*, he comforted himself, *at least we know Lydia won't go near any books.*

93

8
Lydia's Visit

In a flurry of lavender lace and organdy, Lydia Grenfield alighted from the carriage, opened her parasol, and blinked into the afternoon sun. She was not in good spirits.

"What a beastly trip," she commented as she surveyed the lawn appraisingly. Catching sight of Edmund in an upstairs window, however, she waved gaily, smiled brilliantly, and blew him a kiss.

"Oh bloody damnation, she's here," Edmund muttered under his breath. "I can't believe it. Bloody hell, bloody damnation," he continued as he descended the main staircase to the front door. Drawing a deep breath and pausing for a moment on the landing, he caught a few words of conversation drifting through the open doorway.

"But of course I'm not expected, my good woman, I just told you, it's a surprise!" came Lydia's voice.

Remy had come to the front steps when the carriage rolled to a stop to see if its passenger needed some assistance. She had obviously been unprepared for Lydia's announcement that she was a guest of Mr. Symme.

"See that my bags are well-handled, won't you, and placed in my room immediately," Lydia directed.

The coachman had been busy stacking luggage in the drive, and, tiring of the work, paused briefly to wipe his brow with a grimy kerchief. On hearing Lydia's words, however, he made haste to collect his fare, climb back onto his perch, and move his vehicle quickly out the gate. The excessive pile of luggage on the gravel gave credence to Edmund's worst fear.

He strode through the front door and demanded, "Lydia, what is all this?"

"Edmund, dearest, is that any way to greet me?" Lydia pouted as she glided up the steps. She put one lavender-gloved hand on his chest and placed a modestly languid kiss on his cheek. "Haven't you missed me at all?" she whispered, eyes wide with sensuous innocence. "It's been so long!"

Ire rising, Edmund was about to reply when he became aware

of Remy's interested attention. She stood, hands folded, with an admirably serene expression, betrayed only by one arched eyebrow and a slight tilt of her head.

"Pardon my interruption, Mr. Symme," she began. "If a guest room is to be ready for the lady this evening, I must see to it directly. Your instructions, sir?"

Lydia turned to face the servant who had stupidly interfered in her reunion with her beloved, a mix of annoyance and pity on her face. It was at this point that she became aware of Remy as a woman, rather than a servant—a young and rather attractive woman, with a disconcertingly intelligent stare. And, she thought to herself, *he came here directly after leaving me, did he?*

"Oh, Edmund, is there a room close to yours?" Lydia asked. "I do hate late night noises in these country homes and I shall feel so much better with you near me."

She smiled serenely at Remy.

"Not having expected to entertain, Lydia, I've not opened the entire house," Edmund began, pointedly, "and Banks is in the only other prepared bedroom. I fear it will be a dreadful inconvenience for all of us . . . "

"Excuse me, sir," Remy interrupted, "but might I suggest the Camellia Room? It will take me only the afternoon to ready it for the lady."

"Ah, then, it's settled," gushed Lydia, slipping her arm through Edmund's, "and now you must show me this wonderful old house. I haven't seen you in so very long, and you were so dreadfully rude the last time we were together . . ."

Lydia steered him into the foyer.

"Mr. Symme," called Remy, and Edmund disengaged from Lydia and returned to the steps. "Samuel has workers here for the glasshouse repair, and I will see they take care of the luggage."

"Yes, excellent idea," he replied distractedly. Then, finding himself, he continued, "And . . . I would appreciate greatly your making no more suggestions as to the arrangements of guests in my house."

"Mr. Symme, I apologize if you found my suggestion forward, but there was really no alternative and . . ." she tilted her head ever so slightly, " . . . arranging household affairs is why you engage me."

She turned and briskly walked into the house.

"Damned uppity woman. Efficient, but damned uppity. A plague of intractable women is upon me. Why, by God, what have I done to deserve such a thing?" Edmund muttered to himself as he followed.

*   *   *

"Alright, old man, I've had quite enough of this. Any more luggage?" Banks dusted off his hands. "Good St. Therese, does Lydia bring her rock collection wherever she goes? I've never carried a trunk so heavy! My back is about to break."

He threw himself onto the chaise lounge.

"You were under no obligation to help with the bags, Christopher, so it serves you right. I thought you told me she mentioned a 'brief visit'. She looks as though she plans a month, at least!" Edmund frowned. "I will not permit it. She has to leave!"

"Well, I think you should tell her that right now, don't you? Certainly before she unpacks all this! Confront the she-lion on the hunt, as it were. If you don't, no telling what she plans next . . . "

His eyes twinkled merrily at Edmunds disquiet.

"You go down, Banks. Keep her amused for a short while, will you? I want to wash up and collect my thoughts."

And plan an escape, Edmund thought *—could I get to town on foot before the next train? Not a chance.*

"Very well, but if you take too long, I shan't be accountable for the disappearance of that wonderful cognac in the library."

Banks headed down the stairs as Edmund called after him frantically.

"No—not the library! She mustn't go in there, whatever you do!" he almost shouted. In a quieter voice, he continued, "I need one sanctuary, at least, Banks. Keep her in the sitting room, or take her out by the fountain. I won't be long."

For God's sake, Lydia in the library, he thought, *I'm certainly not prepared for that!*

Edmund went to his own room and after a brief splash of water on his face and a good lathering of his hands, a fresh shirt and some stout words of encouragement to himself, he felt ready to confront Lydia and send her immediately back to London.

There's really nothing to handling her, he mused, *I need to be direct. But not too direct. An hysterical female is not what I need. And she's already disrupted my conversations with La Belle Dame! The sooner she's gone and back in Town where she belongs, inflicting herself on some other poor fool, the better.*

A glance in the armoire mirror confirmed that he was indeed suitably dressed to face the upcoming challenge. Edmund left his room and started toward the stair. The door to the adjoining Camellia bedroom was wide open, and as he passed, he looked in. Through the forest of stacked trunks and cases, he saw Remy putting fresh linen on the bed. She stood encasing a pillow with a new slip, the late afternoon sun streaming through the window behind her. Her hair shone a deep auburn red around her head like a crown, and Edmund stood, staring, for a few seconds before she noticed him.

She asked, "Yes, Mr. Symme, may I be of some service?"

Edmund's eyebrows came together in concentration and he moved into the room, coming to stand directly in front of her. "Remy, are your eyes green?" he asked, looking at her intently.

"They are."

Remy was startled, then puzzled, and began to feel uncomfortable under Edmund's stare.

"Is something amiss, sir? What can I . . ."

Edmund took the pillow from her hand and tossed it onto the bed, then placed a hand lightly on her shoulder and gently drew her closer to the window. With his other hand, he tipped her chin up and to the side with a whisper of pressure, all the while gazing into her eyes.

"They are surely green—how strange I did not notice before. And your hair —" his hands moved to the thickly piled tresses "— it's so red! Golden brown and red!"

He continued to look at her as his hands smoothed her hair gently. She returned his gaze and felt there was no end to the clear blue of his eyes; she could look into them forever . . .

A peal of shrill laughter coming from the lawn intruded—Lydia! The moment broken, Edmund dropped his hands and looked disoriented, then flustered, then stern. He turned and strode to the door, stopping for a moment as if he had thought of saying something. But, after looking back at her over his shoulder, he continued downstairs.

Remy stood for a moment, not sure what she was feeling. The memory of his eyes and his hands was like some heady perfume, making her feel light-headed and giddy. Impatient with herself, she remembered the task at hand, moved back to the bed and began to smooth the sheets and blankets. But she was soon lost in reverie of the moment just past. She walked over to the dressing table mirror and looked at her face—at her greenish eyes, at her hair, slightly tousled from Edmund's touch—and she felt in herself that familiar shift of perception that always brought things to "see."

She continued to gaze at the mirror and the items in the room reflected there began to blur, to shift and move, becoming a whirl of color and form. And then all was clear again—except it was not the same room reflected there, but another, dark with shadows—as if the moon were clouded. And in it stood a man and woman, entwined in a passionate embrace. Her hair was loosed and she was dressed only in a long, lacey cloak of some kind. The man's arms were strong and tight around her, and he buried his face in the crook of her neck. After a moment, he released her reluctantly— hands caressing her shoulders—untied his robe and let it fall to the floor. He turned to fling back the covers of the bed, and looked up at the mirror. Those unmistakable blue eyes of Edmund Symme, only now alive with desire, looked almost into Remy's soul. He turned back to the woman, whose face she could not see, and gathered her up into his arms to carry her to the bed. She tossed back her head, and he kissed her throat . . . . The blur came again, then the heady dizziness, and then Remy was alone in the Camellia bedroom again with only real objects reflected in the glass.

Breathless, she turned away from the mirror, and felt the heat rising in her blood. It must be a vision of the future, not the past, if he is in it! And the woman . . . the one who arrived today?

"Why should I see such a thing? It has nothing to do with me!" she said aloud, angrily, and went about her business.

*   *   *

Edmund ran down the stairway and out the front door to where Lydia was ambling in the garden.

After several minutes of polite conversation on the loveliness of the grounds, the arduousness of the trip from London, rustic surroundings and appointments of the manor, and the fact that tea had been overlooked in the bustle of the afternoon, Edmund, Banks, and Lydia found themselves poised on the abyss of awkward silence. Even though she was tired from her unaccustomed travel, Lydia was fully prepared to advance the cause for which she had come, and requested to see Edmund alone for a few minutes. Banks, of course, was delighted to excuse himself and grinned secretly at Edmund as he left.

Lydia settled herself prettily on the bench under the arbor and beckoned.

"Come over here and sit by me, Edmund, won't you?" she requested with her most appealing smile. After he had done as bidden, she continued, "You know, the last time we were together, you behaved in a rather ghastly manner. And all dictates of common decency require you to give me some explanation—especially after all we've been to each other and the hopes of what we would become . . . " She paused and looked closely into Edmund's eyes. "Running off like that and virtually disappearing into the country left Mama and me in a most difficult position—what explanation could we give? And what could have possibly possessed you?"

Her large, violet eyes glistened with gathering tears. Edmund began to respond, but was silenced by Lydia's fingers on his lips.

"But, in truth Edmund, I require no explanation from you. I have made up my mind that the feelings we have for one another more than outweigh the . . . uh . . . incident that occurred. I am willing to be reconciled, with no more said about it!"

The look on her face was so earnest that Edmund felt himself softening. He took her elegant hand in his and began, "Lydia, you are a lady of excellent style and breeding, and the largess of your words moves me greatly. I'm sure I never expected to be forgiven, much less reconciled."

Lydia smiled slightly, and squeezed his hand. "I do care for you, Edmund."

"I know, Lydia, and I am honored." Edmund pushed on. "I have always valued your friendship, and you know I have felt great affection for you. Believe me—as your truest friend—when I say you must return to London immediately."

"But, Edmund, I just arrived! How can I go back immediately?" She looked aghast. "What will people say?" Her mouth formed its renowned charming pout. "Besides, you know, I don't plan to be here terribly long, I didn't even bring my maid with me." Then, struck by a thought, she added, "Do you suppose that housekeeper of yours can find someone to take care of my wardrobe and my hair?"

"Damn your hair and damn what people say!" Edmund exclaimed. "Lydia, how can I explain to you such a great change in my feelings and expectations? I . . . you can't imagine . . . the complexity of my present situation beggars my power to describe it. It is best for you to be elsewhere. Go home."

Lydia looked confused; she was, indeed, often confused in conversations with him.

"Edmund, you say you have held me in some esteem. Has all that changed so very much?"

Yes, he longed to shout, but held himself in check.

"No, Lydia, I still think very highly of you. However, I am not in a position to be . . . to be in love with you. You must be very clear on that point."

He hoped he was making it plain and simple to understand.

Lydia looked incredulous, then puzzled.

"Not in love with me? I'm afraid I don't understand. Everyone's in love with me—even men I don't know. If you knew the letters that are left each week . . . "

"Lydia, please," Edmund continued vigorously, "my change of feelings really has nothing to do with your own self. The complexity of the issue is truly too much to . . . "

"Oh, I know that, Edmund," interrupted Lydia, "I have been talking with a fascinating man Papa brought to dinner recently—a physician who deals with the human mind, instead of the body, isn't that droll? I told him that you had always been bold and impetuous in your legal strategies, (which of course make you the famed man of law that you are), but always the most controlled of gentlemen in social situations. He says that you were probably under a great number of influences that had nothing to do with me but it came out that way. He also says that the changes in your feelings are probably quite real, although they might only be temporary."

"My God."

When Lydia tried to be intellectual, the results were seldom good and often frightening.

"Indeed, he is a fascinating man, Edmund. Can you imagine

anyone being so taken with the human mind? He maintains that breeding is largely a matter of . . . "

Edmund jumped to his feet and began to pace.

"Lydia, you must understand!" he said adamantly. "You mustn't count on me anymore. I am no longer . . . mentally suitable, if you will . . . to be your suitor. I have other directions to pursue, other interests . . . "

"And little interest in me? You must admit, Edmund, that I am used to being the pursued, not the pursuer. And yet I have come to you. All this is rather difficult for me."

She sniffled and raised her handkerchief to her eye.

"I realize that, Lydia. I appreciate your feelings. But, I must be honest with you, as a gentleman and as your friend."

"I know. I am content to be your true and loyal friend for now." She nodded purposefully. "But you won't think ill of me if I remember our . . . closer days . . . with longing and hope for the future?"

Her large eyes looked at him, expectantly.

"There is no hope for more than friendship, Lydia," Edmund continued emphatically. "And you see, don't you, that you must return to London at once. You can't expect to stay on here now, when you know where I stand?"

"Oh, you can't send me packing now that I've just arrived," Lydia smiled prettily. "Besides, friends often visit friends in the countryside. And I've never been here before! Come, we'd best dress for dinner now and discuss the length of my stay later, after we're both refreshed and less weary."

Neither the battle nor the war is yet won, thought Edmund to himself, *but what to do next? Eject her bodily off the estate and onto a passing train?*

"I'm afraid we live a simple life here in the country, and dressing for dinner is not a part of it."

"Oh, really?" Lydia laughed. "Well, I shall certainly dress for dinner, after a lovely hot bath! But of course, since I have left my maid in town, I shall not aspire to my usual standards of evening wear." She looked at him with concern. "You are obviously in great need of a true lady's companionship—rustic surroundings notwithstanding!"

She rose and glided across the grass and into the house, leaving Edmund with a sense of foreboding—and a headache.

101

Three hours later, seated in the dining room with a delicious, fragrant meal set before them, Edmund began to feel better. The cook Remy had engaged was a true jewel, and although the fare was simple by London standards, the flavors and textures were always wonderful.

Tonight was no exception. Banks proved to be his usual genial and entertaining self. And Remy had set the table with fine china and linen, and was quietly providing attentive, confident service. Even Lydia, refreshed by her bath and radiant in her dinner gown, was charming company with her delightfully gossipy tales about the characters Edmund had left behind in London society. She seemed to enjoy her position as sole female at table, even going so far as to call for the next course to be cleared and mentioning that Cook should use a little more savoury in the sauce next time.

She's enjoying playing lady of the manor far too much, Edmund thought, even as he noted how the candlelight was most flattering. By the time Banks suggested adjourning to the sitting room for some brandy, Edmund found himself grudgingly admitting that Lydia had been a delightful dinner guest, especially since she would soon be on her way home.

Lydia insisted that the two men proceed to their brandies without her, and that she would follow directly. When they had left, she took a few moments to inspect the silverware hallmark and the tea service on the credenza before Remy came in to clear the table.

"I wish to review the menus for the coming week tomorrow morning, Remy," she began, "and I'd like you to prepare an inventory of all china, crystal, and serving pieces for me no later than tea time. Does Cook do a decent Wellington? For say, twenty-five? I may wish to hostess a dinner party within the fortnight."

"I am unfamiliar with the extent of Cook's technical expertise, Miss Grenfield," Remy replied. "But I will request from Mr. Symme permission to furnish the information you require."

"Ah, well, perhaps I'd better send for my cook and butler regardless. Oh, please don't misunderstand me," Lydia continued gushingly, "dinner tonight was refreshingly simple and very well done. And I think you do a wonderful job here, my dear, considering the circumstances. But . . ." and here she tilted her head in the direction of the sitting room, "Mr. Symme deserves a household more suited to his social standing and," she smiled brightly, "the place badly needs a woman's touch, *n'estce pas*?"

"*Ce n'est pas ma place à dire, cependent je trouve le style masculin très agréable, Mademoiselle,*" replied Remy as she collected the dinner china onto her tray.

"Oh . . . oh, yes, of course," Lydia's mind raced to find a word she recognized. "How lovely that you speak French. Wherever did you learn?"

"My father was French. Goodnight, Miss."

Remy made her way to the kitchen, leaving Lydia startled and alone in the dining room, a state of being totally unacceptable to her. She was on her way to join her male companions when she became aware of a slight movement of air behind her, almost imperceptible, and a faint rustling of silk. A chill ran up her spine, for what reason she could not imagine; but she took a deep breath (was that gardenia she smelled?) and turned to find . . . no one! Just the shadowy, still hallway all around her. She made haste to the sitting room.

9
Lydia at the Manor

Within a few days, Lydia had proven, despite Edmund's misgivings, a most congenial houseguest and had rather livened up the daily routine at the house with her chattering gaiety and considerable female charm. The diversion she provided eased slightly his feelings of loneliness and loss; for he had neither seen nor heard from La Belle Dame since Lydia's arrival.

On the other side of the coin, Lydia's relentless efforts to induce Edmund to entertain were proving increasingly tiresome. He had successfully resisted so far, claiming that further disruption of his solitude would interfere greatly with his whole reason for being at Owlswood—time for study and reflection. Lydia acquiesced smilingly, gracefully of course—but he noted with self-satisfied amusement her increasing level of frustration at being constantly thwarted in playing the role of lady-of-the-manor.

Remy proved a great ally in his resistance to Lydia's pressure, for although she remained attentive and scrupulously mannered, she absolutely refused to regard Lydia as anything more than a temporary fixture at the house and referred all requests for menu preparation, social invitations, and special arrangements to "Mr. Symme's personal approval."

He could not help but admire Remy's ability to be absolutely appropriate in handling his guests and his household while maintaining her calm, self-possessed manner at every turn. Reluctantly, he had to admit that there was indeed more substance to the woman than he had credited—and became increasingly distracted by her eyes, a most intriguing shade of green.

Now, on this brilliantly cool, crisp Sunday morning, he, Banks, and Lydia were trotting off on his neighbor MacCready's three best mounts to attend chapel before what promised to be a magnificent morning ride. Graciously pious attendance at Sunday Church was another sortie into respectable domesticity, brought on by the determined Lady Grenfield. As if reading Edmund's thoughts, Banks looked over at him, shrugged, and seemed amused.

"Pillars of the community, are we not?" he commented as the small village church tower came into view. "The vicar will be most impressed—if you do nothing during the service to disillusion him."

"Like fall asleep, or fart during his sermon? Banks really."

"That's the stuff, old man. Do you best not to embarrass me, or even worse, your tenacious ex-fiancé. You would never want to alienate her considerable affections."

"Perish the thought, Dr. Banks."

Predictably, the townspeople eyed the unusual trio with unabashed curiosity and took every opportunity to look them over. Each family paid its respects to the young Mr. Symme and company, smiled and curtsied, and inspected each minute detail of manner, speech, and dress. The crowd was absolutely awed by Lydia (partially due to the rumour that *this* was the lady involved in Symme's big London scandal—the one that banished him here to the Old House). Besides impressing them with her highly fashionable riding garb, Lydia dazzled them all with her smile and solicitous interest in their bonnets, their children, their lovely village. Unaware that a reputation had preceded her, she felt that establishing a beneficent presence to the townsfolk, who sooner or later would look to her for social and community guidance when she became Edmund's wife and the mistress of Owlswood, was *noblesse oblige*.

The poor vicar, bless him, was painfully non-plussed by the unexpected addition of such exalted lambs to his humble flock. He stammered and stuttered his way through a sermon that made absolutely no sense and carried on far too long. A spontaneous sigh of relief came forth from the congregation when he as last descended from the pulpit and led the closing hymn.

"There, Banks, I did well, did I not?" Edmund whispered as they filed slowly out of the benches. "No snores or other foul sounds came from my person during the service."

"I wish something *had* broken the monotony—now I know why I gave up the spiritual life: it's bloody hell on earth to sit through these things! The devil does well to keep far away from church services, and so shall I from now on."

Lydia was already outside, chatting with the clergyman and his wife, who stood entranced, with broad smiles and wide eyes, nodding excitedly and hanging on every one of Lydia's words. She caught sight of her companions.

"Ah, here they come! Dr. Banks, did you not truly feel moved by Vicar Creviston's sermon? And Edmund, dear, you'll be so pleased! The Vicar and his wife have agreed to join us for dinner tonight!"

*　*　*

The countryside was just turning to the autumn colors that Edmund loved so well; the sunshine was warm on his face, yet its strength seemed diminished by the coolness of the early September wind. As he cantered his mount through the trees, he took delight in the sights and scents and feelings of fall, all reminding him of the times he had played in these woods as a child on visits to his grandparents. That was before his grandmother had left the house suddenly, vowing she would never set foot in it again, and grandfather reluctantly followed shortly thereafter.

Yet Owlswood was never closed up, as would have been expected, but always remained open and ready to receive the family whenever they should choose to return. How curious that grandfather should leave the place and never visit again during his remaining years, yet provide for its constant maintenance even at his death. Could the old blaggard have *known* somehow that . . .

Suddenly, Lydia drew up beside him, her horse matching the stride of his.

"Stop a moment, won't you?" she called to him.

They slowed the horses to a walk and she continued, prettily, "Edmund, are you still cross? You know I can't bear it when you're angry with me." Her eyes held a look of concern, and when he did not reply, she went on. "Really, the Crevistons won't be any bother, and I'm only thinking of you—you need to be a presence in the town and the vicar could be a very important contact for you. After all, you're the only link these poor souls have to decent . . ." She stopped speaking and looked at him for a moment. "Are you listening?"

Edmund had become rigid in his saddle and was gazing past Lydia, past her words, past the wooded hills and the meadow, far off into the distance where Owlswood stood. He stared, transfixed, and his heart leapt as he heard a faint but familiar silken laugh on the wind and saw in the distance . . .

"What? What's that?"

He was brought back to reality abruptly and looked at Lydia

as if he'd never seen her before. He was struck with her beauty, but untouched by it. After all, honey-blonde hair is far from the passionate red flame that set his heart racing, and blue eyes are so cold compared to sea-green. Even dressed so beautifully in her burgundy riding suit, cordovan boots gleaming, and poised so elegantly on her mount with the ease of an accomplished horsewoman, she was no match for the memory of another elegant, wildly beautiful woman he missed so much. A wave of loneliness swept over him and he felt close to tears. Instead, he covered his painful memories with annoyance.

"Lady Grenfield, you seem to regard me as some medieval lord who has an obligation to vassals on his lands! *Whom* I allow into my home is my own choice, and no one else's. And as I have been clearly and persistently stating, even enough for you to understand, *when* I extend invitations is my sole prerogative as well!"

Lydia looked dumbfounded for a moment and then burst into tears.

"How could you speak to me this way, Edmund, it was only an invitation to dine!"

She looked so miserable in a divinely elegant sort of way that Edmund's heart softened a bit. *If only she weren't so damned comfortable in every sort of situation,* he thought—*on a horse, in the country, in town, wherever—perhaps she'd just pack up and leave if she'd just be sufficiently discomfited. But, by God, I can't keep screaming at her, and nothing I do seems to matter a whit. Discomfited? How I wish!*

"Perhaps I'm a bit harsh, Lydia. However, you must have known how I would feel about it. Have you ever once considered *my* feelings?"

"I always think of you, Edmund. You just are so difficult these days." She sniffed prettily and ventured a slight smile. "But I don't see what can be done about it now—and it's just one meal."

"Very well. What you say is true. But no more, Lady Grenfield, no more."

"And I am forgiven?" She assumed her customary "forgiven?" pout.

Edmund had to smile, although wryly.

"Of course. Now come with me. I'm off to find Banks and get back to the house. It's almost time for the stableboy to collect these beasts."

"No, I think not—I should like to see over that next rise." As Edmund hesitated, Lydia laughed. "Come now, you have no fears for my safety, have you? I can outride any woman in London, or this shire for that matter. There's plenty of time, and I'll be along not a quarter hour behind you."

As she turned her horse and set off, Edmund heard again a faint peal of silver laughter. Thoughtfully, he watched Lydia canter away and then set off himself.

Three-quarters of an hour later, Edmund and Banks came into the drive of Owlswood and dismounted. MacCready's stable boy was due any time, but as usual, the two men decided to cool their mounts themselves with a stroll around the grounds. Banks noticed Edmund's preoccupation, almost as if he were looking into the distance for something or someone, and sought to engage him by asking for a history of the glasshouse they were nearing.

"Samuel—the groundskeeper—is more suited to your inquiry, Banks, but from what I can gather, my grandfather built the place to grow gardenia year-round."

"I had no idea your grandfather was a horticulturist. And interested in flowers? Good lord, I always pictured him a curmudgeon."

"No—not grandfather." Edmund smiled. "A houseguest he had for some time—a . . . a lady. He was quite fond of her, and she was quite fond of gardenia."

"Well, who was she, this houseguest who came to stay? God knows it seems to be an epidemic with this house. Lydia clearly aspires to be such a one," he chortled.

Banks turned to see Edmund grimace at his words, and gaze intently toward the other side of the house, again straining to see or hear something apparently invisible.

"I say, Edmund, what is bedeviling you?"

"Shhh— quiet! Can't you hear?"

Banks cocked his head in the direction of Edmund's stare and listened. He could hear the rustle of trees, and a slight babble from the fountain, but nothing else. He was about to comment so to Edmund, when he did hear something: a woman's voice. It was faint, but coming nearer. Yes, and it was calling Edmund's name!

"It's coming from the other side of the house—by the drive!"

The two men led their mounts quickly around to the front of the house. As they approached, the voice became very clear indeed:

Lydia's voice, in a state of extreme agitation.

"Edmund—my God, can anyone hear me? Halloo the house! Help!"

And there was Lydia, her hair dripping wet around her face, her garments muddy and soaked and forming puddles where she stood, her hat with its magnificent plume crumpled up in her fist. Her horse was looking sheepishly at MacCready's stable boy, whose mouth was wide open as he held tightly to the reins and watched the sight before him.

When she saw Edmund, Lydia moved to embrace him, her cordovan boots squishing as she walked.

"Oh, Edmund, how dreadful—how it happened!"

"What happened?" Edmund asked, holding her at arm's length. "Good heavens, Lydia, what happened?"

"I was cantering back to the house and about to cross the stream when this . . . this animal stopped absolutely dead in his tracks! My stirrup must have come loose and I . . . I fell into the water! What a dreadful beast!"

She looked accusingly at the poor horse, who seemed aware of his disgrace.

"Are you injured?" asked Banks. "Anything need mending or tending?"

"Oh, Doctor, I have no idea. I am extremely fortunate not to be killed!"

"Lydia, you're enough of a horsewoman to know how to cross a creek. What came over you?"

"What came over *me*? Good lord, Edmund, this . . . this filthy animal was seized with some uncontrollable urge to kill me, and you make it out to me my lack of horsemanship! Look at me! Look at my garments! Look at that beast! I haven't been thrown in years!"

Edmund turned to the stable boy and said, "Well?"

"Oh, yes, m'lor, I saw oauld Chex here seem to be runnin' from the devil hisself just a'fore the lady hit the water. But he's no bad'un, sir, he mustuv been bit by a blackie or some such! He's a good horse, he is!"

The stable boy rubbed Chex's muzzle, and the horse nibbled his cheek with his soft lips, glad of an ally.

Edmund assured the lad that no ill-will would be held against the horse, and that nothing would be mentioned to MacCready. He then turned his attention to Lydia, who sputtered and fumed on the front steps as Banks tried to calm her enough so he could assess her injuries, real or imagined. She was such an incredibly sorry sight that Edmund began to smile broadly.

The lady is definitely discomfited, he thought, *and that magnificent steed accomplished in ten minutes what I have failed to achieve this past fortnight.*

He almost giggled, but controlled himself as Lydia's murderous gaze turned on him.

"I'm going upstairs," she said, her voice a dagger, "where Dr. Banks will examine me. Someone, at least, is concerned with my welfare. If all is well, I shall have no trouble attending dinner this evening, Edmund, but I shall rely on the good doctor's advice on that matter. Please be so kind as to alert your housekeeper to attend me in my room."

As Banks took her arm and helped her to enter the house, Edmund remained for a brief moment outside, certain that he heard distant laughter once more. With a thoughtful look, he went inside.

*   *   *

"Absolutely excellent repast, Mr. Symme! The fowl was mouthwatering, and the fish course could not have been tastier. Truly, you have a wonderful cook here."

Vicar Creviston patted his spare little belly and leaned back in his chair.

"But who planned the menu, my dear," added Mrs. Creviston with a solicitous glance at Lydia, "and designed this flavorful medley of foods? Why, I would venture that Lady Grenfield had a hand in it—and after her brush with death today, too."

She gracefully removed the toothpick from the gap between her front teeth and continued, "What a true mark of the finest breeding, to continue to meet one's duties even in the face of pain or adversity."

"Oh, please, make no further reference to my little mishap. I am truly completely recovered and have suffered no lasting ill effects." Lydia's smile bathed her guests in good-will. "And I'm so pleased you enjoyed the meal. Tell me again, vicar, how many families number in your flock?"

"Oh, good St. Bridget, will this never end?" Banks leaned over and muttered in Edmund's ear. "This man looks like a horse and converses about the same way. And his wife! Why does the charming Lydia encourage them so? For God's sake, ring for Remy and let this meal be over!"

Edmund was about to do just that when an overpowering scent of gardenia seemed to fill the room and hang thick in the air, almost like a fog. A look of alarm suddenly came over Lydia's face. Her eyes popped wide open, and she seemed to be struggling for breath. After a moment, she began to cough and choke, and, as the rest of the dinner party sat transfixed, her hand went to her mouth and pulled a long, slender fish bone out of it. She looked at the item as if she could not believe what had happened, then gagged once more, swallowed hard and tried to smile.

"Good heavens, Lydia, are you quite all right?" Edmund rose from his chair and started toward her. "Pour her some wine, Banks!"

"No—no, really, I am fine. I must beg your pardon, all of you—I can't imagine how . . ." Lydia's words were cut short by her shrieking. She began to scream at the top of her lungs, and was then joined by Mrs. Creviston, who also screamed and pointed to Lydia's shoulder. There, making its way down across the fabric of her bodice, was the largest and most detestable looking insect the assembled company had ever seen. The vicar made a sudden move to rise and fell completely over backward in his chair, provoking fresh howls of hysteria from his wife.

Edmund brushed the insect off Lydia's bosom onto the floor, where Banks' heel dispatched it with no further ceremony. But the damage had been done. Both women shrieked and fanned themselves as if all air had gone out of the room, and the poor vicar was struggling on the floor like a beetle on its back. While Banks went to Creviston's aid, Edmund, though nauseated by the heavy-sweet reek of gardenia, tried to comfort Lydia.

Just as he was calming her, she began to fall apart. First, the stay in her front bodice sprang completely out of its casing with a loud snap; then the lace edging around her neckline fell to her waist, exposing her undergarments in a graceful motion. Three buttons from her dress back then popped several feet across the room into the serving dishes on the sideboard. Lydia's eyes opened wide in amazement, and as she moved to rise, her foot caught in the hem of her skirt and tore a large portion of fabric away from the waistline, exposing yards of petticoat and lace.

At this point, Lydia dropped back into her chair, weeping uncontrollably.

Hearing the bedlam from as far away as the kitchen, Remy hurried into the dining room and assisted Banks in righting Vicar Creviston, then poured Mrs. Creviston some port, once re-settled in her chair. Next, she brought a cold cloth for Lydia's head, along with a glass of cool water; finally, she handed Edmund and Banks each a snifter of cognac. She then headed upstairs to prepare Lydia's bed chamber.

Frank admiration shone in Banks' eyes as they followed her up the stairway.

"You don't deserve that creature, Edmund, by all the saints! She is an absolute treasure." Turning his attention to the unfortunate insect, he continued, "Disagreeable item, that one. What the devil is it and where did it come from? And I certainly hope there are no more of them about!"

He quickly looked behind him, up the wall and across the ceiling.

"For God's sake, Banks, just get these people safely on their way while I get Lydia to her room. There'll be time to study nature later!"

Under the circumstances, the Crevistons were happy to hear Edmund bid them a quick good-night. They mustered themselves to be gone immediately, completely perplexed yet thrilled with the prospect of recounting their experiences to the parish as soon and as often as possible. Edmund carried the swooning Lydia up the stairs to her room. He was relieved to note that the scent of gardenia did not follow, and that the room seemed quiet and calm. Remy had lit the fire and turned down the bed, where Edmund unceremoniously deposited his charge and stood to catch his breath. *Why are women always so much heavier than they look,* he thought. He went to the window and opened it wide, then stood in the draft for a moment.

"Oh, Edmund, what is happening to me?" moaned Lydia piteously from her bed. "What dreadful things will happen next? I've never been so utterly humiliated in my life! You were absolutely right, Edmund, I should never have invited those people to your home—they are truly boors, and the woman! My God, she must have drenched herself in gardenia water before they came. I could smell nothing else all night! I am absolutely nauseated." She flung herself back against the pillows and breathed deeply. "But I cannot understand about that fishbone, how could such . . ."

"You were aware of gardenia scent all evening?" Edmund was suddenly alert. "And now? Is the scent gone now, Lydia?" He asked, feeling slightly alarmed.

"Why of course, darling—she's far away from me now."

I wonder, thought Edmund, *I wonder how far away she is.* While his heart beat faster with excitement, thinking she was back at last, he was at the same time seized with a dark sense of foreboding. He shook his head sharply.

"Well, Lydia, you've had quite an evening. Perhaps you should retire for the night—I'll leave you now. You have everything you need?"

He began to back toward the door.

"Yes, Edmund, quite. Will you return and peek in on me a little later—to make sure I'm all right? You know, another woman of lesser character would be making plans to leave this place at once. But I am made of sterner stuff than that." She smiled and stretched on her pillows. "After a good night's sleep, I shall be as good as new, and then we can discuss with Dr. Banks these strange happenings—he's always so calm and logical and he will surely . . . "

"Yes, someone will look in on you, Lydia. Good night."

Edmund closed the door behind him and leaned against it wearily. *Well, at least she didn't suggest that I stay with her,* he thought.

Suddenly, he was alert, for a vague scent of gardenia tantalized him and then quickly disappeared.

My imagination is overstimulated and I need some sleep, he thought. *La Belle Dame will never return to me while Lydia remains under this roof, imagined scents of gardenia flower notwithstanding.*

He entered his room and went to stand by the fire.

What absolutely bizarre happenings, he ruminated as he removed his jacket and cravat. He sat down, took off his boots, and settled into the armchair, enjoying the warmth of the fire and the soothing quiet. He dozed a bit, and was about to fall into deep sleep when he heard a voice cry out, "Edmund—help me!"

"Lydia!"

He jumped to his feet and dashed out toward Lydia's room.

"Lydia!" he shouted and pounded on the door.

10
Lydia's Visitation

"Edmund—EDMUND!" Lydia's scream was full of fear. Edmund could hear her struggle with the door, shouting his name the whole while. When it finally opened, she fell into his arms and cried, "At the window—I saw someone there!"

He disengaged from her embrace and strode to the casement, lifted the pane and leaned out. No one was visible on the lawn below and there were no footholds or handholds to allow any mortal being to cling to the outside wall. He looked around the room's interior and saw no one.

"What did you see?" he asked, closing the window and the drapes, and turning to face her. "What happened exactly?"

"I was almost asleep, and . . . and I thought I heard something. So I sat up and looked around. I left the drape drawn back slightly to look at the moon as I fell asleep, and suddenly in the moonlight, I could see a face! A face, Edmund, directly outside the window! Someone was there!"

She spoke no louder than a whisper, truly frightened.

"It's alright, there's no one here now. Be calm, breathe deeply." He moved closer and placed a comforting hand on her shoulder. He felt her shaking. "Did you see the face well?"

"No, no, not well. But it was there. It was! How could someone be up this high? But someone was there! Someone was looking at me!"

Her eyes filled with tears and she looked at him beseechingly.

"Of course, of course, Lydia. I know." Edmund took her hands; they were icy and trembling. "Did you notice any kind of smell?"

She shook her head and looked perplexed. He looked around the room, but again noticed nothing amiss.

"Come now, and we'll get you back to bed. The night's turned cold and you'll catch a chill."

He walked with her over to the canopied four-poster, speaking soothing words. She held his hands tightly, and even after he threw back the counterpane and made her sit down, she grasped them again and would not let go.

"Edmund, who was it? What did I see?"

He stood by the side of the bed for a few minutes, reassuring her that she was safe, and at last she seemed to relax a bit, enough for him to disengage his hands and ease her gently back onto her pillows. He tucked her feet under the sheet, pulled up the eiderdown and covered her. Then, leaning over, he spoke gently as he would to a child.

"There, now, you're quite safe and settled. Best you get back to sleep. Shall I bring you some water or brandy?"

"No, thank you, but don't leave!" She reached up quickly and frantically wrapped her arms around his neck, pulling him off balance and into bed on top of her.

"Lydia, please, I can't breathe!" he sputtered, muffled by the pillow in his face.

She released her grip slightly, and Edmund rolled onto his side next to her. Annoyed now, he spoke sternly. "Lydia, believe me, you'll be quite all right. There's no one out there! Whomever was there, is gone now, I assure you. You must calm down."

He searched her face for some sign of subterfuge—very like Lydia to fake such a scene—but could find none. Her eyes were still wide and glassy, and she did seem afraid and very nervous as her eyes repeatedly darted to the window.

"Stay, Edmund, just for a few minutes. Please."

Against his better judgment, he nodded and settled into a half-seated position against the plump pillows, with Lydia's iron grip on his arm and her head pressed into his shoulder.

After a while, her breathing became more even, and he thought she might have fallen asleep. Softly, he disengaged her grip on his arm and began to ease out of the bed, but she opened her eyes and took his face in her hands and whispered, "Now that you're here, stay with me."

What a fool I am, Edmund thought with disgust, *it was all a ruse and I walked right into it.*

She kissed him before he could protest. In spite of his annoyance, he felt himself responding to her kiss and the pressure of her lithe body against the length of him. *Get out now, my boy, or you'll regret it*, he told himself. At that very moment, as if in response to his thoughts, the room began crashing down around them.

With a loud series of cracks, the bed beneath them collapsed.

First one leg, and then another, until the mattress slats hit the floor. Canopy posts began to sway drunkenly. One fell and hit the armoire mirror, shattering it and splintering the wood behind it. The heavy brocade canopy itself tumbled down onto them, pulling a second post with it, pinning them to the collapsed bed and floor.

Lydia began to scream, "I can't breathe! Help, help! Someone help me!"

Edmund, startled and angry, lent his shouts to the fray as well.

"Good God, Lydia! Stop that bloody caterwauling and help me here, bloody hell!" Edmund was straining to free himself of the large piece of wood, and of the entangling canopy, but to no avail. The bedpost had smacked him soundly across the shoulder as it fell, and the blow did nothing to improve his mood. "Bloody hell, bloody damnation! For God's sake, Lydia, shut the hell up!"

Lydia continued to scream and groan. Entangled in the canopy and bed curtains, neither of them could see anything. But every time it seemed they were almost freed from one predicament, another would befall—a lamp would fall to the floor and shatter, perfume bottles would be smashed and their contents spilled onto the carpet. By the time Banks and Remy arrived, responding to the thuds, shouts and screaming, the air was so thick with various fragrances that no one even noticed the heavy scent of gardenia in the room.

Remy ran to the closed window, pulled back the drapes, and opened it them wide. Banks, eyes smarting, tried to free the two unfortunates from their tangled state, dragging the post that had pinned Edmund off to the side. Lydia continued to gurgle and scream without pause, and when Remy tried to remove the heavy brocade from over her head, Lydia struggled and kicked even harder. It took both she and Banks to finally free Edmund and steady the hysterical woman sufficiently to remove the voluminous material and expose her to light once again. Lydia clutched her throat and sobbed miserably while Remy patted and murmured to her and helped her up and onto a chair.

It was at this moment that the room became calm enough for Banks and Remy to look around and examine details of the scene for the first time. The likely circumstances that unfolded before their eyes caused them both to look questioningly, Remy with an unwanted blush rising on her cheeks, at Edmund.

"Well, old man," began Banks, clearing his throat, "shall you

117

enlighten us as to what in heaven's name is going on here?"

"What goes on here? My God, you can see for yourself, can't you?" Edmund spat back, testy and extremely aggravated.

"Well, yes—we do see." Banks glanced at the two women and then added, in a lower voice, "Don't you even wish to *try* to convince us otherwise?"

Edmund looked puzzled for a moment, then understood.

"I m-mean, Banks," he stuttered, "it is obvious that a terrible accident has befallen us here." His words began to tumble out. "Lydia cried out because she thought she saw someone outside the window, so I rushed in and could find nothing, and when I got her back to bed she wanted me to wait while she fell asleep—being quite shaken, naturally—and so I did stay, comforting her, as it were, and the room started crashing about us. A stupefying series of events!"

He tried to look amazed and composed at the same time, and succeeded only in looking rather guilty.

Banks stared at him for a long moment. "You were comforting her in a particularly athletic fashion, I dare say," he commented dryly, taking Edmund's arm and drawing him away from the two women. "Really, Edmund, are you out of your mind? I mean all this commotion, not to mention the compromising situation you've created, simply due to a little too much night music! And," with this Banks lowered his voice even more, "I thought you wanted her gone. "

Edmund's eyes grew wide and he began to sputter once more.

"Listen, Banks, that's not what was going on here. I have no interest in Lydia whatsoever. I've been trying to rid myself of her since before I left London!" he muttered angrily. "Don't you understand, I was simply trying to help her. She was so upset! You can't believe that I . . ."

"Doctor, please, will you come here?" Remy interrupted.

Lydia was sobbing softly, still clutching her throat. "Someone tried to strangle me!' she moaned. "Someone tried to kill me!"

Banks came to Lydia's side and gently pried her fingers from her throat so he might examine it. "Come, Lydia, let me see. Let me see, I won't hurt you. "

Edmund, embarrassed, angry, and indignant in equal measure, demanded in his most impressive courtroom manner, "What do you mean, Lydia, that someone tried to kill you? I was the only one here with you. Are you saying that I planned this whole debacle in order to do you ill?"

"No, not you, Edmund. You were already freed. But I felt hands—hands around my throat, squeezing it, trying to crush the life out of me! It was so terrible!" Lydia's voice was scratchy and small, but her eyes were wide with remembered panic.

Edmund dismissed her statement. "No one else was here, Lydia. You must have gotten the curtain pull wrapped around your neck in all the commotion."

"NO! There were fingers at my throat, I tell you! Maybe it was her!" She looked and pointed at Remy accusingly, leaning away in her chair.

Remy looked startled and Edmund was about to protest when Banks said, "Look here, Edmund, do you see these marks?" His gentle fingers pointed out discolored areas on Lydia's throat and neck.

"They look like rope burn to me, Christopher. It must have happened as I described."

"But here—look closely here." And on the side of Lydia's pale white neck were plainly visible pressure bruises as if made by strong fingers.

"It's impossible, Banks. You don't think that I . . . and you surely don't think Remy . . ."

"Of course not, don't be a fool. But what did happen? Was she clawing at a tangled cord that happened to wrap around her neck? Or . . . what, Edmund?"

"I tell you, SHE did it! SHE hates me! My God, why will no one believe me!" Lydia sprang to her feet with sudden fury and pointed at Remy. "She was the only woman here until I came and she's jealous! Jealous of my station, my relationship with you, my breeding, my . . . "

"Enough!" shouted Edmund. "Control yourself, woman! I'll not have you throwing false accusations at my . . ."

"At your WHAT, Edmund? Paramour? Mistress? Oh, you think I'm naïve and stupid, but I see many things, Edmund, many things!" Lydia's voice was shrill with hysteria. She strode over to the armoire and flung open the shattered door. "I will dress now and seek out the constable or whatever authority there be in this pastoral hellhole and . . . *aaaaaahhhhh!*"

Lydia's tirade was halted by a sharp gasp as she saw the contents of the armoire. Where her beautiful dinner gown had hung was a sodden, mildewed, green-and-black mass of rotted lace and silk. A dark, putrid odor came forth, finished off with a sticky-sweet scent of gardenia. On the bottom, among her lace and satin lingerie, a mass of slender black snakes writhed and coiled among themselves. And then, a large, warted toad waddled out from the shelf and onto the floor and defecated before them.

Completely speechless, all of them stared. Then Lydia began anew to scream hysterically.

*   *   *

The following early morning hours were spent preparing Lydia's departure. It was just after daylight when the coach drew up to the front door and the driver knocked. He was shown upstairs by Samuel, and they carried out the baggage for loading. Edmund and Banks stood on the portico, waiting for Lydia to exit the house. When she did so, she walked past Edmund without a glance but stopped to speak to Banks.

Her chin high, she stifled a sob and said, "Thank you for everything, my dear Kit. You have been very kind through this entire ordeal." She lowered her voice slightly. "And thank you for trying to dissuade me from coming here in the first place. I should have listened to your counsel."

Remy came out of the house with a small basket, filled with hastily gathered food for Lydia's trip covered in a white and blue embroidered cloth. "Miss Grenfield," she began, and held out the basket to Lydia, "for your journey."

Lydia eyed Remy coldly, ignored the basket, then turned and entered the carriage without another word.

Remy flushed, went around to the driver and handed up the basket to him. "In case the lady needs this," she directed, and then stepped back out of the way. The driver called to his team, cracked his whip above their heads, and tipped his hat to Edmund as the rig pulled away.

When the carriage had departed, Edmund stared out over the drive for a few moments, listening in vain for a faint, familiar laugh that he alone would hear. Then, without a word, he turned, entered the house, and retired to the library, shutting and locking the door behind him.

Banks watched him go from the front steps, then turned to Remy. "What happened last night, Remy? Have you any idea?"

She shook her head. "No, Doctor, it all still seems utterly inexplicable—almost as if someone, or something, had intended to frighten Miss Grenfield into leaving."

As they entered the house, Banks replied. "Exactly my thoughts. I am confounded as to who or what, though, as I cannot believe Edmund could have planned—much less executed— such a thing. What a night." He smiled ruefully. "I must say, in light of recent events, I'm beginning to comprehend Edmund's troubled state of mind. Owlswood seems to be in a state of turmoil as a result of some sort of. . . delusion that afflicts him! And clearly now, others as well."

Banks looked closely at Remy.

"And you? Besides what I myself witnessed last night—do you have private visions, too?"

She looked away and back and replied, "For a time, yes, I did. When I was younger. But away from Owlswood, they faded into dreams—vivid dreams. I don't really know if what you may be calling 'visions', weren't always just dreams. And now . . . I simply don't know."

Her voice trailed away.

"And now?" asked Banks. "Now that you've returned here?"

"Until the extraordinary manifestations of the past day, I would have said my dreams are my own." She looked at Banks with uncertainty. "But you can now see why I feel unable to evaluate the effect these walls have on Mr. Symme and his memories."

"Well, I am equally perplexed." Banks sighed. "Perhaps I need a bit of solitude and a good walk to settle my thoughts. As does Regis, I think." He noted the big dog, lying quietly outside the library door, ignored by his master again. "Do you need my help here?" When Remy shook her head "no", he nodded back saying, "If you will excuse me, then."

He called to Regis (who hesitated only a moment before scrambling to his side) and headed toward the garden. Remy exhaled deeply and turned toward the stairs to begin the considerable business of righting the mess in the guest bedroom.

The three remaining human mortal occupants of Owlswood went their separate ways for the rest of the day. Remy arranged for the chaos in the demolished bedroom to be cleared away and new furniture moved in; although remarkably, no sign of the toad or garden snakes could be found by the workman who was sent to collect them and return them to the woods.

Around noon, back from his walk, Banks was asked to visit a neighbor's home to examine a feverish daughter of the house and again took Regis with him, coaxing him away from his vigil outside the closed library door. Edmund remained solitary in the library. The day seemed to mirror their collective mood, with low clouds hanging grey and heavy until mid-afternoon, when rain began to fall.

By then, Remy was exhausted. The events of the previous night hung heavy on her mind, and the work of righting the damage upstairs made her very tired indeed. Around three o'clock she stopped for a cup of tea, nestling into the kitchen window seat to watch and listen to the rain.

She loved this kind of rain—soft, soothing, giving everything a gentle wash. As the rivulets traced their way down the window panes, unhurried by wind, autumn shapes beyond them melted into a dreamy blur of earthy pastels. Remy felt herself slip back into the time of her childhood, when she had played on the kitchen floor beside her mother or ran through the long hallways, squealing with laughter in a game. How she loved this house, especially when the Symme family was away in London or elsewhere, and she had the run of the place while her mother worked. In quiet moments, she would sit at the library window, either reading a book or with her forehead pressed against the glass, looking out over the vast expanse of green lawn. On rainy days, she breathed on the surface and then drew flowers in the condensation, or just watched the raindrops run down the panes as they blurred the trees and grass.

Her vision blurred now and out of the corner of her eye she caught sight of a woman's figure, graceful, with a parasol, walking down the pathway that led from the fountain to the gazebo hidden in the trees beyond the lawn. She absently followed the figure with her eyes, pleased by the fluid body movements and contours. The solitary walker reminded her of the "beautiful lady" of her childhood whom no one else could see, who would often come to her and watch her, smiling, at her play. She felt the shift in perception that always announced her 'dreaming' and was too tired to resist. She relaxed into it, and all at once she found herself dressed in a gown of ivory lace, parasol in hand, walking down the same pathway she had just watched. Her hair was loose and fell down her back and over her shoulders, pinned back on one side with a fresh gardenia. She felt calm and happy and expectant as she followed the path out of sight of the house to the gazebo. She heard melodious laughter; it was so pleasing to her ear that it took a full minute before she realized it was her own, light and musical and full of joy.

Now she was in the gazebo, looking out beyond the trees—looking for someone. When will he come, she thought, when will he be here? She saw a man moving swiftly through the trees. He waved and smiled to her. Her heart began to beat faster. In a moment, he was in the gazebo and standing before her, looking delightedly into her eyes. He took her hand and kissed it, then drew her to him and held her gently. She could feel his heart beating fast against her. Suddenly he released her and snatched the parasol from her hand. He jumped up onto the railing, and began to pantomime a tightrope walker, complete with near falls and grimaces of fear. All around the gazebo railing he performed, and she thought she would fall to the floor with laughter. Finally, he stopped, grinned at her, and threw the parasol onto the grass. He jumped down and took her into his arms and began to kiss her, softly at first, but with increasing passion. He kissed her lips, her cheeks, her eyes. And she kissed him back with all her soul. "*Ma Cher*" she breathed. She had never felt such joy, such desire, such . . .

"Oh!" She was brought back to the present with the crash of her teacup on the kitchen floor. She felt woozy, and disoriented, as she usually did after "dreaming." She felt her face flush with color as she thought back over the kisses, so real just a few seconds ago, the warm hands on her body, the deep blue eyes looking into hers . . . Embarrassed that anyone might come looking for her and catch her in such a state, she quickly gathered the broken china, splashed water on her face, and joined Cook in the pantry, offering to assist with preparation of the evening meal.

Shortly after dark, Banks returned, weary but more like his old self, with news that the patient was doing well and should have no difficulty recovering. He retired immediately, taking only a tray of supper and a half-bottle of Bordeaux with him to his room as he bid Remy goodnight.

"I for one, am looking for a quiet bed and uninterrupted night—and I wish you the same. You need rest, Remy, as do we all." She smiled and nodded, as he continued, "And the master of the house—in the library still, I presume?"

Again she nodded, and Banks shook his head and continued to his room. Regis followed his nose to the kitchen, and Cook made much of him as she gathered a goodly bowl of scraps for his dinner.

Remy knocked at the library door several times, but received no answer from Edmund. She had a tray prepared, and left it on the hall table outside. She knocked one last time, calling through the door, "Mr. Symme, I've left a supper tray here for you. I shall bid you goodnight, if there is nothing else you need of me."

"Good night," Edmund responded, almost inaudibly, and she left to go upstairs. She stared at the portrait of John Symme on the landing, and felt a strange déjà vu as she looked at his face. She shook her head. "I'm so very tired," she said softly to herself as she continued up to her room. "I'm beginning to see familiarity in old portraits."

In the quiet of her room she undressed and paused to note that the rain had stopped and a full moon had risen. She sat on her bed, loosed her hair, and began to brush it in preparation for braiding. Suddenly a wave of heat swept over her—such intense, moist, heavy heat that she could not stand to have any clothing, even her light camisole, next to her skin and she flung it from her. Naked, she lay back on her pillow, breathing hard, and thought to herself, *I'm feverish, I must be getting ill. I'm so tired—I must sleep. I must sleep.* Her eyes closed and she drifted away quickly, back to the gazebo of the afternoon and the tall man who awaited her there.

* * *

Below in the library, Edmund, half-lying in his armchair with his eyes closed, head pounding, was equally exhausted. Having paced the room most of the afternoon, waiting—hoping, even exclaiming aloud, "Where are you? Lady, please speak to me!" he felt abandoned and desolate. He had been sure La Belle Dame would have come to him; her presence was so clear in the events of yesterday. But he could do nothing more than wait. He was too restless to read or search volumes on the shelves for more about her, about why she was . . . the way she was. He longed for her.

He barely responded to Remy's knock at the door with the unwanted supper tray, and was glad when she retired and left him alone. He watched the moon rise through the windows until it was high in the heavens and joined by several stars. When the fire had died in the hearth, he wearily unlocked the door and headed up to his room. He carried his lamp up the winding staircase, past his grandfather's stern gaze, asking himself with every step why she had not come. He entered the bedroom, undressed quickly, and got into bed, leaving the room dark except for the fireplace embers. He did not sleep, he just lay, naked and waiting for sleep, watching hypnotic movements of the shadows of trees in the wind outside his windows.

*   *   *

Remy was awake suddenly; she knew not why. Her lamp was still lit and the hairbrush still in her hand. Clothes discarded and still atop the covers of her bed, she continued to feel over heated. The room seemed close and stifling. She stood up and went to the window, opening it wide and standing in the wind that rushed into the room, cool and clean against her skin, in her hair, like a lover's caress or the kiss of raindrops. It bore the sweet scent of gardenia—from the glasshouse, the gardenias in the glasshouse! *He loves me so much to build me a glasshouse for my flowers*, she thought. She stretched and luxuriated in the touch of the air, and then spun around in sheer joy and began to dance about the room. She felt she must still be dreaming, she felt so beautiful, so warm, so . . .

Remy caught sight of herself in the mirror and came closer to look. She saw herself reflected, but she looked different. Her body seemed lusher, somehow, glowing almost with an inner light. Her eyes glittered green and bright, even in the dim lamplight. She turned and twirled and gazed at her image in the glass, then noticed the shawl hanging on the bedpost—the shawl of cream-colored silk and lace that had belonged to her mother's mother, the only material thing that remained of her, so delicate, soft and smooth. Even after all this time, it still smelled so sweetly of flowers—gardenia—and sunlight. She put out her hand to touch it, and heard someone in the hallway. *Him!* she thought. *It must be him! He has come to me at last!*

She ran to the door and opened it a crack, enough to see the figure of a man enter a room far down the hall. Her heart leapt into her throat. She turned back to the mirror and looked at herself

125

again. She ran her hands along her body, up from her thighs across her belly, to the tips of her breasts, to the hollow in her throat. She almost swooned, but closed her eyes and recovered her breath and balance. She drew the filmy shawl around her, and picked up the brush from the bed. She began to slowly brush her long, red tresses, a secret smile playing at the corners of her mouth as she watched herself in the mirror.

*   *   *

Alone in the dark bedroom, Edmund closed his eyes but felt sleep would never come. He kept thinking of the red-haired visitor he longed for with all his heart; but he despaired that his night would be filled only with moon shadows and the sounds of the wind. He rose, put on his dressing gown to keep from catching a chill, and went to sit before the fireplace embers, staring into their glow. Although all remained silent in the house, he became aware of the door to his room slowly opening. Startled, he turned and strained to see.

All at once, the breath caught in his throat, for he saw in the moonlight the figure of a woman in the doorway. Shadow fell across her face, but silvery moonlight revealed the lush curve of her naked breast and the red cascade of hair tumbling over her shoulders. He jumped to his feet and took a step toward her. She stood absolutely still for a long moment, then quickly crossed to stand before him. He saw the filmy lace wrapping her body, and could smell a slight scent of gardenia and lavender when she moved. His breath quickened.

"Lady! Can it be? It . . . it is you . . . "

He took her in his arms and she wound herself around him passionately. He kissed her with pent-up longing, then buried his face in the crook of her neck. He released her after a moment, reluctantly, hands still caressing her shoulders, and she let the lace fall to the carpet. He untied his robe and flung it from him, and embraced her once more. After another long kiss, she broke away from him, laughing, and twirled around the room, dancing and laughing softly. She came to rest, seated on the window sill, and held out her arms wide to him. He rushed to her and began to kiss her feverishly—her lips, her neck, her shoulders —and she wound her legs around his waist and murmured, "*Chérie, ma cher, ma cher*" in his ear. She arched her back and leaned out over the sill, laughing and tossing her head far back. He looked at her beautiful face in the moonlight and saw . . .

"Remy!" he whispered. "You! My God, what . . . !"

"Yes, *Chérie*, it is I. *C'est moi*."

She smiled and wrapped herself more tightly to him.

He felt like a drowning man searching for a breath of air. . . "Wait, no—Remy, no, stop!"

He pushed her roughly from him, hoping his resolve would not melt.

"Give me a moment, I . . ."

Her face in the moonlight looked pained.

"*Chérie*, why do you refuse me? My own, my love . . ." She came closer again and laced her arms around his neck. "*Chérie*, do you not want me, are you not pleased?"

"Oh yes, I . . . no, no, wait!" Edmund's mind took hold of his senses. He looked at Remy, intently searching her face, and held her away from him. "Who are you? What is your name?" he asked in a stern voice.

Remy looked confused, then smiled coyly. "Ah, *Chérie*, you play with me! Who do you wish me to be, I will be that one for you." She shrugged off his grip and moved closer. "Do you not see your very own flower, your own Fleur? It is I, Jean, it is I!"

She caressed his chest and pressed against him, closed her eyes to kiss him, and he felt himself drowning again. He took her shoulders and shook her sharply, his voice louder, "Stop this. Stop right now."

Remy's eyes flew open. She looked at him wide-eyed for a brief moment and then the shock of recognition hit her. Still breathing hard, she asked, "What are you doing here?" She looked around her, at him, at herself. "My God, what is happening!"

"Nothing," he thought it best to lie, "except that you came here and I . . . I didn't think it was you. I thought it was someone else." Recovering himself, he crossed to the armchair, grabbed his robe and brought it to her, "Cover yourself." Then, heeding his own advice, he took the sheet from the bed and wrapped it around his middle.

"I . . . came here?" Remy looked around. "This is your room— why did I come here?" She spoke softly, almost to herself, clutching the robe around her. "I was dreaming and then . . . I came *here*?"

127

"Indeed." Edmund looked at her soberly. "I admit, you did not seem to be yourself, you seemed lost in a dream or . . ." He rubbed his hand across his face, trying to think. "Are you prone to sleepwalk? What were you dreaming?"

Edmund could not see her blush, but he felt her discomfort. "I was dreaming an old dream, it is rather . . . private."

She tried to calm herself, but her chest heaved with embarrassment.

"Mr. Symme, I am sorry for . . ."

"Never mind that," he cut her off sharply, "this is so time for courtesies. You were dreaming of meeting a lover. A romantic assignation, a *rendez-vous*, yes?" Remy nodded slightly. "Who is Jean? Someone from the village?"

"I don't know any Jean. We have no Jean," she replied, embarrassment growing.

"Who the devil is Jean? You called me Jean."

With rising irritation, she replied, "I told you I know no Jean, or . . ."

"Wait!" He again interrupted her. "Wait. My grandfather's name was John. In French, it would be Jean, wouldn't it?" He began to pace the room, as he always did while piecing together evidence, holding the sheet around him. "She knew my grandfather, they spent many hours together, she must have been in love with him! That's why she stayed on, that's why the gardenias were grown. They were lovers!"

Suddenly Remy's knees felt weak and she sat on the edge of the bed. She murmured almost to herself. "Of course . . . the lady of the gardenia and the master of Owlswood. That's why she walks here."

Edmund spoke sharply. "What do you know of the Lady? Remy, tell me what you know!" Suddenly alert, he stopped pacing and stood before her. "This is important. I must know everything. Tell me of the Lady!"

Remy stared at him for a long moment, struggling with the prospect of revealing her innermost experience to a most unlikely audience. She composed herself, then began.

"I have met a lady walking the halls of the house many times in my childhood—not so much when I grew up. She was beautiful and always scented with gardenia. She was very kind to me and seemed to watch over me. She spoke to me in French." Remy paused and swallowed hard. "I have not seen her in a long time, but I have recurring dreams in which she comes to me and . . . it is difficult to distinguish whether I am being myself or being . . . her." She paused again, and then continued. "Tonight, I saw her in my dream and then I seemed to join with her, become her. She—I—was so happy to be meeting my . . . and so . . ."

"I see her also," Edmund stated.

Shock, surprise and skepticism competed for Remy's emotions.

"*You* see her? You? How can you see her? Where do you see her?"

"She visits at night, in the Library." The absurdity of discussing his hallucination with his housekeeper, in the middle of the night, semi-naked, did not escape him, but he pressed on. "I wait for her there."

"Ah, that explains a great deal. But why does she come to you?"

"Why? How can I know—we discuss things." Edmund felt uncomfortably under examination.

"What things?" Remy pursued. "What are these things you discuss?"

"Well, philosophy, music, wine, poetry, art sometimes—and she tells me about times at Owlswood, after she came here when her father died. Beautiful stories, actually."

"But you speak almost no French! How can you discuss art and music?"

Now Remy was incredulous.

"Don't be absurd, she speaks English. Or at least, I hear English in my mind."

Edmund was growing irritated at all the questions. He was not used to being the one questioned.

"Well, it's probable that she spoke English, living here for some time," Remy said, almost to herself, and then more stridently, "But why should she come to you?"

"Well, miss, some people find me less onerous than do you—chalk it up to her poor judgment if you will; she's some kind of phantasm after all!" He stopped to think. "But she was not pleased about Lydia being here and has not come since her arrival, and I had hope she would come tonight since . . ."

Remy felt a shimmer of fear.

"It was *her*, then, all that happened last night? She must be angry. She made the mischief that caused Miss Grenfield to leave? I have never known her to be that way. She . . . oh my God, what is afoot?"

"I intend to find out. Go to your room and stay there. I will dress and demand her presence." Edmund was not certain that would do any good, but he was growing angry himself.

"No! I will come with you. You cannot deny this concerns me, too. Give me a moment and I'll meet you outside the Library."

Edmund could see arguing was useless. He agreed. He pulled on breeches, a shirt and slippers, then hurried downstairs. *I'll get into the library and lock it before . . .*

As he reached the bottom of the stair, he saw Remy already waiting outside the door, dressed in a loose shift and dressing gown. Disgruntled, he opened the door and gestured for Remy to go in, then hesitated. "We may be here for some time; La Belle Dame does not always come when bidden. I will build up the fire, you refill the brandy decanter—I'm afraid I have emptied it."

He stepped inside to the table and seized the empty carafe, then came back and thrust it into her hands.

Remy looked at him strangely, then replied, "It will take but a moment to fetch it, as you wish."

She went past him down the hallway, and he quickly slipped inside and locked the door.

11
Revealing Encounters

After testing the lock to see it was secure, Edmund turned on a lamp and threw logs onto the banked fire, then stood defiantly in the center of the room. "Alright, show yourself! I demand an audience, Lady, and an explanation immediately!" He spoke loudly and with rising ire. "Belle Dame, explain yourself."

"Ah, so now you have time for La Belle Dame, yes? Now that The Lydia has moved on?" The scent of gardenia began to grow strong and a shimmer of light brought a familiar, but unusually cold, voice. "But who are you to demand anything of me, may I inquire?"

La Belle Dame was suddenly visible before him.

Edmund, angry, ignored her question. "Why did you do this—Lydia was no threat to you—she did nothing to harm or offend you!"

"Hah!—*au contraire, Chérie*, she did harm me. She took your attention and your time—and perhaps your affection *un peu*—and I need them." La Belle Dame spoke calmly but her eyes flashed. "The Lydia was detrimental to my purpose. She had to be removed. And you were ineffective in removing her."

Edmund heard the reply, but was too angry to note it as he continued, "And the woman, Remy—why involve her? Why put her in such a position, what has she done to you?"

"And what terrible position was she put into, your Remy?"

"We were about to . . . I thought it was . . . I almost seduced her, ruined her honor, and my own, we almost . . ." Edmund began to sputter. "My own housekeeper, for the love of God! How could you . . ."

"Ah, so was it you who was doing the seducing, *Chérie*? It seemed different to my eyes." La Belle smiled faintly. "It was a gift, no? I wished to make you a gift of love." She clasped her hands over her heart dramatically.

"You saw? You were watching us? Good God!" Edmund exclaimed, but La Belle just shrugged and gave a little *moue*, as if to say, "but of course."

Just then, loud knocking began at the stout library door.

"Mr. Symme, open this door at once!"

Remy was back with the brandy, and angry to have been duped.

"Open at once," she shouted and continued pounding.

"And, it appears she still pursues you, no?" La Belle almost chuckled. "She has spirit, that one, *ma petite fille.*"

"Go away, Remy, go to bed. This is no matter for you. I will see you in the morning," Edmund called. "And stop pounding that door!"

"Let me in! J. EDMUND. SYMME. LET. ME. IN!"

She continued to strike the door with her fist.

"*Zut, alors!* We cannot have this upset continue, eh? *Quelle bruit!*" La Belle was amused. She looked at the door, flicked a finger, and the key turned in the lock. The door swung open, leaving Remy in mid-strike and off-balance as she stumbled into the room.

"*Bienvenue, Chérie, comment ça va ce soir?*" La Belle waved her closer. "*Bon, bon—rapproche toi.*"

Remy entered and bowed her head slightly. "*Madame, bonsoir. Quel plaisir de vous voir autrefois.*" She then turned attention to Edmund. "Why did you lock me out? We agreed we would interview La Dame together!"

"We didn't agree. *You* decided to include yourself," Edmund fumed. "Where's that brandy? We will need it." Remy handed him the decanter and he set it on a table, continuing, "Lady, what is going on? What do you want of me?"

"Of us," Remy added. She then addressed the Lady. "*Qu'est-ce c'est que vous voulez?* My dream of you brought me to this man, I almost disgraced myself with him . . ."

"To make love is no disgrace, if two people both agree and are of a mind to share affection. And it did seem to me that you both agreed . . ." Noting Remy's frown, she continued. "You do not like him? He is intriguing, no? Strong and comely, *if un peu collet monté, sans formación.*" The Lady smiled. "But this can be remedied, we can help him, you and I!"

Edmund had little patience for being discussed like a horse up for purchase.

"Enough, please, ladies. Belle Dame, you said The Lydia—uh, Lydia, Miss Grenfield—you said her presence was detrimental to your purpose. Explain." Her slightly raised eyebrow led him to soften his manner. "Please, if you will."

"*Bon*. Sit. Listen." Edmund and Remy obeyed. La Belle sat across from them, with her hands clasped tightly across her chest, with a look of deep sadness. "I have been betrayed. I seek vindication and revenge—but I cannot accomplish it myself. To achieve justice in the mortal world, I need mortal action. Your action."

"Betrayed? What was this betrayal, and by whom? And to what purpose?" Edmund slipped into barrister persona, and began questioning. "Please continue."

La Belle became agitated, her gaze intense, her entire body shimmering. "Betrayal of the most heinous kind—betrayal of one loving and beloved, a dagger into the heart of one who did not deserve it." She began to move, as if pacing, across the room. "Oh, there are some who deserve what they get, *bien sur*. But I did not deserve what happened to me."

"Please—can you say more? Details, if you will—what happened? Who did—whatever they did?" Edmund the man of law had no use for emotional outbursts, just facts.

"Who? *Who* betrayed me? Are you *un bête, un stupide*? Who? The Symme family—those magnificent men of business, those merchant princes—all of them! Alistair, John, Nigel. All of them, vipers! Even," her voice faltered slightly, "even my beloved Jean, *mon cher, mon coeur . . .*" She began to rock forward and back, as a child seeking comfort would rock, arms wound close around her torso. "*Le poignard en pierre, la place de la trahison, le poignard, poignard…*"

Edmund was frustrated. "Lady, take hold of yourself! I cannot help if I do not understand. What happened? Who did what? Tell me!"

He turned to look at Remy, hoping she would reinforce his demands, and found she had risen and was moving toward La Belle, arms outstretched, eyes filled with tears. She moved closer and closer and, slowly, La Belle, too, reached out a hand. They seemed to touch, and La Belle looked at Remy searchingly. "*Ma petite fille, ma petite fille…*" she whispered softly.

"Ladies, this is all very touching, but it gets us nowhere!" Edmund almost shouted. "What the bloody hell happened, Lady?"

The two women, one specter, one mortal, turned to him with the same look of disgust.

"Edmund Symme—what is wrong with you? Can you not see

she is distraught!" Remy exclaimed.

"Distress gets us nowhere, miss; we need facts!"

La Belle, composing herself but matching Edmund's anger, began to speak.

"Brilliant man of law! You tease out justice from thin threads of fact, or no fact at all, for men who employ you! Can you bring me justice? Can you find truth, buried in the facts? Can you clear my name, avenge my outrage? Can you?" She drew a deep breath. "You, last of the Symme lineage. It is true, *n'est-ce pas*, that you have no son, no one to carry on your name and your disgrace. Only your brilliant mind matters to you—brilliance unsullied by emotion!"

She seemed to spit out the words, and continued bitterly, "Such brilliance—and yet, you expect that I spoon-feed you my cause for vengeance! Use your brains! What happened here over sixty years ago is no mystery—you can learn the 'facts' from any village gossip. But are the stories true? What can you believe? Look into the glasshouse, the *orangerie*! Look to the *poignard, le poignard en pierre… le temps venant . . .*" She looked around frantically, then seemed to glide to the far side of the room. She looked over her shoulder and shouted, "*Le temps venant! Bientot!*"

She disappeared.

The air seemed to shudder, then settle into a shroud of stillness over Edmund and Remy. The silence was heavy. Neither spoke for some time.

Remy slumped onto a chair, confused and weary.

"She has set us a task—but exactly what task, I am yet unclear."

"It's simple enough, Remy—she wants to be vindicated, revenged, her name cleared. But of what, and why, and why now?" Edmund shook his head. "And why the two of us?"

"She was always thought to have been mad, at the end. There are stories about her told in the village." Remy sounded sad. "I have heard she went mad after the birth of her child, and that she killed herself out of grief."

"Grief? What grief?"

"Because John Symme abandoned her."

"Was the child his?" Edmund asked. "It makes no sense. He could have married her and no one would have been the wiser."

He flung himself into an armchair and rubbed his eyes.

"The stories say it was not. They say she was a 'loose woman' of questionable character. A fallen woman."

Remy smiled bitterly.

"Hah—a fallen woman driven mad by grief. Well, in earlier times, anyway, she was apparently a lady of more tender sensibilities. She hardly seems so fragile now," Edmund mused. "So—what is missing? La Belle certainly seems to feel remorse about something, but she also feels hard-done-by. What is that about?" He rose and began to pace around the room. "She could regret taking her own life, but from whence comes this fierce anger about buried truth and the need for vengeance?"

"Perhaps she did not commit suicide. Perhaps she was murdered." Remy spoke thoughtfully. "Nobody saw what happened, that I have heard; one morning, her body was found in the clearing and a bloody dagger was in her hand. Perhaps it was murder!"

"If that were so, why was this alleged murder not investigated when it happened? Even callous villagers cannot have a dead body appear without raising the hue and cry, and then an inquest comes. Why was the crime, if there had been a crime, not discovered then?" Edmund was becoming engaged, his brain lurching into motion. "And what became of the child?"

Remy thought for a moment. "I'll tell you why—no one looked for a crime because no one thought a crime had been committed. They considered it suicide." She stared at him. "She had no champion to uphold her honor."

"Hmmm." Edmund began to think out loud. "Item: French girl, a foreigner (never to be understood or trusted), falls from the righteous path despite the shelter and loving care of her guardian. Item: said girl finds herself with child, and is cast off by her prominent fiancé. Item: after the birth, in a fit of shame and remorse, she kills herself." He ticked the items off with his fingers. "End of story. Who needs trouble, why look for foul play? Idiots." He swung around to face the fire. "If I had tuppence for every district coroner who had half a brain, I'd be in debtor's prison. Where do they find these people, they must be inbred to moronic . . ."

"But what if she didn't stray?" Remy interrupted. "What if she were coerced?"

"Rape?" Edmund frowned. "By whom? Why? How? She was living in the bosom of the Symme family, who could get to her . . . unless . . ." His frown deepened.

"Someone who stood to gain from her death, or her discrediting. Who would that be?" Remy continued.

"Who indeed? What happened to the child?" Edmund asked. "What happened to her money and lands? How was my grandfather involved?" He continued to pace, brow furrowed, eyes downcast in thought.

"Mr. Symme, I cannot think any more, my brain is muddled. It is only a few hours until light; shall I make coffee?" Remy asked quietly.

"No—go to bed, Remy." Edmund stopped, turned to her, and raised his hand in admonishment. "No, I insist—there was little sleep for any of us the night Ms. Grenfield made her departure, and this past night was no better. No—Cook will be here at dawn and coffee will follow then. I am exhausted, and so must you be." She made a gesture and he quickly continued. "No objections. Sleep will aid us. We will continue this discussion after breakfast. Now, please, go upstairs and take what rest you can."

Remy nodded and rose from her chair. "Mr. Symme, I must ask you this, even if I offend." Afraid to hear, and yet needing to know, Remy steeled herself and continued. "About earlier this night, can you assure me that neither one of us engaged in any action to compromise ourselves in any way? Do I owe you apology of any kind?" She looked at him directly. "You can tell me; I am prepared for whatever answer comes."

Edmund saw her earnest expression and would have laughed had he not been so deeply weary. *Well, if you consider coming to a man's room in the middle of the night, stark naked and exuding passion, to be compromising, then . . .* Instead, he said without hesitation, "I assure you, Remy, it was obvious that you were not yourself. You did nothing for which you need feel disgraced, and I will never speak of this matter to anyone. You have my word. You owe me no apology, rather, I thank you for precipitating our very interesting meeting with La Belle Dame."

"Ah," she nodded slightly, and with a wry smile replied, "And once again, I find that I must thank you for being a gentleman. Goodnight, then, or rather, good morning."

Edmund retired to his room and found a few hours of sleep. When he woke, it was already light, and he lay in bed staring at the ceiling, remembering the events of the previous night.

He felt unsettled and full of conflicting emotions. A mystery had been given him, and his mind was primed to investigate and follow whatever trail lay before him. He knew how to do that. He excelled at doing that. He reviewed every word, every nuance of movement La Belle Dame presented in that most extraordinary conversation. He began to formulate a plan, a clear and . . .

But disquieting thoughts intruded. He knew himself to be a man of intellect and logic, and yet he had been prepared to believe at first the woman who entered his room last night had been . . . a phantom? Spirit? Hallucination? Was he going mad? And when it turned out to be his *housekeeper*—his housekeeper, for God's sake— what a disappointment! But . . . was he truly disappointed to have a real woman in his arms rather than an apparition? Memories flooded back, and it was not so disappointing at all to have Remy in his embrace, clinging to him, the touch of her lips on his, the look of vast tenderness on her face, her incredible skin, her smile, her throaty laugh as he . . .

He snorted in disgust!

How can all this have come to pass? Was I truly about to make love to a servant, whom I don't even like particularly and who certainly doesn't like me? So absurd as to be insulting!

He got out of bed, annoyed and grumbling, ran his hand through his hair and looked down at his naked body. *All these thoughts of last night have produced an interesting effect*, he thought as he looked downward. *I haven't responded like this to the thought of a woman in some time.* He smiled slightly in spite of himself, and began to dress.

Banks was already seated at breakfast, enjoying a plate heaped with rashers of bacon, eggs, roasted tomatoes and a huge kipper, with his normal excellent appetite.

"Good Morning, Edmund," he began, "By God, I am glad to see you! You've been so elusive, I half thought you had taken off after the disgruntled Lydia to make amends."

"Have pity, Banks, and constrain your dubious wit and ill-conceived humor at least until after breakfast. Please," Edmund replied as he sank heavily into his chair.

"Hmm, you seem to be back to your old grumbling self. Not a good night?" Banks stopped slathering his toast with marmalade and spoke earnestly. "Although nights around here have been poor indeed of late—Edmund, what the hell happened with Lydia?"

Edmund brought his hand to his forehead, rubbed it wearily,

and said, "I cannot begin to say. You were there, you saw and heard what I saw and heard. I have suspicions, but . . . really, I cannot discuss it now. May I please have some breakfast?"

Edmund's attention turned suddenly to the doorway, where Remy stood with a pot of steaming coffee and a pitcher of hot milk.

"Good morning, Mr. Symme," she said, as if this were just another morning. He looked at her for a long moment, noticing the familiar curve of her breasts and her tight waist. She looked pale, but otherwise composed and she met his eyes calmly and smiled.

"Good morning, Remy—that coffee is most welcome," he replied. She set the hot liquids before him and brought a cup and saucer from the sideboard.

"I hope you slept well, sir," she continued. "May I bring you anything else?"

"Well, since the good Doctor seems to have inhaled all the available toasted bread, please ask Cook for more, if you will," he told her.

"Of course," she nodded and left for the kitchen.

Edmund poured himself coffee and drank half the cup.

"Ah, I feel life returning."

He rose and gathered some food, idly slipping Regis a piece of bacon, then settled at the table. "I need another translation. Your French improved any of late, Banks?"

"Oh, it's not that credible, as you know, and certainly not like Remy's, but I get along. Doing additional research on the laws of jackass ownership, are you?" Banks began to chuckle.

Edmund grimaced. "Can you not leave that incident alone? Be useful, for a moment—tell me, what does *'le poignard en pierre'* mean?" Edmund took a forkful of roasted tomato and waited expectantly.

"Hmm—*poignard en Pierre*...sounds suspiciously like 'Peter's prick' to me." Banks began to grin. "Oh, no, Edmund, don't tell me you've come across a stash of those saucy French postale cards in your wonderful library! Good photographs? Do they comment on Peter and his..."

"Oh, for the love of God, Banks, there are no postale cards—it is just a phrase I would like to understand."

"Ah." Banks was not convinced. He thought for a moment. "Well, in any other situation I would remind you that Remy speaks

French quite well but . . ."

"Yes, I have occasion to know that fact," Edmund grunted. "I will ask her when she brings my toast." Edmund replied through a mouthful of egg.

"Really, Edmund, I don't think asking a lady about Pierre's . . ."

"Don't be such an ass, Banks—your French is about as good as your . . . it has nothing to do with . . . Ah, Remy, back so quickly."

Remy entered the room with a napkin-covered basket.

"Cook had anticipated the need and was already toasting," she explained and set the basket in front of them. She smiled slightly and asked, "Anything else, Gentlemen?"

"Yes, as a matter of fact—please tell me, what does '*poignard en pierre*' mean? The good Doctor and I cannot translate the phrase."

Remy arched a brow and looked at Edmund. "It means, 'dagger in stone'."

"Hah—see there, Banks, nothing about Pierre at all!" Edmund looked smug.

"In this shire, however, it has a special meaning as a place name among the local folk," Remy added.

"Really?" Banks asked, "Tell us more—please, be seated and speak with us."

When Remy hesitated for a moment, Edmund urged, "Yes, please take a chair; I may have a number of questions for you. Please, be seated."

She took a place across from them at the table and continued, "There is a legend about the days of the early Celtic tribes who lived in this area, when the Romans were engaged in conquest of Britain. You have heard of the Queen Boudicca, no doubt, who actually did rule somewhere south of here. However, there were many tribes and it was not so unusual to have a warrior queen rule. Legend has it that such a queen ruled the tribe here; her name was Linosea, and she was fierce and unyielding against the hapless Romans who came for her kingdom. Until . . ." She paused.

"Until?" Banks asked.

"Until she lost her heart, and thereby her reason, to the commander who had been charged with negotiating a 'peace' and the takeover of her lands. She trusted him. He betrayed her. Many of her people were killed in the battles than ensued. Finally, she told the Romans she was ready to surrender, but only to that commander. The meeting place was a very large stone, a landmark and sacred place to the tribe. When the two delegations came together, Linosea drew her sword to deliver it to the man, and as he came closer she requested one last kiss. He took the sword from her, leaned close for the kiss, and she drew her dagger from her bosom and plunged it into his stomach. He managed to wield her sword and wound her mortally. In her death throes, she cursed him and all his kind; and legend says the heavens opened with a bolt of lightning that struck the stone, leaving in it a deep imprint of a dagger. So Linosea's bravery and her betrayal by the Roman would live forever. Thus, the Dagger in Stone—*le poignard en pierre.*"

"But what has this to do with Owlswood? What does it mean to me? Why does it have a French name?" Edmund asked sharply.

"The stone is on your property, Mr. Symme. And . . . there is more." Remy replied.

"Good God, tell us please!" Banks was mesmerized.

"Go on. What more?" Edmund asked gravely.

12
The Dagger in Stone

Remy continued with the tale. "A more recent story about the Stone concerns someone who lived at Owlswood, many years ago now. She was a young French girl from Martinique who came to live with the Symmes when her father died suddenly. He—the father—and Alistair Symme were great friends and business associates, and the girl became Symme's ward. She loved to walk the grounds, and especially loved the boulder and the story of the courageous woman warrior of old. All was well until she encountered . . . difficulties and had a child out of wedlock; and the expected betrothal to John Symme was discarded."

Edmund inserted, in response to the questioning look on Banks' face, "Alistair was my great grandfather, and John my grandfather." Then to Remy he said, "Continue, please."

"The story says the lady in question went mad with grief and despair; she killed herself at the Stone. It was a favorite place of hers, she always referred to it as '*le poignard*'. Nothing is said about the child, so it's possible it, too, perished." Remy sat quietly.

"By jove, that is a story," Banks commented softly. All three of them were lost in their own thoughts for a few moments, until he continued. "And you say this all happened here, at Owlswood?"

"Yes, on Symme property," Remy replied.

"Well, we must see it—right now! How far away is it?" Banks' imagination was captured and he spoke with emotion.

"A good walk only—perhaps half-way between here and the village," Remy told him, suppressing a smile at his eagerness, "Why are you so curious, Doctor?"

"Why? How could I not be curious—such drama, such history! Mystery and doomed romance, even if not entirely factual—do these stories not touch your soul, Miss Remy? And it's a fine day for a walk and a discovery, and a look at the Poignard en Pierre. Is it not, Edmund—we'll go, shall we?"

Edmund stared at them briefly, and then agreed.

"Hmm. Mystery and romance? Doom and betrayal, more like. But yes, I would like to see this monument. Very much. Remy, can you guide us there?"

Regis had risen to his feet at the word "walk" and was now at Edmund's side, looking pleased indeed. Remy took a moment to tell Cook she was leaving, grabbed her bonnet, shawl and basket from the mud room, and joined the two men on the back lawn.

They set off at an easy stride, Remy keeping up with no effort, and Regis dashing off to track wild fauna. Edmund lagged, deep in thought. As they walked, Banks asked questions about the story, and about the scenery. Remy explained what she knew about the legend, the grounds, and the general family history. After a half-mile or so, Banks dropped back to walk with Edmund and let Remy go ahead, the big dog now at her side and very interested in her basket.

"Pretty rum of your grandfather to abandon this girl, if that's what happened—was he that much of a bastard?" Banks queried. "Was the child his, do you think?"

Edmund laughed ruefully. "Oh, yes, he was that much of a bastard, and worse. But," and he paused for a moment, "I don't think the child was his. He would have married her, if only to protect the family name. And . . . it's possible some affection . . . I don't know." He shook his head.

They had lost sight of Remy and Regis, and it was not until they had turned up a hairpin curve of the path that they caught sight of them. Remy and the dog were waiting, both looking toward a slight rise of a hill to their left, to a small copse of trees.

As they reached her she said, "Well, gentlemen, we have arrived."

She took off up the rise, and they followed, and as they reached the first tree they saw it. A boulder about chest-high, wider than a wagon, the color of grey dawn, lichen-covered in patches and flattish on top, sloping slightly toward the ground on one side. The trees formed an irregular ring around it, and made it difficult to see from the path. But it was there. Huge. Grim. Commanding.

"Big rock, 'tis," Edmund commented wryly. As they drew nearer, cracks and fissures became visible. When they stood beside it, Banks murmured, "Good God."

There, in the very center, was a fissure the exact size and shape of a dagger of war; the hilt, the guard, the tapering blade and sharp point—all clear and visible. Moss and lichen radiated from the dagger's edge as if they traced the flow of blood, across the face and down the sides of the rock to the ground. The air seemed to grow still and a chill settled. Light seemed to fade but no cloud could be seen in the sky. Both men stared, mesmerized, not speaking, barely breathing.

Remy, ashen and hoarse, broke the silence. She stood several yards behind them, reluctant to move closer to the Stone. "It is a place of grave superstition for people here, who say the Stone holds some power, tells some story, wants something. But no one cares to find out more." She paused. "I never feel at ease here. And now I must be off. I have business in the village, and Cook asked for a few things." She turned briskly, adding, "I trust you can find your way back to the house without me."

"And if we could not—would that concern you at all, Miss?" Edmund spoke with some irritation, not certain why the thought of her leaving them made him angry. "And what of the matter you and I were to discuss this morning, as we mutually decided?"

Remy looked at him calmly.

"That matter is part of my business in the village, and I will speak with you about it upon my return. Is that satisfactory?"

"Edmund, no cause to be testy, old man—we'll be all right, even if we must rely on Regis' nose to lead us home." Banks turned to Remy. "Or would you prefer one of us escort you?" he asked.

"That is very kind, Doctor, however I am fine on my own. I will be only an hour or two."

She smiled at him, nodded at Edmund, and started away. Banks watched her leave, hoping she might change her mind about wanting company. She didn't, and as she disappeared up the path he turned back to Edmund.

"What's come over you, now?" he asked brusquely. "You seem to be exceeding even your old rude self, but . . . Edmund, what's the matter?" Banks saw the look of concentration of Edmund's face.

"There is something about this rock, something about this place. I find it . . . rather disturbing." He frowned as he reached out his hand to touch the Stone lightly, then withdrew it. "Don't you feel it?"

"Well, after all, it is a place where two women came to sticky ends—a sobering and unhappy thought, certainly, even though so long ago. I do feel something. But . . . are you falling under a spell?"

Banks asked, not lightly. "Edmund, is something troubling you about all this? Edmund?"

"I think it's time we went back. Shall we?" Edmund turned away from the Stone and strode rapidly toward the path, Regis and Banks at heel.

*   *   *

Remy reached the cottage just as the village men were heading back to fields and workshops after their midday meal. The women would be in their kitchens, cleaning and preparing for the evening meal—kitchen work was never-ending—and she was likely to find Nana Cooper at home, hopefully with Annie and Molly tending to the chickens out back in the toft. She wanted a word in private. She knocked on the open door.

"Jeannie, come in, girl," said the older woman, looking surprised but pleased. "Good to see you on my doorstep."

They embraced and Remy said, "I hope you have time to speak with me. Alone. I need your advice."

Nana's face became serious. "Of course, the girls are working out back, won't be coming in for a while, unless I call to them. Sit."

She pulled out her own chair, laced her fingers on the table in front of her, and waited.

Remy pulled a chair close and sat down. She looked boldly into the elderly but piercing grey eyes and began, "What is the connection between the French Woman of Owlswood and my family?"

Nana returned her stare, then replied, "You were never one to mince words, my girl. So you are seeing things again, up at the house, are you?" Remy nodded, holding the woman's gaze. The old face became worried and distant, almost as if Nana were seeing the past and not liking it much; she looked away from Remy and seemed lost in thought. "What else happened?"

"Why do you ask me that? What kinds of things could have happened?" Remy bristled. "Very well. I had one of my spells last night. It was very strong, and I might have acted rashly had not . . . had not something stopped me. And then I saw her again." She looked at the woman beside her. "You know something about all this. Why do you not answer my question?"

The old woman shook her head and looked sad, seemingly far away.

Remy pursued. "Nana, I was born and raised here, in this place, among people I love and respect. But I have never felt a true part of this village. There has always been something . . . else." She continued, "I never knew my grandparents; they died when I was so small. Mother used to tell me stories, and I have some fleeting memories of them, but not much more. You must have known them. You must know my family story. What have you not told me?"

Nana spoke slowly. "It's true, your mother married late in life, and her parents were joyful to see you born but didn't live many years after. No one thought she would bear a child—but you came, and she was so happy. Your father, too, doted on you as a rare gift from heaven. He was a rough French merchant marine man, but with you he was so gentle."

"But what of my forebears—they were cousins of Samuel's, were they not, and also worked at the House? Am I not related to him by blood? Am I not?" Remy pressed.

"In truth," Nana hesitated, "in truth I am not certain who is your blood kin. No one is certain, nor can they be."

"What is this mystery?! Why do you not speak plainly?" Remy erupted and rose from her chair. "Someone must have the answers I seek!"

"My mother knew, but she is buried these thirty years. She was the midwife for the three villages hereabouts. She knew, but she told no one. No one." Nana looked hard at Remy. "Even when I asked her where the squalling bundle of ginger-haired baby came from, she wouldn't tell me—and swore me to never tell a soul it was not the natural offspring of the two she gave it to." The woman paused for an instant. "So, you see, you will never know. Best to leave it."

"Damnation! I will not leave it. It is my right to know from whence I came! Why will you keep such a secret?" Remy began to pace the kitchen. "Things are happening, strange things. I must know what is going on, can't you see that? The moment for truth has come!"

Nana rose and stood facing Remy, and grasped her shoulder.

"Quiet yourself," she said. "We'd best have some tea. Set the table. And then I will tell you what I know."

She turned and stirred the fire in the stove and added water to the tea kettle. Remy bridled at the delay, but did as she was bidden.

Ten minutes later they were again seated, and Nana began.

"Samuel's mother had an elder sister—by many years—who was married and already with a half-grown daughter when Samuel was born. The girl reached marrying age and took a husband, and they got tenancy acreage on the Willows property and a small cottage here in town. She worked as kitchen maid, and then housekeeper at Owlswood while her husband worked their land. Things went well for them; except she could not conceive. They both grieved mightily over that, especially after all the rest of us began our broods and they were left the only ones childless. It's a hard path—you know how people will talk and blame hidden sin and all that nonsense. Gossips and biddies."

She snorted with contempt and blew on her tea before going on, "As midwife, Mam had great herbal knowledge, of course. She tried to help Lily—that was her name—and in time, Lily finally found herself with child. She carried it almost to term, but one night her pains started, too early by weeks, and she labored two full days but the child would not be born. Mam was at her side the whole time, but late the second night was called away by an urgent summons from the Reader." Nana checked to be sure Remy knew who that was. "Mam was good friends with the Reader and respected her—even though some thought she was a witch, and most thought she was daft, and she was so old! But Mam got on with her, learned Tarot from her and then she taught me, both midwifery and Tarot."

She paused and sipped from her steaming cup.

"Mam sent for me to watch with Lily so she could attend the Reader. Just before she left, the child was stillborn. Lily was exhausted and distraught, barely conscious, and she began to slip away toward death. Mam told me to stay with her and said she would return soon, with herbs to brew a tonic, after she saw the Reader. I wondered if Lily would live until then. And what could be so important that Mam would leave her side? But my place was not to question.

"Mam wasn't gone long, and when she returned, she had with her a very young baby—a girl with a fuzz of red hair on her head. She placed it in the crook of Lily's arm and didn't say a word. When Lily heard the baby cry, she came out of her stupor and smiled like she was looking at the Lord himself. She took the babe as her own—maybe she thought it was her own. Mam never said a word more. When the husband came back to see his family, everything was settled." She paused. "Mam and I buried the stillborn in the garden, under a rose. It couldn't go to the churchyard, you see, because it died before it was baptized, poor mite."

Remy turned pale, and searched the other woman's face. "The red-haired babe was my mother?" Nana nodded. "Whose baby was she?"

"Mam ne'er told me, nor another living soul. And she told me never to ask her, ever, and swore me on the blood of Christ that I would never tell anyone that the babe was not Lily's." Nana rose from the table. "And nobody ever crossed my Mam, least of all her daughter."

She went to the stove and added a log.

She watched the fire burn and continued, "Your mother used to ask me, sometimes—in jest I think—how she could be the same blood as the rest of Samuel's family; she was so different. Fey, almost, your mum was, and otherworldly. But I never said what I might have thought. Not until now." She poked at the fire vigorously, then turned to face Remy, poker in hand. "But now you're a grown woman, and you ask me, and you deserve to know. You are meant to walk a different path than the rest of us, and the silence does you no good. I hope my Mam will look down from heaven and forgive me for breaking my oath." She waved the poker around above her head slowly three times, as if signaling to some celestial being. Then she put it down and said, "Drink your tea, and tell me what happened at the House."

Remy sighed and shook her head.

"Many things happened. Too many. And I saw her, spoke with her. Why might the spirit of the French woman be concerned with me? Did she trouble my mother?" she queried.

"Trouble? No, never a trouble. She . . . well, your mother felt some . . . patronage, maybe? That some blithe and bonny spirit looked after her, but she never had the visions you have. Except once." Remy raised an eyebrow and tilted her head as Nana continued. "She was frail, your mother, afraid of village talk, and of bad places; of witches and ghosts and evil spirits; and she was afraid of dark forces down to the marrow of her bones. She would never even let me read for her; she was so fearful of the Cards. One day she saw . . . well, something or someone at the House, and shouted at it in the name of Christ to never return. It didn't."

Remy frowned. "Hmmmm . . . Maybe that explains why I was

punished so severely when I insisted I saw the beautiful Lady—then forbidden to even be at Owlswood. I thought it was the old Symme banishing me, but it was Mother." She thought for a moment. "Was the child given to your Mam close to the time the French woman died? Could she have been the baby's mother?"

Nana paused, then answered. "Her body was found the morning after the babe came to us. Do you think your mother was her child?"

Remy replied, "I do. Last night the Lady called me granddaughter."

13
Family Connections

With the dark influence of the Stone still upon them, and Remy off to the village on her errands, Edmund and Banks made their way back to the house—Edmund in a brooding silence most of the way. Banks walked beside him, lost in his thoughts; even Regis seemed subdued and quiet. When they had almost reached home, Edmund spoke.

"I have in mind to research this episode in Owlswood history—this strange death and this French woman of some notoriety."

"Do you now?" commented Banks with a frown. "So the library will continue to claim your attentions and your time, will it?"

"No, actually, I will be rummaging through old John Symme's personal papers, up on the third floor—and I wonder if you would assist me?"

"What? You want help?" Banks came to an abrupt halt, truly surprised. "By all the saints, abandoning your solitude and requesting aid, are you!" Leaning on his walking stick, he added wryly, "And what an honor, to be the one selected. This holiday in the country continues to produce unexpected delights."

"Come along, Banks—although you don't have to help if you prefer not. It will be boring, probably, however there is the chance we'll discover some lurid and interesting facts."

"Such as? You have no idea what those papers contain—wouldn't they most likely notate old accounts, inventories, business negotiations?" Banks thought for a moment. "Did old Symme keep a diary, do you suppose, and would he include such matters as Remy described if he did? Matters of immorality and untimely death? Somewhat unappealing matters for a personal memoire, no?"

"Well, after all, the woman was ward of the family; there must be records of her finances, official papers for her wardship, perhaps letters between bankers or even some from her father—or from herself. You said it was a romantic story back there at the rock, I heard you."

"Yes," Banks admitted, "but I said that before I knew of a

research project."

"Oh, come on, aren't you a bit curious? What do you say?" Edmund grinned at him.

Sighing deeply, but with a smile, Banks replied, "How can I refuse such an intriguing offer? When do we begin?"

"Immediately!" Edmund crowed, triumphant. "I have keys to the upstairs rooms, and we can begin this very afternoon."

"Not before lunch, we won't! I know you rarely eat at midday; however, I require some food." Banks was adamant. "And so does Regis!" The dog wagged is tail, looking grateful.

"For God's sake, you and your stomach are worse than a child, or a dog. Very well, we'll get Cook to make you some sandwiches and take them up to our work. You can have a feed while I see if there is some organization to the records. Fair enough?"

Edmund was determined to begin at once.

"Agreed—first stop, the kitchen. Come on, Regis, let's go see Cook!"

Banks and the big dog trotted ahead to use their considerable charms on the lady of the larder, and see what she might provide for their meal.

*   *   *

Some half an hour later, Banks made his way up the stairs to the third floor, carrying a basket filled with ham sandwiches, a large wedge of cheese, an onion tart, three fruit muffins, a jug of water, and two bottles of beer. He looked down the gleaming, polished hall, noting fresh flowers on the side tables, and saw a door standing open about halfway down. Drawing nearer, he heard Edmund swearing and scuffling around.

"This must be the archive in question," Banks commented to Regis, who had received his own ration of ham in the kitchen but kept a close eye on the basket nonetheless. Man and dog continued into the room.

Musty, dusty, and filled with shelves and cabinets bursting with tightly catalogued papers, the room smelled of old vellum and mildew even though Edmund had tied back the drapes and set the windows wide open. On some shelves, and on two tables, motheaten taxidermy of badger, fox, and hawk snarled and grimaced.

"Hells bells, where to begin, old man," was all Banks could say.

"Where indeed," Edmund agreed, then sneezed loudly. His sleeves were rolled above his elbows, his coat hung on an ancient coat rack. "This is like a mortuary vault! And the adjoining chamber is almost worse. The housekeepers were forbidden to enter these rooms, and could only clean the hallways. It must be years since anyone aired them out. I'm surprised there are no rats." Just then a rather sleek black cat peered into the room from the hall, saw Regis, and disappeared.

"There's your rat-catcher, appearing quite well-fed." Banks looked around and then said, "And I know exactly where you should begin—here!" He handed Edmund one of the beer bottles from his basket and took the other for himself. After a long swallow he said, "Really, Edmund, what do you propose we may find here? This seems a morass of ancient information, sixty years or more of it! What promise does it hold? And how the hell do we know what we are looking for, even if we find it?"

"This is a treasure-trove for my purpose. These bound volumes cover two years each, so we can choose the one from, oh, say…1830 for a start. However, I somehow feel the documents I want are stored in a more secure and valued manner. This was a personal matter, the wardship of a young woman, as well as a financial one. Especially if there were difficulties, the usual cataloguing would not suffice." He looked around. "There may even be a Bible or something, traditionally where one might find a record of births and deaths. You start on that locked cabinet, and I'll look around for a safe. Here."

Catching the tossed key, Banks headed for his assigned task, sandwich in hand. While he fiddled with the lock, he commented, "I may find a Bible, but I doubt we'll find sensitive or romantic missives in this case. Why do you think we shall?"

"Oh, she said that old John Symme was deeply in love with her, and she with him, and there were many letters and tokens exchanged," Edmund replied absently. "We're bound to find some. Damn—this footstool is heavy!"

"Remy said this? Remy was in love with the old man? How could that be, she . . ."

"No, you fool, La Belle told me about the love affair. I doubt Remy . . ." He stopped abruptly and stood up, wishing he could take back what had just slipped out.

"La Belle? La Belle Who?" Banks turned to Edmund and saw

151

his look of dismay. When no response came, he continued, "Who is La Belle? Is she connected to why you spend so much time alone in the library?"

When Edmund remained at a loss for words, Banks went on.

"Don't you think it's time to confide in me? What is happening here? What turns you into a hermit each night? What makes you irritable, sleepless, ill-tempered? Why do you talk to yourself all evening behind a closed door? What has this to do with your obsession with research? Tell me."

They stared at each other for some moments in silence. Edmund began to pace anxiously, stopping to peer out the window several times, almost at the point of speech once or twice. Finally, he began.

"Banks, I . . . I may be losing my mind. I may be a fool. I cannot explain what has happened to me. But I . . . I don't speak to myself in the library, I have a companion. She is extremely beautiful, very well-read, and truly delightful company. And . . . she is dead." He shrugged and looked helpless. "And thereby lies my problem and conundrum."

Banks set down his sandwich, drained his beer, and leaned against the cabinet.

"This is news, indeed. Do you care to tell me more?"

Over the next quarter hour, Edmund told Banks the story of his meeting La Belle and the very many interests they shared. He spared no detail of how charming and intelligent she was, carefully omitting, however, any mention of the almost-tryst she had arranged between him and Remy. Banks asked a question or two, listened carefully, and paid close attention to the unfolding story. Edmund finished by saying, "It is clear to me now that she orchestrated the events that caused Lydia's departure. Banks, she must be the French woman of the Stone! And now she wants me to clear her reputation, I think. But of what, and how . . ."

He shrugged, shook his head, and opened his palms in a gesture of frustration.

It was Banks' turn to be speechless.

Edmund continued, "As my friend, and my physician, tell me please: am I mad? Because I can't decide."

He watched his friend's face closely, anxiously, hopefully, but said no more.

Banks took several moments to think before he answered.

"You know, Edmund, probably fully half of the country houses in England have resident ghosts. I doubt that all of the most prominent families of the realm are mad—I can think of several who are, mind you—but this situation in itself proves nothing." He rose and looked at Edmund intently. "You are my friend. I know you. I don't know what is happening, but I will stake my professional standing on the fact that you are as sane as you ever were." His eyes began to sparkle, and suddenly they both burst into loud guffaws. "Not much of a testimonial, I know, but the best I can do!"

A minute or two later, their laughter spent and eyes watering with mirth, they returned to the task at hand. Soon, two large volumes filled with miniscule script and numbers lay open on the long table, exposing interminable inventories of storerooms, cargo ships, household goods, receipts for expenditures, servant's wages and accounts due. After an hour, they looked at each other and decided to rest.

"This is excruciating, old man. I never knew so many barrels of molasses and sugar even existed, much less crossed the sea from Martinique. By God, my brain is beginning to solidify," Banks complained, rubbing the back of his neck.

"Yes, I agree" Edmund sighed, "this seems a bit futile, I'll grant. But there must be something here. Where is that blasted safe? You distracted me when I was searching for it earlier!"

Suddenly Regis' ears stood up and he came out from where he was lying under the table. He trotted to the doorway, tail wagging.

Remy appeared in the doorway, caressed the big dog's head, and entered.

"Oh my, what is going on here?"

"Miss Remy, have you come to rescue us from this Hades of cataloged minutiae?" Banks was pleased to see her. "Edmund recruited me as research assistant in his quest for knowledge of the erstwhile and ill-fated Symme ward of long ago—with whom he is well-acquainted, I understand." He looked at her with mild amusement. "Did you complete your business in the village with success?"

"Ah, yes, well . . . to that matter, Mr. Symme, I have some information to discuss with you and perhaps you could release the good Doctor for a bit, that may speak privately?"

She tried to hide her excitement, but her heart was pounding.

"You may speak freely here, Remy. I have informed Dr. Banks of my—our—most interesting and ephemeral acquaintance," Edmund told her. "Although, not *all* the details," he added with a knowing look.

"Damnation!" Remy was taken aback. "You told him? You told him of the Lady?" Remy's her eyes widened in disbelief. Not used to feeling nonplussed, she looked from one man to the other, not knowing what else to say. "You told him? All of it?"

Edmund cleared his throat and replied, "I repeat, I shared only what was relevant to our research, to be sure."

"Damnation!" Remy repeated and stared at Edmund another moment. "Mr. Symme, may I have a brief word with you?" She moved toward the window farthest away from where Banks sat. "Over here, please?"

Edmund joined her.

"Well—what is it?"

She spoke in little more than a whisper. "Is it wise to spread word of the Lady before we have made more progress? And, forgive me if I seem concerned, what have you said about my . . . involvement with you last night?"

She began to flush, whether from embarrassment or pique, Edmund could not say.

"Oh, honestly, Remy, do you take me for a fool? Why would I tell Banks that we almost . . . that my *housekeeper* and I were . . . I stated clearly just now that I did not include all the details! Confound it, Banks is my ally here, and yours as well! Do you not see that?"

Edmund was annoyed.

"I have little concern about the trustworthiness of Dr. Banks. It's your attitude and actions that prompt my inquiries!" Remy's annoyance rose. "I question the wisdom of your recent decision."

"You question *my* decision? Hah—this from a woman who came to my bedroom almost completely naked in the middle of the night!" Edmund was losing his temper and control of his voice as he continued to whisper louder and louder. "How in the name of all that's holy can you . . ."

Sensing an awkward situation brewing, Banks called over to them. "I must say, I feel quite slighted that you, too, are gifted with this vision as well, Miss Remy, while I am excluded."

He put on a face of disappointment, but his eyes shimmered in jest.

Edmund was glad to leave the subject at hand. "Oh, and Regis sees her, too, by the way," he called back, smirking. "I forgot to mention that before."

"By all the saints, am I the only one to be left out of this phenomenon?" Banks asked, incredulous. "Damnation, indeed!"

Moving back to where Banks was seated, Edmund continued. "As I made quite clear, La Belle is a woman of taste and fine sensibility, why should she want you?" Edmund was enjoying himself. Then, becoming brusque and business-like, he asked Remy, "Come now, what is this information you have uncovered?" He gestured her to come closer. "We may as well hear your news."

Recovering herself, Remy began.

"I spoke at length with a long-time resident of the village, and then went to see the reverend Mr. Creviston. Apparently, while there is no absolute proof, it is almost certain that my mother was the infant the French woman left behind at the time of her death." She paused for a heartbeat and took a breath. "I cannot come to any other conclusion but that La Belle Dame is that unfortunate young French woman, and moreover, that she is my grandmother." Remy spoke with quiet intensity. "The Rev. Creviston was little help; he did consult his parish records, but he stated that in all likelihood, the French woman was of the Roman Catholic faith so no mention of her would appear. He was even more certain that, had she been Church of England, as a suicide, she would never have been permitted burial in his churchyard, and in light of her questionable character, no predecessor of his would ever consider affording her services or record her passing officially." Her face showed disdain. "Fie on him and his predecessors. What a magniloquent fool."

Edmund shared a surprised look with Banks, smiled slightly, and replied, "Quite an apt and elegant description. I have no great opinion of Creviston myself. But this is a significant discovery—La Belle is your blood relative!"

Remy nodded. "So it appears."

"It certainly casts new light on your childhood here at Owlswood," Banks commented, "and on the provision in the will that your family stay on as caretakers."

"And why La Belle was so adamant that you remain!' added

Edmund. At Remy's inquiring look he added, "She was most upset to learn you wanted to surrender your post to another, and made me promise to prevent that from happening."

"I see." Remy was thoughtful. "However, all this throws little light on the task of discovering what truly happened to her, and what she needs of us."

"To that end, you see us here. We have reviewed page after page of tedious information, but have encountered nothing relevant to her wardship, death, or the father of the child." Edmund grumbled. "What next?"

"It has been a long time since I've been in these rooms," said Remy, looking around. "Your forebears were prosperous men, and this all looks to be records of business dealing. Would what we seek even be here?"

She swayed slightly and leaned against the table.

"But where else to look? Do you know of a safe or some other likely place to keep valuable records?" Edmund was growing frustrated. "There must be a safe or a strongbox or....."

Just then, noticing how pale Remy had become, Banks broke in. "Miss Remy, please, sit down and pause a moment. Edmund, fetch a glass of water, quickly."

He rose and moved his chair nearer to Remy, then took her elbow gently and guided her to it. Edmund, not liking to be ordered about, nevertheless provided the water and handed it to Remy. She nodded thanks, and drank thirstily.

Banks took her wrist gently and felt her pulse. He searched her face quietly for a moment.

"You are a strong and resilient person. Nevertheless, these discoveries have taken a toll on your emotions and physical resources. Will you permit me to advise you as a physician?" he asked. When Remy nodded, he continued, "Go down and get Cook to make you a strong cup of tea, plenty of sugar. Drink it in the kitchen, seated at the table. Then go up to your room, remove your shoes and any other constricting items of clothing, and lie down for at least an hour. I will check on you then." Banks spoke definitively, his face serious. "No objections, please. We may continue discussions of our plans after you have taken rest. Do you need our assistance with the stairs?"

"No, of course not, I am . . ." She rose to her feet and swayed again. "I can get to the kitchen by myself, thank you. And . . . thank you for your kind concern." Remy moved toward the hallway and stopped, turning to smile at Banks. "But really, I don't need to lie down . . ."

"Lie down!" Banks commanded. "I will see you in little more than an hour. You need to take my prescription seriously. Will you?"

"Yes, Doctor, I shall." She smiled shyly, and headed for the stairs.

"Well, your medical degree seems to have worked some magic, Banks. That woman has not once taken my direction without major discussion, not to mention, complete resistance," Edmund grumbled. "Good of you to notice her flagging, I noticed myself that she seemed off her mettle. Perhaps she is affected by all this news. Women are such emotional creatures." They returned to business matters without delay. "So, there is one more volume I wish to review before we call an end to this for now. Are you with me?"

"Hmm? Hold on a moment." Banks had gone to the hall to observe Remy's progress down the stairs. When he had decided she was steady enough on her feet, he came back and replied, "And if I say no, we shall do it anyway, I'm sure. So, let's get to it so we can put this dreadful chore aside for the day." He settled again at the long table and pulled the volume labeled 1837-39 toward him. "Now, I can hardly wait—how many tons of sugar did we import in '37?"

Edmund had just retrieved another Ledger book for inspection when Banks commented, "Well, here's something unusual—a receipt in the amount of 500 pounds, issued by Alistair Symme and witnessed by John Symme, to a person named Ian Llewellyn. Payment in full for services rendered. No mention of what services." Banks looked up at Edmund. "A sizeable amount for 'services', especially 60 years ago. Who was this Llewellyn chap? Any idea?"

"None. Why is this of interest?"

"Well, half the amount is noted as paid in cash, and half in a bank draft issued for the purchase of Burgess farm in Middlevale—that's the next town over, isn't it? Very unusual transaction, based on what we've found to now."

"Indeed. Do you think it sufficiently significant to merit investigation?" Edmund asked.

"Well, I'd like to know who this Llewellyn fellow was, and why his services were so valued. It seems very strange. How shall we pursue this?" Banks continued to read the document. "Dated September, 1837."

"We will need to find some elder of the community who might remember him, and we can send to the county registry for information on the recorded deed, if it seems like a promising line of inquiry." Edmund paced a bit, then snapped his fingers and said, "Perhaps we can ask Remy whom she recommends we ask."

"We will ask Miss Remy nothing for several hours, at the very earliest," Banks replied. "But I agree she may know to whom we should speak."

Banks marked the receipt page with a ribbon and continued scanning the records of 1837-39.

*   *   *

Remy followed Dr. Banks' prescription to the letter. After a restorative cup of tea with plenty of sugar, and a freshly baked scone from Cook's ever-busy oven, she excused herself and went up to her room. Shoes off, hair loose, stripped to her shift, she climbed into bed and nestled into the softness. Almost immediately, she was asleep. She heard a soft voice, murmuring endearments and then, crooning a familiar lullaby.

> Dodo, l'enfant do,
> l'enfant dormira bien vite.
> Une poule blanche est là dans la grange.
> Qui va faire un petit coco?

Her eyes fluttered behind her lids; her lips curled into a soft smile. "Grandmère..." she sighed.

*   *   *

Edmund and Banks continued working for more than an hour, turning pages mostly in frustrated silence, until Banks blurted, "By St. Milberga's bones, here's another interesting item!"

"Oh yes—now what?" Edmund asked wearily. "And how is it that you discover all the interesting items?"

"Were either your old granddad or his father seriously ill at any time? One of them an invalid, perhaps?" Banks was perusing another document.

"Good lord, no—they were too full of venom and vitriol to ever be ill, although they made others around them wish they'd be afflicted and pass on. What have you there?" Edmund replied.

"A bill—from a doctor Crandall in London. A very expensive bill, dated around the same time as this Llewellyn item." He paused to think. "Why on earth would they pay such an exorbitant fee to a physician so far away? Why not use the local man? This has to be some major illness." He turned to Edmund. "Was the Lady seriously ill, d'you think?"

"I have no idea—but she looks hale and healthy now—in spite of being dead of course—so I would doubt it. Hmmm . . . the old misers were very mean with money. At least my Grandfather was. So, I agree, paying a London man sounds highly unusual." He came around the table to take a look. "Does it give a specialty?"

"None stated here. But I gather from the rather large amount that he was a specialist of some kind—prominent enough to secure vastly inflated fees." Banks continued to peruse the document. "Let me take this one in hand. Perhaps I shall run down to the village and use the Post Office telephone to contact a knowledgeable friend of mine. He can find out what kind of medicine this . . . Randolph Crandall . . . practiced." He rose and stretched extravagantly. "Do you mind if I take Regis with me on the walk? But before I leave, I will take a look at my patient."

Banks first went around to the kitchen to return the provisions basket, Regis at his side. He paused a moment to chat with Cook, thanking her for the delicious lunch and her willingness to create it on a moment's notice. Her smile was wide and her cheeks blushing as she bustled the basket out of his hands, saying, "Oh, get on with you, sir, t'was just a bit of a mid-day feed. Young men need regular meals, I always say." She hesitated, then continued a bit shyly. "And, if I may be so bold, I am most obliged that you sent my Jeannie up for a bit of a lie-down. She would never listen were I to suggest it."

Ah, thought Banks, so *her given name is Jeanne*. He smiled at the knowledge. "Well, she was looking somewhat fatigued, I thought, and under no little strain," he explained.

Cook, never before garrulous, was feeling bolder today. "Strain, indeed, the poor girl! What with her mother's passing so hard on her, and havin' to give up her city life and all—though, mind you,

I never approved of her going so far away and going to that doctoring school! And then tryin' to get his place ready for the young Master, of course he's entitled and all, but still! And then that run-in with that bunch of Llewellyn ruffians at the pond, what a disgrace! She's worn out, I say!"

Cook was working up a fair lather of umbrage.

Banks' ears pricked-up. "Llewellyn—is that a local family?" he asked.

"They have a farm out on the other side of the hill. Not too far—and not far enough, if you ask me! Very fine horse stock, some good bulls. They are tolerable when they keep to themselves, and they mostly do." She came a bit closer, and lowered her voice. "I don't hold with gossip, lord knows, but the men of that family have a bad reputation, and those boys need a good caning. Always into some kind of unpleasantness when they come to town. Especially troublin' the girls—if you take my meanin'?" She picked up a spoon and waved it. "They'll come to no good, mark my words. I thought Molly's father was about to kill that eldest one with his own fists, until the men pulled them apart. Would have been good riddance. Nobody'd miss that one at all. Humph."

Banks listened with interest.

"Well, how very interesting—I appreciate the cautionary word about the Llewellyns. And I am so delighted you agree with my medical advice!" He flashed her a smile and turned toward the door. "I'd best check on my patient. Many thanks, again, for the most appreciated lunch basket."

Cook almost melted in pleasure.

From the kitchen, he jogged up the stairs to the corner room where Remy slept, knocking softly at the door and then, when no answer came, opening it carefully to take a look. Remy looked peaceful and comfortable, and he was about to leave her undisturbed when Regis pushed through the opening and began to nuzzle her hand where it lay on the counterpane. The big orange cat curled on the bed in the hollow of her knee did not take kindly to this disruption and growled menacingly. Remy opened her eyes. She saw Banks and smiled.

"Oh—apologies for my overly-enthusiastic companion," Banks began, "I was hoping to leave you asleep but he had other ideas."

"Not at all, Doctor, I think I was half-awake anyway." Remy

caressed the big dog's head. "I had been dreaming about my childhood here, and my grandmother."

"All this must be a great deal to absorb, not to mention become used to. You have had quite the discovery today." Banks looked at her closely. "Were your dreams good ones, may I ask?"

"Oh, yes—and even more, I believe I've made sense of some things that happened when I was a child, that have puzzled me for many years!" She adjusted her head against the pillows, and continued. "When I was a child, I played on these grounds quite freely. My mother was in charge of the house, and often I would help her as I could—folding and putting away linens, changing the flowers in the smaller vases, such things as a child could safely do. As I played in the kitchen, or walked the halls on my errands, I would often see a beautiful lady who would smile and sometimes speak to me very kindly. Sometimes she would teach me little songs, or add a flower or two to my bunches. She was very lovely, and I wondered who she was—especially because the Symme family was very dour (when they were here at all) and aloof from the servants. I was the only child around most of the time and not welcome underfoot, but the lady seemed always glad to see me. And she smelled so good, of gardenia and new-cut hay." She paused. "I must be boring you, forgive me."

Banks quickly replied, smiling, "No, not at all. Please, continue."

"I told no one except my mother, who chastised me for making up stories. Then, one day, she took me home from Owlswood unexpectedly and forbade me ever to come to the house again. She seemed so frightened, and so angry with me when I protested. I was certain one of the Symmes had demanded that I be banished from the house—but I learned today that it was because *Maman* had seen the Lady, and was sure she came from the devil. What nonsense." Remy looked sad. "So the Lady began coming to me in dreams, away from the house. Sometimes disturbing dreams, and sometimes even frightening ones, and ..." She looked at Banks sheepishly. "But today, the dream was quite comforting."

"I'm so glad to hear that. May I have Cook bring you something?" Banks asked.

"No—I'm ready to be up and about."

"Not so fast, Jeanne Remy!" Banks moved a chair over to the bedside and sat. "May I?" he asked, and when she nodded, he

161

took her hand, put his fingers to her wrist and felt her pulse. "This is much better; the nap has done you good. I'm glad to see some healthy color back in your cheeks. And you feel . . . ?"

He released her hand.

"I feel very well. Ready to be about my duties." She sat up in bed, careful to keep the sheet about her, and asked, "And curious—how do you come to know my name, Doctor Christopher Banks?"

"Ah—I have my sources. My great charm enticed Cook to tell me your first name. Actually, she called you Jeannie. I assumed it was for Jeanne." He lightly felt her forehead. "Do you feel strong enough to rise?"

"Yes, indeed. However, you are in error—neither one is my *first* name. I am called Jeannie, or Jeanne, by my friends and family." She smiled at his puzzled look. "Another mystery for you, and your charm shall have no effect on me."

"I am called Kit by my friends and family—except for Edmund—and since I am now your kindly old physician I would like you to call me Kit. What do you say?"

He placed his hands on his knees and waited for an answer.

"I think if the gentleman at hand were to leave me on my own, I would rise and get dressed. I generally do not need assistance with such matters. And to call you Kit would be most unseemly, Dr. Banks."

She looked at him sternly.

"Aah—you are most concerned with being seemly in all things, is that correct?" Banks noted her blush as she laughed and replied, "Not in all things, as you have learned."

Banks chuckled, too. "Very well, can we agree that we shall observe proprieties in all social and household matters, but when we converse privately or work together we are Jeanne and Kit?" He asked. She nodded. "And this gentleman at hand wants to assist you to get onto your feet, and when you are steady, he will leave. This is the prudent course of action." He lowered his voice conspiratorially. "And I assure you, as a physician I have seen many women in a greater state of dishabille. There is no impropriety here."

Remy laughed again, swung her legs over the edge of the bed, and allowed Banks to take her hands and steady her rise. When she was on her feet, he released her.

"Thank you, Kit," she stated. "I will see you downstairs."

"Not before meal time—I have an errand to which I must attend. Till then, Jeanne."

Banks nodded slightly, smiled, and with a "Regis, come along," he and the big dog were off and away.

* * *

Dressed and on her way to inspect the dining room, Remy encountered Edmund on the stairway.

"Ah, Remy, you look much better," he greeted her. "You are feeling yourself again, I trust?"

"Thank you, Mr. Symme, I feel quite myself. And I assume you have finished your research for the day?"

"Not entirely—I have a question for you. I want to gain some information about a local man mentioned in my grandfather's papers. Is there someone who would know about that?"

Remy thought for a moment. "There are elders still in the village, but someone involved with the Symmes in a business matter might not have been common knowledge. A local man, you say? Have you spoken with Samuel—he was young in your grandfather's time, but he might . . ."

"Of course, Samuel!! He's the very one!"

Edmund left her standing in the hallway and trotted out toward the glasshouse area.

"You are very welcome, sir," Remy said to herself as she watched him go. Then she shook her head and got on with her tasks.

Side-stepping renovation debris on the lawn, Edmund had to admit the work was coming along swiftly. A half-dozen or more local craftsmen and workers bustled around; glaziers and carpenters, apprentices, and young lads serving to fetch and carry seemed to be everywhere. He strode toward the side entrance nearest the place where the glass walls attached to the main house, and called, "Samuel—Samuel Gardener! Are you here?"

"Aye—young Symme. I'm inside, hold and I'll come around," a voice called in response.

"No—stay where you are, I'll come in and find you."

Edmund entered and was amazed at the transformation: timbers replaced, panes of new glass gleaming in the daylight, and the formerly rotted and broken plant beds scraped clean down to bare earth. Samuel was perched on a high stool, looking at a sketch of the floor plan stretched out on a makeshift potting bench, in discussion with one of the hired groundsmen. There were still some old work tables, plant stands and small mounds of rubble along one short wall.

"Come to inspect our progress, are ye?" Samuel asked. "What think ye?"

"Absolutely amazing—amazing! What you have done in just a few days—I could hardly have thought it possible! Very nice, Samuel." Edmund looked around in real pleasure. "However, I need a word with you. Let's find a place we can speak privately."

"We can stay right here, if you've no objection—Thomas, bring that other stool over for the gentleman." The other man quickly complied, and Samuel thanked him. "You should go out and speak to the other lads, you're clear on what's needed," Samuel told him. With a nod and tip of his cap, Thomas left them. "Now, what do you need, young Symme?"

"I would like you to think back to the time my grandfather was a young man and old Alistair Symme was master." Edmund leaned on the back of the stool, but did not sit. "Do you recall a man named Llewellyn doing business with them?"

"Hah—Yes, of course I remember Llewellyn. Ian Llewellyn—he was master of the stables, a very good horse man. Very good with all kinds of livestock, in truth, but the Symmes had horses. Old Alistair liked to fancy himself a breeder. Had some beautiful animals here at that time."

"I remember the horses. I learned to ride here. You say this Llewellyn worked for my family?" Edmund asked.

"Yes, for a number of years. Until he was sacked." Samuel's eyes were hard, "Good with horses, not with people, he was."

"What happened? Did he get into it with one of the Symmes?"

"Well, I was maybe twelve years old at the time. Llewellyn was ex-military—cavalry. Welsh, out of St. Asaph. His people were farmers and stockmen there since before the Commonwealth. Ran a good stable. All the grooms feared him but learned aplenty. He got on wi' my dad, as long as he kept to his horses."

"And . . . why was he sacked?" Edmund asked.

"Ah—I tell you, I was young then, but we all knew that Llewellyn fancied himself irresistible to the ladies and wouldn't take no for an answer. My da knocked him down once—and threatened to take the pruning shears to his bollocks—when he cast his eye on my cousin Lily and he laid a hand on her against her will. She wasn't harmed, but after the second housemaid had to be sent away to have her baby after being forced by him, John Symme took issue with him. He was sacked and sent packing. I think t'was the spring of '37 when he got the boot. Nobody missed him."

"Hmm, the spring, you say? Are you certain? Wasn't it more like September that year?" Edmund was trying to make sense of the discrepancy between the September payment made to Llewellyn and being sacked a few months earlier. "And are you sure he left in disgrace?"

Why pay a man if you have sacked him, he wondered.

"It was spring. He got sacked, I tell you, but he stayed in the area. They took him on over at the Burgess place—a good stockman can always find work in these parts. Sometime later he must have come into some inheritance. He bought the place, and did well by it. Good horses, good bulls. Not too long after, he married and settled down. Family is still there."

Edmund thought for a moment. "I'd like to speak with him—perhaps I shall ride over to this Burgess Farm and see him. "

"Beggin' your pardon, ye cannot speak with him. He's dead these five years. His family still runs the place; his daughter owns it now. Her husband is gone, but she has boys to do the work. You know them." Samuel pronounced.

"I know them? How do I know them?"

"Those charmers ye routed away from the pond when you first arrived—the older Llewellyn boy was with 'em. Made in his great-grandfather's image, pretty much." Samuel tsked and shook his head. "Their animals are thought highly of; the folk themselves, not so much. I wouldn't plan a visit to Burgess Farm any time soon, young Symme. But if ye must, take a stout horsewhip and reinforcements with ye."

14
Ancient Betrayal

Banks completed his business in the village and returned to Owls-wood as twilight was falling. Edmund awaited him, eager to share news on their respective lines of investigation. They had the pleasure of dining together that evening.

"Good God, old man, your appetite is back—I think this may only be the second time we've dined together since my arrival (not counting the Creviston debacle)—and I'm pleased Miss Remy's little herbal tonic has been salubrious," Banks commented. "No repast in the Library tonight? No assignation with your charming specter? I must admit, I feel honored to take her place as dinner companion."

"I have business in the Library later, Banks," Edmund replied. Looking thoughtful, he continued, "Please don't mention that to Remy, although you insist we need tell her of your inquiry to London. I would rather speak with La Belle privately, without my housekeeper's intrusion."

"Why? It seems she is vitally concerned with what the Lady can tell you, does it not? And as a relative, isn't she entitled?" Banks asked.

"Yes, surely, however . . . the two of them become so emotional! They weep and croon at each other, as women will do, and it gets in the way. I need facts. Information, not heartrending sobs and commiseration. Facts!" Edmund declared.

"May I be of some assistance, gentlemen?" Remy asked as she entered the dining room with after-dinner coffee service. "You are seeking facts, Mr. Symme, related to our mutual inquiries?"

"I am always seeking facts, Remy. It is who I am and what I do. However, right now I will ask Dr. Banks to share some information we—he—uncovered this afternoon after you left us," Edmund pronounced, giving Banks and then the floor a meaningful look.

"Yes, I neglected to tell you earlier when we spoke, as I was in a rush to use the telephone in the village. Please, set your tray down." Remy quickly complied, and Banks continued. "In reviewing those most fascinating accounting and company ledgers in the Symme archive," he rolled his eyes, "I found two curious items: one was mention of a large amount paid to a London specialist physician in '37. Since Edmund could recall no serious maladies in his forebears, I decided to make inquiries of my colleagues to see what we could learn about this specialist. I was able to reach two of my physician friends, but they were not themselves familiar with the name of Randolph Crandall. This is hardly unusual, as they hadn't yet been born at the time in question, but they agreed to ask around and consult with various records at the Medical school and licensing bureau. It may take a day or two, but they will send word to me here."

Remy replied, "The name means nothing to me. You feel this doctor might have treated my grandmother for something, something that may throw light on our queries?"

"It's possible, and the monies paid him were exorbitant enough to merit a closer look."

"You mentioned two curious items; what is the second?" Remy asked.

"Ah, I will leave that to Edmund, if I may," replied Banks.

He and Remy looked at Edmund expectantly.

"The other unusual matter discovered in the archives today was a large sum of money, and the purchase of a farm, afforded to one Ian Llewellyn in that same year. The man had apparently been Master of the Stables at Owlswood. He had been sacked for immoral behavior, yet a short time later he was paid a substantial sum," Edmund explained. "We as yet do not know why."

"Llewellyn! There is a family near here who owns a farm, and the name is Llewellyn. Might they be one and the same?" Remy asked.

"As you say. You know this family, I believe."

"I do, and you do as well, Mr. Symme. Not a week after your arrival at Owlswood, you sent one of them hastening away from the pond, after they had menaced me. I remember it well." Remy colored slightly as she spoke.

"Indeed. Unsavory individuals they were, to say the least." Edmund continued, "However, the fact still remains that one's great-grandfather was paid a goodly sum and given a farm by my grandfather John and great-grandfather Alistair Symme. Why? Why such largesse to a man they sacked? "

"Are you thinking blackmail of some kind?" Remy asked.

"I don't know what to think, although blackmail seems a likely guess. I'll need to speak with these Llewellyns. Who runs their farm and business dealings? Not that ruffian I tossed in the pond, I'll wager."

Edmund almost chuckled at the memory.

"The farm now belongs to Gwyned Llewellyn. She and her elder brother were the only two children; her brother inherited from their father and she inherited from him when he died. Kane, the one you met in the woods, and his brother, are her grandsons. They work the farm for her, under their father, Owen, who will inherit when she dies. They breed fine horses and bulls," Remy explained. "They are not known for their hospitality."

"So I understand from speaking with Samuel. But they will speak to me, or face the consequences." Edmund's face was set. "I'll make arrangements in the morning." He glanced at Banks. "Would you care to accompany me?"

"By the saints, I wouldn't miss it!" replied Banks. "Besides, someone may need medical attention."

After dinner, Banks retired with correspondence to complete and Edmund retreated to the Library, Regis at heel. Remy watched him go, and followed down the hall.

"Mr. Symme," she called as she approached, "do you expect to speak with La Belle Dame tonight?"

"I have no idea if she will make an appearance. She comes and goes as she pleases, and she certainly seemed irritated the last time we met—at me, Lord knows why. She may not wish to engage again so soon." Edmund hoped to discourage any further questions, especially a request from Remy to be included, and he spoke with some pique. "I plan to review another ledger or two over a brandy and then seek my bed."

Remy continued, smiling slightly. "I have no wish to intrude. However, if she should make herself available, she will surely have key knowledge of the London physician. She might provide useful facts, should you ask her. And," she looked at him appraisingly, "I would appreciate your giving her my respectful greetings. Will you do so?"

"Of course."

"Then I give you good night, and my thanks. Sir."

Remy turned back to the dining room and was gone.

Edmund watched her go. "Give you good night," he simpered, imitating her words. "Blasted women are so damned unpredictable! 'Give her my respectful greetings', good Christ! Messenger boy to a specter, am I now? On my housekeeper's errands of courtesy?" He turned to enter the Library. "Regis, come," he barked, directing the dog ahead of him.

He paced for a moment and came to stand in front of the fireplace. His mood was truculent. Regis settled at his feet and looked around, seeming expectant.

Edmund called to the air around him.

"Alright, Lady, present yourself. I have a number of questions for you!"

Nothing.

He took a deep breath. In a quieter voice he tried again.

"Belle Dame, I need your help. I have many questions in the matters you set me to investigate. And I . . . I respectfully request answers." He paused for a moment. "And I bring you greetings from your granddaughter. If you please . . . appear."

He paused for a moment.

"*Oh, la la la la*, you are in a bad mood, *Chérie*, yes?" The silvery voice made him smile in spite of himself. "What is all this about questions? What questions may I possibly answer for you, eh?" In a shimmer of light, the Lady appeared. "And *ma petite fille*, she is well? She has recovered from the *attaint* of her new-found ancestry?"

"She has recovered, Lady. She seems to have inherited some of your tenacity and strength." *And perhaps those mesmerizing green eyes, as well*, Edmund thought but did not say.

La Belle cocked her head and looked at him closely, the shadow of a smile upon her lips.

"*Bien, alors*, of what shall we speak?"

She settled herself in her favorite spot on the mantle, skirts rustling, and assumed an attentive mien.

The heady scent of gardenia wafted around Edmund, and he felt calm, his mood much improved. He took a moment to collect his thoughts, and then said, "We have ascertained that the year of your untimely death was 1837. Is that correct?"

The Lady nodded.

"In that same year, a London physician came to Owlswood. Did he come to examine and treat you?" Edmund continued. When the Lady remained silent, he continued, "Were you ill, Madam, and did you require specialized care?"

The air around La Belle began to quiver, and her face grew stony.

"The man was called to attend me. He did examine me."

"I see." Edmund paused. "Was it a difficult pregnancy that required this care? Was Randolph Crandall a specialist in women's maladies and gynecological ills?"

"*Pas du tout.*"

"No. Well, did he treat you for some other serious condition? Were you ill, Lady?"

Edmund started to feel slightly anxious, and began to pace again.

"I was *desespereé, le cœur brisé, abattu*. I was sick at heart."

Her face grew even harder, and she seemed to be remembering something distasteful.

"Well, I understand." Edmund tried to be suitably sympathetic, then began to probe. "You were heartsick, yes. However, was there also some major illness, some condition that caused your despair? And Dr. Crandall was called upon to assist you? He was a specialist of some renown, was he not?"

"He was a viper—a pig! *Cochon!*" Stony no longer, her face became a mask of anger, eyes blazing. She spat into the fire and it popped and sizzled, alarming Regis. The big dog got to his feet and went to her, whining softly. She looked down at him and her manner softened as she reached to stroke his huge head.

"My gallant friend, you comfort me, eh? Not like some of my own kind."

Regis whined again and then sat.

Edmund, frustrated, took her words as a barb at him.

"Lady, I must press you for answers if you wish me to clear this matter! Now attend me! I cannot accomplish a task I know nothing about!"

The Lady erupted in anger.

"So, you know nothing, then, about honor, nothing about justice, and law? Do you not make a name for yourself discovering the truth of men's actions, and persuading others to believe it? Why can you not do this for me? Or, perhaps you *will* not do it for me. Perhaps you belong back in London, among your own kind — men without souls!"

Her agitation seemed to make the entire room quiver and move, causing Edmund to feel slightly nauseous. He tried to soothe her.

"Lady, calm yourself! I only try to find out if you had some kind of terrible malady that drove you to suicide!"

"Suicide! You believe this?" She looked at him, aghast. "That I am the mad French woman, the girl who loved gardenia and then killed herself! That I am the one who abandoned my child and embraced death! Do you think this of me — you, who have shared my thoughts and seen into my heart. Do you think I am such a one?"

Edmund tried a straightforward approach once again.

"Lady, calmly. Please be clear. Are you saying you did not take your own life? There are those who . . ."

She cut him off in disgust.

"You swallow rumor whole and do not choke? Or do you think me such a one as noble Lucretia, to end my life in despair to make a point?"

"Lucretia?" Now Edmund was stymied. "Who in blazes is Lucretia? Do you speak of Lucretia Borgia? Did she do that?"

"*Bon Dieu*! No, Lucretia of ancient Rome, who was dishonored like a piece of meat! She brought about the founding of an empire because she took her own life to protect her family's honor, and to prove she spoke truth! She murdered herself because the only way her words carried weight was underlined with her own blood! After all, she was only a woman!" She paused for a moment. "Well, I could have been such a heroine, I suppose, but . . . my darling *enfant*, my *Aimee*, how could I leave her motherless by my own choice? How could I leave her alone in this world? Where is honor in that?"

She looked at him with entreaty in her eyes.

Edmund replied with unusual gentleness.

"No, of course you could not . . . quite right, Belle Dame. I *do* know your heart that well." He smiled sadly at her. "So, what did happen? What caused the despair of which you speak? And why was that doctor summoned?"

The moment of calm evaporated.

"*Sacre bleu*, must I spoon-feed you? I cannot tell you! You must reveal it for yourself! Can you not see—it is a curse you must break, a curse on your head and on your house and on your descendants forever—if you have any descendants, solitary man, last remaining Symme! I cannot do it for you." La Belle swirled away from the mantle and hovered above him. "You ask of maladies, of cause for despair—does forced sexual congress, betrayal and abandonment qualify as cause to the great man of law, last scion of the Symme family?"

Then she was gone.

*   *   *

Despite being mightily perplexed by his encounter with the Lady, when Edmund took himself to bed, he fell into a sound sleep almost immediately. Finally, on this night, after several eventful days, Owlswood manor house felt at rest. Even the walls seemed to slumber peacefully. All was calm.

Then a small light appeared in the darkness, a single hand-lamp on the second-floor landing. It began to descend, illuminating the path for the woman who carried it. Remy silently made her way downstairs, through the hall, pausing only a moment as the clock struck two. She hurriedly entered the Library, and caught her breath.

"*Grand-mére?*" she breathed. "*Grand-mère, s'il vous plait, apparaissez?*" She waited. "*Grand-mére?*" All was silent. Remy glanced at the stars through the tall windows, shivered, and spoke again. "*Belle Dame, un mot, s'il vous plait?*"

A shimmer of apricot-colored light caught her eye, and she turned toward the fireplace. Slowly, little by little, the glow intensified and La Belle Dame appeared.

"To what do I owe this honor, *Chérie*, that you come seeking me?" La Belle hovered above the mantle. "You have not sought me out for many a long year, *petite fille*. What do you wish?" she asked, with a wistful half-smile and sad eyes.

"*Grand-mére*—Lady—I am ashamed. I come to beg your pardon." Remy began. "I know now that I abandoned you—that Mother and I both abandoned you—so many years ago. I wish it had been different. My childishness drew me away from you." Her mouth was dry, her throat constricted. "I am so sorry."

Fleur smiled and shrugged slightly. "You were a child, *oui,* and

172

childishness is neither strange nor culpable in children. No pardon need be begged." She arranged herself more comfortably. "It is my dear Aimee that I fault for the estrangement. She was always so frightened, so reluctant. Such a product of this place. This village. These people. *Mon Dieu*—my own daughter decried me as a messenger from hell!" She sighed deeply, sadness emanating from her very core. "And I know what hell is, *bien sur*, I know hell."

Remy tried to explain. "*Mamán* was caught up in a web of ignorance and religious shame, as many village people are, and she was not very strong. When she saw you she . . . she was consumed with fear. I think mostly for my sake." She paused. "But she was beautiful, as you are beautiful, and loving. She married a French man—did you know that?—and we spoke French at home. She knew the lullabies you sang to me, and she sang them, too. Were she here, she would also beg your pardon. She never knew you, not even your name! Nor do I."

A moment's pause hung in the air. "Shall we then introduce ourselves, *Chérie? Je suis Fleur Marie Victoria DuPlessis, a votre service.*" A slight sparkle lit her eyes as she gracefully inclined her head. "*Et toi?*"

"I am Flora Jeanne Remy. *Enchantée.*" Remy replied, and bowed slightly. "And I am so pleased to meet you." A solitary tear rolled down her cheek. "So honored to meet you. And I am your namesake. How can that be?"

"Ah, your *mamán* was not completely impervious to me," Fleur chuckled, "she was not in complete control of her dreams, eh? Who of us are?" When Remy's eyes widened, she continued, "You have had interesting dreams from me, yes, from time to time? *Bien*, your *mamán* would not permit my visage to grace her sleep, but my thoughts . . ."

"And you brought my name to her in her dreams?"

"*Mais, oui*! And she took it as her own idea, to my great pleasure, and I believe, the pleasure of your father. However, she pronounced it in the British way," her lips formed a slight pout, "She called you Flora. *Domage, ma fleur, ma petite fille.*" She smiled slightly and continued, "But you have never liked that name, Flora, eh? You prefer Jeanne, do you not?"

Remy responded sheepishly. "That is true, I have never felt much like a flower, or a fragile, pretty thing—so I use my middle name. With all respect, it seems to fit me better." She paused, slightly embarrassed, and then continued. "Would you consider..." she hesitated but a moment, "...telling me about yourself? Your life, your family?" The words tumbled from her mouth. "Because you see, I have always felt apart from my people here. There is some distance, some chasm between my thoughts and desires and the life I have lived among them." She looked at the Lady earnestly. "Please don't think they lacked love or care for us. They never led either of us to think we were not their own. It's just . . . we were so different from them. So different." She looked at the Lady wistfully. "Will you not tell me about yourself?"

"Ah . . . to tell you, perhaps no. Words have their limits. But I will show you."

"Show me? How can you possibly . . ."

Remy was silenced mid-sentence.

"Enough! *Tête-toi! Ferme la bouche, et les yeux!*" The Lady commanded, and gestured, "Sit there!"

Remy seated herself in the wing-back leather chair, the one Edmund used so frequently, closed both her mouth and her eyes, and waited.

"*Enfin, bien.*" Fleur glided closer and placed her hand on Remy's brow, to smooth an errant lock of hair back into place. "We begin. Softly, now, breathe slowly and clear your mind."

She caressed Remy's brow lightly.

Remy complied and settled into a feeling of calm, warmth, and the sensation of drifting off to sleep. Then, all at once her senses were brought to alert, as she felt herself moving with the wind. She looked around in a place of riotous colors and odors—she could smell the sea, and a series of floral scents so strong they almost made her swoon. She saw bright red flowers, burning oranges, yellows that rivaled the dawn all framed against lush leaves in a hundred hues of green and the sky of crystal-clear blue. She felt wind rush past her face and against her body, whipping her hair all around.

She was on a horse, a beautiful white animal, cantering through what must be a jungle. She looked around and saw a young boy waving to her, and blew him a kiss. She continued to ride, now along a sea cliff with crashing white waves against ragged rocks below her, water stretching out blue and green as far as her eye could see. Soon, a house came into view, surrounded by hedges of white

174

gardenia, their fragrance borne to her on the breeze. A man came out onto the front portico; he was distinguished and handsome, with a graying mustache and silvering hair, and he laughed with joy as he opened his arms and waited for her.

"Papa!" she cried, as the horse slowed to a stop and he came to help her dismount. "Papa," she said again as he wrapped her in his arms and said, "*Ma Fleur, ma belle, ma chere fille!*" She felt such happiness she thought her heart would burst. "*Ou est ton frère?* Where is Armand?" the man asked, and then the boy who had waved at her came running up the path. "Ah, *en famille, eh?*" the man cried as he wrapped an arm around the boy. "And now, lunch you ruffian children—come inside!"

The scene faded away, and another came. Remy now gazed with excitement at *L'Arc de Triomphe* looming above her! A kaleidoscope of images and experiences washed over her: drinking coffee in the petit café, watching elegant ladies promenade with their chevaliers; walking the halls of the Louvre, surrounded by paintings of the Masters, coming face-to-face with *La Joconde*. The streets of Paris, bustling, exciting, the people so elegant, the shops so delightful. She smiled as she sat for her portrait, not by a painter of canvas, but by a man who sketched with charcoal who produced her image in little time.

Then Papa's face, stern and serious, frowning in concern as she said, "*Non*, Papa, I do not wish to leave—why may I not stay here? Take Armand back to Martinique with you, he is homesick, I am not! You will return when your business is complete—if I stay, I can go to the libraries, I can learn so many things! I wish to learn of all the exciting new things coming to pass, I wish to . . ." Remy felt her foot stamp impatiently. "*Non*, Papa, please listen . . ."

Then she was weeping, her heart athrob with pain. Through her tears she saw another face, a portrait from the Symme family gallery come to life. "My poor child, I know you must be in great pain for the loss of your father and brother." Alistair Symme, cold sympathy on his features, continued. "But as my ward you will be well cared for. Studies? What is there for a woman to study, a waste to spend time and money on that kind of nonsense. No more now, we will leave that discussion for another time, perhaps when you are less distraught." The cold grey eyes bored into hers. "London may be too stimulating for you, my dear. We leave for my country house in two days. Be ready." And then the young face of John Symme, concern in his eyes and a smile on his lips, saying, "My darling Fleur, you will like Owlswood—there is a wonderful library there, you can continue with your philosophy reading! And we will be together and I will look after you, I promise with all my heart!" He took her hand and kissed it. "I promise you will be happy!"

Then darkness. Fear, anger.

"Fleur, you must understand—he forbids the marriage! Then what shall we do?" The same John Symme looked haggard and pale. "He will disown me. What can we do?" Then she was running, through the night, screaming to heaven, *"Ayez pitie de moi! Ayez pitie, mon dieu!"* Running, running, a knife in her hand, running . . .!

"Enough." The Lady removed her hand from Remy's face and backed away. "Perhaps too much. *Chérie*, do you come to know me any better now?"

Remy was shaken and confused. She caught her breath in great sobs, gradually calming and settling back into the present. She had no idea how much time had passed, several minutes or several hours.

"My God!" she breathed. "So much happiness, and then so much loss. Your family, gone. Your plans . . . you had a mind to follow a profession, to study the classics, to learn portraiture. I, too, crave my own path, in that we are alike. Everyone, especially men, block my way."

"Ah, men—they are a problem, yes," Fleur commented sadly. She paused for a long moment. "But you have the chance to do it. You are strong, and alive! You must follow your heart, *Chérie*, but will it not somehow include a man?"

"Never, *Grand-mére*, never in this life!" Remy muttered. "Times have changed since you . . . things have changed."

"Ah, not so much. A woman still needs a man as protector, even today, *non*?"

"I don't want a man, protector or otherwise! That path is not for me!" Remy countered.

"I did not say 'want', *Chérie. Ecoutez plus bien.*"

"No, *Grand-mére*—how can you say that?" Remy was becoming angry. "You had to abandon your dream because of those faithless men!"

"Abandon? Abandon my dream? *Non*, I did not abandon it, it

was stolen from me!" Fleur's eyes flashed dangerously. "First my father and brother, then my plans to become an artist, then my marriage, my child, and my very life. All stolen!" She spoke in a hoarse whisper. "They must pay now. It must be brought to light." She tightened her fists. "The Symme blood must avenge me, and soon! There is only one left." After a silent moment, she looked out the window. "Dawn is beginning to light the sky. It is enough for now, *petite*, I must leave you before the sun rises. We shall speak again, another time."

"Why do you leave with the sun? Is it . . . required?"

"In daylight, the living have no time for the dead. We whisper amid the business of the world but are not heard. Only when the quiet of darkness comes, when the world slows and opens its portals to another consciousness, may we intrude upon the pathways of those alive, and be noticed," the Lady explained. "It is the way of things."

Remy paused. "You spoke with Edmund Symme tonight as well, I believe. Did he give you my regards?" she asked, with curiosity.

"Ah yes, he gave me your greetings, and seemed much impressed with your strength of character." La Belle smiled, now slightly mischievously. "He also mentioned green eyes."

Remy ignored the compliment. "Well, I dislike the man but cannot fault his integrity," she replied. "I must credit him with keeping his word." She continued earnestly, "He will honor his word to you, have no fear, and is moving with great intention toward clearing your name. And I will do all I can to help him."

"Ah, *petite*, but this is no task for you!" The Lady became serious again. "This shame falls on the head of the Symme—and it is dangerous, this path he treads. You must not put yourself in danger. You owe me nothing!"

"But *Grand-mére*, you are my blood. You are my family!" Remy was passionate. "I will work to clear your name; you cannot tell me no!"

The Lady was silent. "What does the Symme propose to do next, do you know?"

"He and Kit will pay a call to Burgess Farm; there is some record of an unusual act of largesse from the Symme forebears to the family there, and they will investigate. Kit has also made inquiries regarding the physician, Crandall, and will have information soon."

Remy wanted the Lady to know how seriously they were working on her behalf.

"And who is this 'Kit' of whom you speak?"

"Doctor Christopher Banks, a good friend to Mr. Symme. He is a guest here. And a fine gentleman, from what I see." Remy continued, a smile in her voice. "He is very disheartened that you do not include him in your company. He would be honored to meet you."

"*Bien*, we will see. But you like him, this Kit, much more than the Symme, yes?"

"Much more!" Remy exclaimed. "He is true, charming and most trustworthy."

"Hmm—well perhaps I must meet this Kit." The Lady looked at Remy thoughtfully. "You say they will visit Burgess Farm. You will not go with them, *non*?"

"I have no plan to go, unless you would have me join them." Remy replied.

"*Non*! It is the nest of the Llewellyn spawn. Stay away from them—do you mark me?" The Lady's face was cold as ice. "Stay away from them! "

Remy was taken aback at the change in the Lady, and a bit frightened as well. "But why? They have little to commend them, a very bad reputation—but . . ."

"Mark me!" The Lady's eyes blazed. "If you hear no other of my words, hear these and mark them well!"

"As you wish, *Grand-mère*." Remy acquiesced, frowning in confusion.

"Good." Her eyes softened as she spoke, "And now *adieu*—I will look for you again. I will send my love to protect you, such as it may, wherever you are. Be well. Be happy. Be careful."

15
Llewellyns

By midmorning, Edmund, Banks and one other were mounted and on their way toward Burgess Farm. MacCready was skeptical toward their errand, but nonetheless loaned them two magnificent hunters from his stable.

"They'll recognize these beauties; they sold them to me not two years ago. But information, nay, you'll probably get none. Short fuses, they have, and primed for taking offense. Mind now, watch your back, and don't let the horses come home riderless," he cautioned with a laugh. He insisted on sending one of his grooms along with them, a barrel-chested man with a soothing voice, large hands, and no-nonsense manner. "They know Clive, so he will be a bit of surety—at least for my horses," he added. "And he's a good man in a fight, should anything go awry."

"By God, who are these people—and what in bloody hell do you intend to say to them?" Banks looked at Edmund askance as they trotted along. "Is this not a fool's errand?"

"Well, two more worthy fools than we are not to be found hereabouts, I'll grant you," he replied wryly. "I intend to ask them about the man who formerly headed the family—Ian Llewellyn—and his ties to Owlswood and the Symmes."

"Should we have brought firearms, d'you think?" Banks asked. "And my medical bag?"

He chuckled somewhat nervously, Edmund thought.

"Perhaps. We'll soon know." Edmund smiled ruefully. "Come now, Banks, you were always the optimistic one regarding matters of human nature—you shall surely charm them into cooperating, will you not?"

"You have a plan, perchance, not leaving all to my charm?" Banks queried.

"I plan on approaching them as a potential customer. It is common knowledge around here that I've returned to Owlswood, and having a good mount or two would not be amiss if I planned to stay. Which I do not," Edmund emphasized. "But the family Llewellyn doesn't know that. Then we can hopefully steer the conversation to the history of their business, etc. and learn how their dicey forebear came to have it."

"And we think that will work, do we?" Banks looked dubious. "Clive should be informed."

"Right. Give him a call up here, will you?" Edmund replied.

Banks signaled to the groom to join them. He trotted up abreast with them and Edmund gave him the word on what was to pass at the farm. He tipped his cap and nodded in understanding.

"Aye, Guv'nor. Let me know if I need do something."

*　*　*

The farm was a beautiful place of rolling hillocks and well-kept buildings. Large fenced areas held various kinds of livestock: bulls and stallions individually penned, mares in foal and some with newborns held in larger communal areas. Further up the hillside were pens with cows and calves. Several large dogs of indeterminate breed ran to greet them, careful not to alarm the horses but sounding the alert to their masters.

Within a moment, a workman came out of the main barn, brushing hay from his clothing, and walked over to the visitors.

"'Morning, gents. How may I help you?" Catching sight of a familiar face, he continued, "Ay, Clive, how do you?"

A small boy ran out to join them as they dismounted, taking the reins from Edmund and Banks and leaving Clive to hold his own.

"'Morning, Brax, I do well, thanks," Clive extended his hand, and the two men shook. "This here is Mr. Symme, from over at Owlswood, and his guest Dr. Banks. Come to look at some horse-flesh."

Brax nodded slightly and touched his temple in a salute.

"Gentlemen, you'll wish to speak to the owner, then. I'll get him."

He turned and walked out of sight behind the main barn, toward the forge and other outbuildings. The boy followed, with all three horses now, to water them at the nearby trough. Clive strolled over to keep the boy and horses company.

Edmund and Banks looked around admiringly.

"Beautiful spot, and these animals are very fine, indeed," Banks commented. "So far, so good." They both turned attention to the old but beautifully maintained two-story main house, freshly painted. Flowers bloomed in window boxes and hanging baskets. "Looks quite prosperous, wouldn't you say?"

"Indeed. And tranquil. Ah, our host approacheth," Edmund commented, nodding toward the man striding across the lawn toward them. He was a large man of around fifty years of age, well-muscled and clean-shaven, dressed in work clothes of good material and fit, with a leather apron tied at his waist. As he walked, he took it off and hung it on a fencepost, then continued toward them and held out his hand.

"I'm Owen Llewellyn, you're looking for me?"

Edmund took his hand. "I believe we are. I'm Edmund Symme." They shook hands. "And this is my friend, Dr. Christopher Banks." Banks and Llewellyn shook hands as well. "You are the owner of this most impressive place, I take it?"

"You might say. My mother owns the spread, but I run it for her and someday it'll come to me and my sons. Looking for a horse or two, are you?"

"I very well may be. I have recently come back to my family's estate, Owlswood, after a long time away. My plans are yet uncertain, but I remember many fine rides through this country from my youth," Edmund explained. "My neighbor, MacCready, has nothing but praise for your animals."

"Aye, he got himself two beauties, maybe eighteen months ago—looks like the ones you rode here. Tell me," Llewellyn continued, "would you be looking for a basic mount or a hunter—maybe fifteen hands, for yourself—or do you have in mind hitching the beast to a rig—dogtrap or curricle? What have you in mind?"

Since Edmund had nothing in mind, he was caught off-guard by the question, but was able to recover enough to maintain credible discussion for several minutes. He agreed with Llewellyn that he would set aside a day within the next week or so to view, and then ride, several horses of Llewellyn's choosing.

"I'm very pleased we can do business, Llewellyn, as there is a long-standing association between our families." Edmund smiled.

"Oh? Why do you say that?" Llewellyn's face remained impassive, but his manner quickly became guarded. "What association is this?"

Keeping his tone light and friendly, Edmund replied, "Well, you know, your grandfather used to work for my family out at Owlswood—for my great-grandfather in fact. He was stablemaster there for many years, until some Symme money set him up here. Isn't that right?"

"My grandfather has been dead some years now. I don't know that he ever mentioned employ with the Symmes. You seem to be mistaken."

His voice remained level, but his eyes narrowed.

"Really! Well, how could that be?" Edmund laughed. "I'm sure I understood correctly —that he worked at Owlswood for many years and that they must have thought most highly of him, to stake him in this property! Very highly indeed. Right Banks?"

"That's what the record books say, certainly," Banks replied, smiling widely.

"Well, the records are wrong. I don't know what you're up to, but we owe the Symmes nothing—not this place, and not this business." His voice was raised now. "And you may take your custom elsewhere, for all I care."

Banks noticed two young men coming toward them from one of the outbuildings to investigate, having heard their father's raised voice.

"Company coming," he said softly to Edmund.

"Anything amiss here, Father?" The larger of the two stood beside Llewellyn, looked at Edmund with disdain, and said, "No dog this time?"

"We meet again—no women or children to abuse this time?" Edmund met the young man's glare coolly with his own.

"Oh, bloody hell," Banks muttered under his breath.

"What, Kane, you know this gentleman?" Owen Llewellyn asked. "What's this about women and children?"

He cast an annoyed glance at his son.

"Oh, nothing, Father, I was just renewing my acquaintance with an old friend when this . . . gentleman . . . came upon us and got the wrong notion." He grinned malevolently. "That's all."

The elder Llewellyn turned to his son.

"What friend? When was this?" he demanded.

"Jeannie Remy, some time after she returned." He looked at Edmund and sneered, "I was asking her what she had learned there, in London—you never can tell what new skills a woman like that might pick up in a big city, and I was interested in her progress."

"Shut your mouth," growled Llewellyn. "Where's your sense, boy!"

"Your son here was trespassing on my property, threatening a member of my household staff, and terrorizing a child and her pet," Edmund shot back. "It seemed he needed a lesson in courtesy, so I gave him one." He paused and looked Kane up and down. "Doesn't seem to have taken."

"And are you ready to teach me more, you . . ." Kane's fists curled ready at his sides. Banks slowly reached into his jacket pocket, eyes fixed on the second young man who was moving closer to them.

"I said shut it!" barked his father, then turned to Edmund. "These gentlemen were just taking their leave, as it is clear we won't be doing any further business. Isn't that right, Mr. Symme?"

Before Edmund could answer, Banks took charge.

"Ah, yes, we are indeed just leaving, are we not?" and grabbed Edmund's arm, pulling him backward as Clive walked briskly between the two factions, leading their mounts. "What a pleasure it has been."

He tipped his hat, made certain Edmund was in the saddle, then swung up into his own seat. Clive waited a moment, until Edmund and Banks had started back toward the road, then mounted and took his leave of the Llewellyns.

Looking over his shoulder, Banks could see a figure on the outer stairway of the main house watching them leave, a stout old woman, plainly but elegantly dressed in some dark fabric, a blotch on the whitewash of the house. He urged his horse into a slow canter and caught up with Edmund.

"Well, that went swimmingly, did it not?" he commented. "Very touchy, they were, about association with your family." He paused. "And I was somewhat concerned by that second fellow—did you see him moving up?" When Edmund just grunted, Banks continued, "All in all, I'm pleased I was not required to enlist the aid of my small friend here."

They slowed to a walk and he opened his palm, showing a small pistol with a walnut grip.

"By God, you did bring a firearm! What the hell is that little thing?" Edmund exclaimed.

"It's called a Little All Right, made in America, you know." When Edmund looked at the weapon dubiously, Banks continued, "My cousin brought it to me as a gift after his time in Boston. Very handy, don't you think?"

"And you believe that thing would be protection, do you?" Edmund asked wryly. He leaned over his saddle to the pannier, unbuckled it, and drew from it a small but impressive gun. "Webley Bulldog, .32 caliber. This would be protection."

"You bastard, Edmund, you might have said." Banks was nonplussed. "And what good would have that done; it was in your saddlebag!" He grumbled. "I was worried for us."

"Ah, ye of little faith. Let's get on back."

Edmund urged his horse and was off to Owlswood.

*　　*　　*

"We're breeding fine livestock, but fools instead of men now, are we Owen?" the woman spat, with a cold and angry stare. She eyed her son, and grandsons, with scorn. "What was all that about?"

"Mother, it was nothing. The man wanted to purchase some horses, so he said, but . . ."

"But what? Your idiot boy queered the whole thing—and more!" The old woman turned her gaze to the grandson standing before her. "And what is this about the Remy woman? Did you accost her?"

"T'was naught, Grandmother, just . . . I just spoke with her. Nothing happened." He spoke in a sulk, his eyes shifty. His younger brother said nothing.

"But if this Symme man had not come along, then what? Have I not told you to leave her be?" The woman's eyes blazed. "Do you want to be the ruin of this family, you fool?"

Kane replied angrily, "I don't understand why you fear her so!

184

She is nothing—a stupid woman, full of herself, she went off to do a man's job and then . . . now she's back and working in the Owls-wood house! Why should she be treated with concern?"

The old woman looked at her son. "So, have you not made it plain to these whelps of yours why they'd best tread lightly? Have I not made things clear, Owen Lewellen?"

"It is clear to me, Mother, very clear."

"Well, it's not clear to me! Why do I tread on ice with this up-start woman who thinks she is better than everyone else?" Kane cried.

"Because, you fool, she can take this farm, and put you into the gutter before her."

Gwyned spoke softly, but with menace in her voice.

16
Invitation to Meet

Back at Owlswood, after returning the horses and bidding Clive farewell, Edmund puzzled over what could be gleaned from their visit.

"Why did that Owen become so piqued about his grandfather's time at Owlswood?" Edmund asked Banks. "Seems a harmless enough fact, does it not?"

"Indeed, he seemed to infer some insult from your query." Banks swung his walking stick at a bush. "He's none too pleased with his sons either, is he?"

Edmund snorted. "Ruffians and ne'er do wells, what's to be pleased with? No, Owen got the brains in the family, at least some of them. Did you see that woman who came out of the house?" he asked.

"I did. Must be the grandmother, don't you think?" Banks replied.

"I do. And I think it is she we should have been talking to," Edmund mused. "I think she is the brains in the family, and the reason they are so prosperous. And she may know about her father's dealings."

"Another visit?" Banks asked, not relishing the thought. "Blimey."

He swatted another hapless shrub.

"Perhaps—but I wish we knew how all this might tie into La Belle's demise. Or even if it does tie in."

Edmund shook his head.

"What to do next?"

"Well, next for me is to get packed—remember that I leave for London tomorrow," Banks stated, far more cheerily than Edmund appreciated. Seeing his dour expression, Banks went on, "Now don't tell me you forgot—I need to present a paper at the Institute day after tomorrow, as I informed you weeks ago!" Noting Edmund's scowl, he exclaimed, "By St. Anne's holy knickers, I've been at Owlswood for almost a month, and I need to get back to my responsibilities! Some of us, at least, are not gentlemen of complete leisure."

"Damn it, Banks, I need your help here!" Edmund snapped. And then continued, more amenably, "Shall you return?"

Looking at his friend's anxious expression, Banks smiled slightly.

"I shall. After presenting the paper—and the attendant conference *fal-de-rol*—I need to see several patients. I also intend to pursue information about this elusive Dr. Crandall, so . . . perhaps a week before I return." A twinkle appeared in his eye. "Will you miss me, darling?" he grinned.

"Like a sore tooth," Edmund muttered, then grinned back.

*   *   *

"Don't be daft, Grandmother, that uppity Remy woman just needs a lesson in . . ."

"Enough." One word, spoken low and fast by his grandmother, brought an uneasy silence to Kane. "Hear me, and hear me well. I will not lose what I have poured my lifeblood into because of your stupidity, or anyone else's. Understood?" Her eyes narrowed as she looked at the three men. "Does it not strike you strange that the famous Barrister Symme came back to Owlswood after all these years, and somehow found his way to our farm? "

"He wants good horseflesh—we have the best—and he has money to buy. What's strange about it?" Kane grumbled.

The old woman looked at him in disgust.

"Owen, what think you?"

Her son took a moment before he spoke.

"She knows. She told him."

"Aye." The old woman nodded. "She's the housekeeper now, since her ma passed on. I was certain Aimee knew nothing but . . . who can tell? They spent many long days together at the end, talking . . ." Her expression darkened. "Maybe the girl wants her due. And for all we know, she has the paper."

"Grandmother, what is all this—why fret about . . ." This time, the woman silenced him with a look.

"Get away with you, you have work to do—or will the farm run itself? I must think—leave, all of you. But Owen—brandy, and quickly."

187

All three men left the room, Owen leaving a large glass of tawny liquor on the table beside the rocker. He looked at his mother, nodded curtly, and was gone.

Gwyned Llewellyn sat in her rocking chair, brandy in hand. She mused, softly, "What is their game, by God, what is next?"

*   *   *

The next morning, Banks strolled into the kitchen just as Cook was heading out to speak to the dairyman, and bid her a cheery "Goodbye, most excellent woman, and I'll be dreaming of your scones until my return!"

She flushed with pleasure as she hurried out the back door, calling, "Don't tarry and miss your train, Dr. Banks, and don't forget the parcel I made for you!"

"How could I forget it?"

He bowed slightly and blew her a kiss.

Remy began to laugh.

"Cook is one of your greatest admirers, Dr. Banks, and she has packed you enough scones here to last all the way to China!" She picked up the carefully wrapped bundle and presented it. Then, reaching into the pocket of her apron, she handed him a thick letter. "And thank you so much for taking this—please drop it in any postbox when you arrive in London."

Banks took the letter and read the address: Sophia Jex-Blake.

"Ah," he laughed, "a missive to the elder she-dragon! You are still in contact, then?"

He glanced at the letter briefly and carefully placed it in his breast pocket.

"Indeed, she is a good friend to me as always. I appreciate her calm and experienced advice, even from afar." Remy smiled. "I must admit, I am sorry to see you go away, and very glad your return will be soon. I need not tell you I wish you Godspeed and great success at the Institute. I only wish I could hear your paper with the rest of them!"

"Thank you, and I have little doubt I shall see you one day in the auditorium, along with your sister physicians, shoulder to shoulder with 'the rest of them.' And have no fear of your post going astray." He looked at her fondly. "I, too, look forward to my return to Owlswood next week." Searching her face he continued.

"Jeanne, is there something amiss with you? You are pale and have seemed . . . distracted since our return from the Llewellyn place yesterday. Nothing happened there that should cause you concern, as we have already said." He smiled ruefully. "The Llewellyns were . . . strange and difficult, as promised."

"Yes, I understand that, and I'm sorry your time there was not more profitable." She paused just a moment. "It's just—I feel so off-balance, Kit. My dreams now are so vivid, so real, I can hardly tell them from events in waking life. And even when I am awake, I am swept up in feeling and seeing things that *she* felt! It is hard for me sometimes to know what it is I feel, and what I am feeling through her. It worries me. I seem not to be entirely . . . myself, almost like I am two persons in one body sometimes."

Banks took her hands in his.

"All this has been a great deal to experience and understand in a very short time. My head is reeling, and I am but on the periphery of things! It may be wise to leave the house for a day or two, go back to the village and rest, be with people you know." He looked at her earnestly. "Dealing with Owlswood, and Edmund, is not easy. It is a great strain on you, on top of your newly found spectral grandmother and her accompanying mysteries."

"Oh, Owlswood is like an old friend to me, and Mr. Symme seems to be settling down a bit." She looked at him doubtfully, and they both began to chuckle. "Well, at least he seems somewhat more human these days!"

The chuckles turned into laughs.

"Yes, he likes a good problem to keep him occupied. It calms his mind," Banks told her, "but you, Jeanne Remy, must take care of yourself. You are human, as well."

"I heed your advice. One thing you should know—the Lady hates Llewellyn. No, more she feels extreme revulsion toward him. There must be something to uncover there, perhaps I can . . ."

"That is not a wise idea," Banks replied. "Best leave that lot to Edmund and me. We will pursue this matter and make headway soon. I can assure you that your reformed employer is most serious about solving the mysteries around the Lady, and Owlswood." He dropped her hands. "And I am serious as well—rest! I expect to see you rosy-cheeked and hearty upon my return. Take care," he admonished.

"Yes, sir, I will take care. You as well," Remy smiled.

Banks picked up his valise and medical bag, and headed to the village where his ride to the train station awaited. Remy gathered her pencil and paper, preparing to finalize the coming week of menus as soon as Cook finished lecturing the poor farm boy about forgetting her extra pint of cream yesterday (almost jeopardizing the special batch of scones for Dr. Banks). Remy was adding water to a fresh pot of tea when Samuel came through the kitchen doorway.

"Jeannie, have a moment for me?" he asked.

"Always, of course," she told him with a smile, "and your timing could not be better. Sit and have a cup with me."

"Ah, ye don't have to ask twice, girl," he replied, "and I'm glad to see the Queen of Pots 'n Pans is busy elsewhere." He sat at the big table. "I have something private for ye."

Remy brought cups, milk jug and the cozied teapot to the table and sat with him. "What might that be?"

"A note was delivered to me by one of the Llewellyn boys, and it's for you."

"Kane brought a note for me?" Her eyes were wide with surprise. "You're joking!"

"Naw, not Kane, t'other one—the young Bran came to see me. I asked him why not deliver it direct to you—and he said he didn't like to come right up to the house. Thought maybe Mr. Symme would be around. Here—take it." He handed her a folded piece of paper. "I asked him what it was about, but he said he would never read it or his granny would kick his backside all the way to Thornton Dale." He took a sip of tea. "So, it must be from the dowager stallion-gelder herself."

Remy took the note and unfolded it. Her brow furrowed as she read.

"Well—what does it say, for the love of heaven?" Samuel prodded her.

"It says, 'I must speak with you. I will walk to town and stop at the spring just past the north signpost at noon tomorrow. Gwyned Llewellyn.' She wants me to meet her, apparently."

"Ha, and in a place not too likely to have prying eyes at that time of day," Samuel commented. "I don't like it. Why would she talk to you, and about what?"

190

He sipped his tea again.

"Miserable old harridan biddy," he muttered.

"Samuel, where is your Christian charity?" Remy asked in mock sternness. "She is an interesting person, though off-putting certainly. It always impressed me that she refused to give up the Llewellyn surname when she married, and kept it for her son. She's a proud woman, and proud of her heritage."

"Did she even marry, then?" mused Samuel. "I never knew the father of the boys." He continued, "Listen here, I don't like it. Don't go, or take someone with you—the note doesn't say to come alone. I'll go with ye."

"Hmm. Let me think on this. But thank you for your gallant offer, I will decide and let you know."

"And another matter that might interest ye: the lads found something in the potting area of the glasshouse. A big metal box, with a righteous large padlock on it."

"What kind of box? Did you open it?" Remembering what she had seen in her recent dream, blood drained from Remy's face and her entire body tingled with a chill.

17
Gwyned and Remy

Remy felt off-balance and heady as she accompanied Samuel to see Edmund. Could the box she had seen so clearly in her dreams have now appeared in reality? They found Edmund in his study deep in thought, papers spread out on the desk, Regis resting beside his chair.

"Sorry to disturb, but there's a matter in the glasshouse that needs your attention, Mr. Symme," Samuel began.

Frowning, Edmund called his thoughts back from whatever weighty matter they had been considering, and replied, "What is it?"

After explaining, Samuel summed it up, "So, ye see Mr. Symme, the chest is somewhat walled-up inside a bit of a recess—brick and mortar, 'tis—and the boys will need to chip away a fair amount to retrieve it. I didna' want to cause any further damage without your approval. Although," he scratched his chin as he continued, "'tis a might bit strange that the smallish edifice, like, is in perfect condition, since the rest of the place was in a state of rubble. Almost like…it was protected, or some such." He shook his head slightly and shrugged. "We found it only after some rotted timbers and dried brush had been cleared."

"And this 'edifice' as you call it, is against the wall of the house near the former gardenia bed?" Samuel nodded and Edmund continued, "I cannot take time to go see for myself right now, but I trust your judgment in the matter. Will they need to knock it down completely?"

"Not at all, they can just chip careful around the opening until the box may be taken out. The damage will be as small as will serve," Samuel assured him.

"Very well, and please, tell the men to destroy as little of the structure as possible. I would like to examine it at another time." Edmund thought for a moment. "Can the work begin this afternoon? How long will it take?"

"Aye, we'll start today and use a light touch. Sometime tomorrow, you'll be opening the chest, at your convenience." Samuel bowed his head slightly. "Thank 'ee, Mr. Symme. I'll be off now." He looked at Remy. "Coming, Jeannie?"

"I need another moment of Mr. Symme's time, Samuel. I will see you later," she replied.

"Don't forget that other matter, you'll let me know, yes?" Samuel pressed her.

"I will. Thank you." As he left the room, Remy turned to Edmund. "Something of interest has happened."

"Indeed. It seems I can scarcely draw breath around here without something of interest happening," Edmund muttered. He set down his pen and crossed his arms on his chest. "Well, shall you enlighten me, Remy? Please, do you care to sit down?"

He gestured to a chair near the desk.

"Thank you. " She sat. "There are in truth two matters of interest. First, I have seen this recently discovered chest, I believe, in one of my . . . encounters with my Grandmother's memories. In one of my dreams. When it is freed from its alcove, I believe it will be a leather-covered smallish metal foot-locker—a small hope chest, if you like—with intricate golden filigree hinges, and painted with vines and flowers. There are handles on either side." She caught her breath. "I have seen it. I believe it belonged to Fleur at one time."

"Do you? Have you been to the glasshouse to view it?"

"Not yet. I have just learned of it. Samuel came to see me on another matter of interest—a note from Gwyned Llewellyn." She reached into the pocket of her dress and offered the note. "Would you care to read it?"

Edmund took it and read. "Well, what prompts this? A reaction to our recent visit, no doubt." He looked at the note thoughtfully. "This is not a safe thing for you to do. If you choose to meet her, you must have an escort."

"So I've been told," she stated with a wry smile, "however I doubt anything would come of our conversation were I to bring a companion. Besides," she continued with some resolution, "I am not a child and may take care of myself."

"Ah, indeed—and if her charming entourage of grandsons are with her? I seem to recall a bit of a problem once, even though you may take care of yourself." He looked at her appraisingly. "Remy, do not let your pride lead you into a foolish action. You must be accompanied. "

"Samuel has offered—but I think no use will come of the meeting with a witness present. This must be obvious to you, Mr. Symme!" She was becoming annoyed.

"You have a point there," he allowed. "However, I believe I have a solution. But first, tell me why you are so certain this newly discovered chest belonged to La Belle. You say you've 'seen' it?"

"Yes, I have seen it." Remy took a moment. "You, of all people, should know what happens when these . . . dreams, or encounters . . . come over me. I am not truly myself. Or, rather, I am not only myself, but also living the thoughts and feelings of another—and we now know they are the memories of La Belle Fleur." She looked away briefly, then again met his gaze. "Since revealing she is my own blood, these dreams have become even more vivid, and sometimes I think I cannot tell where La Belle leaves off and I begin. But even before that, I saw the chest—saw it in her bedroom, more than once. It is hers."

"I see." Edmund found himself caught up in the emotion of her words, then shook it off. "And you think there is some significance to the chest, some reason it now appears? What might it contain?"

"How can anyone know? But as to significance—do you not wonder why it should now come to light? Why it should have been hidden away in an obscure, abandoned part of Owlswood? There must be something of value to our purpose within it!" Remy spoke earnestly and placed her hand on Edmund's desk.

"Well, then, tomorrow you may have the opportunity to witness its contents revealed, if all goes as planned. Tomorrow we may know more."

They were both silent for a moment. Then Remy asked, "And the solution you have in mind for my meeting?"

Looking just a bit smug, Edmund shared his plan.

* * *

The woman dressed in dark green linen paced slowly to-and-fro, her eyes scanning the road toward the village. She wore a large-brimmed straw bonnet against the sun; it had a matching green grosgrain ribbon around the crown. Her fingers toyed restlessly with the top of her walking stick. She occasionally turned to watch the water rippling down the rock face of the small spring nearby, then resumed her pacing.

Catching sight of an approaching figure, she stopped to greet it. "Jeanne Remy," she called.

"Gwyned Llewellyn." Remy answered, drawing near. "Good day. You wish to speak with me?"

"I do." The woman looked piercingly at Remy, and her companion. "That's a fine, handsome dog. A bloody big dog," she commented. "I don't recall you having a dog."

Remy smiled slightly, patting Regis as he came to heel and sat at her side. "We live together at Owlswood."

"Ah—then I've heard about that one." She continued. "Will you walk with me?"

Remy nodded and the two women fell into step, slowly strolling along the road, Regis at Remy's side. For a few moments neither one spoke.

"My condolences on the death of your mother," the older woman began. "It is never easy to lose family."

Remy inclined her head slightly in acknowledgement. "I thank you; she is greatly missed." She smiled sadly. "Sometimes I even expect to see her at the cottage."

"Yes. The dead never really leave us, do they?" The older woman paused. "I may owe you an apology, as I understand you had an unpleasant meeting with my grandsons shortly after her passing."

Remy's eyes grew hard. "More than unpleasant; they threatened me, manhandled a small child and abused an animal. It was only good fortune that saved us."

"Aye, t'was Sara Archer's bastard child that the Coopers took in, the crippled one. I heard about that." The woman's eyes were just as hard. "It should not have happened."

"Yes, it was Jack and Annie Cooper's adopted daughter, who is lame. You heard correctly." Remy's voice remained steady. "And no, it should not have happened."

Gwyned looked at her appraisingly. "My grandson Kane took quite a walloping from someone after that."

"Jack Cooper does not take kindly to anyone who harms his family. Can you blame him?" Remy replied coolly.

"No, in truth, I cannot," the Llewellyn woman agreed. "I thought it might have been your employer who took out his ire, as he seemed to have played a large part in your rescue." She eyed Remy from beneath her bonnet brim. "But that's over and done. I want to know—why did Symme come to my farm?"

Remy kept her expression bland. "Mr. Symme hardly discusses his business with me, but the obvious reason is he wanted to look at your stock for purchase," she replied. "He has money, and he has suddenly taken a shine to Owlswood. He may want to have horses again, and Burgess Farm horses are reputed to be the best."

"Maybe." Gwyned's eyes grew wary. "But he asked many questions, questions about my father and his purchase of the farm. Why would he do that?"

"I have no notion. Your father purchased that spread long before I was born. What could I know about it? " Remy looked puzzled. "Should that upset you, the questions?"

Gwyned was quiet for several heartbeats. "Did your mother ever mention me, or my family, before she passed?" When Remy looked at her in surprise, she continued, "Was there ever any discussion of some distant connection between our families?"

"What? Never! What connection could there be?"

"Ah, I cannot rightly say—just some passing comments I recall from my younger days, when Da' was still with us. Probably nothing to it. I regret not asking your mother before she passed, that's why I ask you now." She stopped walking. "No, it may be more than that— I have reason to believe there is some connection. Did you come into possession of your family's Bible when your mother passed? Or any other like documents—that might mention ties? Anything addressed to me, perhaps?"

"To you? I don't recall you ever speaking to my mother past a greeting in the market, much less treating her like a possible family connection!" Remy became agitated. "Now, after her death, you look to establish some kind of kinship? What are you up to here?" She continued, angrily. "Whatever came to me upon my mother's death is no concern of yours. And anything that belonged to her is mine now. Is this why you asked me to meet you?" Her voice rose. "This interest in my inheritance?"

The older woman paled and caught her breath, but answered in a steady voice.

"My curiosity sometimes overcomes my sense. But if there were some truth to the matter I would want to know—wouldn't you?" She recovered herself and continued, "Think on it—if you know something about our families, I want to know. Then, too, I want you to press your employer not to file some kind of complaint against my grandsons. It would be unwise. He is, of course, a man of law and he mentioned he had found them trespassing. Does he intend to bring them up?"

"I have heard him say nothing about that," Remy replied and then stopped short. Regis had begun a low, menacing growl in his throat, hackles rising under her hand, and took a stance of warning. Remy looked up and saw Bran, Gwyned's younger grandson, driving a small wagon out from behind a copse of trees. She suddenly felt nervous.

"Ah, my ride home, " her companion stated, then turned to face Remy. "If you have any knowledge of your family history that relates to me and mine, I advise you to share it with me. I dislike dissembling."

She called to her grandson, "Whatever took you so long, boy?" then said to Remy, "Thank you for your courtesy in meeting me. I will be off."

Bran jumped down from the driver's bench to assist his grandmother up into the wagon. He cast a quick glance Remy, as Regis continued to growl and move in front of her, blocking access to her with his taut body. Bran just as quickly jumped back into the wagon and turned it toward home.

"Gwyned Llewellyn," Remy called to her and the wagon stopped. "I dislike intrusive and rude attempts at intimidation. I advise you and your family to remember that. Good day."

She turned with Regis and headed back to town.

She walked quickly, not knowing if she was more puzzled, amazed, or angry. Regis kept pace, until a well-dressed figure striding toward them whistled, and he bounded off to Edmund's side. When she got close enough, Edmund took off his hat in greeting and said, "Well, still alive and with all limbs intact, I'm glad to see. How did it go?"

Remy shook her head, not knowing how to start. "I'm not certain. She thinks we may be related—distant family! Can you credit it? My God, what a thought!"

"You and the Llewellyn bunch, related? You're joking!" Edmund exclaimed, then continued, thoughtfully, "Does the woman drink—or use opium?"

"Who can say," Remy answered, "but she was quite sober just

now and quite serious." She smiled ruefully and continued, "She also hopes you will not bring a charge of trespass against her two grandsons."

"Does she indeed! Lucky for her I've more pressing things on my mind right now," he huffed. "So . . . apparently my choice of companion was a good one?" He smirked.

"The absolute best, of course!" Remy smiled and caressed Regis' huge head. "And may I ask how you come to find yourself on this very road, and this very time?"

"Ah—just a bit of serendipity." The remark could not be left to lie, so he added, "Despite my faith in Regis, I thought perhaps an able-bodied passer-by would not be amiss, toward the end of your appointment. So here I am. Unneeded, but enjoying a fine stroll."

"Your concern is appreciated, Mr. Symme, and you have my thanks. As it happens, this meeting presented little threat, but many more questions than answers." Remy shook her head in puzzlement. "Why would she think that somehow there was kinship between us, and why would she care? She said she had reason to believe it. She asked if there was a letter addressed to her or if I was given a family Bible when my Mother passed." Remy paused and then continued. "She seems to think I received some inheritance along with hidden information. What could she be after?"

"A woman like that is either after advantage to her and her family, or trying to assess a threat. She might be afraid of something," Edmund pronounced.

"Afraid of me? " Remy scoffed. "A Llewellyn afraid of Jeanne Remy? The only notice that woman would take of me would be to crush me like a bug under her heel!"

"And yet, she came to you in a most genteel manner; *she* came to *you*. This bears further analysis." He slowed his pace slightly. "I plan to stop by the Post Office; I have had no word from Banks and I want to send him a wire—he must have found some kind of relevant information by now, unless he is too distracted by carousing with his medical cronies to tend to important business."

"He's only been away for two days, and his presentation is scheduled for tomorrow. Surely he is very busy with preparation and patients!" Remy was surprised. "I have no doubt he will be in touch as soon as he has the chance!"

"Possibly. But I intend to check anyway. No sense in passing up an opportunity." Edmund was a bit rankled by her expression of faith in Banks. "He does sometimes get caught up in carousing, you know."

"Ah." Remy thought it best to limit further discussion. She waited outside with Regis while Edmund conducted his errands at the Post Office. He joined them outside after just a few minutes.

"Just as I had thought, no news yet. But I did wire him. And now," he settled his hat and turned to her, "I think we should return to Owlswood and check on the progress of Samuel's work crew, and see if we can get a look at this chest—don't you?"

* * *

"It's more than perplexing, Mr. Symme, and it's got the best of me," Samuel shook his head, fuming. "Hey, Tom, making any progress w'it?" He was addressing his question to the aft end of one of his workers, who had the upper half of his body crammed into a small brick opening at floor level, only his haunches and legs visible to onlookers.

"Nary a move," came the muffled reply. "Hard work in here, so small!"

"Come on out, then, why don't you—hardly your best angle we're seeing, lad, and there's a lady present."

Samuel sat back down on a low stool as the man wriggled out of his awkward situation. Perspiring and face covered with smudges of grit, Tom got to his feet. He tugged at his forelock as he saw Edmund and Remy, then said, "Sorry, guv'nor, I cannot budge it. There's little room to see clearly, but I think the box is mortared in—most likely around the entire bottom side. Maybe even the back of it, too."

He drew a large kerchief from his back pocket and wiped his face.

Edmund stared at the brick opening of the "edifice"—as Samuel called it—and scowled. The men had chipped away several inches of bricks and mortar to gain better access to the box enclosed inside. Although the opening was now large enough to permit a man to reach the box, lying on his belly, it would not come free.

"You've done as I requested and used a light touch, but it seems there's no help for it: we need to take the entire top off and expose this well-concealed box." He turned to Samuel. "I don't know that

I want it sledged to the ground, but certainly we need clear access. What do you," and he included Tom in his query, "propose we do now?"

As the three men discussed various next steps, Remy began to inspect the brick opening. She got on her knees, then made her way into the small opening. Very little light entered with her, but she inched toward the box and finally her hands found it. She explored with her fingers and confirmed Tom's findings.

"Yes, it is clearly embedded in something and held fast."

Samuel looked toward the sound of her voice, then sputtered, "Jeannie Remy, what the devil are you . . .! You get back on your feet, young woman, 'tis most unseemly to be showin' yer ham end to the world like that!"

Remy's rump swayed slightly exactly at the moment the other two men turned to see what was happening.

"Just a moment, I think I may have found something . . ."

"Jeannie Remy!" Samuel bellowed. "Get yourself upright without delay!"

He looked at Tom, whose eyes were open wide and not unappreciative of the view, and then at Edmund, who was plainly staring.

"What have you found?" he asked.

Remy backed her way out of the opening, saying, "Ah, false alarm—just a broken piece of mortar." Standing and smoothing her skirts, she nodded at Edmund. "It is the box I anticipated."

"Alright, then, are we agreed? The top two layers of brick will be completely removed, plus more around the actual alcove opening, and then we'll see?" Edmund recapped.

The other two men nodded in agreement, and Tom went off to obtain the necessary tools.

"I suppose we will have no choice except to wait until tomorrow. This will take some effort and it is already tea-time. Do you reckon things will be finished by noon?" Edmund asked.

"That would be my guess," Samuel replied. "We won't destroy any brick we can save, but that mortar—very strong it is for something over half-century old. But then again, it was always the best of everything for this glasshouse, 'twas." As Edmund started toward the door, and had his back to them, Samuel turned to Remy and lowered his voice. "You should know better than to be crawling around like a child, Jeannie, showing your ankles and petticoats to God and all the people! And you a university student and all!" he scolded.

"And shall I believe that you find the sight of my ankles to be unpleasant, Samuel Gardener? I take great pride in my petticoats, and show them only to the most fortunate and worthy of men!" Remy teased him, as, sputtering again, he waved his hand and said "Off w'ye, foolish young woman!"

Neither one of them noticed Edmund's smile, or his soft chuckle as he listened on his way out the door.

Edmund and Remy had already decided to try their luck seeking answers from La Belle that night, and saw no reason to change their plan even without the box being freed from its snug sanctuary. After dinner was cleared and Cook had left for home, Remy made sure the library decanter held sufficient port and ensured the fire was fueled for the evening chill. She had agreed to meet Edmund there just before 10pm, and was securing her shawl around her shoulders as she knocked at the door.

"Mr. Symme, may I come in?"

After entering and finding Edmund and Regis settled in their usual places, she brought a chair from the writing desk and sat with them.

"Have you requested the Lady's presence?" she asked.

"I was waiting for you before doing so," Edmund replied. "I've been thinking about that box—why should it be so securely fastened in that spot? I also meant to ask you before, did you actually touch the box earlier, I wonder, and if so what…"

"I did touch it," Remy answered, "and I felt no particular effect. I could see that the filigree was exactly what I expected and could only feel the tooled flowers on the top rather than see them. Very little light made its way into that small place."

"How could it, when the space was filled with such luxurious crisp white petticoats and finely turned ankles?" Edmund looked at her boldly.

"*Oh, la la la . . . !*" the silvery voice exclaimed and the scent of gardenia filled the room. "What is this talk of petticoats and charming ankles, eh?" Between one heartbeat and the next, La Belle Fleur was at her usual place. "Ah, tell me more of this." She smiled and her eyes sparkled merrily. "Whose ankles? Whose lingerie? *Les cho-*

ses tant délicieux!"

"Good evening, Belle Dame," Remy answered, hoping the blush on her cheeks was not noticeable. "We are very pleased to see you. We—Mr. Symme and I—have things to discuss with you."

"Ah, *oui?* Better things than ankles and lace? *Bien.* What things?" Fleur fluffed her gown and her hair. "Have you progress to report?"

With little ceremony, except for a deep breath, Edmund began.

"A visit to Burgess Farm and some conversation with the Llewellyns seem to point toward a strong connection between that family and Owlswood—specifically with my grandfather. It appears they may have done business, or the relationship may have included blackmail of some kind. It involves a large sum of money and the purchase of the farm. Do you have any idea what could have occurred between John Symme and Ian Llewellyn?"

La Belle took a moment before responding. "Between Jean and scum Llewellyn, nothing occurred—although there should have been a great reckoning, *tant pis.*" She paused again. "Between Alistair Symme and Llewellyn—may they be chained together in the eternal stench and fires of hell— there is where you should look. There was the unholy alliance."

"Alistair Symme—my great grandfather," Edmund murmured thoughtfully. "He and Ian Llewellyn—what connects them? Why should they burn in hell, Lady?"

"Because they deserve it!" She snapped. "Do not forget you must find the truth yourself, not get it so smoothly from me." She seemed to soften slightly. "Do you recall why the Roman Lucretia died? Why your author Mallory was sent to prison? Think on it!"

She moved as if ready to disappear.

"Wait!"

18
Mysterious Chest

"I'm putting tea on." Remy moved with vigor toward the door.

"Tea! *Tea*? Stay right here—how can you mention bloody tea when there is so much to talk about, so many questions," Edmund exclaimed.

"Yes," Remy interrupted, "I always think better with tea." She turned to face him. "And I'm cold. Coming?" She left the library and headed for the kitchen.

"Tea. For the love of all the bloody saints!"

Edmund took a last look around the library, swore again softly, thought for a moment, then scooped up the brandy decanter and followed.

After tending to the kettle, Remy set herself to assembling the necessary items—including two thick slices of bread and a crock of butter. She seemed lost in thought, hardly noticing Edmund as he entered and seated himself at the kitchen work table and set the brandy next to the sugar bowl. There was a second bowl, too, with some dark, rust-colored substance in it. While Remy's back was turned Edmund wet his finger and dabbed a bit—cinnamon!

When the kettle whistled, she poured steaming water into the readied teapot and set it on the table. Another spouted pot was filled with water and cozied, and after warming the cups, it too sat on the table. She poured two cups of tea, added sugar and cinnamon to hers, took a first cautious sip and closed her eyes in relief. Only then did she speak.

"Rape." She stated. "It can only be rape of which the Lady speaks. Lucretia of Rome, Mallory of the Arthur tales. Clearly."

She gazed absently at the fire.

"Yes, clearly, I agree. And Llewellyn did it."

Edmund sipped his own tea, then added a bit of cinnamon.

"This is quite interesting, spice in tea!"

He eyed the brandy.

"This will be even better," and he poured a dollop into each cup.

Remy looked at him critically, and he pronounced, "Try it—it is very fine, indeed, and we can use some warming up. Try it!"

She took a sip and smiled. "It is good. And warming." Then her face clouded in thought. "So that is why La Belle regards Llewellyn with such anathema—he assaulted her and . . . could he have left her with child?"

"There is a chance of that, especially in view of the old matriarch's approach to you. But why do something so stupid as to rape the ward of your employer? And how did he get the farm? Why would money come his way from the Symmes?" Edmund shook his head in confusion. "I had felt so certain he was blackmailing them."

"It is strange," Remy said. "Were they involved with him, somehow, perhaps in some business venture?" Remy mused. "Three diverse men, sixty years ago . . . what were they about? What were they thinking? And how was Fleur entangled?"

She reached for a slice of bread, buttered it, then used her teaspoon to sprinkle cinnamon and sugar as she spoke.

"The Symme family was wealthy and fairly prominent—what was the source of their money?"

"The very thing you are consuming at a rather alarming rate, I may say—sugar. Other commodities. Wool." Edmund eyed the other slice of bread, then seized and buttered it as he spoke. "They were nouveau riche, *parvenue*, not old titled money—traders, shippers. With some moneyed marriages thrown in." He took a big bite of bread and butter. "That's probably how they met La Belle's father—not the marriages, the trading. He was a sugar planter in Martinique. Shiploads of money in sugar." He paused to swallow, then asked, "How do you come to use so much cinnamon?"

"Oh," she smiled a bit self-consciously. "My father was in the French merchant marine and brought cinnamon home after his time away at sea. I developed quite a fondness for it. He brought other spices, too, and different kinds of plants. He would keep an eye out for unusual flowers or herbs, and then bring them home to my mother. She was a skilled herbalist and had a wonderful gift with the garden." She noticed the cups were empty. "More tea?"

"Please," Edmund told her, and as she poured, he added more brandy to each cup. "I think I shall pass on the cinnamon—not my spice of choice."

"Hmm—I picture you more of a strawberry-preserves-in-tea kind of person," Remy declared.

"Indeed!" Now it was Edmund's turn to smile. "My nurse always gave me strawberry tea when I turned fractious. And I did like it tremendously."

"And I imagine you obtained quite a lot of it," Remy replied. "Would you like some now—no fractiousness required?" She rose and fetched a small ceramic pot of preserves, and set it on the table before him. "With my compliments!"

Edmund laughed.

"Many thanks, but this shall go on my bread and butter!"

He set to adorning his slice of bread.

"Remy, you will forgive me for saying—you do not impress me as one who has chosen domestic service as a living. I have no complaint about your work—Owlswood is managed quite smoothly and efficiently under your hand, but . . . you don't think or act like a servant."

"How astute of you, Mr. Symme." Remy spoke wryly. "I am performing this role as surrogate for my mother, in respect for the living Owlswood provided her in her lifetime, and in deference to the Symme will. You are correct, however—I have no aspiration to be in service. I am a student of medicine, and hope to return to my studies soon. You will recall, a few weeks after your return here I had requested the codicil of the will be extended to allow my cousin to assume housekeeping here, and me to return to London. You may also recall, you refused to consider it at the time."

Edmund swallowed his mouthful of strawberry-bread and washed it down with a long swallow of tea.

"I do recall, very well, and the main reason I refused to consider the matter at the time, although I admit I had no idea of your educational aspirations, is because La Belle felt very strongly you should remain here." He paused. "In hindsight, my refusal seems unfair, but . . . she—quite frankly—intimidated me by suggesting she might remain 'disappeared' should you leave."

"Really?! So she had some plans for including me in this matter even then."

Remy looked thoughtful.

"However," Edmund continued, "since we will no longer be engaged on her behalf after the coming month—apparently—I will definitely reconsider some accommodation that suits all parties. After the month is gone."

"That would be much appreciated." Remy acknowledged, surprised but gratified. "What is this month deadline about? Less than a month, she actually said. What is significant about these next three weeks or so?"

"That is one of the things I hope to find out from whatever is in this blasted uncooperative chest. Tomorrow will bring answers, I have every confidence." He drained his tea and stood. "However, today is almost gone, and we may be glad in the morning of a good rest in what's left of this night. Do you agree?"

Remy nodded, then rose to quickly tidy the kitchen and bank the fire for the night.

They used the back stairway from the kitchen to the first floor, Edmund carrying the lamp and Remy following close behind. At her bedroom door he turned and bade her good night.

"Thank you, Remy. Tea was a good idea," he granted. He smiled slightly, then quickly put out an arm to steady Remy, as her eyes began to roll upwards into their lids and she stumbled slightly. "Careful!" he cautioned.

She opened her bedroom door and he grabbed her arm more firmly, set the lamp on the hall table, and guided her into the room. He led her to sit on her bed, asking, "What's wrong?"

"My apologies," she murmured, "I'm so sleepy and so . . . so warm." She tugged at the buttons of her dress clumsily and opened the collar, breathing deeply. "So . . . hot in here . . ."

Not used to brandy in her tea after a long day, Edmund thought, *perhaps my hand was too heavy in the pour.*

"Here—lie back and take your rest. You need sleep."

He gave her a gentle nudge and she settled back onto the pillows, opening more buttons on her dress. He sighed, wondering what to do, then bundled her skirt around her legs and tossed them up onto the bed. One of her shoes had come off, and he took off the other one.

"There. At least you are safely in bed. I'll leave you now."

She made no reply. Somewhat concerned, he bent to feel her forehead, to assure himself there was no fever, and she smiled slightly at his touch.

"Remy. Miss Remy. Jeanne Remy," he spoke louder each time.

"I am leaving you now. Stay in bed. Good night."

She seemed not to hear him, but looked peaceful enough. He brushed a lock of hair off her temple, and was suddenly seized with the urge to kiss the smooth skin of her throat, in the hollow where the blood pulsed. *Steady, man*, he told himself. Then, before he could stop himself, he bent closer and brushed her cheek with his lips. At that moment she turned her head and her mouth found his. She hesitated only a moment, then kissed him deeply, wrapping her arm around his neck and her hand in his hair. Then she relaxed, sighed, and was fast asleep.

Edmund quickly turned and headed toward his own bedroom, perplexed and a little shaken. In the dark hallway, lit only by the moon, he heard faint words, *"Bonne nuit, mes enfants, mes chèrs enfants."*

* * *

The morning dawned crisp and clear, and Edmund and Regis enjoyed a long ramble in the wood before breakfasting somewhat later than usual. Nevertheless, time seemed to slog toward mid-day and the anticipated release of the chest from its glasshouse prison. Edmund tried to busy his mind with reading, and Remy attended to routine duties that required no real attention.

Finally, Remy heard Samuel's voice call to her, "I'm on to see Mr. Symme, the box is coming!"

She left her work and hurried out the kitchen door to see Thomas crossing the lawn, long-awaited prize in his arms. She left her apron on the chair and followed him to the library, where Samuel was placing a clean strip of canvas over the long table.

Thomas set the chest carefully on the canvas and stepped back. The lock had been sawn- off. Each one of them—Samuel, Thomas, Edmund, and Remy—stood silent for a long moment, just looking at it. It seemed to have cast a spell over them all.

After a minute Samuel said, "If that's all for now, Mr. Symme, we'll take ourselves off. We still have some rubble and sharp edges to clear off, back at the site."

Edmund thanked him and the two men returned to work.

He looked the chest over carefully, taking in every detail of the fine leather tooling and filigreed fittings.

"Shall we?" he asked, and put out his hand to lift the lid, then hesitated. He looked at Remy. "I think it would be fitting if you opened it. Please."

She didn't hesitate, but came to the chest and ran her hands over its top, smoothing the leather and caressing the tooled flowers. She carefully loosened the front hasp, then placed a hand on each side of the top and lifted it. When it was fully opened, the scent of gardenia and lavender was faint but unmistakable.

Edmund came to stand beside her. The chest was lined with cambric to protect the contents. Remy carefully unfolded the fabric to expose the interior.

The first item was a delicately sheer silk nightdress with embroidered flowers at the neckline and hem. Then came an elegant evening reticule in the shape of a gardenia, sewn with small seed pearls. Another layer of fabric came next, and when it was lifted, an oval gilded picture frame—of a size that only just fit into the chest—was exposed. Remy carefully lifted it out of the chest and caught her breath; it was a portrait of Fleur as she had been when first at Owlswood—vibrant, mischievously smiling, red hair wildly framing her lovely face.

"Oh!" Remy breathed, "she is so beautiful. And I can see my mother in her face!" Tears filled her eyes. She walked nearer to the window to catch more of the light. "This is wonderful."

Edmund peered into the chest, impatient for what else might be there.

"Ho—what have we here? This is strange!" He reached in and brought out an old, worn, leather scabbard with a large knife inside. "Great bloody hell, what is this doing here?" he murmured. He carefully slid the weapon out of its sheath and examined it closely. Too broad to be considered a dagger, this was a working knife: well-balanced, skillfully made, tapered, and very sharp. "I'd be surprised if this belonged to La Belle," he commented. "Her hand would barely fit around it." He held it up to the light. "There is an initial engraved here. Remy—come look at this!"

She set the portrait down carefully on the table and came to look. "My God," she breathed.

"Yes," Edmund agreed as he turned the blade to highlight the engraving of the letter "L." "Can we agree this is most probably Ian Llewellyn's knife? And if so, what the devil is it doing here?" He continued to examine the knife and scabbard. "Who packed this chest? We know it wasn't the Lady, and I cannot imagine it was

Llewellyn."

"Is there more inside?" Remy asked. "Perhaps something will tell us." She lifted a large envelope, tied with red ribbon to a notebook. "This looks more promising." She set the packet on the table and untied the ribbon, separating the two items. She opened the envelope first and found several sheets of thin vellum paper, folded in half. She unfolded one, and found a long, thick curl of red hair, secured with a ribbon, and a pressed gardenia of unusually large size. Tears again filled her eyes. "These must belong to Fleur," she whispered. Her fingers caressed the beautiful hair and gently prodded the flower, and she raised both close to her face to capture their fragrance. "Someone who loved her put these here."

Edmund reached for the second sheet of paper, unfolded it, and read. It was written in a flourishing script; a poem. He looked at Remy, and read the page out loud.

> I am chained to the earth, not brave enough to follow
> As each day crumbles to ash in my mouth, to cold steel in my heart
> Because you are gone!
> If only I could turn back cruel time, to when
> You smiled and breathed into my kiss
> My flower, ma fleur, my only lovely one
> To before the lack in me took you away forever.
> Forgive me! I dread life because it is without you.
> I dread death, for when I cross to eternity you
> May turn away. My sins are many
> But none greater than those against you,
> My betrayed, beloved, crushed and bleeding Fleur.
> Your own, yours only,
> John

"Well, I think we now know who packed this chest," Edmund said quietly. "That old bastard of a grandfather, John Symme. It seems as though he might have had a heart after all."

He tossed the poem onto the table, and Remy picked it up and read it again.

"This does seem . . . heartfelt. He appears to be truly heartbroken. But what are these sins of which he speaks?" she mused. "Why do you dislike him so much, your grandfather?"

"Why? Because he was a rude, pedantic, cold, mean-spirited,

bullying, amoral piece of work who, after producing my completely worthless father, never gave him or his wife a moment of consideration or human kindness. And he hated me. So . . ."

Remy looked quietly at him for a heartbeat. "He always seemed
ineffably sad to me."

"No doubt he was sad, after whatever he did to her, among others," Edmund snorted. "Sorry for himself, more like."

"And yet, Fleur loved him." She thought for a moment. "Whatever changed him?"

Edmund sighed impatiently, then noticed the notebook, picked
it up and opened it. "Oh ho," he cried, "more here—this book belongs to John E. Symme and, at first glance, is much like a diary." He
flipped through the pages. "This will take some time to read—but
what else is left in the chest?" He peered in and reported, "Nothing." He again looked at the notebook. "I would like to spend some
time with this. There may be important information in these pages,
something to help us with our task. I have no issue with your reading it, but I would like to examine it first."

"Of course. The book is your grandfather's. You should examine it first." Remy agreed.

Just then someone tapped at the door, and Edmund called,
"Yes? Come in."

The door opened slowly and Cook, looking ill-at-ease, said,
"Pardon the interruption, but the boy just delivered this telegram
for you, Mr. Symme. I thought, maybe, bad news?"

Telegrams rarely brought good news.

"Ah—finally, Banks remembered us and sent a wire at last! Give
it here, Cook, come, come!"

The woman nervously entered and held out the envelope, curtsied, and looked around, her eyes wide. She had never been in the
library before.

"Thank you, Cook!"

Edmund took the envelope and the poor woman curtsied again,
and left quickly.

He tore open the wire and read aloud: "Crandall mad doctor
stop Ticehurst house stop old dragon came through stop see you
Sunday stop Banks."

Edmund tossed the telegram on the table in disgust.

"Ticehurst! So that's where they were going with all this—they planned to put her in an asylum! Crandall got his enormous fees by helping men put their wives, daughters—wards—in with the insane, to get them out of the way."

"And get control of their money." Remy added. "No wonder Fleur called him a pig." She shook her head. "Could this be one of the 'sins' your grandfather regrets?"

"I must read this notebook! Banks will be back day after tomorrow. He may have details we can use. But who is this 'Old Dragon' he mentions—do you know?"

"Sophia Jex-Blake, my professor and mentor. He must have delivered my letter in person and asked her about Crandall." Remy smiled ruefully. "If anyone would know the dark practices of male physicians, she is the one. But, you know this Ticehurst House— what is it?"

"A very exclusive, very expensive, madhouse for the use of men who wish to be rid of troublesome women in their lives. At least they weren't considering Bedlam," Edmund replied. "And now, if you will excuse me, I have work to do."

Remy nodded and took but a moment to replace the contents of the chest—all except the portrait, which she left displayed on the table. She closed the box and turned to Edmund.

"Please let me know if you need my assistance, and please keep me informed."

She turned and left the library, closing the door softly behind her.

Edmund made a place for himself at the other end of the table, retrieved writing paper and pen to make notes, and settled in to read. And read he did, for the rest of the afternoon.

While the notebook was not a diary in the conventional sense, his grandfather used it to record important thoughts and events. It seemed clear that this volume was one of a series, identified by calendar year. There were also various papers and letters stuck in among its pages, apparently relating to the matters addressed therein.

It was more or less chronological, and the first entry of interest to Edmund was dated in August, 1836. John Symme would have been in his late 20's, perhaps even close to 30 years of age; already established as a man of business and society. It referred to a meeting with a solicitor in London, one Peter Hoffman, Esq., and contained a list of points John Symme intended to make in his next letter to the man. In his precise, smallish handwriting, he had written:

1. It is understood as per our last meeting that my father is within his rights to disinherit me for marrying against his will—although the reason given (the fact the woman is Roman Catholic and therefore unacceptable to my family and business associates) seems archaic. So be it.

2. You are enjoined to keep my plan to go ahead with the marriage in strictest confidence, but you will prepare the needed documents. My ownership of Owlswood is absolute, according to the will of my maternal grandfather, who, having no other blood family left after the death of my mother, entailed that property to me along with sufficient monies for a comfortable income. Prepare two additional certified copies of that ownership document, verify the inheritance, and secure all in my bank in London.

3. Shall you prepare an audit of the inheritance monies now kept in Wardship by Alistair Symme for Miss Fleur Marie Victoria DuPlessis? I am aware that my father's personal lawyer has charge of that information—may it be accessed on my behalf, discretely? Miss DuPlessis comes into her money in approximately 14 months, upon her 20th birthday.

4. Ascertain to the best of your abilities that all documents for the transfer of those funds to Miss DuPlessis are in perfect order and ready for her to assume ownership. Alert me of any discrepancy.

5. You will make no mention of my involvement in these requests to anyone unless and until I give you permission in writing. This specifically includes Alistair Symme.

Note: instructions to be hand-delivered to Hoffman by courier.

Note: how to tell Fleur we must postpone nuptials? She will not be happy to wait, but I must convince her. We can do well without Symme money, based on my resources and her inheritance. After she reaches majority, my father loses control of her fortune. Important she understands we must keep plans secret.

Edmund took a moment to think. "Well, he seems to have been fairly attentive to details, at least where finances were concerned," he said out loud. "And the Hoffman firm is still extant and well thought-of. And . . . he doesn't trust his father more than a tinker's dam. Interesting." He jotted down a few more notes and continued to read, then paused. "Perhaps he really loved her," he mused.

He continued to read until late evening, taking his dinner on a tray in the library. He shared a few words with Remy at that time, but she left him to his work as agreed. Nothing more of great interest caught his attention until a seemingly small household matter came to light. It was not actually written in the notebook, but on a scrap of paper lodged between two pages.

"Louisa has left our employ to marry. Fleur has decided that this Meghan woman from Grassington is her next maid. Difficult to get references, she is new to service and living here with distant relatives. I must look into it on Monday. Wages? Character?" There was a bold slash in red ink across this writing, and block letters that read, *"HOW COULD I HAVE BEEN SO BLIND!"*

Edmund sighed and rubbed his tired eyes. What the devil could that have been about? Such a trifling domestic matter but such vehemence in the post-script.

*   *   *

"Interesting reading, *Chèrie*?" a silvery voice inquired. "Any progress? What have you there?"

The scent of gardenia instantly enveloped him.

"Good evening, Belle Dame. I am reading the notebook John Symme left in the chest—your chest—discovered in the glasshouse." He rubbed his eyes again and asked, "Who was Louisa?"

"Ah! The little book speaks of Louisa? I have not thought of her in some time. Louisa was my maid—my personal lady's maid. She joined the household when we were in London, and came with me to Owlswood." As usual, Fleur settled her gown around her on the mantle. "I liked her very much. She was lively and very sweet—and she could dress my hair like no other!" She sighed. "I was very sad to see her go."

"She left you to marry?" Edmund pursued.

"Ah, she did indeed. Her young man remained in London where he was employed in some bank and they finally could not bear to be so far apart. He received a higher post, she received a proposal, I received her notice—it was a matter of absence making the heart grow fonder between them, I believe." Fleur shook her head. *"Quel dommage, vraiment."*

"But you soon found her replacement, am I right?" Edmund consulted the scrap of paper. "This Meghan?"

"Meghan, *bien sur*, she came to me. John was not pleased, she had no references but—*mon dieu*, who can one find in the middle of such a place as Yorkshire?" She waved her hands in irritation. "Yes, she came and she was quite good with wardrobe and jewelry, and she finally did learn to make the evening chocolate drink *assez convenablement*, but... I do not like to remember her."

"Why is that, Lady?" Edmund asked.

"*Parce-que . . . parce-que . . .* she was with me when it happened." Fleur's face clouded.

"It—what was 'it', Lady," Edmund queried. "What happened?"

"*L'enlèvement.*"

When Edmund's face remained blank, she added, "My abduction."

He looked stunned.

"My abduction—I was kidnapped. *Comprennez*—kidnapped?" The air around her began to quiver and she trembled. "Kidnapped."

"Lady," Edmund spoke almost in a whisper, "tell me what happened."

She paused for a long moment, her eyes seeing something locked deep in her memory. "I do not like to speak of it. It was the beginning of the end for me." She was quiet again. "But since you have made progress in your investigation, I will tell you. We went into the village because I wanted some sweets and to post a letter. I was bored, as I was often in those days." Her smile was sad. "John and I were supposed to marry that year, but his father forbade it . . . *cochon*! We had a plan to pretend to acquiesce until I attained my next birthday. But it was so far away . . . bien, I was restless and so Meghan urged me and we took the dogtrap wagon into the village. We had a basket with us for a picnic, so after I purchased my sweets she offered to post my letter and meet me at the spring just outside of the village. I took the dogtrap and had just taken the basket to a big flat rock when—the world went black and I with it. When I woke, I was in a strange place and . . . they kept me."

"Who kept you, Lady?" Edmund asked gently.

"Some man and woman I did not know. I was kept in a root cellar, or old smokehouse. Very small, very dark, very silent." She shivered again, more violently. "They fed me, gave me water, let me wash and walk each day. But as a prisoner. They kept me as a prisoner. I was there for more than a week. And then . . ." She hesitated. "He came."

"Who came? Who was it?" Edmund pressed. "Please, I must know if I am to help you."

"I did not know who he was then. He was very tall, very strong—a young man. He came into the cellar one night and told me I would be released the next day. I thought he had been sent by John, to rescue me! He seemed somewhat drunk, and somewhat unhappy. He told me . . . he said that he must make sure I was not returned in a 'marriageable' state and he was sorry but . . . He tore at me and I struggled, and I struck him with the water jug. Then he hit me very hard and I fainted and when I woke . . . I had been dishonored. He was gone. The next day I was blindfolded and taken to the edge of Owlswood, filthy, bloody, and no longer a virgin." She paused. "It was the next month that I missed my courses. *Enciente*. Pregnant. Unfit for a decent marriage." Her face contorted in anger and she raised a fist. "It was then I swore a solemn oath to find him and kill him."

"Who was this man? Do you know his name?"

"Oh yes, I know his name. His name was Llewellyn. Ian Llewellyn."

She looked at Edmund with the saddest smile he had ever seen, and was gone.

215

19
Terrible Secrets

"We need to dig deeper, I'm afeared. Perhaps take the structure down to the ground—and maybe even under." Samuel shook his head. "T'is the damnedest thing; I thought I knew everything there is to know about this place."

He had come to the library to bring Edmund word of a strange development.

Edmund frowned.

"What exactly have you found, man?" he demanded.

"T'is another strongbox, smaller certainly than the chest, sunk into the mortar and brick. And, there looks to be a heavy brass plate of some kind, aside it and down below the brick." Samuel shook his head. "We can get it, but not without taking up most of the ground level masonry. What is your will?"

Edmund thought for a moment. He cast his eye out toward the glasshouse and decided to take a chance.

"Samuel, you were a boy when the French woman died, is that right? Do you remember anything about that time—anything unusual or remarkable? Can you remember?"

Samuel took his time responding. "You know it was a very bad time here, do you?" He noted Edmund's nod. "I might have been ten or eleven—not of an age to eye the ladies, you understand. But she was so charming and a real beauty, and always kind to me, and then . . ." He shifted on his feet and Edmund motioned him to be seated. "One day she just disappeared—gone for almost a fortnight! Her maid came back here with some story about 'losing' her in the village, that she later saw her go off with some man—a man, for pity's sake! Why would she go off with some man, when John Symme was wrapped around her finger, so in love with her that . . .?" He grunted in disgust. "But that was the story the maid told. The household was mightily astir but the Old Symme wanted no scandal, so the search for her was quiet. And then one day, she came back." Samuel paused. "But the damage was done."

"What damage?" Edmund prompted.

Samuel looked pained. "She was never right in her mind after that. Disgrace, gossip, and whatever had happened to her—oh, she was with child, no gettin' away from it, but . . ." He waved his hand angrily. "The Symmes were no comfort, ye can be certain of that! She was left to her own pain, and a little and a little she went mad. Or so it seemed to me. Started wanderin' all about, nobody could control her. My half-sister, Lily, was housekeeper here during that time, with child herself then, and she was the only one who could comfort or even touch her, keep her clean, get food in her. Poor thing. She never told Lily what had happened, but I have my suspicions . . ."

"And they are?"

"Some felon took her, and she was forced to have congress with some piece of work that should not have been left breathing!" Samuel was almost shouting.

"But why take her—to what end?" Edmund asked. "And then why let her return?"

"Money! Ransom, that's why, but she escaped before they could demand payment!" Samuel spat, disgusted. "She never should have suffered so—she was driven mad—it should not have been permitted, and John Symme should have been man enough to find the bastard and kill him, to marry her and save her name, to make things right!"

"But he wasn't man enough, and he didn't do what was called for—did he?" Edmund stated.

"Ye know the answer to that—he did not. And then she killed herself! It should not have ended so." Samuel eyed Edmund appraisingly. "Young Symme, what is your interest here? Reconstructin' the glasshouse is one thing, but you are delving into dark matters long past about people long dead. To what end, if I may ask?"

"You have had information from Jeanne Remy, I gather?" Edmund asked.

"I have—and I'm not happy about it!" Samuel responded. "She's all aflutter about this French woman being her grandmother! Cock and bull, that's what it is! And that Llewelyn . . . witch . . . talking about some kinship between them—them, those well-off n'er-do-wells and our own Jeannie!" He sputtered with indignation. "How could that be? Jeanne is my great niece. My half-sister Lily was her grandmother!"

Edmund paused but a moment. "Samuel, did the French woman give birth before she died? What became of the child?"

He took a deep breath and quieted down. "I can't rightly say—no one really knows. The Symmes were most secretive toward the end, and Lily had left the house right about then to have her own baby. She felt bad that she couldn't stay on, but her own time was near, and she was not the strongest woman—took her so long to conceive, she was old to be birthing and we were afraid for her. As it was, she had a difficult time; we almost lost her and the child."

"What about the village midwives? Did they say the lady had given birth?" Edmund pressed.

"Oh, the Symmes wouldn't have any village midwife up at the house. If the baby was born, they would've had a medical man to attend the birth—if it happened." Samuel shook his head sadly. "It may be the poor mad thing did for herself before the child was born. There was nary a sign of a newborn at Owlswood, to my ken." He paused again. "Lily wasn't long away from her duties, and by the time she returned to the house it was over. No sign of a baby, no sign of the lady. Almost as if the poor young woman never even existed."

"Why not believe the child was John Symme's?" Edmund asked.

"Because of the way the poor woman was treated—like a leper! Like a pariah out of the scriptures! If there was any chance the child she carried had been a Symme, you can be certain she would have been cared for, even in the face of scandal."

"Who found the body? Who buried her—and where?"

"My Da' told me it was John Symme himself who found her—out at the Dagger Rock— but it was kept hushed. Plenty of gossip and tale-telling, but nobody knew for sure. And as to where she was buried, I cannot say." Samuel looked at the floor. "No churchyard would accept a suicide. There was no funeral that I heard of. The poor lady as good as disappeared from the face of the earth."

"Did no one from the authorities look into the matter—no inquest, no coroner inquiry?" Edmund wondered. "After all, a woman was alive, and then she was dead."

Samuel looked as if he had swallowed a bitter herb.

"As I said, the old man Symme wanted it kept quiet and he had the money and power to make sure it were. Besides, all were assured the woman went mad and did away with herself—t'was a family matter, and kept private."

They both remained silent for several minutes.

Then Samuel asked, "Why are you digging in this dirt? You gave me no answer before."

Edmund looked him squarely in the eye and replied, "I am acting on behalf of a client. I have been engaged to find the truth."

"The truth? What good will that do now? What purpose can it serve? And why involve our Jeannie?" he demanded. "Don't tell me she is your client!"

"No, Samuel, she is not my client and yes, she did involve herself in my research. I had naught to do with it. And you must know how difficult it is to dissuade that woman once she sets her mind on something," Edmund answered.

"True enough," Samuel admitted. "But I can't see much good coming from all this."

"I can't see much of anything yet, not clearly. But that may change." Edmund rose. "Do what is needed to retrieve this strongbox and report progress to me."

"That I will," Samuel rose also and turned to leave.

"Samuel, one thing more—what of the lady's maid who told the tale of going off with some man? What happened to her?"

"Oh, she did well enough for herself. She married Ian Llewellyn and got herself a farm."

* * *

Edmund felt confused, disconcerted. He needed a walk. He did not relish the idea of further discussing with Remy the evidence pointing strongly toward her being not only Fleur's granddaughter, but Ian Llewellyn's as well. And it was also impossible to discount entirely that Fleur's child might have been John Symme's, and in that case, Remy and he were cousins; a disturbing thought. He would have to question La Belle on that point, a task than inspired no joy.

Regis, at least, was in high spirits, pleased to be out and about. They walked for an hour or more before turning back. Interestingly, Edmund found they were nearing the little knoll upon which rested the Dagger in Stone. He paused for a moment to look at it, a looming presence that had unsettled him when first he saw it. With Regis at his side, he walked close to the boulder and confronted it.

"So, what can you tell me about all this?" he asked aloud. "You seem to play a big part in the troubles of Owlswood, do you not?"

He walked all around it, inspecting it carefully, swinging his walking stick to give himself courage. The Rock seemed to eye him back.

"What is the secret you know? You must have seen much!" He stopped and drew closer, feeling the chill he experienced before. He tossed his stick aside and placed both hands on the huge rock, one on each side of the figure of the Dagger. "Tell me! Tell me what you know!"

The surface of the stone felt almost icy beneath his hands; a cloud must have passed before the sun, for the light changed and grew dimmer. Then, almost imperceptibly, the rock began to warm beneath his palms and he closed his eyes.

"Tell me!" he whispered.

The heat under his hands built and he felt a jolt of energy. Rain poured down in a torrent, cold wind whipped around him as if to tear him limb from limb. He felt he was in his body, but also apart from it, suspended in time—all his senses were aroused.

Suddenly he heard a woman scream, "*Aie pitié de moi, mon Dieu*"' and then a man spoke roughly, "Nobody will believe a madwoman, you cannot hurt me with words!" The woman again, "I will tell all, and ruin you—who will buy from a rapist, eh? Give me money—so I can take the child away from here and never see you again!"

Thunder roared above them. The man roared with it. "You crazed bitch, you would blackmail me? Don't try it!" Edmund saw her move closer to her opponent, her gauzy gown soaked and plastered to her lush figure so recently with child by the driving rain, her long scarf wrapped around her arms. "Just the money, and one last kiss—and I will trouble you no more," she shouted above the storm. She pressed herself against the strong body and the man put his arms around her, pinning her to the boulder.

"I was wrong about you. You liked this, didn't you?" he kissed her hard, then pulled away with a howl of pain as rivulets of blood ran down his back. She had stabbed him deeply with a dagger concealed in her scarf, and stabbed him again as he pulled away. He writhed in pain and struck her with a huge fist, reached around in his belt for his own knife and drove it into her chest. "Bitch!" he screamed.

"NO!" cried Edmund, unable to move.

Another voice screamed "NO!" as a man came rushing out of the shadows, soaked by rain and buffeted by the wind. "Llewellyn!" the man shouted as he grabbed the injured Llewelyn, spun him around, and slammed him to the ground. "What have you done?!"

Then he turned to gather the lifeless body of the woman into his arms, her blood running down the stone into puddles on the sodden earth. "My God, Fleur—Fleur!" He held her limp form, great sobs wracking his body, and wept for a time. Then gently placing her on the rock, he turned to the other.

"You'll hang for murder, I'll see to it!" he rasped.

Llewellyn grimaced in pain.

"It was self-defense, Symme, she stabbed me!"

"Was it self-defense to assault and rape her, you bastard?"

John Symme shouted and kicked the other in the ribs where he lay.

Lewellyn howled in pain. "Stop! Stop—you know your father paid me to . . ." His words were cut off by a fist to the chin, then he was dragged up by his shirt and slammed against the rock.

"What are you saying?! Liar!"

"No, no, you know it's true—it was his idea! The old man paid me to take her and make sure she was ruined!" he put his hands up in a gesture of surrender. "If you tell the police, I'll destroy you both!"

Llewelyn grimaced in pain and desperation.

John Symme looked at him in horror; then at the dead woman.

"Coward! Filth! Take yourself away, man, before I finish what she started." Llewellyn staggered to his feet and stumbled off toward the village. "Take yourself to hell, man!" Symme screamed after him. "To hell!"

The rain grew even more fierce. Weeping, Symme gathered the body of the dead woman in his arms and said, "Let us go home, Fleur. We should go home."

Struggling with his heavy burden, he turned toward the trees from which he had emerged too late, and disappeared.

*   *   *

All at once, silence.

No rain, no wind, no thunder.

Edmund opened his eyes, expecting to see himself bloody and wet; he was not. The sun was shining, the ground and the Dagger Rock were perfectly dry—and so was he. Regis nudged him gently, softly whining in concern; he stroked the dog in relief, grateful to be back in his own time, his own body, his own thoughts.

Then he sunk to sit on the ground, back against the rock, head in his hands.

"What in God's name just happened?" he asked aloud.

He took a moment to catch his breath, then rose to his feet. Turning to face the boulder, he slowly backed away and nodded to it, respectfully.

"I may myself be mad, but I think you . . . Oh my God, I am speaking to a rock. Or, the spirit of a rock."

He shook his head, confused and unbelieving, but then . . . then he said, "Thank you," retrieved his walking stick, and on unsteady legs started back to the house, Regis at his side.

Soon he was crossing the lawn of Owlswood, a bit steadier on his feet, and he saw a familiar figure on the terrace.

"Banks!" he called out.

Banks turned at the sound of his name and walked to meet him.

"You weren't expected until tomorrow!" Edmund exclaimed, taking his outstretched hand and then embracing him.

"Well, I knew you must be missing me terribly, so I finished my business and took an earlier train. How are you, Edmund?" Banks looked at him closely. "Are you quite well? You look a bit pale!"

"Yes, well, I am . . . we have much to discuss, some new developments." Then he added, "Do you have more news?"

"None past what my telegram contained. Say, are you certain you are all right?" Banks' physician's eye looked hard at his friend. "Come inside and let's have a glass of wine, shall we, and you can recover yourself and tell me what's going on—-don't try to deny anything. Come inside and let us talk." Then, seeing the big dog, he added, "Regis my friend, I haven't forgotten you, look what I have!" He brought a leathery-looking item from his breast pocket. "A pig's ear, my lad!" Regis politely accepted the tidbit, tail wagging, and headed onto the grass to enjoy it.

Settled in the small drawing room with glass of wine in hand,

Banks took another appraising look at his friend.

"Hmm, well, color is coming back into your homely face, so I think this wine was just the right thing!" He smiled and took a sip of his own. "So, what have you been about this afternoon that made you so pale and wan?"

"Banks, I'm not sure I even know how to tell you."

Edmund paused for a moment, and then recounted not only his last conversations with La Belle and Samuel, but also his experience at the Dagger Stone.

Banks listened attentively and asked no questions; he noted the emotional turmoil that played across Edmund's features as he spoke of the encounter at the Stone. It seemed best to let him pour out information without pause. When Edmund had finished, exhausted, Banks nodded and frowned.

"Well, the fact she had been abducted and raped certainly fits with the work of the esteemed Dr. Randolph Crandall—he would have been called in to initiate and medically authorize the commitment proceedings with the County Judiciary. Based on her obvious moral turpitude and the accompanying lack of mental capacity." He paused a moment. "Maybe Crandall was even to be present at the birth. I could see him strangling a newborn."

"Maybe." Edmund responded glumly. "But according to the village midwife, the baby lived and was given to the Owlswood housekeeper, who happened to be Samuel's half-sister, Lily." He shook his head and added, "The baby grew up to become Remy's mother, and then Remy came along, viewing Lily as her grandmother."

Banks leaned forward. "You will forgive me, Edmund, but while pieces of the puzzle seem to be coming together—some from Samuel, some from Remy, some from writings and unearthed objects and others from this spectral woman with whom you seem to have regular conversations—no, no, hear me out, man—I find it difficult to comprehend that you have actually had a vision of your own at this damned rock!"

"You don't believe me, then?" Edmund protested. "What do you think happened?"

"I have no idea—overstimulation, too much claret . . ." Banks waved his hand in the air.

"You bastard, I had not been drinking this morning—I never

drink until evening! What do you take me for—some feeble-minded sot who cannot tell real from fantasy, truth from fiction?" He brought his fist down hard on the arm of the chair. "I know what I saw, I know what I felt!"

"Ah, well then," replied Banks, with a slightly mischievous grin, "I'm pleased to hear it. You always know the precise and clear facts of any matter, but if you know what you *felt*, well, that is progress indeed." He raised his glass to Edmund, who glared at him in return. "Has Miss Remy heard of your findings?"

"Not all of them, no. And certainly not those of this morning— I want to satisfy myself that she is not my relation before moving ahead with any plan. If Fleur had been intimate with John Symme, it is possible her baby was his and Remy is my cousin. A long-lost family member may present serious complication."

Banks frowned. "If the child had been Symme's—by his beloved betrothed—I doubt it would have been shunned or abandoned as it was. It has to have been Llewellyn's."

"Nevertheless, I must confirm the matter with La Belle Fleur." Edmund paused. "Where the devil is Remy? She is usually hovering around—have you seen her?"

"No," Banks replied, "but your charming Cook—who was the only person here when I arrived, you being engaged in a vision— told me she is in the village, visiting some family member who has taken ill. She is expected before the evening meal." He took a sip of wine and soberly addressed his friend. "Edmund, where is all this going? What does all this mean? And more importantly, what will you do about what you find?"

Edmund sat back in his chair and took a moment to compose his thoughts.

"Something is not right. Why would great grandfather Symme take so much trouble—actually risk criminal charges—to keep control of Fleur's assets by having her assaulted and committed? Her money would have come to her and then to his son, John, when they married, still within the family, still available for family interests. Why be so set on holding onto control himself ... unless ... hmmm ... unless he had already spent the money or some other fraud was afoot? No, something stinks like last week's fish and if that is the case, Remy is due recompense for that which Alistair Symme stole from her grandmother. The obligation to make that right is mine."

He got to his feet and began to pace.

"But you ask apt questions, Banks, and I have been giving matters a good deal of consideration. First and foremost, I want to know the truth about all this, about my family, about the decisions made in the past that now affect my life. I want to know what the current Llewellyns are about, and why that old woman has made overtures to Remy—what does she know, how does she know it? I want to learn what happened, and I want to bring justice to La Belle Fleur, who has been in the shadow of disgrace these many years."

"And for Jeanne Remy? What do you want for her?" Banks asked.

"As I said, the obligation to right whatever wrong was done her grandmother is mine."

Banks took a deep beath.

"Edmund, you seem to have taken on quite the quest. How long do you intend to stay here at Owlswood?" Banks said in dismay. "This was to be a brief respite from your work in town, a lark out to the old family estate—but let me tell you, people are clamoring to know when you will return to London! I could barely turn around without someone asking me what had become of you. Not to mention your poor head clerk, God knows he is running himself to ruin preparing briefs and fending off clients who wonder where the hell you are!"

Edmund stopped his pacing. "Oh, no, Banks, I have but three weeks to solve these questions."

"Three weeks? By the blessed toenails of St. Martin, how can you possibly . . ."

"La Belle herself set the deadline," Edmund continued. "It is some date of significance to her and her story. That's why I need your help, and Remy's, and why I hope what is buried in this strongbox will prove illuminating."

"You have my help, of course, but . . . I wonder if you have thought this through. What happens in three weeks? What if you cannot solve this mystery by then? Or, if you can and you satisfy yourself on all these counts—will the Lady be satisfied? Will she remain at Owlswood or..."

"What do you mean, remain here? Remain here or what?" Edmund cut him off sharply.

"Or will she disappear into wherever avenged and satisfied

country-house specters go?" Banks rose to look him in the eye. "Or what if the 'truth' you find is not so clean or simple as the Lady implies? What if it shows some duplicity on her part or even..."

"Then so be it. I will know, and I will resolve matters, and I will be satisfied. And she needs be satisfied as well." Their eyes locked for a long moment. "And, if she chooses to leave Owlswood, that is her right."

Banks rose and laid his hand on Edmund's shoulder. "Well, I am with you, for what that's worth." They both smiled grimly. "But now I feel I must get outside and walk before the light fades. Spending hours on a train does little for my back or disposition. Might you spare Regis for an hour or so?"

Banks had left his traveling coat and walking stick in the entry foyer and headed out in that direction, leaving the door ajar. Apparently, he met Remy en route, as Edmund heard their voices in the hallway.

"Jeanne—good to see you! Everything all right in the village?" Banks said warmly.

"Kit!" Remy replied, "We didn't expect you until tomorrow! Welcome back!" Her voice was filled with delight. "Yes, she seems better now—I was concerned because of the fever, but the herbs I brought calmed her stomach and she seems cooler. Did Cook tell you where I had gone?"

Their voices faded as they made their way back toward the foyer and front door.

Kit? *Jeanne*? thought Edmund. *What-ho with such familiarity*? Disgruntled and feeling much excluded, he nonetheless turned his thoughts to strategizing for his meeting with La Belle later on that night. *Kit, indeed*!

But his thoughts would not cooperate. Stewing in his own juices, Edmund began to pace again, stopping at the window to gaze absently at the rustling trees across the lawn.

"Kit, indeed," he muttered to himself.

A soft rapping on the study door caused him to turn abruptly and find Remy standing in the half-open doorway.

"Mr. Symme, I wanted to be certain you knew I had returned. I trust Cook let you know why I left while you were out this afternoon."

Edmund looked at her with some annoyance, hoping she had

not heard his words, and replied drily, "She did not. However, *Kit* informed me that you were needed for some emergency in the village."

He hoped his voice sounded normal; he felt nonplussed and feared that perhaps he was blushing.

Remy nodded.

"Yes, I saw Dr. Banks when I returned. We did not expect him today, but his room is ready and Cook has sufficient for dinner."

"And your emergency—all is now well?" Edmund pursued, feigning polite interest and a calm he did not feel.

"Yes, Molly seems to be bettering and thankfully, our concern may have been a false alarm." She smiled. "I am much relieved."

"Molly! What was wrong with her?" Edmund asked, concern in his voice. He couldn't hide his warm feelings for the child, and did not try. "She is not seriously ill, I trust?"

"No, she had fever and the flux—which is always troubling in a young child—so her mother asked me to come. But after taking the tea I prepared, she napped comfortably and upon waking, her fever was much reduced. She is recovering well, thank you for your concern." Remy smiled mischievously. "She asked about you, by the way."

"Did she?" Edmund was pleased. "Well, we are old comrades-in-arms, so to speak. She does well, otherwise? And the gander—has he recovered from his wounds?"

"Oh, my, yes—he cannot strut quite as proudly as he used to, but he has mended well. He, however, did not inquire about you at all."

She began to chuckle and Edmund could not help smiling.

"Yes, well," Edmund began, "um, in regard to our mutual concern, I have information to share with you. However, I am involved with another matter now and am not free for discussion. I would prefer to speak with you about it tomorrow morning." He paused and took a breath, hoping his nervousness did not show. "That is acceptable, I assume?"

Remy looked at him for a brief moment, then replied, "Of course, I am eager to hear at any time. I wonder if you will be at table this evening—or would you prefer a tray in the Library?"

She's assuming I will be looking for La Belle tonight and will go to the Library, Edmund thought. *How can I keep her away? I need private*

227

conversation with the Lady.

"Neither." He said aloud, and frowned. "No, well, a tray, now I think, perhaps with just some cold meat, bread and cheese will do. No dinner for me this evening. And a pot of tea, perhaps. Just ..." he attempted to sound casual, ". . . just bring it in here. I will remain working here and I . . . my appetite is not, um, I'm not very hungry."

"Are you all right, Mr. Symme? Is there anything I may do for . . ."

"No, no, I am quite all right, Remy, just the tray when Cook can manage it. And uninterrupted time for my business. That is all, thank you," he stated. "Now I must work."

"Yes, sir. Of course."

Remy eyed him with mild concern, turned, and left the room with the door ajar as she had found it. No more than twenty minutes later, she returned with the requested tray of food and set it on a side table. After confirming nothing more was required, she bade Edmund a good afternoon and returned to her duties.

Edmund waited a moment to be sure she was gone from the hallway. He wrapped up the food in his napkin (Regis might be glad of it later), drained the teapot into the ever-suffering sitting-room aspidistra, and set the emptied tray on the hall table. Looking down the corridor again, he then slipped out and headed for the Library. Once there, he took up pen and paper and settled himself in his chair. "Now, what must I learn from La Belle," he mumbled to himself. He set himself to write, but had scribbled only a few lines before heaving a tremendous sigh in a wave of fatigue. "Just the events of the day catching up with me," he grumbled, "perhaps if I close my eyes for a few minutes…"

Almost immediately, he was deeply asleep.

He may have dreamed, but no trace of any dream remained when he opened his eyes. The room was dark, chilly, and silent. He must have slept for a few hours, as the afternoon had passed into night. He shifted in his chair, stiff from slumber; his papers fell from his lap to the floor. Then he heard a soft lullaby and the air began to shimmer.

Do do, l'enfant do,
l'enfant dormira bien vite
Une poule blanche est là dans la grange
Qui va faire un petit coco?

The voice hummed, and a dim light emerged over the fireplace mantle.

"Even men look like angels when they are asleep, no, *Petit?*" Fleur spoke quietly. "But what a disguise that is, what a cruel ruse. They are no angels, *les hommes, non, non*…" The light grew stronger and she emerged more clearly.

Edmund sat upright and rubbed the sleep from his eyes. "Belle Dame?" he asked.

"*Oui,* who else, *Chérie,* who else but me?" came the reply.

But the image before him was not the Lady he expected. It was Fleur, but pale and drawn, with disheveled hair and darting eyes. She seemed ill-at-ease, agitated, upset.

"You have news for me, you have found something—the Truth, perhaps?" she snapped. "What can you tell me?"

"Lady, I…" Edmund responded, "I have learned much, but not all, about the manner of your death. Please, may we . . ."

"What?" she demanded. "*Dis-moi vit!* What have you learned, great barrister Symme?" The light around her trembled and grew stronger.

Edmund drew a breath and began. "I know you were murdered at the Dagger Stone by Ian Llewellyn, and that John Symme was too late to save you. I know you went there to kill Llewellyn in revenge, but he overpowered you. I know you are no suicide." He got to his feet and spoke quickly and clearly. "I know your name and honor were besmirched by Alistair Symme—why I have yet to discover. I know you were betrayed by men you trusted, my grandfather and great-grandfather, and therefore it is my responsibility to make these things right."

The Lady quieted slightly and replied, "And how do you propose to make things right, barrister Symme? What can you possibly do for me that will make any difference?"

"I can clear your name, as you have requested," Edmund stated. "I can levy a charge of murder posthumously on Ian Llewellyn. I can make sure Jeanne Remy is afforded her due and . . ."

"Her due! Had John Symme made good his promise, my granddaughter's due would have been Owlswood!" Fleur spat at him. "Would you have her inherit a stinking livestock farm run by a nest of vipers and call it her due?"

Edmund seized his moment. "So you are certain your child was

229

sired by Llewellyn, not John Symme?" He steeled himself for her answer.

Fleur began to laugh maniacally. "Ah—you will clear my good name, you will cleanse my honor, you will make the Truth known and yet—you can ask if I was some kind of libertine to sleep with men before marriage and a pig such as Llewellyn, no less!?" She flung her arms in the air angrily. "Why would I stop with John, eh, why not Alistair? Why not the vicar? Just because Llewellyn forced me does not mean I didn't give myself freely to half the village men, *non*? Frenchwomen are all whores, this is widely known in England, yes?"

She hugged her arms close around her body and began to shake violently with laughter, then began to cough and soon her body seemed to melt into a picture of grief itself as she was racked with shuddering sobs and tears poured from her eyes. "Oh you are my champion, *bien sur*, you will vindicate me, oh yes, I can see that clearly . . ."

Edmund was dumb with shock. Had this been a woman of flesh and blood, he would have slapped her to bring her to her senses, or consoled her in his arms. But what could he do for Fleur? Cautiously he moved close to her, arms open, and said softly, "Lady . . . Belle Dame . . . Fleur . . . you must know I hold you in great esteem, more than any woman I have ever known. You must know why I had to ask that question. You must . . ."

His words were cut short when Fleur turned her face and met his eyes with the most heartrending look of sorrow and pain. She was suddenly down from her mantle perch and standing before him, shaking with sobs, trying to press herself close against his chest and nestle her head into his shoulder. He could not feel her body, as he would have felt a living woman against him, but he felt her emotions course through him, become part of him, and he experienced her pain, sadness, and desolation as if it were his own. His arms closed softly around her as he began to rock gently and murmur.

"There. It will be alright. It will be alright."

The scent of gardenia, unnoticed before, permeated his senses, and he, too, began to weep.

Edmund could not tell how long they remained together, but finally the Lady disengaged from him, smiled slightly, and returned to her customary seat above the fireplace.

She looked at him, still sad. "No, *Chérie*, I was never with John in that way—nor any other man save my rapist. John and I shared physical affection, many kisses and caresses, but he cared too much for honor to do more. And, we had a lifetime together ahead of us, *non*? He would not press his advantage." She tilted her head slightly and asked, "Is that answer enough?"

"*Merci*, Belle Dame. I regret causing you this pain, but your answer is important." Edmund felt slightly giddy and suddenly seized with weariness, but continued. "There is a strongbox being uncovered in the glasshouse. I should have it tomorrow. When we examine its contents I have no doubt we shall make progress in our endeavor."

"More documents? Hmm. perhaps they will help." Fleur did not seem hopeful. "Examine one other thing: why was John Symme too late to save me? What kept him?"

Edmund's fatigue again became intense and he felt faint. "I shall do that, as you direct. But now, I must beg your pardon, I need to rest." He bowed slightly. "I hope you will forgive me, for everything."

"Not at all," Fleur replied, "it is you who must forgive me. I am not myself, or rather, I am too much myself. It is . . . the time draws near." She smiled, a little less sadly, and bade him goodnight. "Until next we meet. Be well."

She was gone.

* * *

The next morning at breakfast, Edmund asked Remy to join him and Banks at table to discuss their progress, taking that opportunity to bring her current. He was direct and thorough, even explaining his experience at the Dagger Stone in detail. She listened intently until he had finished.

She seemed to be considering the matters at hand, and not lightly. Then her expression softened slightly and she commented, "What I find truly astonishing is your vision at the Stone. The Lady must have had a hand in that, and it shows she is opening to you— and you to her."

"I am 'opening' to her as I would to any client, and as to her sending me the vision, she seemed unaware of it. Besides," Edmund said impatiently, "she sent me dreams even before I left London, so a vision is hardly a large step—if she had been involved at all."

"By God's pearly teeth, I had forgotten that—you were having troublesome dreams before this all began!" Banks exclaimed. "It's what pointed you toward Owlswood in the first place—you told me that the night of Lydia's soiree! By God, what a night that was—do you remember that tavern. . ."

"Enough, Banks," Edmund interrupted, "that has nothing to do with this matter."

"But you have had dreams from the Lady before? I had no idea!" Remy looked thoughtful. "So she was planning this all along—to bring you to Owlswood to help her." She turned her eyes to his; they seemed to indicate an unspoken, "And me."

Edmund held her gaze for a brief moment, then continued. "As I say, we digress. Back to the point. For good or ill, it is fact that this Llewellyn man was your grandfather—which must be at least part of what the Llewellyn matriarch was getting at when you met. Can you accept that?" Edmund searched Remy's face, then continued. "Even more, the same man killed your grandmother."

"The past is what it is, Mr. Symme," she replied with cold calm, "there is little to be gained in railing against it. And I agree, Gwyned must know, or at least suspect, that she and my mother were half-sisters." She rose and began to pace. "But why she would bring this forward now I cannot tell—my mother is gone, and I want nothing to do with her and the Llewellyn kin." She frowned slightly. "I doubt she knows about the murder, for she was not yet born, and who would tell her—not her father, surely, and perhaps her mother didn't know."

Suddenly, she made a fist and hit her other palm, once, twice, three times. She continued to pace. Her eyes flashed dangerously.

"But what I cannot accept is that my grandmother was murdered, the Symme men knew, and nothing was done!" She came back to the table and slammed it with her palm. "Your grandfather did nothing, he did nothing to avenge her or clear her name!" she hissed, her voice hoarse with disgust.

Edmund and Banks, both open-mouthed and staring, were speechless.

"How could any decent human being allow such a thing to go unacknowledged and unpunished? How?" she demanded. "Alistair Symme took on a debt of honor as her guardian, and John

Symme claimed to have loved her . . ."

"Remy, calm yourself. I assure you I will use every possible leverage of the Law to . . ." Edmund managed to croak.

"Calm myself! You must be mad—I'm angry! I'm damn bloody angry!" The quiet intensity of her voice was frightening. "Where was your esteemed Law when all this came to be? All that rot about protection of women and children for the sake of the Country?" Her eyes burned through him. "Your precious Law permitted Alistair Symme to have Fleur declared incompetent, to steal her life and her reputation, to condemn her to a long slow death in an asylum—which is exactly what would have happened if she hadn't been killed! Your precious Law, Mr. Symme, wasn't worth a spoon full of shit to my grandmother and it's not worth even that to me!"

"By the balls of St. Jude . . ." Banks murmured, transfixed.

Edmund's emotions were rising, as was his temper.

"What can we hope to do if not give Fleur justice—the justice she deserves? The Law will do that, I will make sure it does!"

"Justice! What good will justice do her—will it make her murderer pay, put him to death? No, he is already dead." Remy's voice was low. "Will it show the Symmes for who they were, callous and greedy men with no souls—will it make them pay? No, they are dead too, long moldering in their elegant graves. Justice has been done, it seems, not by law but by Nature. What I seek is to right this wrong against Fleur. Can you do that? Can you make things right for her?"

"By God, woman, I just said I would and I shall!" Edmund rejoined. "Do you think I haven't wracked my brain about what to do—how to make things right for a woman who's dead? What does 'justice' mean for such a one? What weighty responsibility that brings me, much more than if she were living—if she were living I could perhaps effect some change in her fortunes but . . . what can I do for her now except bring some kind of acknowledgement of wrong-doing for whatever it's worth, some kind of equipoise at best?" He rose and leaned across the table, "I'm angry, too, and ashamed of the past. Ashamed of my forebears! It does not sit well with me, as a man of Law or as a man, period!"

Remy opened her mouth in retort but a sharp rapping on the door frame of the dining room stopped her.

It was Samuel, a large, rusted strongbox under his arm and

crowbar in his hand.

"Sorry to break into your meetin'. We have it."

20
Crime and Conspiracy

When the flurry of activity caused by Samuel's words was done, the remains of breakfast were cleared and a large linen cloth spread across the table. The strongbox lay, pried open like a huge mollusk, before them. A strong musty smell of old paper mixed with the dark scent of earth that clung to the box, clods now scattered on the cloth, all eyes fixed on its contents. Everyone was silent.

Samuel spoke. "More papers, as ye expected," he commented, "Didn't want to open it where the lads could see in, so . . . I think I'll take myself off now." He picked up the crowbar and looked at Edmund. "Anything else? If no, I'll be gone."

"No, nothing else. Thank you, Samuel, well done." Edmund muttered.

Remy eyed the box with disdain.

"More papers—more heart-rending, self-pitying poetry, perhaps, from the bloody cowardly bastard John Symme?"

Samuel turned back and looked at her sharply.

"Mind yourself, young woman. You were never brought up to use such language. And mind your temper, as well."

He gave her a dire look, shook his head, turned, and left.

"I must say, I am impressed by your ability to swear with such ease," Banks mused, "whenever did you . . ."

"Oh, Kit, please . . ." Remy had the good grace to blush slightly, then explained. "Medical lecture halls are not for the verbally faint of heart."

Edmund seemed unaware of all conversation, fixating on the contents of the box and carefully placing papers into piles on the table.

"Here we are . . ."

He pushed a pile toward Banks, then one to Remy, and centered one before himself.

Nobody spoke, but each began reviewing the papers placed before them, reading for some minutes in silence.

"Well, this is interesting," Banks said absently. "Apparently

Symme the Elder forbade the marriage between John and Fleur because she was Catholic—a papist—and it would cast a pall on business dealings." He rubbed his eyes. "I suppose in the '30s, there was still high sentiment about that—do you think, Edmund?"

"What are you reading?" Edmund asked sharply.

"Some vituperative letter from Alistair to his son John, explaining why the marriage is a poor idea. He informs that he will not give his consent as her guardian, and should the marriage take place after the girl attains majority, he will cut John out of the will completely. Hmm. Nasty piece of work, the old man." He read on for a moment. "Apparently, he was an admirer of Shaftsbury and shared his great antipathy toward papists and the Irish, but not his devotion to social reform."

"So that's why they made plans to marry in secret before she came into her money," Edmund commented. "But she still would have become a rather rich woman on her twentieth birthday, regardless of marital status, and they would have no need of John's inheritance—except, perhaps, to soothe his ego." He paused briefly. "And the Catholic Relief Act had long been enacted—I think it was in '29. All those Roman Catholic Irish were asserting their rights to sit in Parliament, if elected, and it almost came to civil war until McConnel and Wellington convinced the House of Lords to pass it. Even so, if John had political aspirations there might be taint from having a Catholic wife—although, I think money was the main concern."

"So then, why all the upset? Fleur's money would be part of the family assets if they married, even though John would have more direct access to it than would his father." Banks shook his head. "Would the mere presence of popery in the family be so detrimental to their interests?"

"Well, anti-papist sentiment was still quite high in certain factions in those days. But I can't help but feel there was something else behind all this religious bluster. Something rotten." Edmund turned back to his reading.

"Have you found anything, Miss Remy?" Banks asked. "I mean, apart from heart-rending poems?" He smiled mischievously. "You seem unusually quiet."

She looked up from her work and made a face. "No poetry, but rather cloying love letters I can do without. Ugh. In light of what we know happened, they make me cringe."

"My apologies, Remy, it was not intentional that they came to you," Edmund said absently, focusing on his own reading.

Things went on for some time, punctuated by sighs of fatigue and yawns none took pains to stifle. Banks finally rose, rubbing his eyes and stretching his back, then returned to the table and absently reached for the small, leather-bound Bible setting apart from the other papers.

"Whose is this, I wonder?" he mused, opening the cover and fanning through the pages. "What's this?"

His attention was caught by an envelope, slipped inside the back cover, containing two handwritten pages on cheap paper. He took the envelope and sat down, removed the papers and began to read.

"By God and all the saints!" he cried, after a few minutes. "Holy Blessed Mother, Edmund, here it is!"

"What have you found, Banks?" Edmund was instantly alert, and Remy upright in her seat.

"This is a letter addressed to John Symme, written by one Meghan Llewellyn." Banks replied.

"Meghan, Fleur's maid?" Remy asked.

"The self-same one. She seems . . . disabused of the notion of her husband's enduring affection. She is, how to put this properly, ratting him out!" Banks was amazed.

"Come on, man, what the devil does it say?" Edmund growled.

"All right—dated September, 1837, she writes :

Mr. Symme:

My name is Meghan Llewellyn. You know me as Meghan Parry. Some months ago, I left employment at Owlswood to be married to Ian Llewellyn. We now await the birth of our first child together. But I had a son before, who is now 5 years old. I left him with family so I could take the job in your house as maid to Miss Fleur. None here knew of him.

I took up with Ian and he offered marriage, and to adopt my son as his own. Now that my belly is big, he has gone back on his word. He will not take my boy as his own or to inherit any of our property. Only children of his body. I have seen the will. He has also taken up with another woman, with no remorse. I feel it is time that his sins, and my own, be known.

Miss Fleur told me that you were planning to secretly marry just after her birthday. She told me not to worry, she would find a place for me when you moved to London. She trusted me to keep this secret. But I told Ian, fool that I am.

He went to your father, and was hired to make sure the marriage did not occur. I know this, because I helped him take her. For this, he was paid a great deal of money. That is how he purchased his farm. He would have thrown me over after the deal was done, but I knew his misdeeds so he went through with the marriage. Now he betrays me again.

Ian Llewellyn is a kidnapper and rapist. If he is transported or hanged I will not be sorry. I know the child Miss Fleur carries is his, and has a claim on Burgess Farm. I am prepared to honor that claim.

"And then she signs it." Banks looked up and shook his head. "So, your grandfather knew this."

"By God, it appears he did. And before Fleur's child was born, and before she was murdered." A darkness came over Edmund's face. "So why did he not bring charges against the man?"

"Because he was a bloody cowardly bastard?" Remy replied, grimly.

"Do you mind holding your righteous sputters in check while we discuss this question rationally?" Edmund was annoyed. "Your opinion on John Symme's character is duly noted. And I am certain there is more to this than his lack of moral courage."

"Are you?" Remy was skeptical.

"No, no—I agree with Edmund," Banks interjected, "assuming John Symme was a passably decent man, what would persuade him to let this horrible thing go unpunished? After all, he was in love with the woman, with Fleur!"

Edmund rose and began to pace.

"Money. Greed. Family loyalty." He looked grim. "Or some of each." His hands waved aimlessly. "How can we discover what was in his mind?"

"We can continue through these documents, for one thing," Banks answered," and we can look wherever else holds promise—county archives, maybe the archives upstairs again. We've hardly exhausted *that* treasure trove of fascinating business records." He grimaced. "If old man Symme was misusing his Ward's money, there may be some clue in his ledgers—although I for one have had my fill of those things. But I'm willing, if necessary."

"What kind of business did the Symmes conduct?" Remy asked. "Where did their money come from? I don't even know."

"Diversified, as with many *nouveaux riches* of the time," Edmund replied. "Property, some inherited monies on both sides through marriages. I think my great-grandfather imported a good deal of Spanish silver and finished jewelry at one time, plus some commodities—sugar, where he must have met Fleur's father, wool, and such. I believe the Symmes even had shares in a ship that traded in Caribbean goods."

"So, they must have needed capital to invest in such voyages, and ran the risk of some calamity at sea wiping out their money," Banks commented. "Storms, piracy, or privateers could always strike."

"Yes, but they would have been heavily insured, if I know my forebears, and quite ready to make claims if needed. But that is a good avenue of inquiry; we should pursue it." Edmund was thoughtful. "Maybe a return to those archives is a good idea."

Banks groaned.

"Perhaps we have another choice as well," Remy said quietly. "If you want to know what was in John Symme's mind about this, why not try to experience it—as you experienced events at the Stone?"

Edmund looked at her, amazed. "You can't be serious! What a ridiculous idea!" He stopped his pacing, hands on hips. "We need evidence, records, historical information, hard facts—not some vision brought on by emotional distress!"

"Do you forget you gained important information at the Stone with your 'emotional' vision, later confirmed by Fleur as accurate? Why do you discount the possibility of learning more?" Remy argued.

"The idea is absurd."

"Just a moment, Edmund, why dismiss this so quickly?" Banks asked. "You are always talking about logic, and if it worked once it's only logical that it can work again. Why would you—a man who communes regularly with a ghostly lady—object to seeking a vision? What is there to lose?"

"My sanity? My intellectual honesty? Banks, what nonsense! This vision or whatever I had was a fluke, some anomaly of my mind, not something to draw upon at will. You of all people, a physician, should ..." Edmund sputtered.

"I should what, Edmund, discount what I don't entirely understand? Including the power of emotion? How would that be helpful to me or my patients?" Banks pressed. "Why not explore an avenue that so recently bore fruit?"

Edmund sighed deeply, looked aggrieved, then said, "I will not seek any more visions. What I will do, is return to the archives upstairs and see what I may uncover. You stay here and finish with all this," he swept his hand toward the piles of documents still on the table. "Agreed?"

"I think you are adopting an exceedingly foolish stance, Mr. Symme," Remy stated flatly, "but there is no way to coerce you into thinking differently. I shall continue here, as you suggest."

Both Edmund and Banks noted the use of the word "suggest" rather than "direct." One of them was pleased and slightly amused.

"Please don't call if you need reinforcements," Banks chirped as Edmund rose to leave, then returned to perusing the letters and papers in his pile.

*　　*　　*

The day had been unusually warm, and the third-floor archive was overly hot and stuffy; there was hardly a breeze even with the windows thrown wide open. Still fuming, Edmund attempted to work, but found himself speaking to Regis.

"Those two downstairs—'Kit' and 'Jeanne'—how can we make headway when they propose only foolishness! I never should have told them what occurred at the Stone."

Regis listened attentively, but soon became bored and settled onto a small rug under the window.

Edmund stewed for a few more minutes, then finally applied himself to the task at hand, locating a thick volume titled "Private: Alistair Symme 35-37" and began making his way through the myriad entries in crabbed handwriting.

"Lord have mercy," he muttered to himself, stifling a yawn. He pressed on, and came across an entry on the debits column. "Brigantine Mary Elizabeth, out of Tortola, confirmed lost SSW of Sullivan's Island, August 12, 1836. Value, 120,000 pounds sterling."

"Well, well, well, this is interesting . . . and what was the Mary Elizabeth carrying, I wonder?" he mused. "And where in blazes is

Sullivan's Island?"

He knew Tortola was a large island in Britain's Caribbean holdings, so he glanced at the world map hanging on the wall facing him. He had to rise and move closer to make out the words, and soon found what he was looking for.

"By God, a shipment of something to the Americans."

He returned to the table and decided to look for a ship's manifest, and any claim made to the insurance company.

Having no luck with locating either a claim or a detailed manifest, Edmund felt frustrated. "This is a fool's errand!" he muttered, flipping the pages of the journal in irritation. A loose piece of paper dislodged and fell onto the table; it was a short letter that read:

"Brother Alistair, I write to confirm that the Mary Elizabeth has sailed with a manifest of unspecified commodity, expecting to reach port within three weeks. Depending on the factors at the Island, cargo should reach Charleston Mart and be auctioned in September. Your share of proceeds to follow. Stay well. Johnathon."

"Well I'll be damned—the old devil had a brother! I had a great-uncle. Hmm." Edmund mused aloud. "What in blazes was he doing on Tortola? And what was he sending to our former colonies that would qualify as 'unspecified' on a ship manifest?"

His interest and energy renewed, Edmund spent several more hours searching records and even browsing the history shelves in the Library below. By the time he, Banks and Remy gathered in the dining room that evening, he had sobering news.

"Had a productive afternoon, Edmund?" quipped Banks as he took a seat at the table. "You were amazingly industrious and particularly well-mannered—I was most appreciative not to hear any loud cursing or the like wafting from the upper floors."

"Good of you to be concerned, Banks. I may have some news of interest." He paused as Remy entered with a soup tureen. "Well met, Remy, you should hear this too. Please join us."

He motioned for her to be seated. Remy set the tureen on the sideboard and took a chair at the table.

"During my time in the archives today, I came to find out that my great-grandfather, Alistair Symme, had a brother, Johnathon, who owned a plantation on the Virgin Island of Tortola. I haven't found much more detail about him, but I can only assume he farmed sugar and perhaps processed rum for export. Alistair joined him in

241

ownership of a vessel, the Mary Elizabeth, and they were success-
ful in that venture for some years, until she was wrecked in 1836."

Edmund took a sip of his wine.

"A newly discovered uncle on a plantation on Tortola! Now,
that brings to mind landowner wealth. And slaves—he must have
been a slave-owner," Banks commented.

"But slavery was abolished in Britain, and all her territories, in
1834," Remy said. "How could he still own slaves to operate a plantation in 1836?"

"Interesting point, Remy, and I questioned the same thing. I
was able to research the matter a bit," Edmund responded. "The
Emancipation Act took effect in 1834; however, it immediately
freed only individuals who were no more than six years old. Any
older slave simply became an 'apprentice,' continued to work for
the same master for no pay, and was not freed until 1838. So, in essence, slavery continued for four more years—until Her Majesty's
Government paid the 'owners' over 20 million pounds in compensation for loss of their 'property'. Over 700,000 slaves were freed,
and their former owners compensated, but not a penny went to
the newly-free." He shook his head in distaste. "So Virgin Island
plantation owners had labor for their operations until '38, although
they had other problems."

"Hmm—were those isles indeed teeming with virgins, do you
imagine? Could that be considered a problem?" Banks asked with
a serious expression and twinkling eye.

Remy laughed, and even Edmund had to smile as he replied.

"Unknown, Banks, but the name came from that renowned Ital-
ian, Columbus. He stumbled upon the Islands in his travels and,
being a good son of the Church, named them for St. Ursula and her
11,000 martyred virgins. A bit macabre, but . . ."

"Indeed, martyred virgins would have no appeal at all . . ."
Banks grimaced.

"But you mentioned problems. What were they?" Remy asked.

"Hurricanes, for one—apparently a series of severe storms over
several years tore up the islands and caused widespread destruc-
tion. Rebuilding was slow, production suffered. Also, because of
the craving for sugar and increased ability by the middle classes to
purchase it, by the mid '30s both England and her former colonies
had invested heavily in the planting of sugar beets locally. So, the

demand for Virgin Island cane sugar and rum greatly diminished. Their free labor was soon to disappear, and their markets declined as well."

"So that means a significant source of Symme wealth was in jeopardy, even before the ship was lost. But they must have insured the vessel and the cargo, so could they not recover at least some money?" Remy pressed.

"One would think so, and I believe, ultimately, some of the cost of the ship was recovered. But I cannot find any record of a claim for the ship, or the cargo, made to any insurer! The only mention I find is of an unspecified cargo—how can one claim payment for something that is unknown? Usually the manifests are quite specific." Edmund shook his head. "It's maddening."

"But it could explain why old man Symme was so adamant on keeping control of Fleur's money," Banks said thoughtfully. "With a significant source of income drying up, and the loss of a ship and some kind of cargo come to pass, he might have used her inheritance to keep his business solvent."

"Perhaps. But something just doesn't make sense." Edmund mused. "The family business dealings, and wealth, seems to have recovered sufficiently fairly soon after this apparent disaster. So, what happened?"

"Well, it appears it's back to the archives for you, my friend. And may we please have dinner now?" Banks requested. "The soup smells excellent!"

Remy rose and served, then left them.

After enjoying dinner with no more talk of business, ancestors, or unsolved quests, Edmund leaned back in his chair and spoke.

"I don't suppose you would like to join me in looking for more information on Symme deeds and misdeeds—would you?"

"What, this evening?" Banks replied. "Sorry, Edmund, but I think I'm for a brief walk around the grounds with Regis, if you don't mind, and then for bed. Why don't you come with us?"

Edmund agreed that was an excellent idea, and the three of them strolled through the darkening evening for almost an hour before coming back into the house.

"Are you really going to work more tonight, Edmund?" Banks asked. "It's been a long day."

"Yes, well, I'm feeling rather anxious about finding out more and not ready to give up yet. But I will keep the loud swearing to a minimum, so as not to disturb your beauty rest." He smiled at this friend. "Good night."

They both walked up the stairs, Banks heading to his room at the first landing, and Edmund and Regis continuing up to the archive rooms above.

Edmund was determined to find the one piece of information that would make sense of it all.

21
The Hurt of Truth

"Father, you've damn well gone too far! How dare you interfere with the woman I had chosen to marry?'

After almost two hours of fruitless searching, Edmund's eyes and spirit had grown weary. He sighed and rubbed at his forehead, then decided to rest for a moment. Slowly his head slipped down to his folded arms on the table. He was soon asleep.

He was startled awake by the slam of a hand on the table near his head, and angry words. He sat up to see a vaguely familiar figure pacing in front of the window. The figure stopped and spoke.

"You disgrace her, and me, and yourself! I was dissuaded by you once, but now I will report him—and you—to the law! Now it is not only rape, but murder!"

Edmund felt disoriented. He could not believe what he was seeing: his grandfather and great grandfather, there in the room. *This is impossible*, he thought, *am I losing my mind? Or is this another dream?*

"And you think the scandal will leave you untouched?" Alistair Symme, angry and looking formidable in spite of physical frailty, replied to his son. "John, think with your brain for once. The woman is dead and virtually forgotten—nobody cares what has become of her."

"I care—I care a great deal," John replied, just as angry. "And I have not forgotten her."

"I stand corrected: besides you, nobody cares nor will they remember Fleur DuPlessis. And so it must remain." Alistair leaned heavily on his cane. "Do you think I have influence enough to keep myself out of prison if charged with being an accessory to murder? Well, perhaps. But what of the Mary Elizabeth? Will fraud against Her Majesty's government be so easily excused? And can you escape the tarnish of my disgrace? Unlikely." He paused. "And if you think all my assets, the business, my connections will then be solely yours while I swing from the gibbet or rot in gaol, think again. Everything we have will be gone—they'll confiscate it all. Do you think you will be able to recover under that kind of pall? Scandal dies hard in the world of business, and people have great appetite for the misfortunes of others. Will they excuse the son for the sins of the father—or believe the son was also involved, not merely tainted by the disgrace?" His face twisted in an ugly leer. "Be realistic, you have just as much to lose as do I. And for what—a dead woman?"

John's fists closed menacingly as he faced his father. "I could kill you myself," he stated coldly.

"Go ahead," Alistair replied, "it might be the best favor you could do me."

Edmund felt violence in the air; cautiously, he got to his feet and as quietly as possible edged his way against the wall in the far corner of the room.

The other two Symmes were silent for some time, eyeing each other warily. Then Alistair spoke.

"John, I'm not proud of my actions, and as it turns out, I had no need to take such drastic steps. Who would have thought that most of those half-drowned black heathens would have made it to Sullivan's Island and then to the Slave Market in Charleston after the ship went down? And that your uncle would die so suddenly, leaving me that hellhole plantation and all the compensation monies for those same slaves, plus the ones we didn't ship? And then that fool neighbor of his, within a year paying top dollar to set the land into cotton again?" He laughed mirthlessly, shaking his head. "At the time, the girl's money was the only thing between us and disaster."

He hobbled heavily to the chair Edmund had just left and heaved himself into it.

"But what about forbidding our marriage? Why?" John still had murder in his eyes. "Why? Did you take her in just for the money, father? Did you see gold in her veins, profit in her footsteps, money in her smile? Even then, did you not feel for the girl, the orphan, the life entrusted to you?"

Alistair lowered his eyes and remained silent, then glared at John.

"For the reasons I gave, you fool!" his father snapped. "That damned Catholic Relief Act did nothing to change public opinion— nobody does business with papists or those who consort with them. It would have ruined us! And I had to keep control—the money was gone by that time, down with the ship and covering our losses." He met his son's stare. "And if I had taken you both into my confidence about it, maybe you might not have raised the hue and cry, but that girl could never keep her mouth shut for a minute. We'd have been in prison before you could whistle! And then, what would have become of her—papist, penniless, no guardian, no fiancé, making her way alone in this backwater hole. She might have welcomed Llewellyn's attentions then!"

John moved to strike his father, but held himself in check. "You bastard," he growled.

"Perhaps." Alistair sighed. "I do not regret my decisions, but I do regret the outcome—it was not my intention for things to go so badly for Fleur. Believe or not, as you will. But at least, John, you are now a very rich man, able to make an influential and lucrative marriage. At least you have that."

John shook his head. "I have no taste for it. It is ashes in my mouth." He sighed deeply, again gathered his hands into fists at his side, then spoke. "Father, I hope you burn in hell, but I will not put you to the judgment of the law." He turned away. "I will also never speak to you again, and, I hope to God, never set eyes on you again. You'd best take yourself away from my house—Owlswood is my house—never come back, and stay far away from me. If I see you again, I may kill you."

He turned and seemed to look directly at Edmund, then left the room.

*   *   *

"Well, by God, Edmund, it's not every day one discovers one's forebears are felons—and by way of a vision, no less!" Banks commented drily as he slathered a scone with jam. "Ye of little faith, we told you it could happen."

He, Remy, and Edmund sat at the breakfast table as Edmund related his experience.

"Yes, you were indeed right, both of you," Edmund admitted, with some annoyance. "I have come to such strange experiences in this matter I hardly know what to think of myself—am I a fool, idiot, victim of feeble-mindedness?" He grumbled. "No matter whether dream or vision or the onset of insanity, the information rings true with what I researched. And for the love of heaven, simmer down your gloating that we may move forward with some plan."

"Mr. Symme, let me be sure I understand," Remy began. "What

you have gleaned is that in 1836 Alistair Symme colluded with his brother to sell a number of slaves—then called apprentices—to the American states where slavery was still legal, but somehow to also claim Emancipation Act compensation for them as well. Those 'apprentices' were the 'unspecified cargo' on the ship Mary Elizabeth, and they were not lost in the wreck but made their way to the Charleston Slave Market. By their actions, the Symmes defrauded the British government, gained a good profit, and possibly recovered some compensation for the lost ship. Then, upon his brother's death, Alistair inherited and sold his plantation for another goodly sum."

"You have it." Edmund replied, then continued. "And in the uncertain time between the loss of the ship and the ensuing events, Fleur's fortune was used to keep his business afloat. The old man was already determined to prevent the marriage—and resultant loss of control over his Ward's fortune—because he feared that public and political opinion against Catholics would damage his business dealings and social standing,"

Remy spoke. "In service of that fear, Alistair Symme had Fleur abducted to prevent her marriage to his son and sully her reputation enough to have her committed—thereby ensuring her fortune remained in his control. After she was raped and impregnated, he would have used that to reinforce the diagnosis of Crandall, the 'mad doctor' hired from London, that she was immoral and incompetent. Only she was murdered. And when she was murdered, he hushed it up." She paused briefly. "His son, John Symme, affianced to Fleur, did nothing to bring all this to light, nor did he assist Fleur's child except for providing employment at Owlswood or her family in perpetuum." Her face had become deathly pale. "Does that sum up the situation?"

Neither Edmund nor Banks could find words; they both nodded silently.

"And now that we know all this, it is our charge to make things right for my grandmother," Remy stated, quietly. "Her wish is to have her name cleared and the truth known."

"Indeed. It sounds straightforward enough. But what will satisfy her, and why must it happen within the next fortnight?" Edmund mused. "Remy, on what date was your mother born?"

"October 18, 1837. We would have celebrated soon. " Remy answered.

"You said your mother, Fleur's child, was substituted for a still-born by the midwife." Edmund thought for a moment. "This happened on the night Fleur met her death, by our best reckoning. It would not be impossible to consider a babe just a few days old to be a newborn—especially in the confusion and exhaustion of a difficult birth. So . . ."

"So you think this deadline Fleur has imposed on us is the anniversary of her murder?" Banks finished the thought. "By God, it makes sense."

"By God, it does!" Edmund agreed. "But why impose a deadline at all? She has waited this long, what causes the urgency?"

Remy thought for a moment, then replied, "Perhaps because her time hovering between the Earth and the afterlife is waning. And because you are the last of your bloodline, as I am the last of mine. You are the last Symme, and I am her only blood kin, and if we do not avenge her, she is lost."

"If the Lady's name is to be cleared, then it strikes me that Llewellyn's must be further sullied," Banks began, "and even the name of Symme will not come away unscathed." He looked at Edmund solemnly. "What think you, Edmund?"

"I think you are correct." He thought for a moment. "And in all honesty, I feel no hesitation about taking on the responsibility. I must account for my forebears, regardless of shame or other unpleasantness that may result. However," he glanced at Remy, "the Llewellyn clan will not be pleased, and that may bring problems of its own."

"Hmm, most unpleasant and possibly dangerous problems from what I can gather." Banks looked concerned. "We'd best take precautions. Those people are not to be disregarded when they take umbrage."

"You're right, of course," Edmund agreed, "but we have little choice. Now that we know the truth, we must act on it. All must come to light, regardless of the consequences." He smiled ruefully. "As the Bible states, 'The truth shall set you free'. I have also found that, while possibly painful at first, truth clears the air and permits welcome resolution to begin."

"Don't be so glum, Edmund, you accomplished what you set out to do—find the Truth of this serpentine affair!" Banks exclaimed. "Now we have but to . . ."

Remy's face darkened and she interrupted. "You, both of you, cannot be such fools as to think this Truth will be welcome, that truth is always welcome no matter what it looks like!" She rose from the table. "When she has a lovely face and brings solace, the world bows before the truth—but when she is hard and ugly, who opens their arms to her? When she brings trouble and pain, who welcomes her?"

"What are you saying—explain yourself, Remy!" Edmund demanded.

"So, these facts, this Truth, about what happened to Fleur will have devastating effects on many people—people whom I love and esteem. Can you not see?"

She was quiet but vehement as she continued.

"A family very dear to me, my family, believes that my mother was Lily's daughter, Samuels's niece! And that I am his grand-niece and that we share blood and family bonds. But this is not true!" Her eyes blazed. "The truth revealed means that a very respected woman whom I love, midwife to half the village, will be exposed as a liar, as will her legendary mother before her. I will lose the only family I have ever known, because the truth is that I am not one of them. The truth is that I am the descendent of some foreigner from France and a most despised local landowner, Ian Llewellyn, and so am kin to his most unpleasant progeny!" She placed her hands on the table and leaned in closer. "Is this the Truth that will set me free? Cast me adrift, more!"

Tears filled her eyes.

"For God's sake, Remy, what the devil are you talking about?" Edmund erupted. "Were you not completely devoted to clearing Fleur's name, so entranced by the idea of a spirit grandmother that you could hardly think? Now *she* means nothing?" He, too, rose to his feet. "Now you are filled with remorse for the local townspeople who may need to reconcile to the fact of your lineage? Where was this concern for your supposed family when we embarked on this search for the truth—only now it comes forth?" His voice was harsh. "Well, I say too bad! I say they can jolly well take themselves all to hell if they cannot handle the truth!"

Remy's eyes blazed through her tears.

"Edmund Symme, the fact that you despised your own family and found little comfort with them has turned your soul! Not every family elder is a cold, angry, empty shell of a former self, or a simpering dandy, or a feckless female ninny! You cannot see what you never had, what a decent family looks like! How dare you paint my people with that same brush, sending them off to hell . . ."

Banks quickly rose, put his hand on her shoulder, and said, "Miss Remy—Jeanne—listen to me." His voice was soothing. "Please, may I tell you something?" He took his handkerchief and handed it to her, then turned to Edmund and directed, "Sit down."

Edmund sat; Remy nodded, took the handkerchief, and quieted as she wiped her eyes. Then she, too, sat.

"Good," he smiled and began. "I have a sister, Dolly, younger than I, and we grew up together. She was always following me around, getting in the way—as younger siblings will—and angry that I had more freedom to get myself into trouble than did she. But, nevertheless always the first to come to my defense and comfort when I got in a mess." He shook his head in remembrance and smiled wider. "I love her incredibly—along with her children now, my niece and nephew. I will do anything for them. I can't imagine what life would be without them." He paused for a moment. "If I were to learn that, somehow, Dolly was not my blood kin—had been adopted, perhaps—it would make absolutely no difference to me. She is my sister. No accident of birth or destiny could or would change my feelings for her and her children." He continued, gently but earnestly, "Do you understand? This will make no difference to your people, none." He looked at her intently. "Do you understand?"

Quieted and more in control of herself, Remy nodded and ventured a half-smile.

"I wish I could be certain of that. I am not."

Edmund was not appeased. "I still cannot believe that, after all this time and effort, you would abandon Fleur to languish in disgrace and obscurity! She is your blood, after all, if you are so concerned with family!"

"This is not about abandoning my grandmother. I would never do that, as you are so quick to assume, and I little appreciate . . ." Remy's anger returned.

"Please—both of you! For pity's sake calm down!" Banks said, exasperated. "Listen and listen well. Your adoptive family will not turn against you, Miss Remy, nor will they shun you. It will come as a shock, of course, but that will settle soon enough. As for damage to their reputation and standing in the community, perhaps we can come to some happy accommodation with the Lady about how much, and what, becomes known. We may find a way to clear the Lady's name and satisfy her concerns without vast damage to the living community." Now he looked sharply at Edmund, then back to Remy. "Yes? Shall we pursue such a path?"

Edmund grudgingly replied, "Yes, well, of course, that is the worthiest option."

Remy agreed. "Indeed, we should do that."

She glanced at Edmund. There was a moment of quiet as they collected their thoughts, and their emotions.

"It occurs to me," Edmund began, "that the Dowager witch Llewellyn knows of this blood tie with you, and that is what prompted her surprising request to meet you—why else would she make such an overture? But to what end, and how did she catch wind of it?"

"Yes, it seems obvious she knows something," Remy replied, "but what exactly and how did she learn of it? And why would she care? She was most circumspect when we spoke." She paused. "I must find out. Another meeting with her is in order. It will be tricky."

"Hah! Tricky and dangerous, by God. How can this be managed, and is it worth the risk and trouble?" Edmund wondered. "Still, we need the information and where else may it be obtained?"

"If I may be so bold, haven't you both forgotten one very important thing?" Banks inquired.

"And that would be?" Edmund asked, turning to Banks.

Banks replied calmly, "By the milky white breasts of St. Ursula's virgins, the next meeting anyone should have is with the Lady Fleur herself."

22
Respect for the Dead

Flames in the fireplace danced as the night wind came up and cast a soft glow on Fleur's face. Unusual for her, Fleur had abandoned her perch on the mantle and was slowly floating by the bookcases, absently drawing her hand across the volumes in a light caress, her feet seeming to skim the air above the floor. She did not look well; dark smudges under her eyes and a firm set to her lips made her seem even paler than normal. Her usually glorious red hair was dull and untidy. She turned to face Edmund.

"So, what do you propose?" she asked softly. "It is enlightening, to find Alistair Symme behind my undoing so directly. And you say John knew nothing of the plot until after my death? Yet . . . yet he did nothing when he found out. Hmm." One hand rose to her temple, as if with pain. "Again, what do you propose?"

Edmund had set out the entire story for her, informing her of what he had uncovered. In prior encounters, he had not been certain she had understood, nor perhaps even listened. Now he knew she had followed every word.

"Here is what I propose," he began. "Since there was no inquest into your death, I cannot file a legal inquiry to reopen the matter. Some may have assumed you simply returned to France. Many others, no doubt due to a campaign of gossip encouraged by the Symmes, thought you killed yourself and probably your child as well." He took stock of her reaction, then continued. "However, I can make all the information I found public, and we can claim assault, kidnapping, and murder. Because it happened so many years ago, statutes may prevent official charges from proceeding. But even if dismissed, the truth will be known." He searched her face. "Regardless, I will file another suit on behalf of your living relative for recovery of your fortune. It would be most unusual but not difficult."

She continued to move slowly through the room for some minutes, almost as if in a trance. Edmund was startled when she spoke.

"A legal matter would require a hearing and evidence. You

surely do not expect me to testify, and all other witnesses to the abduction and murder are dead." There was a brief flicker of a smile. "And you, the one living witness, through a vision or—from a logical viewpoint—perhaps through alcohol-induced delirium, came to this knowledge. You as barrister, you as witness. How can you win such a case?"

Edmund shook his head. "There is one other witness still alive: the midwife who placed your infant with the village woman. It will be unpleasant, but we can exert pressure that will force her to testify." He walked toward her. "And we have other evidence: letters, journals, business records, and Llewellyn's knife. Mostly circumstantial, however enough to make a credible argument." He saw her shudder slightly at the mention of her murder weapon. "There may be some trouble from the Llewellyn people, but we can deal with that." He pressed on. "There will be no contest to the facts. The intent is for the truth to be made public, to expose your betrayal and murder. And for your granddaughter to be made whole."

"*Tellement stupide*! How much weight will all that carry after sixty years? And who will care about me or my granddaughter?" There was an angry flash to her eyes, welcome after the former deadness of her stare. "And this is your idea of adequate justice for a murdered woman? What about clearing the blood from the name of Symme?"

Edmund was startled. "What do you mean?"

Fleur smiled ruefully. "Does not the Bible command 'an eye for an eye and a tooth for a tooth', in the cause of justice? What you propose is within your great renown within the law, but that is too easy. What I require is avengement for my death—the death of a Llewellyn as recompense for mine." She watched him coldly. "Can you understand that? You must clear the stain of cowardice and bad blood from your line. A Llewellyn must die."

Edmund, speechless for a moment, slowly replied, "I cannot promise—or even seek—a death sentence for an innocent citizen today for the crime of his forebear many years ago. No court would hear it."

"There are other ways to effect a death, *nest'ce-pas*, than through the law."

Edmund gestured impatiently.

"You are not yourself tonight, Lady, and I bring you back to the matter at hand. We can clear your name and return your fortune to your granddaughter with little resistance. You forget, the Symme family will be defendants in the case. There will be no contest to the testimony. There will be no dispute of the facts. You will prevail." Reluctantly, Edmund continued. "However, you must consult with your granddaughter. She seems to have some hesitation about revealing your relationship and the details of her mother's birth."

"What! I do not believe you! She would not turn against the truth, turn against me!" Fleur cried. "*Impossible!*"

Edmund had no taste for this issue. "I will let her discuss it with you. I have told you my intentions. You, and she, must decide. She waits now to see you."

He bowed slightly and said, "Belle Dame, *adieu* for now. I will leave you, and your granddaughter will join you." He turned and walked out of the room. A few moments later, Remy entered, closed the door, and walked to her grandmother.

"Good evening, *Grandmère. Comment ça va?*" Remy smiled sadly, alarmed to see how haggard Fleur appeared. "Are you well?"

"I am not well. I am not certain how to feel, *Chérie,* as I hear you plan to abandon me, now that the truth is known!" Fleur replied coldly. "I could not be more astonished or appalled."

Remy was nonplussed. "*Grandmère*, please, it is not the case. I only wish . . . only wish to do what is right, to do what is merciful!" Angry now, she asked warily, "What did he tell you?"

"Mercy! You speak to me of mercy?" Fleur turned away and clenched her fists. "Where was mercy when I was alone and afraid, cast out and reviled? Who deserved mercy more than I? This is no time for mercy." She spat out the word with bitterness. "Now it is time for justice, for revenge!" Fleur shook her fists toward heaven and trembled. "I deserve revenge!" Cold with anger, she turned her eyes to Remy. "And you want to leave me?"

"No! Not at all. Please, let me speak." Remy pleaded. "I must tell you what is in my heart and in my thoughts. Then you can judge." She tried to remain calm. "Will you listen?"

Fleur looked at her for a long moment. "*Bien.* Say what you have to say." She nodded her head toward the fireplace and the chair before it. "Let us sit and I will listen."

When Remy was seated in the winged armchair, Fleur glided effortlessly to her normal place on the mantle. She settled and turned a stony face to Remy, who took a long breath, then began. "First,

I must ask you—did you love my mother, *Grandmère*? Or hate her because of Lewellyn?"

Fleur's eyes grew wide with surprise. "How can you ask—I loved your mother so very much! She was my own dear child, my Aimee." Her eyes grew soft with tears. "I carried her and grew her with my own life blood for nine months, then gave her to this world. I was determined to protect her, to teach her well—I was determined that the sins of the father would not be visited on the head of the child!" She began to weep. "When I feared I might not return from meeting Llewellyn at the Stone, I gave her to someone who would keep her safe." She sighed deeply. "And as I watched her grow, she had no trace of that pig in her nature, no hardness or anger." She paused and her face hardened. "How can you ask such a question? It was she who rejected me, who turned away every time I appeared to her here, every time I reached out to you in these halls. She hated me!" She began to weep.

"No, *Grandmère*, she was just afraid," Remy felt caught in the middle. "She was taught to fear what she could not understand, and to distrust things of the spirit that could not be explained. But I saw she was much like you in her love of natural beauty, and love of her child. And she tried to be a good daughter to the woman who took her in—Lily, the housekeeper here—and to the people she thought were her family. *Were* her family. They raised her with village superstitions and folklore and foolish beliefs, but also with protection and love. Even though she seemed strange and did not look or act like them, they cared for her. For us both."

Fleur's sobs abated and she quieted. "Ah—Lily! I remember her! She was the housekeeper here, and always very kind and helpful to me when I lived at Owlswood. She, too, was *enceinte* when I carried your mother, and then she was the only kindness I could find." She paused as memory came back to her. "Do you know why John Symme came so late to the Stone at the time of my death—too late to save me and bring Llewellyn to heel?"

Remy shook her head.

"I will tell you." Fleur leaned closer. "I went to him and told him I would meet my rapist one last time, to kill him as he deserved. He was shocked, of course. Then I pleaded with him that, if I should not return from the encounter, to promise to raise my lovely baby as his own, as the child he and I would have had together. I asked him to do this out of his love for me."

She pulled away again, her eyes angry and cold. "He refused. He told me I was a fool to take such a step, he spoke to me disdainfully, he called me mad. He forbade me to go! Perhaps he thought I wanted other from Llewellyn than to kill him." Her faced clouded with remembered shame and anger. "He took my hands in his and told me not to go. He said we could leave Owlswood, leave all the sorrow and disgrace behind, travel and be happy together . . . without the child. We would leave the child at some kind of place that took unwanted children, and live a happy life without her." Her eyes became wild. "Can you imagine? Can you imagine him saying that to me?"

"What did you do, *Grandmère*?" Remy whispered.

"I slapped his face, spit on his shoes, and called him *cochon*." Tears ran down her face. "I left him there, I took the small dagger my own *Maman* gave to me, hid it in my gown, bundled your mother in my shawl and went to see the Tarot Crone on my way to kill Llewellyn." She wiped at her eyes. "She was the midwife who cared for me when my time was at hand. She often read the cards for me, and—it was to her that I entrusted my Aimee when I went to the Stone that final time." She became slightly calmer. "That was the last time I saw John Symme. Perhaps he thought I would not go through with it, so he failed to follow me. Until . . ." She seemed unable to speak for a moment.

"Until what, *Grandmère*?" Remy prodded.

"I believe the Crone told him where I had gone and what would happen. She tried to save me. But . . ." Fleur gave a shrug and smiled sadly, "she was too slow, and he was too late, and too faithless."

Remy rose from her chair and reached up toward the mantle where Fleur still perched, taking her hands in her own, feeling not flesh but warm vibrating energy. "I am so sorry, *Grandmère*, so very sorry."

They wept silently together for a time.

Then Remy spoke. "The Tarot Crone who helped you was very old and she, too, had a daughter who helped women birth their children." Remy continued. "Her daughter brought your child to Lily after Lily's own baby died at birth, and you had lost your life. She told no one, except for me just recently. She kept us safe, kept the secret, and that family became our family. Lily thought I was her granddaughter, Samuel thinks I am his niece, Annie thinks I am her cousin."

"Ah, Samuel! He was but a boy when I knew him, a good boy, and always respectful to me." Fleur mused. "They were good people, even to a stranger such as I."

"I will not say that my mother seemed happy as part of that family, or that I have myself fit with these people, but I was cared for and loved." She paused. "Lily and my Mother are both dead now. But you must understand, when the truth of my mother's origin is revealed—perhaps through the legal action Edmund Symme wishes to pursue—a very good woman, the midwife, will be labeled a liar. Perhaps she will lose her livelihood, certainly Samuel will lose a niece, and I will lose my family." Remy took a deep breath. "My father used to tell me a saying from his youth: *On doit des egards aux vivants, on ne doit aux morts que la verité.'* "

"Ah!" the word escaped in a sigh from Fleur. "Yes, I see." She smiled slightly. "As your father told you, 'We owe the living respect, we owe only truth to the dead.' So, you have found the truth of my death for me, but you feel that by revealing it to vindicate me, you will be showing disrespect to all these others." She paused. "And you feel that you and I owe much to these people, do you not? A dilemma." She grew thoughtful. "What shall we do? The time grows short! There are only a few days left. Symme owes me the truth, and a life, and he must do it or all is lost!"

Remy drew her hands away from Fleur's and asked, "But I don't understand! Why is time so important? Why do you say we must act so quickly? And what is this talk of owing a life?"

Fleur became agitated. "The anniversary approaches—the day of my death. Every year it is harder. I begin to lose my grip as the date comes near." Her eyes grew wilder. "You must understand how hard I have tried—through the years, every year!" She shook her head. "Each time I tried to gain a champion I was rejected. First my beloved John, who preferred to wallow in his misery and guilt; then his son Nigel, the fainting one who saw me and fled. Many times I tried . . . and now this last Symme."

She tore at her hair in frustration. "This is the last chance for me. What will happen? I feel I can no longer hold onto the existence I have, and the chance to move onto another realm—it has vanished, too. I feel I will enter oblivion. This last Symme, will he . . .?" She flung her arms out in frustration. "And to simply file a claim at law, tell whomever might wish to listen how I was wronged—will that be enough? What kind of expiation will that be for decades of

Symme betrayal? What kind of bravery and strength of spirit will that show?" She shook her head and looked distraught. "He must kill a Llewellyn to avenge me!"

Remy caught her breath. "What is this you say—Edmund must kill for you? Explain!"

"But it is simple, *Chérie*, as the holy scriptures direct, 'An eye for an eye and a tooth for a tooth' is the way of Justice. There is no other way to redeem the Symme bloodline. How else can I be truly sure of my vengeance, of his determination, of his commitment to Justice?" She paused. "Of his commitment to me and righting the wrong against me."

Remy spoke quickly. "But there must be some other way than murder, you cannot demand that Edmund become a criminal!"

"Hah! A criminal?" Fleur laughed. "Is not the great Law of society based upon the Law of God, the Law of Scripture? How can fulfilling Scripture be criminal?" Her gaze hardened. "I demand retribution, I demand justice. Edmund Symme must be the instrument of my revenge. He has promised."

"No, *Grandmère*, he never promised murder and he would not now." Remy shook her head, angry. "Why do you take this stance—why force him to choose his loyalties? Why force me to choose between the living and the dead? Have you become so much like the Symmes you claim to despise that you use the pain of others against them, use their pain to gain something you want? How could you be that person?"

Fleur's eyes blazed but her voice was icy. "How do you dare speak to me in this way! I could drive you all mad, make you all grovel at my feet should I so choose. Why do you turn against me now, why does Edmund Symme fail me?"

Remy tried to remain calm. "You are wrong. Edmund has not abandoned you. He is on your side; he will fight for you. And I, *Grandmère*, I have your blood. I will be your champion!"

Fleur's smile seemed calmer, but infinitely sad.

"Dear child, only a Symme can erase the stain from his house, his blood, and my being. Only a Symme can avenge these wrongs, and your Edmund is the last Symme."

She faded from view, and all was quiet.

23
Eye for an Eye

"How's the old lady today?" Kane asked as he entered the room, gnawing an apple. He leaned against the door frame and looked the maid up and down appraisingly.

The young woman carried a small tray holding an empty medicine bottle, drinking glass, and soiled face towels. Her face betrayed no emotion.

"Your Grandmother, Mrs. Llewellyn, is in comfort, Kane Llewellyn—now she wishes to rest." She looked at him severely, her pretty face in a frown. "You've left it too late for a visit this morning."

"Ah, too bad—but then maybe I could have a bit of a visit with you, Janie?" He chewed and smirked at the same time.

She tilted her head and returned his smirk.

"Then my brothers would cut off your bollocks and toss them to the hogs, before breaking every bone in your body. Out of my way, please."

She met his gaze with no falter.

"Bloody hell, you don't have to get all pissy, woman, I was just being polite, like," Kane moved away past her into the room and watched Janie walk on without a backward glance.

He shook his head at her disinterest.

"Can't even pass the time of day with some people," he muttered. "Say, Bran," he called as he caught sight of his brother leaving the sickroom, "come down and tell me how Gran is doing."

"She seems better today, but still can't move her left side," Bran answered as he came downstairs. "A little easier to understand her when she tries talkin'." He looked worried. "I've never seen her weak like this before, and just struck down so sudden! Is there a cure for apoplexy?"

"Bah—she's strong as an ox. She'll recover," Kane scoffed. "But I'll grant you, it did come on sudden. Right after she talked to that Remy woman, wasn't it? She was pretty bothered by that little talk they had—did she tell you anything?"

"Not me. But she wants Da to go and see Miss Remy and do some kind of business with her. It has something to do with money and some claim on our place." Bran was uncomfortable with this line of inquiry. "Da will know what to do."

"Now wait a minute, you know more of this than you're saying—what's going on?" Kane moved closer to his brother. "Tell me what you know—tell me!" He grabbed the front of Bran's shirt and shook him. "You know better than to cross me, little brother." He let Bran loose and pushed him away. "What did she say?"

"All I know is that there's some kind of family relation with Miss Remy—we're cousins or some such. Gran doesn't want her to put a claim on our farm, to get her rights or some money or something! Now that Gran is sick, she wants Da to handle things with the woman. That's all I know!" Bran lifted his chin defiantly. "And you'd best not get in Da's way, I'm thinkin'."

"That's all you do, brother, think!" Kane laughed as he gave a not-too-gentle slap to Bran's face. Then his face darkened. "There's no fancy, citified, prissy woman who's going to threaten my inheritance, not any small part of it! I'll deal with that Remy bitch, and she'll leave us alone when I do. Da can be damned!" He thought for a moment. "You take a message over to Owlswood, sayin' Da wants to palaver—but it'll be me that shows up. He'll be gone the best part of this week, deliverin' that livestock to the Squire next parish. By the time he's back, it'll be done."

"No chance, Kane—I'll not go against Gran and Da, not even for you and your fists. You'd better keep out of it! Da can still take you down." Bran looked defiant, but moved out of range of his brother's fists nonetheless. "I won't bring no message. And what will you do?"

"Ah, you fool—I don't need you to bring a message, somebody else will go. But you keep your mouth shut, hear?" He tried to soften his tone. "What're ye in a tizzy for—I'm just going to make it clear to the Remy woman where her true interests lie—and they lie in leaving us alone. I'll convince her to return to her big city pursuits, won't I?"

"But that barrister, Symme, he might be trouble," Bran said over his shoulder as he left the room. "He won't scare easy. He could help her with legal matters—a claim and such. Don't start trouble for us, Kane. You'd best leave it alone—you'd best leave it to Da. You mark that!"

Kane watched his brother leave, then mused out loud.

"Well now, that woman might just decide to let the matter drop. Or, if she chooses to be stubborn, the truth is, she can't file much of a claim if some accident renders her terrible injured or, even, God forbid, dead." He shook his head. "T'would be a shame, but there it be."

He shook his head as if regretting the thought, but there was a smile on his face.

*   *   *

Banks was incredulous. "It is ridiculous; it cannot be true; you must be mistaken!" He paced to-and-fro across the terrace. "She demands a death?"

"Not 'a' death, Kit, a Llewellyn's death," Remy answered. "The only way, she says, to avenge the wrongs against her and clear the stain of cowardice from the house of Symme."

Edmund was dismissive. "You must have taken her words too seriously, Remy—she was upset and highly agitated," he countered, "She must have been venting. No more." He sprawled in his chair in front of the remains of their breakfast al fresco. "Oh, and many thanks for the reminder of my family's failings, lest any of us forget."

"I strongly disagree," Remy replied, "she was absolutely serious and very clear. She cited scripture to support her cause."

"Oh, please," Edmund waved his hand in the air.

"She feels legal action is too easy, too weak, too likely to be disregarded—she feels you are abandoning her and retreating into the law to mask your weakness. Our weakness. Our retreat from her." Remy frowned. "Abandonment."

"Which Llewellyn does she wish Edmund to do for?" Banks inquired, interested. "I know the one I'd choose, but it's not for me to . . ."

"Oh, for heaven's sake, she did not name names, and I don't think it would matter, really, it's retribution!" Remy was annoyed. "Neither of you take this seriously. She demands a death, by your hand, Edmund Symme," Remy pointed at him, "and she was not swayed by other concerns."

"So . . . what do we do?" Banks let the question hang.

"Well, I know what I will do—feckless coward that I am—and that is to proceed with filings in court." Edmund rose. "I have sent word to the justice of the peace and my clerk; documents are being prepared. And I have no intention of planning an execution of retribution, regardless of the moral imperatives involved. Regis, come."

He nodded to both Banks and Remy and headed into the house, the big dog following.

Remy watched him go.

"He will not listen to a word I say. He is so certain of his own . . . oh, why bother to think of it!" She clenched her fist against her skirt. "I am off for a walk."

She turned and took off across the lawn.

"Do you wish some company?" Banks called after her. "I'm glad to join you."

Not bothering to turn and speak, she just waved her arm in negation and kept her steady pace past the gazebo and through the hedge.

24
Truth for the Living

"So, what are your thoughts about how to proceed with the charming family Llewellyn, your newly revealed relations?" Banks asked gently. He and Remy were seated at the large kitchen table, having arranged to take lunch together and compare notes. He had again been called to London for a patient emergency and had returned only that morning. "This seems like sticky business to me, and you can't be serious about doing it on your own."

"It was a rather strange meeting I had with Gwyned Llewellyn last week, I must admit," Remy reported. "She seemed wary of me, as if I would pose some kind of a threat to her and her family. That was not my goal." She paused. "She seemed to think I wanted to exploit our connection in some way."

"That hardly surprises me. What did you discuss?" Banks asked between bites of a delectable slice of Stilton from the after-lunch cheese plate. After a few days away, he reacquainted himself with the excellent provisions of Owlswood with gusto.

"Well, I first told her of the evidence that she and my Mother were half-sisters. She did not seem at all surprised—in fact she stated that her mother had told her as much before she died. She's known about it for some years." Remy paused. "She had no desire to establish any kind of relations with us while my mother was alive, and certainly has no interest in considering me family—mainly, I think, because she feels I may lay claim to part of her business." Again, she paused. "I made it most clear that I had no interest in pursuing a share of her family's assets, and she seemed to believe me, somewhat reluctantly. But I know she'd be very troubled by the thought of her father being publicly labeled a murderer."

"She was devoted to the old bas—-er, gentleman, was she?" Banks asked, surprised.

Remy smiled. "It does not seem so. She says her reputation will be badly affected if such news gets around—even though it was so long ago, she fears people won't like to deal with them with a stain of murder on the family." She shook her head. "I really don't know how to resolve the issue. We must make the truth of Fleur's death public to clear her name, and yet . . ."

"And yet, why do you concern yourself with the effects of the truth on such people?" Edmund asked, joining them after his usual mid-day walk of the grounds, Regis at his side. The big dog padded over to Remy and was torn between laying his head on her lap, or on the table close to the cheese. "They are truly not worthy of your sympathy, are they?"

Remy bristled. "They are difficult people, hard people, unpleasant people, but I don't believe they are as unworthy as you think. Gwyned has been forthright with me, and she and her son have built a good reputation for quality livestock—you must be fair-dealing to do that. Her grandson Bran is a decent enough young man, when away from his brother. Kane, is not worth much, I grant."

She also thought, but did not say, *And of course, they can make unpleasantness for my family, should they choose.*

"Hah!" Edmund puffed. "Our friend Kane is a braggart, bully, and mangy cur—I would not trust him with mucking out the barn!" He reached over to the cheese and grabbed a morsel, prompting Banks to wave his knife in protest.

"But for her to be so unsettled by my words, I cannot understand it." Remy mused. "What next?"

"She was more than just unsettled, Remy. She had an apoplectic seizure three days ago and has become an invalid," Edmund stated. "You knew this, did you not?"

"I had heard she was taken ill—but apoplexy! Is she paralyzed?" Remy was concerned.

"Bettering now, I think."

"It is truly not called apoplexy anymore, Edmund, rather a brain embolism or brain bleeding," corrected Banks. "Sometimes people recover from the after-effects quickly, and sometimes not. Do you think I should offer to visit?"

"As you like, Banks, but she has her own physician and is under care," Edmund replied. "If you go, take your gun, won't you?" He smiled sardonically, then paused. "But it is rather an obstacle to our moving forward with the Lady Fleur's business, wouldn't you say? Even I feel badly, kicking an opponent when downed."

"But what should be our next step? We have little time to consider before we act," Remy worried.

"I've sent word to the District Magistrate and will meet with him tomorrow," Edmund informed them. "It would be best for him to lodge a request for an inquiry into Fleur's death—remember, there was no formal proceeding conducted at the time, as far as we know, and it was so long ago. Someone would have signed the death certificate as 'suicide,' and I have people looking for that document. Then we can present evidence of the murder, officially change the cause of death, and file a formal claim to restore Fleur du Plessey's inheritance to her only living relative."

"My God," Remy murmured, then bit her lower lip. "Do you think Gwyned Llewellyn is right, that the news will ruin them?"

"I truly have no idea, and I hardly care," was Edmund's grim reply.

"Must it be made public?" Remy continued.

"By God, woman, this will be public record—do you think murders are kept secret? Do you think the Law is some kind of parlor game?" Edmund bristled.

The air in the room crackled, like the moments between thunder and lightning.

"Could the charge be something less than murder—manslaughter, perhaps?" Banks interjected. "After all, it could have been unpremeditated, done in the heat of the moment. Is it really so clear that Llewellyn intended to kill her?"

"What the hell are you blathering about?" Edmund exclaimed. "A large man against a slight woman who'd given birth not two weeks prior, a woman he'd forced himself on? A woman who threatened to expose him? If this is not murder aforethought . . ."

"Edmund—peace! Please, did you not tell us that Fleur struck the first blow, that she stabbed him first? He may have just responded as the dirty street-fighter he was!" Banks retorted. "And for the benefit of Miss Remy's family in the village, would not a softening of the matter serve best?"

"How can you say such a disastrously stupid thing to me . . ." Edmund was almost shouting.

"Stop!" Remy stood up and bellowed. "Enough!"

The two men looked at her in amazement.

"I have spoken with La Belle Dame about this, and I have given it a great deal of thought," Remy began. "Causing undue uproar is not what she expects, nor does she demand unnecessary pain."

25
Le Poignard en Pierre

Edmund strode into the kitchen to find Cook at the big work table, flour dusting her forearms as she kneaded bread for dinner.

"Cook, have you seen Remy?" he asked. "I have need to speak with her and cannot find her."

He tried not to sound curt.

"Well, sir, you can't find her because she's not here—she's out walkin' in the dusk." Cook shook her head. "I told her she was daft to traipse about like that, but she was determined, as our Jeannie often is."

The last words were almost muttered to herself.

"Out walking—where did she go?" Edmund pressed.

"That's the most daft of all—she said she was headin' out by the Stone! Can you credit it, the Stone almost at dark and with a nasty change in the weather coming on!" The woman looked at him with concern. "I didn't like to bring it to your attention, sir, it's not my place. But . . ."

"Was Dr. Banks with her? Regis?" He felt a strange heaviness in the pit of his stomach.

"No, sir, the good doctor and the great doggie left together some time ago, also daft to be walking so close to nightfall! But they were only out to gather a brief after-tea constitutional before the rain comes." She paused, then said, "Can I help you with something?" She began to wipe her hands. "Is there some trouble, sir?"

"No, no, that's all right—please get on with your work. And…" Edmund tried to sound composed, "you are certain she said the Stone, are you?"

"Oh, no doubt about that—she was very brisk about it, too, almost like she was on an errand or such!" Cook returned to her bread. "I'd best be getting this into the oven if we want it for your dinner tonight." She smiled up at him. "You're certain I cannot be of help to you?" she asked over her shoulder as she bustled away to the oven across the room.

"No, thank you very much. Carry on." Edmund felt another wave of anxiety course through him. *She couldn't possibly be trying to fulfill Fleur's hare-brained mission on her own...could she?*

He attempted to think calmly, but his thoughts ran wild. What to do now? He felt a surge of relief when he heard Banks' voice calling from the other end of the long hallway and the scrabble of Regis' paws on the wood floor.

"I say, anyone left alive or awake in this place? Where is everyone?" Banks appeared, shaking droplets from his coat and hat. "Feels like the wind is picking up and the rain with it! Ah, Edmund—what's the trouble? You look like you've seen a ghost. Oh, sorry, wrong thing to say."

"Which way did you walk—did you see Remy while you were out?"

"We just walked down the road to the village apiece—and we did not see Remy. What's going on?" Banks asked, concerned.

"She told Cook she was going to the Stone. Of all the infinitely, egregiously stupid things . . .!" Edmund shook his head and spoke softly. "You know what night this is, don't you?"

"How could I not?" Banks was grim. Catching sight of Cook across the big room, he lowered his voice. "The anniversary of La Belle Dame's murder. Let's go."

"Wait." Edmund took a breath. "Regis and I will go. You stay here, in case she comes back or Cook was mistaken." When Banks opened his mouth to protest, Edmund put up a hand to stop him, "No, this is for me to do. Just me."

*　*　*

Remy drew her collar close and draped her shawl tighter. She had almost left her walking staff in the mud room, but as small brush was blown across her path she was glad she had it with her. *Je dois être une folle!* She thought to herself. *I'm crazy, no doubt about it.* The sun had just dropped behind the hills and the sky was darkening, even without the arrival of rain-laden clouds. *Only a matter of time before the heavens open and I'm drenched.* But she kept her pace, getting closer to the Stone with every determined step.

What possible difference could her presence at the Stone make, she wondered? But she felt compelled to be there, to be present at the place where such an atrocity had taken place sixty years ago to-

268

night. Why? Would it make any difference to her Grandmother, distraught as she had become? Would this night mark the end of existence for La Belle Dame Fleur?

"Someone must stand for her!" she said aloud. "Someone must remember with her, remember for her—perhaps for the final time." She looked up as she felt a splash of rain. "That will be me."

She saw the Stone ahead and quickened her approach. Moving steadily, she walked to the huge boulder and placed her hands, palms spread wide, on the cold surface.

"I'm here," she said softly, "I'm with you."

"Yeah, well, I'm here too," came a voice from behind her. She started and turned, just in time to see a figure stroll out from behind the trees. "Fancy meeting anyone else here, much less such a lovely woman, on such a blustery afternoon."

"Kane! What are you doing here?" Remy demanded.

"The same as you, I suppose, just out for a bit of a walk," he replied lazily. "You don't seem pleased to see me." He smiled wickedly.

Remy felt her annoyance rise. "I'm not. And I ask again, why are you here?"

"Ah, so you're seekin' a bit of solitude, are you?" He smirked. "Well, I could say I'm sorry to disturb, but that's not true. I came to talk to you—knowin' you often walk this way of an evening." He looked around. "It seems a private enough place for a talk."

Remy tensed, noticing he had been inching closer to her as he spoke. She tightened her grip on the staff. "What have we to talk about?"

"Ah, well, my Gran is still fair much under the weather, so she sent me to discuss a matter with you in her stead, a very important matter."

He came closer.

"Your grandmother never sent you to talk with me," Remy countered. "What do you want?" The wind had grown stronger, whipping dead leaves around her feet.

Kane chuckled and kicked at a stone.

"No, Gran doesn't know I'm here, it's true. Nevertheless, there is an important matter to discuss. The matter of my inheritance, and what claim you think you have on it." His face grew hard. "I intend to see there is no claim made against what's mine."

"Claim? I make no claim on your property, and I never will! I don't care a fig for your inheritance! What I want is to clear my Grandmother's name and see she has justice!"

"Oh, really? A woman dead for two generations and all you want is to clear her name? Do you think me a fool to believe such a tale?" He sneered, moving ever closer. "There's talk around that your rich tongue-padder snipe friend from London is filing charges against my family, the first step in you stealing our land—and I intend to put a stop to that!"

"Mr. Symme is considering legal action, but not for your inheritance, and not to charge your family with anything. He has uncovered the truth about her death—not suicide, but murder! Murder by Ian Llewellyn," she blurted, regretting it almost as the words left her mouth. Feeling hemmed-in by the Stone against her back, she raised her staff across her body. ". . . a man dead many years." She added cautiously. "The Symmes are greatly to blame for what happened to her, and he will take responsibility for that." She breathed a great sigh. "Your great-grandfather is dead. There is no claim being made against you, your living family or your property."

"Maybe, maybe not, but you'll blacken our name!"

She shook her head.

"I'm sorry but that can't be helped. The truth must come out. My Grandmother did not kill herself, and she did not kill her child. Her name must be cleared."

"And our name blackened," he sneered, "and then nobody will buy from us, we'll lose everything, and your barrister friend will buy up our worthless farm for pennies! And we'll be cast-outs! And you'll be rich!"

"Kane, that's not true! This will be a matter mostly in the courts, in the records! I don't want your farm. Symme doesn't want your farm, he doesn't want anything from you!" Remy stated emphatically.

"Maybe he doesn't, but he wants you, doesn't he? He wants to make you beholden to him! You'll be so much friendlier to him if he makes you a woman of means—you'll owe him, won't you?" He paused and spit on the ground. "But what if his little Miss Remy goes back to the city and forgets about us, or even better, what if she meets with some terrible accident—she could even die? Then he won't have no reason to start legal actions or anything else, will he?"

"Do you really think 'disposing' of me in some way will stop Mr. Symme?" she asked, equal scorn and fear in her voice. "You'll only make your situation worse."

He looked around as if searching for someone. "Well, now, I don't see anybody else around here who could witness whatever *might* happen. Do you?" Again, he smiled with malice. "Were it to come down to it, it would be my word against yours, wouldn't it? *Should* anything happen here? And *should* anybody but me be able to speak about it at all, yeah?"

Feeling more threatened every moment, Remy tried to keep her voice even.

"Do you suppose that suspicion would fall on anyone in the village besides you?" she countered. "You've made quite a reputation for yourself, and not a good one. If some woman came to harm, the first place anybody would look would be at Kane Llewellyn."

"Unfair, people are, aren't they? That's why it's so good that I have a person who will swear I was far away from here this day." Eyes downcast, he shook his head humbly. "My brother has a much better reputation than do I."

"Bran would never lie in such a manner!" Remy exclaimed. "He's well thought of because he respects the truth, and other people!"

"And I have various methods of persuasion with little brother, so we'll see what wins out, won't we?" He edged closer. "So . . . what say you? Leaving this area first thing tomorrow? Heading to London and shelter with your uppity friends? Keeping your mouth shut and your hands off what's mine?"

Remy's mind raced. *Let me stand with La Belle Dame tonight,* she thought, *and deal with what besets me tomorrow.* "I see there is little choice, so I must agree. So . . . I will leave," she replied.

Kane's face settled into a satisfied smirk. "Very wise. Very smart." He held her eyes with his own. "Too bad I know yer lying."

Speechless, Remy held her breath.

"Yes, too bad. I may have a bad reputation, but it doesn't include being simple-minded." He put his fists on his hips and leaned toward her. "So . . . what's it to be, Jeanne Remy? A little roughing up to convince you, maybe 'ruining' you so you have to disappear and keep your mouth shut, or is the best thing for me to shut your mouth for you permanently?"

He swiftly drew his hunting knife from its sheath at his back, and grabbed her staff with his other hand. Pointing the knife at her throat, eyes glinting with pleasure, he crooned, "Would you like to try to persuade me one way or the other? I'm sure you have some sweet, persuasive ways about you."

His smile was cruel as he tugged at the staff, pulling her off-balance.

Stumbling, she scrabbled for her footing and said sharply, "Kane, you don't want to do this! This won't help anything!"

Trying to keep the desperation out of her voice and off her face, she grappled with him for control of the staff, buying time to maybe push him away so she could run.

"Oh, but I do." His knife point pricked the skin of her throat, drawing a trickle of blood. "And I shall!" She smelled his rancid breath and felt his hard body against her. "Persuade me to be kind."

All at once, a figure dashed swiftly toward them from the direction of the path and Remy felt the impact of Kane's body pushed against her, forcing her flat on the Stone. She almost lost breath from the force of it, then heard Kane scream, "Goddamn you!" and a dreadful growl.

Kane tried to turn, but struggled in vain and groaned as his body was shaken side to side.

He managed to turn and face Regis, who crouched slightly, growling louder and readying for a lunge at his throat. Kane thrust his knife out blindly as he tried to make it past the huge dog, but Regis leapt toward Kane and grabbed his shoulder, just missing his jugular.

"Get off me—get away, you bastard dog!" Kane screamed in pain as they tussled.

"Regis—drop it!" A voice cut through the chaos and the big dog immediately retreated, padding to Edmund's side.

"Well, Kane, we meet yet again." Edmund walked slowly toward him, his voice cold with fury. "We've seen how brave you are fighting women, and small children, geese and dogs." He came closer. "Let's see how brave you are against a man, shall we?"

"A man? You mean a lily-livered London-bred lying snipe passes for a man where you come from? Bring it on, nancy-boy—did you bring your little gun with you today?"

Kane laughed maliciously.

I damn well wish I had, Edmund thought. *Stupid!* He spread his hands out, palms up, and shook his head saying, "No gun. Just me. Frightened?"

Rain fell, bringing wet leaves down in a swirl..

Kane squared his stance and raised his knife.

"No knife either? Pity."

He began to move slowly toward Edmund.

"Now, to be fair, I should drop this knife but, well, you might sic that dog on me again and," he chuckled, "nobody ever called me fair."

He rushed at Edmund.

Edmund blocked the attack and landed a punch to Kane's mid-section, but as he crumpled, the knife tore through Edmund's left forearm in a shallow but painful gash. Seeing the blood, Remy ran toward the two men, staff raised, and swung it stoutly at Kane's head—missing it and hitting his wounded shoulder instead. He roared and turned on her, slashing wildly, and caught her side with the blade.

Edmund grabbed him in a choke-hold with his right arm, pulling him away from Remy, momentum taking both of them to the ground. Kane lost his grip on the knife and dropped it on the muddying dirt. He roared and elbowed Edmund viciously in his wounded arm, then staggered to his feet and stomped on Edmund's left hand, to break the fingers. Then he turned and began to wrest the staff from Remy's grip. She struggled and fought with all her might.

Edmund saw the knife and grabbed it in his injured left hand, rising unsteadily. On his feet, he moved toward the struggling pair near the Stone. But a crash of thunder stopped him in his tracks, and a brilliant flash of light almost blinded him. Not lightning, but a harsh white light emanated from the Stone itself.

Suddenly a figure emerged, bathed in bloodlike light, broadcasting rage and malice. Fleur, hair electrified like a huge halo around her, hands raised in claws, rushed toward Kane screaming, "You! Llewellyn! The taint of murder in your blood! I will crush the life from you myself!!"

She flew toward him, crazed and manic.

Kane's mouth dropped open in fear. He let Remy go, pushing her aside, and backed away from the menacing presence before him. "Who are you? You're a ghost—get away! Get away!"

Fleur continued toward him as he turned to run. But Edmund was behind him. Kane ran into him; they both fell. Kane fell onto the knife held in Edmund's injured hand. It plunged deep. Deep enough. Rain lashed down.

Neither Edmund nor Remy had noticed Banks arrive, but here he was, seamlessly applying his trade. He helped Remy to sit and bound the slash in her side with her scarf. He turned to Edmund and examined the gash on his forearm.

"Not so bad," he commented, "the bleeding has almost stopped."

He wrapped his handkerchief around Edmund's wound.

Banks saw that Regis was injured, and so was Kane. Which one should he attend to first? He was torn. But as a doctor he must first care for the human.

He knelt over Kane, who had lost a lot of blood. His eyes were turning upward. Banks detected a disappearing pulse.

"He's a goner! Loss of blood. Knife penetration just below the heart."

"Edmund. Regis is in a bad way."

"What?!" Edmund looked around desperately. He saw the dog lying on the ground, Bank's belt providing a tourniquet but blood all around.

"Tend to Regis," he croaked. "Please. My dog."

Remy was already with Regis, holding up his head. Banks turned Regis over to see the wound. Regis looked up at him, and at Remy, and at Edmund.

"That bastard knifed him! That bastard hurt Regis!"

Edmund slipped in the mud and knelt beside him. "Alright boy, you're alright—take it slow, you'll be fine."

Banks spoke softly.

"He must have taken a bad plunge of the knife. I've tried to staunch the bleeding, but it looks like a main artery, my man—he, he doesn't have much time."

Edmund looked at Banks in anguish.

"No, no, no—he'll be alright, he's strong. You can stitch him up, can't you? We'll go back and get the pony cart—we have to get him home! We can't…"

"Edmund! Stop." Banks held his arm. "Edmund, he won't last. He's fading quickly." He looked at the big dog, panting quietly. "The tourniquet, it just—he's lost too much blood." He stroked Regis gently. "Hold him, man, be with him now. He doesn't have long."

Tears pooling in his eyes, Edmund caressed the big head, smoothed the blood away from the quivering shoulder. "Regis, my friend, my . . . don't go." He bowed his head close to the dying animal. "Not you, my friend, not you!"

The great dog whined softly.

Remy covered the huge animal with her cloak. "You need to say goodbye. He . . . he doesn't want to leave you. Edmund. Let him go."

"No! We've got to save him, we will save him." Edmund spun around. "Banks, don't just be your idiot self, man, take this…"

Suddenly from the Stone a light began to glow, emanating more strongly and turning almost apricot in color. Shimmering, the familiar figure appeared, no longer the picture of wrath but more her former self.

Fleur cried, "*Tiens! Mon Dieu*, what is this? Edmund, *ne sois pas stupid*! Let your friend be free from pain, let him pass."

She turned to Regis, caressing his head and bowing low. She crooned gently, "*Courage, mon brave, mon héros! Regis, mon brave, a moi ! A moi* ! To me, now, *doucement*!"

She held her arms open and smiled.

The big dog looked once more at Edmund with longing, then sighed mightily and relaxed into death. He was still. All was still. Until the silence was shattered by Edmund's primal howl. Loss and anger echoed through the trees, drowning out the sound of rain.

In anger and frustration, Edmund stood up and kicked the corpse of Kane as hard as he could.

*   *   *

Fleur appeared, sitting on the stone, next to the dagger crack. She appeared very different. Older. More frightening. Like her inner demon was emerging.

"Mr. Symme has avenged my death," she pronounced. "On the anniversary of my demise."

The three of them stood, looking around at the carnage and

death.

"My God, what have we done?" Edmund exclaimed.

The enormity of the event began to sink in.

"We have a dead man here," he said. "I killed him."

"It was self-defense," said Banks. "And he fell on the knife."

"Edmund was trying to defend me," Remy said.

Edmund sat and stared for a moment.

"We'll have to inform the constable," he said wearily. He bent over toward the knife lying on the ground. "Look at this. A murderous weapon."

"Don't touch it," said Banks. "Leave it lie."

"Look at the initials on the haft," Remy said, bending close and holding the lantern that Banks had brought. "K L. It's his all right."

Remy's two wounds were oozing blood through Banks' makeshift bandages.

Edmund said, "Banks, you must tend to Remy. Let's get her back to the house. Then I'll go into the village. Llewellyn isn't going anywhere."

Banks objected. "Remy cannot walk to Owlswood. We'll have to carry her."

Edmund looked incredulous. "How? That may be take more of a toll than walking. I could run back and retrieve the pony cart."

Banks shook his head.

"That would take too long. We need to get her back to the house where I can care for her properly. Could we rig a stretcher from shirts and jackets and two strong poles?"

Edmund scoffed. "Yes, if we had an axe to cut the poles from these trees."

"Then we'll have to do the soldier's carry," Banks said. "You and I link arms, creating a seat, and Miss Remy sits on our arms. Edmund, you take this side to keep pressure off your wounded arm."

Edmund shook his head but could think of nothing better. He and Banks fumbled on how to link arms to create a seat.

Remy demurred. "That would be very unladylike."

Edmund said, "Jeanne Remy, as your employer, I insist. Now please ease yourself down onto our arms. Wrap your arms around our necks."

Remy sat on their linked arms, and the men immediately realized that even petite women are not weightless.

Edmund stifled a groan, then said, "Now lift. Up we go."

Banks, already breathing heavily, said, "By the time we get to the house, I'll need a stretcher, myself. It's not you, Remy; you're light as a feather. It's the crablike angle we must walk."

Edmund turned back for a second. Fleur stood on the stone, gazing intently at him, her wraps flowing in the wind.

"An eye for an eye, Edmund Symme," she uttered in the voice of doom. "An eye for an eye."

He shivered at the memory of what he had just done, but Fleur seemed at ease, demonic but happy.

"Belle Dame, we depend on you to guard Kane Llewellyn," he choked. "And Regis."

Fleur, still in her demon mode, said, "I will stand guard. No man nor beast shall dare challenge me. Only if I could summon the hounds from hell to tear him limb from limb would he be unsafe."

Fleur drifted over, picked up the knife, carried it back to the stone, and placed it in the dagger crack. Was it imagination? Or did a ghost of a dagger appear there?

"And besides, I have a brave dog here with me," she said, looking more like her old self. At that, the ghost of Regis appeared beside Fleur, wagging his tail.

The three humans stood aghast at these actions.

"How is this possible?" Banks cried out.

Finally, he, too was privy to the spectral sights Edmund and Remy had shared for the last several months.

26
Constable Pryce

Edmund and Banks carried Remy back to the house, huffing and puffing, stumbling and slipping in mud. When they reached the bottom of the hill, Remy squirmed and demanded, "Gentlemen, please put me down now. I'll walk the rest of the way, thank you."

They were surprised to see that Cook was still there, but she had prepared dinner and was trying to keep it warm. She met them in the entryway and Samuel soon joined them.

Cook said, "I couldna go wi'out knowin' what happened to my dear Jeannie—Miss Remy—now could I? Jeannie, wha' happened to you? You have blood—blood on your beautiful gown! And Mr. Symme, your arm is bloody as well!"

"Yes, indeed, they both have wounds," said Banks. "And temporary bandages which I will soon re-wrap. Let us first sit a moment and catch our breath. And eat something of the magnificent supper you have prepared."

"Samuel, something unfortunate has happened." Edmund said, still breathing hard. He took off his wet outer clothing and sat down for a moment. "I'll tell you in the dining room as soon as I've washed my hands."

He resumed addressing Samuel a few minutes later. "There has been a serious accident involving one of the Llewellyn boys. Kane is dead. After you have a bit to eat, would you go to the village and fetch Constable Pryce? He'll be off for the evening, but hopefully not too deep in his cups at the pub. He will want to come."

Samuel looked shocked, and curious for more details, but said, "Yes sire, Mr. Symme. Right away. I done ate a'ready."

Edmund, Remy, and Banks huddled in the kitchen and ate hot fresh bread with slabs of butter and honey, not that they tasted it but that their bodies needed sustenance. Cook hovered and fussed around them. "I'm dyin' to hear wha' happened to tha' Kane lad."

Remy put her hand on Cook's arm and said, "I will tell you all. But I beg of you; please don't tell others until Constable Pryce can take charge."

"Cross my heart, Jeannie."

After this repast, Edmund said, "Remy, you must go to your room now, and allow Dr. Banks to minister to your wounds. We can't take a chance of infection."

She didn't protest.

Banks guided Remy carefully up the stairs to her room with his arm around her waist. This irritated Edmund, but he said nothing.

He returned to the kitchen where Cook was cleaning up.

"Cook, an unusual request. Miss Remy will need to remove some items of clothing for Dr. Banks to treat her wounds. Could you help her in this? It's not for the doctor or me to help her in that way."

"Gor blimey. Of course. Let me get a clean apron."

She bustled about and Edmund went back to Remy's room. He and Banks waited in the hallway while Cook tended to her.

Cook helped Remy out of her torn, bloody dress, making noises of distress and sympathy at the blood oozing from the temporary bandages. She helped Remy put on a robe that would allow Banks to access the wounds.

As Banks removed bandages and various tools from his bag, Remy said, "Dr. Banks, allow me to suggest some herbals and unguents to place against my skin beneath the bandages. I keep them in that top drawer in clearly marked packets." She pointed at her dresser. "They should provide a strong aid to healing."

"You are the green woman, Miss Remy," said Banks as he went to retrieve the items she described. "I learn from you in this regard."

Edmund stood out of the way and remained silent, but watched intently every move Banks made.

"Remy, this wound on your side requires some stitches. I have everything I need here—well-boiled and clean. I'm renowned for my stitching that doesn't leave ugly scars, or you'd look like you had your appendix removed. Except it's the wrong side."

After Remy was well bandaged, she insisted on going back downstairs. She thanked Cook profusely for staying and helping.

"When Samuel comes back, he can accompany you into the village."

"I'll not wait. Poor Samuel has taken enough late-night walks. I know well the way home."

Remy gave her a lantern.

Edmund stayed behind as Banks re-assembled his bag. Banks noticed that Edmund was shaking, and asked, "What's wrong, old man? Are you having a reaction to what happened to Kane? You could have been killed. Let me now tend to your injury."

"No, it's not myself I'm concerned about. Not me." He looked at Banks with great sadness and a touch of fear. "Kane came within an inch of killing Remy. What a loss that would be."

"So, you have a soft spot in your heart for your housekeeper after all." He ribbed Edmund with a smile. "I cannot but agree with you." He put his arm around Edmund's shoulder. "This entire strange episode has taken a toll on all of us."

*   *   *

Samuel soon returned to Owlswood with Constable Pryce in the constable's buggy. They met in the sitting room.

Edmund, Remy, and Banks told their stories, what happened and where.

Edmund said, "So, there's a dead man's body up there." He added with a catch in his voice, "And my dog." He was tempted to say they were being guarded by a ghost.

The constable wanted to see Remy's bandaged wounds. And then Edmund's.

"You see the bandage on my throat, but I cannot show you the one on my midriff. It's right here," she said, pointing to her side.

Since Samuel was still staying close by, Edmund said to him, "Samuel, would you rouse nephew Seth. We need to retrieve Regis, who was killed by Kane while defending Remy. Perhaps rig a stretcher. Or take the pony cart."

"Regis is no more? Why that bas—. I was jes' gettin' to love that big hound. We will go forthwith."

Edmund said to the constable, "We'll have to walk to the stone, since there's no buggy track, and we don't have horses."

Fortunately, the rain had let up, but it was quite muddy trekking up the hill. The three men tramped up to the stone in the dark with lanterns, arriving just as Samuel and Seth were lifting Regis and gently placing him in the cart.

When the three reached the stone, it looked like an ordinary boulder. Edmund wondered if Fleur was still standing guard, and if the constable would see her. But no, she was not to be seen. Edmund realized he'd have no idea whether or not she was still lurking about.

"There's Kane," Edmund said to the constable.

"Where's the knife?"

They looked around. Banks spied it. "Over on that rock," he pointed out.

"How did it get there?" the constable asked with hands on hips. Edmund and Banks stumbled over their words, not telling a credible story. How could one say a ghost carried it over there?

Banks finally said, "Constable, we suspect there's a spirit in this rock, and it moved the knife to that crack."

"Is that the best story you've got?"

"It's not that absurd, my good man, there are many spirits in these woods. There's a tale that one of the Symme predecessors was murdered here some decades ago. Perhaps her spirit is haunting this place."

"I'll ignore this line of poppycock. Let's look at the knife."

Constable Pryce saw the initials and the blood. Then, holding his lantern close, he looked at the wounds on Kane and Regis.

He looked through Kane's pockets. A chaw of tobacco. A folding blade knife. A quid and a few pence. Nothing helpful. But then, he pulled out a crumpled piece of paper. He flattened it out and saw that it was a note. Banks and Edmund craned their necks to get a look. Holding it close to the lantern, the constable read aloud, "Kane, don't go to that stone, you understand? Obey me. Don't go there. Let the Remy woman be. Da."

The constable nodded and gave a humpf, folded the note, and stuck it in his breast pocket.

Edmund and Banks looked at each other.

The Constable turned to Edmund. "It's hard to imagine that you two gentlemen lured Mr. Llewellyn up here in the evening to murder him. What's your motive? Nor would you kill your dog and wound yourself and your housekeeper. Llewellyn was known as a hothead and he's been reported for accosting Miss Remy not that long ago. Thus, your story, as unbelievable as it sounds, might actually make some sense. Especially if I may verify this note. But the knife lying on the rock—that's going to take some explaining, it will."

The constable looked closely at Edmund and Banks to see how they reacted to his statement, but both retained impassive faces, not wanting to complicate matters further.

Satisfied, he said, "I will summon men to retrieve the body tonight. It's late, but if we leave it, animals may disturb it. Please excuse our intrusion when we return later. On the morrow, I will pay a visit to Mrs. Llewellyn. Perhaps you should join me. There will be an inquest. So, I ask that you two and Miss Remy stay at your property for the nonce."

Ignoring the contradiction between staying at Owlswood and accompanying the constable to see Mrs. Llewellyn, Banks nodded. "Yes, sir. We must care for Miss Remy. And a ceremony for dear Regis."

"Mr. Symme. Your family has been here for many years, and I don't recall any trouble between you and the Llewellyns."

"Yes, the grandfather Ian worked for my great-grandfather Alistair, who helped them buy their property. There's a story to be told. Perhaps it will come out at the inquest. But not tonight. Not sure it would shed any light on our current situation."

Edmund knew he was telling a blatant lie.

They walked in silence back down the dark, slippery trail to the house and bade the constable good night. After he left, both went to check on Remy. Banks looked at her bandages, felt her forehead for fever, and checked her pulse.

"Jeanne, I'm quite sure you will recover with no incident, but I will keep close watch over you. Now you should go to bed and get some well-deserved rest."

"I thank you, Doctor—Kit—for your care. We are indeed fortunate to have a medical doctor on the premises."

After the household had settled down, Edmund made his way to the library. Closing and locking the door, he looked around and asked, "Where's Fleur, I wonder? Belle Dame, are you here?"

But La Belle Dame did not make an appearance.

Edmund was concerned. Was she still up at the Stone guarding Kane? Had she finished her work on this world and passed on to the next plane—wherever it is that freed ghosts go? Would he ever again see her, and have delightful conversations with her? Edmund waited for a while, talking to her but receiving no response. Eventually, he gave up and went to his room.

*   *   *

Dawn was approaching before those at Owlswood finally slept.

Edmund dreamt of Regis with Fleur, standing next to the Stone. The dagger was stabbed into the stone, like Arthur's sword.

Remy dreamt of being attacked near the Stone. But she held a knife; the perpetrator was another man; and she was dressed very strangely.

Banks dreamt of Remy in his arms, smiling up at him.

27
Llewellyns and Villagers

A tired and sore group huddled around the breakfast table early next morning. Cook brought hot coffee, ham and eggs, thick buttered toast, fruit, and kippers, to restore their souls.

Sniffing the coffee, Edmund remarked, "Ah, the eternal elixir! Thank you, Cook, from the bottom of my heart."

She twittered in embarrassment.

Banks flexed his arms. "My muscles are complaining of unfamiliar demands."

Edmund sighed, "I certainly hope the constable returned and retrieved Kane. I confess I heard nothing after falling asleep."

Remy gently patted her side and said, "Dr. Banks, you patched me up so well last night I'm hardly sore."

Edmund agreed. "Nor am I, my friend."

After breakfast, everyone present gathered for a remembrance of Regis. Samuel and Seth dug a grave near the *orangerie*, where Regis had lounged in the sun when he wasn't with Edmund.

Edmund spoke.

"Regis was my companion, my protector. He loved to be with me wherever I went. I was so fortunate to have him, and I shall miss him always." He held Regis' leash and started to place it in the grave, but then hesitated. "You'll need no leash where you've gone, old boy. Run free."

Tears shone in his eyes.

Then Remy spoke.

"I met Regis chasing my cat and was angry with him. But since then, he was always a gentle and loving companion. And protector. More than once, he came to my defense and it was he who saved my life."

She threw a bouquet of flowers and herbs into the grave.

Banks took his turn.

"Edmund and Regis went together like brothers. Regis calmed Edmund and forced him to exercise. Regis loved Owlswood and was a good companion to anyone out for a stroll."

Banks threw a big piece of Stilton cheese into the grave.

"Samuel, would you like to say something?" Edmund asked.

"Yes, sir. Regis were a well-trained and friendly hound, and had a fine sense of telling friend from foe. I also noticed that with him livin' here, not as many night beasts came sniffin' around."

Samuel threw a rabbit skin into the grave.

Cook was blubbering and could hardly speak.

"That great old dog. He would eat all the table scraps, no matter what."

She threw a ham bone into his earthy covering.

They took turns shoveling dirt into the grave, then Samuel finished the job.

"I'll make a fine plaque worthy of him, Mr. Symme," he said.

*   *   *

Edmund, Remy, and Banks walked soberly to the village to meet the constable.

"Let's get this unpleasantness out of the way, shall we?" said Constable Pryce. "Mrs. Llewellyn is housebound, so if you please, would you accompany me to her farm? I know there has been some bad blood between the families, and now a deceased son. I shall therefore go as much to keep peace as to investigate what the son was up to in the first place."

Edmund, Remy, and Banks joined him on the walk to Burgess farm. As they approached, they saw the Llewellyn clan arrayed in a line on the front porch—Owen with hands on hips, Bran with arms crossed, stable boys looking nervous, and Gwyned in her rocking chair, impassive.

Owen spoke, "How ken we help you, constable? And why bring this lot?" He thrust his chin towards Edmund.

Constable Pryce began to relate his understanding of events of the preceding evening.

Gwyned, in her rocking chair, glared at Remy and hissed, "You murdered my grandson!"

Had she been mobile, she may have inflicted more than words.

"He tried to kill me!" responded Remy. "He cut me with his knife and Mr. Symme, too, before I was rescued. He even killed Mr.

285

Symme's dog."

Owen stood beside Gwyned, glowering. He held a stout walking stick almost like a weapon.

Irish blackthorn, useful as a cudgel, Edmund thought, measuring distance between his group and Owen.

"Now, ma'am, I'm here to keep the peace," repeated the constable, moving closer to the Llewellyns. "I've told you what we know. There's no grounds to believe Kane was murdered."

Gwyned trembled, as if she might have another seizure. "These ghouls," she muttered, wheezing and coughing, "they've come to take our land."

Owen wrapped her shawl more tightly around her shoulders.

Remy thought, *she seems to be drawing inward since we met that day in the village.*

Just then, Gwyned cried out, "You killed my grandson! Why?"

"It's your grandson who was out to kill *me*!" Remy's voice bristled in response. "Kane attacked *me*. I fought him off, but he cut me . . . right here and here." Remy showed the bandage on her throat that still had a stain of red, and pointed to her midriff. "He would have killed me, had Edmund—Mr. Symme—and Dr. Banks, and Regis the dog arrived a moment later. They saved me. She took a deep breath and continued, "Regis jumped on Kane, who fought him off, stabbing the poor dog with his knife. Kane fought with Mr. Symme, but dropped his hold on the weapon. Mr. Symme picked it up. Kane leapt on him; they fell backwards. The knife penetrated him. He was killed by his own blade."

Gwyned seemed to rise in her chair like a hot air balloon though she could barely move.

"That Miss Remy wants our farm," she accused. "And she killed our Kane. She thinks she has a right to it from my father. And now my grandson is dead."

"Now, now," said Constable Pryce, mopping his forehead with his handkerchief. "The evidence points to Mr. Llewellyn having been stabbed with his own knife. The same knife he had used to injure others, including the dog, who also died. Kane fell onto his own blade after attacking both Miss Remy and Mr. Symme here. We have no proof to the contrary but much to support these facts. Kane suffered from Mr. Symme's act of self-defense. I shall recommend no crime be charged."

Owen stood erect and glared at Remy.

"What about her claiming our land due to some inheritance? That's a motive, ain't it? And these two here," he pointed to Edmund and Banks, "could be telling a tale. No one else was there to see what Kane did or didn't do."

Remy shook her head and looked him in the eye.

"I told your mother, and Kane, and now I'm telling you: I make no such claim. None of you have believed me."

Owen ignored her and once again tilted his head toward Edmund.

"Egged on by your fancy London barrister here."

Edmund stepped forward.

"Now see here. My great grandfather helped you grandfather purchase this land. Why would I wish to take it over?"

"Because that's what you landed gentry do. Take advantage of us hard working folk."

"Look here, Mr. Owen," said Constable Pryce. "I have something that may help you believe what the young lady says. And the barrister, too." He opened a leather pouch and removed an official looking document. "This here is a quit claim deed drawn up by Mr. Symme for Miss Remy. I shall read the pertinent part:

"I, Flora Jeanne Remy, hereby relinquish any and all claim on the property known as Burgess Farm, owned and controlled by the family Llewellyn, now and in the future, as may have come to me by inheritance from my mother, whom, it has recently been determined, is the eldest daughter of Ian Llewellyn."

Mother and son mirrored each other with deep frowns, absorbing words that had never before been said out loud.

The entire company seemed to hold their breath. No one spoke or moved until Owen shook his head as if he'd been slapped.

"What's this about my grandfather siring . . . just who, now?"

Gwyned pulled herself together.

"Don't be daft, Owen. Now it's all spilling out. Why d'ya think this has been kept secret? A shame and a disgrace upon our family."

Another frozen silence followed.

"Mrs. Llewellyn," Remy began, startled at the sound of her own voice. "This document states that I eschew all claim to your farm."

287

"A shoe?" Gwyned was indignant. "Something you do to a horse? What's that got to do with anything?"

Edmund coughed. "Ah. Yes. Eschew. Similar word, different meaning. In this case, a public record of releasing a claim to ownership. Your farm shall not be challenged by Miss Remy nor by myself."

The constable interrupted. "Right then, Mrs. Llewellyn. Here's something else for you to see." Once again, he drew a paper from his pouch, this one small and wrinkled. "I found this note in Kane's pocket," he said. "Apparently written by you, Owen."

Owen took the note and looked at it. Color drained form his face. "I gave this to Bran to give to Kane. Bran, what say you?"

"I gave that to him," he stuttered. "And I told him not to go looking for Miss Remy. I told him not to cross you. That if he did, it would cause trouble." Bran hung his head. "And now he's dead."

The constable asked Bran, "What did he want from Miss Remy?"

Bran mumbled at his shoes. "He didn't say. He just said he needed to find her."

"Miss Remy?"

"Kane said he wanted to dissuade me from claiming the Llewellyn property. But I told him I had no intention of making a claim. He didn't believe me. Then he threatened me—he came very close and pressed against me. He brandished his knife, and said vile things. He cut my neck. He would have killed me if Edmund— Mr. Symme—and his dog, had not arrived at that very moment."

Owen looked around, fire in his eyes.

"And just what happened to your grandmother?" he asked.

Remy wondered, *did Gwyned know that her father had killed Fleur?* She had to tell Fleur's story.

For the next several minutes, she recounted Alistair Symme's heinous intervention to prevent his son's marriage to Fleur, the terrible violation that made certain his goals were met and the financial arrangement that seeded Burgess Farm. Remy told the assembled party of Fleur's abduction and rape, of John's renouncing the baby Fleur was devoted to keeping and raising, and the desperate encounter with Ian at the Stone that had cost Fleur her life.

Owen turned on her.

"You want to pin a murder on my Pa? And ruin my family?"

Her temper flared.

"Your grandfather and my grandfather are one and the same. And yes, he killed my grandmother with his knife, just as Kane attempted to do to me . . . at the same Stone."

Once again, the air stilled.

"My son is dead," Owen said. "And I'm supposed to believe it was he that wounded you, and your fancy friend, and that he killed the dog, too." He turned on Edmund. "And that before my time, your great grandfather hired my grandfather to rape a woman to keep her from his son, and that he killed that same woman."

Owen shook his head as if to clear it. Bran had sat down in a daze. Gwyned's rile had utterly deflated. The three looked at each other.

"Well, this is quite a bit to take in, now ain't it?" Owen said. "If even the half of it is true, ain't nobody blameless."

"Right you are," said Edmund, his chest heaving with pent-up emotion. "Should you care to see evidence from the past that verifies what Miss Remy just explained, I have the proof in my possession. I am certain you will be convinced of the truth of her words. As I am."

"And I," said Banks.

"But I have no desire to make public any such information," said Remy. "My sole desire is to clear the name of my grandmother for what happened two generations ago. We're not here to visit the sins of the father on the daughter and grandson."

Gwyned raised one trembling hand.

"Gimme that piece o' paper you read from, Owen. And make sure it's all signed and official, would you?"

Owen took the document from Constable Pryce, squinted and moved his lips while reading to himself. As he did so, Edmund deduced that Gwyned—and perhaps Owen, too—was less concerned about the past than keeping the farm and their reputation. Perhaps they knew enough to believe the truth themselves. And they feared what others would make of it.

"Mr. Llewellyn, for this to be binding, it must be signed and witnessed at the courthouse. If we sign it now, I'll get the seal affixed over the next day or so. Miss Remy and you or your mother will sign, then the good constable and I will bear witness. As you see, there's a copy for you to hold until it becomes official."

Owen looked at Gwyned, who was non-committal, then nodded his head in acceptance, and spoke through his scowl, "Constable, you gonna proceed against my son?"

"Can't arrest a dead man."

Owen stared at the ground.

"I canna believe my son killed a dog. And now he's dead, too." He looked over at his younger son. "Bran, it's high time you step up."

The three took their leave and headed back toward the village.

Edmund said, "Constable Pryce, thank you. I must say, that went better than I expected.'

"It certainly did. I'm a bit surprised myself. Glad it's behind us. Like I said, Mr. Symme, my desire is to keep the peace among the good folk of my township."

* * *

Back home, the three gathered around the kitchen table.

Remy asked, "Will La Belle Dame be satisfied?"

Edmund responded, "She bloody well should be! And you, Remy, have resolved a long-standing dispute with a neighbor."

Banks said, "And you must admit, old man, that you have accomplished her demand — an eye for an eye."

Edmund flared in anger, but quickly subsided to sadness.

"I am not proud of taking the life of another, even by accident. I keep thinking, I could have turned the knife aside. Kane Llewellyn was not responsible for the misdeeds of his great-grandfather."

"Oh, but he was responsible for the attacks on us," Remy retorted, pointing to the bandage on her neck. "I would be dead if you gentlemen — and Regis — hadn't come to my rescue."

"Yes, I know that, and it troubles me sorely," Edmund said, looking down so they couldn't see the tear that appeared at the corner of his eye. "I am so relieved you were not seriously injured."

Remy pretended like she didn't notice his tear.

"There's one more task. I must confront a fear I've had my whole life about who I really am. I must speak the truth to my loved ones in the village. And that would include Samuel."

Banks shook his head.

"I know you are concerned that they will reject you when they discover the truth about your heritage, but I do not believe it. The feelings of family are deeper than blood."

"I hope you are right, my good doctor. Mr. Symme—Edmund—may I ask Samuel to hitch up a buggy and take me into town? I must face the thing I most dread."

"By all means. He'll need to get a horse from MacCready, but that should not cause much delay. Are you going now?"

"Yes, while I have courage. And before evening falls."

*   *   *

Samuel soon brought the horse and buggy back from the Mac-Cready farm. He and Remy rode into the village with little said between them. Samuel could tell something was troubling her, but didn't probe.

Annie was home with Nana. They sat in Nana's kitchen, sipping tea and enjoying fresh-baked bread with jam. Like Samuel, they noticed that something weighed on Remy, but didn't press her.

Remy screwed up her courage.

"I have something I must tell you, Annie," she began. "Something important that Nana already knows. That I recently discovered on my own." She paused to take a breath. "My mother was not the blood daughter of Lily. My grandmother was Fleur Duplessis, the ward of Alistair Symme, and betrothed to John Symme—the grandfather of Edmund Symme.

"My maternal grandfather was Ian Llewellyn, through a terrible deed. My grandmother Fleur, who has long been rumored to be a suicide, was in fact killed by Ian Llewellyn after he had fathered her child.

"This is the hardest part for me to say." Remy took a deep breath and wiped a tear before going on. "Lily's baby was stillborn, so Fleur's newborn babe—my mother Aimee—was substituted without Lily's knowledge, and was accepted as her daughter. When I was born, I was then Lily's granddaughter, your cousin, Annie, and Samuel's grand-niece.

Remy looked around to gauge the impact on her listeners. "I know some have been sworn to secrecy never to reveal this, but I must. And besides we around this table, all others involved have passed to the Great Beyond and beyond caring.

"We—Mr. Symme, Dr. Banks and I—have uncovered these

facts through exhaustive research into old documents held in safe-keeping by the Symme family. Samuel is aware of the discovery of some of these."

Remy choked up and sobbed, unable to speak for several minutes. In a rush of words, she blurted out, "What this means is—is that—I am not truly your family." She broke down again. "I have been living a lie."

Nana stood up and came around behind Remy and kneaded her shoulders.

"My dear, dear child." Nana let her touch speak for her. "Yes, I have long known this. You and I recently spoke about the spirit who called you granddaughter. But you are family. How could you think otherwise? You are loved. We love you."

Annie nodded in agreement, teary-eyed, and reached over and took Remy's hand.

Samuel sat open-mouthed.

"You tell us your grandmother was young Fleur, who resided at the Symme estate when I was a wee lad? I recall her well."

He shook his head and frowned in surprise.

"What you tell us explains a lot. But it doesn't change a thing. You are my beloved niece."

Annie, who had sat quietly, spoke up.

"The same with me, my dear friend. Who among us has a family tree without crooked branches—going all the way back to Adam and Eve?"

Samuel said thoughtfully, "So your grandmother was dishonored by Mr. Llewellyn and then killed by him when the baby was newborn?"

Nana spoke softly.

"I see now that your mother, Remy, would be the eldest of Ian Llewellyn—and would thus have a claim through inheritance of his farm. This explains much about the dislike—fear almost—of his daughter Gwyned toward Miss Remy. Fear that your grandmother, then your mother and you, have a prior claim to their farm. I see more. That's why the Symme family created the position for your mother and you, Remy, at the Symme estate."

She moved toward the wood stove and refilled the kettle.

"This calls for another pot of tea."

"And a spot o' brandy, if ye ask me," said Samuel.

Water heating, Nana returned to sit, then reached across the table and took Remy's hand. Then so did Annie. "Come on, Samuel, put your paw out here. You afraid of three women?"

Samuel timidly added his hand, and the three held onto Remy's hand, who was bawling uncontrollably.

"Annie, hand Jeannie that towel if you would."

Remy wiped away the tears and managed a smile. "I thank you all so much. I love you from the bottom of my heart."

They sat in silence for a time.

"One more thing," said Remy. "I have told the Llewellyn clan that I have no interest in laying claim to their property."

"What about damage to the Llewellyn reputation, if word of this gets out, which it will," asked Samuel, as Nana poured his spot of brandy from a venerable flask.

Nana shook her head.

"What damage? Besides, beyond those in this room, as Jeannie says, all the others—Lily, Mam, the Reader—have passed to the Great Beyond. No point of visiting the sins of the father on the son."

Samuel said, "Mr. Symme and Constable Pryce say there will be an inquest. The results will be a public document."

Nana stuck out her chin and replied, "Owen and Gwyned will have to eat some crow and be extra nice to people for once. I see no lasting damage. If need be, I'll give them a talking to."

*   *   *

Samuel stood. "Miss Jeannie, better get you home."

On the way back to Owlswood, Samuel broke the silence by asking, "You telling us the Symme place has been haunted by the spirit of Miss Fleur all these years?"

Remy smiled at him. "Both Mr. Symme and I have spoken with her. As would have my mother, if she hadn't been so fearful."

"Well, I'll be. I'll wager that there are some fascinating tales waitin' to be told."

After a minute of silence, Samuel went on.

"Mr. Symme never struck me as the type who would be communin' with spirits. But perhaps that explains his interest in restoring the orangerie. And retrievin' those boxes embedded in the mortar."

After Remy was reunited with the two men, and had shared the conversation in the village, Edmund put his hand on Banks' shoulder.

"Banks, my friend, I believe this next episode is for Remy and myself. We must attract our guardian spirit in the library and relate what has transpired. We're hoping beyond hope that she will be satisfied so she can be at peace. And so can we."

28
Squaring Accounts

That evening, Edmund and Remy shared concerns that Fleur might be gone forever. They sat with a bottle Edmund had retrieved from the cellar but had no enthusiasm for more than a taste. They sat in the library in agitated silence, jumping at very rustle of the wind outside. Exhausted after half an hour, they gave up.

"Well, we tried," said Edmund. "It seems the events at the Stone must be the final chapter. We've seen your grandmother's spirit for the last time."

"How sad," Remy said, preparing to gather the practically untouched wine. "If only she knew what happened the day after at Burgess Farm."

Just then, Fleur materialized upon the mantle in a flurry of pink and gardenia. She looked restored to the condition in which she had first appeared: stately, healthy, well put together, and mischievous.

"To what do I owe this honor, *mes chéries*?" she asked, smiling and tilting her head.

They rushed to greet her.

"Oh, my," Remy gushed. "I'm so glad to see you!"

"I'll say," said Edmund, visibly relieved. "One doesn't quite know when a ghost may have had enough of earthly conditions, does one?"

"There is much to report, *Grandmère*," said Remy.

"*Ah, oui*? Please tell," said Fleur, turning to Edmund. "Shall we settle comfortably to discuss? Sit, sit." As she gestured to the chairs recently vacated by Edmund and Remy, she perused the bottle Remy had removed from the table. "Fill your glasses, *mes chéries. What are you drinking this evening? Ah, a Chateau du Bordieu to celebrate the anniversary of my death?"

She ushered them back toward their chairs and gestured to Edmund to their wine glasses. When they were seated, she addressed Edmund.

"My dear Mr. Symme," she said. "You have avenged my murder by the death of a Llewelyn."

She bowed in front of him. She lifted his wine glass, swirled and sniffed the contents, nodded in approval and replaced it on the side table.

"Mmm," said Edmund, after taking a sip himself. "Let me say, I'm distinctly not proud of taking a life. It was an accident."

"But it happened. An eye for an eye. Kane Llewellyn deserved his fate. Like his grandfather before him, he brought it upon himself."

She rustled her gown and paced for a moment.

"*Quoi d'autre?* And what else, pray tell."

Remy spoke.

"Mr. Symme, Dr. Banks and I visited the Llewellyns at their farm. The constable escorted us there in case there would be trouble. And to advise them of my releasing all claim to their farm. They have admitted that Ian Llewellyn wronged you in the worst possible way. Gwyned was well aware that Ian was the father of your child—and that your child was my mother. And we told them that he killed you. None of them had known this. They were shocked. Yet they did not protest."

Fleur nodded and floated to her perch on the mantle.

"Do go on," she said.

"I went to the village and told my close friends the truth about my heritage—my relationship with you. And the wrongs committed on you. They were not concerned with my surprising lineage, nor were they surprised when I related the shocking events surrounding the end of your mortal life."

"All well and good," replied Fleur with a hard look. "Easy conversations. You let them off too easily. The Llewellyns are not suffering, from what you say. The villagers are not outraged. And few even know."

"*Grandmère*, who else needs to know? All the others that you wish to inform and be outraged are long since passed. Perhaps you are more in touch with their spirits. The record has been corrected. It was not a suicide, but murder and rape. Those still living now know that. Yes, there was secrecy at the time, with the transfer of a baby, but that was all for the best, given the circumstances, and people were acting in the best way they could. Local people are the only ones who would care; few are still alive. And they don't care; they welcome me as family."

Fleur glided back and forth like she was pacing the floor.

"You talk with a few people and think this makes everything all right? But what about my distress at their treatment of me? My rejection by John Symme? For many years, I have awaited this moment of retribution, and now I see it is half-hearted. I am disappointed in you."

Remy stood up and faced Fleur, eyes blazing.

"*Grandmère*, we have done everything you asked—everything we can do. Do you not see this? You cannot punish the living for the sins of the dead. You cannot make people feel shame for events they had no part in. What do the living owe the dead? Truth. You said this yourself. We have told the truth. That's what you asked for, and what you are due. We can do no more. Can you accept this? Can you rest in peace?"

For a moment, there was no sound except the heavy breathing of Edmund and Remy as they awaited Fleur's response to Remy standing up to her.

Fleur looked at Remy, then at Edmund, in great sadness. Then she spoke.

"*Regarde-ça!* I see my granddaughter has grown into her power. What can I do but accept what you say? I am nothing but a tired old woman. Very tired. I desire rest. I deserve rest."

"What else would you have us do?" Remy asked with sympathy.

"You have not mentioned reparation from the Symme family."

Edmund stepped forward. "I have offered Remy recompense for the loss of her inheritance. She has refused. I have put substantial funds into an account in her name, should she ever change her mind. Regarding your abandonment by my grandfather, I can only offer Remy my friendship." He looked at Remy. "Yes, I consider you my friend. I hope at some time I can be yours."

"Edmund Symme, that is quite a shift in attitude."

"Yes, you and I have been through a lot together, far beyond master and housekeeper."

She blushed, knowing they were thinking of the same things.

Edmund turned back to Fleur.

"Furthermore, La Belle Dame, you are welcome to remain at

Owlswood at your pleasure, and have Regis as your companion. The library will remain your sanctuary."

"Regis is already my companion," responded Fleur. She looked pensively at Remy, then Edmund. "We shall see. We shall see."

She gradually faded from view, leaving behind only a trace of gardenia.

Edmund looked at Remy and nodded his head. She shrugged her shoulders, and said, "Indeed, we shall see."

Edmund and Remy repaired to the sitting room, where Banks had been waiting impatiently, despite snacks provided by Cook. They recounted what had happened.

"You made a strong argument, Remy," said Edmund. "You would make a good barrister."

"Doctor," she rebutted.

Remy asked, "If we have satisfied La Belle, will we ever see her again?"

"Who can say? I confess, I would miss her presence."

"Mr. Symme—Edmund—you conducted excellent research in most unusual circumstances."

"Perhaps it is easier to discover obscure facts when guided by spirits and visions?" Banks conjectured. "How shall any of us fare back in the hubbub of London? Perhaps you should retain Owlswood as your base of operations."

They looked at one another, each immersed in a crush of impressions from recent events.

"Shall we make one last visit to the stone?" Banks asked.

"Yes," Remy agreed.

Edmund nodded. "Good idea, old man. Let's gather our coats and sticks and confront our nemesis one last time."

On the way, Edmund couldn't help himself from looking and listening for Regis. Remy and Banks did the same.

"How I miss the old beast," said Edmund as he trudged ahead of the others, wet leaves squishing below his feet. "well, let's take another look at this mysterious Stone."

The three gathered around the site. What they saw was an ordinary-looking flat boulder with a prominent crack from which no mysterious energy escaped.

"No sign of our lady," Edmund observed, "but I would not be

surprised if she made an appearance."

She didn't. The three turned away after each had paid respects to the spirit who had shown them a realm beyond what they previously believed as real. As they hiked back to the house, Banks looked back and said, "Yet another tale of the *poignard en pierre* to be passed down through the ages."

*   *   *

Later that afternoon, the three sat in the dining room as Cook brought them dish after dish, indulging appetites that had paused for several days.

"Mr. Symme, I thank you from the bottom of my heart for pursuing this otherworldly matter to a satisfactory finish." The three of them clinked glasses. "And I am grateful that you have freed me from my contract to care for Owlswood. I shall return to London to pursue my studies. Dr. Banks—Kit—will support me in the endeavor of becoming a doctor."

Edmund sputtered involuntarily. "A doctor?! One day it's women's suffrage, the next women doctors! Where does it end? Shall females be admitted to the clergy, too?!"

Banks sprang to her defense. "Now see here, old man, many women would prefer having a female doctor."

Remy smiled at him, then turned toward Edmund with eyes blazing.

"Mr. Symme, I would ask that you limit your approval or disapproval to my work here at Owlswood. I have no need to justify my pursuits outside of this realm." She took a moment to calm her ire. "As you know, I have spoken with several potential replacements, and my cousin Anne, whom you have met, is ready to take over my duties. She would move into my quarters as soon as I depart, with your permission. Which I hope you will grant immediately."

Edmund looked as if cold water had been thrown on him.

Remy looked away to compose herself, then continued, "Since I shall be leaving Owlswood, I take this opportunity—if you will give me more of your time—to say a few words on parting."

She took a deep breath. Edmund nodded.

"The Symme family bequest that provided for my mother and myself has been most welcome, and I very much appreciate it.

"I am also grateful that you have applied yourself to the plight of my late grandmother, and cleared the stains of our separate and common ancestry. You have been generous and professional to the end.

"Regarding my personal pursuits, however, take heed: your attitude is nearly universal among men, but it cannot continue. I should have hoped your character, so worthy in other respects, would prevail over ordinary male arrogance, and guide you to disavow such obstinate, aggravating and outmoded notions."

She stared directly into his eyes, then went on.

"Dr. Banks will accompany me to London, where I have arranged modest accommodations."

Edmund once again was taken aback. His eyes welled up with tears, so unlike him. He turned away. He couldn't think of a single response. Edmund Symme, at a loss for words!

The image of Lydia flashed before his eyes, then Remy superimposed. *My God, this is a real woman!* he thought. He'd be a fool to let her go. A doctor? Well, he'd had doctors who weren't nearly as capable and level-headed as Remy.

But Remy was headed out the door on the arm of Banks, who had the biggest smile Edmund had ever seen.

"Some friend you are," muttered Edmund, taking a deep breath. He ran behind the two as they reached the threshold.

"Remy, I . . . I look forward to working with your cousin Anne." He breathed again and said so softly, hardly anybody could hear, "And, and...I don't want to lose you."

Remy and Banks continued out the door. Edmund followed them outside.

Standing on the front step, he spoke as they walked away. It was hard to get the words out, but he said loudly enough for the retreating couple to hear. "Jeanne Remy, I . . . I love you!"

She turned and looked at him in total surprise. Banks freed her arm and she stood facing Edmund.

"Mr. Symme—Edmund—are you in your right mind? No, I think not. You cannot be. I shall pretend I did not hear you."

"Remy, stop!" Edmund shouted. "You did hear me. And you must hear me out. I can't let you go like this."

He rushed down the steps, took Remy's hand and knelt before her. She looked at him skeptically.

"I love you," he said, holding her hand to his heart. "I see now what I a fool I've been. Thank you. You've allowed me to see my own stupidity. I'll learn, I promise I will, if you'll only give me the chance. If you do—please do—I'll support you in whatever endeavor you choose."

Their eyes locked with soul-piercing intensity. She urged him to stand. With one hand, he awkwardly wiped his tears with his handkerchief, still grasping Remy's hand with the other.

He pulled her to him in an embrace—no help from Fleur needed. She peered into his eyes with a questioning expression. Edmund said softly, "Really, I would support you in any endeavor you choose. I want to be with you forever."

Banks raised his hands in a gesture of surrender.

"By the holy girdle of St. Gertrude, I see which way the wind is blowing."

"I appreciate these sentiments more than I can say," Remy said with a lingering smile. "But at this time, sir, I am off to London to re-commence my studies. Perhaps I shall see you again before too long."

"You will!" cried Edmund as Remy turned to leave with Banks once more. "I shall visit in London shortly. Yes. See you, too, old man," he said as he touched Banks' shoulder. "Safe travels. See you in town."

As he watched them enter the waiting carriage, the scent of gardenia was unmistakable.

Epilogue

On a fine spring day, Christopher Symme drove his Humber with the top down from Cambridge up to Owlswood during a break between semesters. As he parked in the circle, he honked and waved at Molly, who was pruning in the flower garden. Rex came bounding up, tongue hanging out, and leapt up against the driver side door, glad to see his walking partner after a long absence. Chris clambered out, knees first, and knelt down to wrestle with the dog, ignoring the scratches just left by its paws. Together, they headed up the steps to the front door, Chris almost pushed over by Rex. The housekeeper, Aunty Anne, greeted him at the entryway. He threw his dust-covered goggles, leather jacket, and driving gloves on a chair, and gave her the huge smile he had inherited from his father.

She stood back with her hands on his shoulders and looked him up and down.

"So good to see you, Master Chris. Come, come, I'll get you some tea," she said, picking up after him. "Your sister Fleur will be glad you are finally arrived. Here, a letter was just delivered for you."

She held out a silver salver.

"A letter? Who would post to me here?" He scooped up the envelope. Strange stamps! From America. Postmarked Philadelphia, March 20, 1914. With a smile, he glanced at the return address: *Dr. Jeanne Remy-Symme.*

"It's from Mother!"

Fleur appeared and wrapped her arm around her big brother's waist.

"What's from Mother?" she asked as he hugged her in return, then focused on the letter.

"This letter," he said, tearing it open and scanning it quickly. "Good, she'll soon be home," he sighed. "Father will be delighted. He tries to hide it, but he misses her so." He sniffed the paper. "Mmm... smells so good. Like those flowers in the *orangerie.*"

Fleur grabbed for the letter. "Let me read it now."

He teasingly held it away from her, then relented. She sniffed, then read.

"It does smell dreamy. Like gardenia. That reminds me, my pesky brother, last night I had the strangest dream. A beautiful lady—with wavy red hair like mine . . ."

Families of the Main Characters

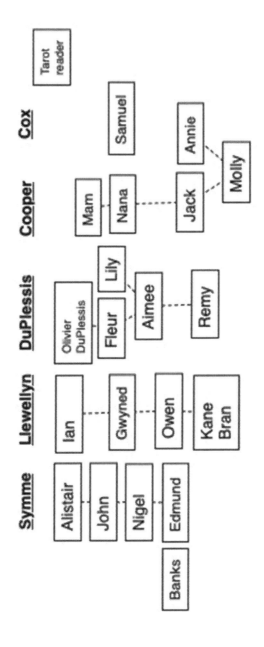

Author and Ghosts

BJ Van Horn (1949-2023) was a writer of easy-reading tales of ghosts and other fascinating beings, as well as an in-demand human resources consultant. She lived in San Rafael, California with husband Mike, had two daughters, and three grandkids. Mike is also a writer and consultant. A two consultant, two writer family! They worked together, played together, wrote together, and traveled the world together. BJ passed away unexpectedly in the fall of 2023.

The "ghost writers"

Mike Van Horn advises small business owners and writes science fiction. The sci fi is much more fun, he says! His trilogy—*Aliens Crashed in My Back Yard*, *My Spaceship Calls Out to Me*, and *Spacegirl Yearning*—is available on Amazon. Also at galaxytalltales.com. Mike lives in San Rafael CA

Becky Van Horn writes tales on the theme "Down and out in Marin County," mixing self-reflection with commentary on the various weird and ordinary people she encounters. Becky also lives in San Rafael CA

Eva Shoshany writes about her adventures in learning to manage stress. She ran a printing business with her husband Barry Toranto in Marin County for thirty-one years and has been involved in the Inner Research Institute, School of T'ai Chi Ch'uan since 1986. She and Barry live in Mill Valley CA.

Fonts
Text, Palatino. Chapter titles, Palatino Linotype. Book title, Sidhe.

Our Other Fiction Books
Mike Van Horn's science fiction trilogy +1

Read the space exploits of our quirky heroine, singer Selena M, and her cast of very non-human aliens. galaxytalltales.com

– Aliens Crashed in My Back Yard
– My Spaceship Calls Out to Me
– Space Girl Yearning
– Alien Invasion: There Goes the Neighborhood

Made in the USA
Columbia, SC
18 June 2024

36913807R00174